Miranda Frank

MW00717080

A World Turned Upside Down

J. M. Dent

PublishAmerica

Baltimore

© 2006 by J. M. Dent.
All rights reserved. No part of this book may be reproduced, stored in a retrieval system, or transmitted in any form or by any means without the prior written permission of the publishers, except by a reviewer who may quote brief passages in a review to be printed in a newspaper, magazine, or journal.

First printing

Portions of shape-note hymns from *The Sacred Harp* used by permission, Sacred Harp Publishing Co., Chelsea, AL.

ISBN: 1-4137-7055-X
PUBLISHED BY PUBLISHAMERICA, LLLP
www.publishamerica.com
Baltimore

Printed in the United States of America

For MKD, with all my love

Preface

It is historical fact that when General Cornwallis surrendered at Yorktown in 1781 to the revolutionary forces of George Washington and the Count de Rochambeau, neither army actually played "The World Turned Upside Down."

The legend, though—its perfection more perfect than plain historical fact—will probably never die. For it reflects a sense at the time that truly all things were made new again; that a *Novus Ordo Seclorum*—a New Order of the Ages – had begun; that new values, of a breathtaking power and rightness, could be implemented for the first time in man's history by a nation being born.

But all that's young grows old and dies. And a once-revolutionary land, grown dissipated and corrupt over the years, may discover that although *it* has stopped, *history* hasn't. So again comes a time of upheaval, when men and women in whom the founding values are still alive face the need to implement them once again—in *A World Turned Upside Down.*

Readers might enjoy hearing the Revolutionary tune from which this book's title is taken, played on fife and drum, at http://www.contemplator.com/england/worldtur.html

If buttercups buzz'd after the bee,
If boats were on land, churches on sea,
If ponies rode men and if grass ate the cows,
And cats should be chased into holes by the mouse,
If the mamas sold their babies
To the gypsies for half a crown;
If summer were spring and the other way round,
Then all the world would be upside down.

Foreword

At first the water covered everything. Gradually, as more of the water was locked up in the Earth's polar icecaps, and pressures from deep in the Earth's core began forcing bulges of its rock mantle upward, land began to rise from the water. Assorted marine creatures were stranded and died, to become interesting fossils collected by hikers and picnickers on the tops of West Virginia's mountains in millennia yet to come. (The hikers and picnickers did not pity these trilobites, or mourn their deaths.)

Eons later, the slowly receding waters made room for countless non-marine organisms—insects, amphibians, reptiles, giant fern-like plants—the progenitors of the "dinosaurs" which would become so popular with children of the hikers and picnickers of millennia yet to come. Nearly all these early life forms died off, as did their descendants the dinosaurs, thick piles of their corpses creating, over geologic time, the vast coal deposits of West Virginia. (In millennia yet to come, neither the miners supplying coal to power plants nor the users of the electric power pitied these immense masses of once-living organisms, all dead so long ago.)

Eventually, the earliest mammals began to evolve. But most of evolution consists of false starts, dead ends and blind alleys, ending in permanent extinction for that luckless line of creatures. Nature went on producing many forms of mammals, in this cold and lethal way for eons, before the first recognizable humans completed their long wanderings across the Bering Strait, across the North American continent, and onto the land in question. (They felt no particular anguish about all the countless extinctions that had occurred there before their arrival.)

Stronger bands of savages—long before any such bands had names, or probably even much speech beyond basic grunts and cries—killed off the

7

original bands and took over the area for themselves. (They were not especially distressed at having done this perfectly natural thing.)

Then other bands killed off those bands, and still others killed off those. And so forth, many, many times, before things reached the point where there were even names to distinguish the killers from the killed. Eventually, groups such as the "Shawnee" were victorious occupants of the land—but they felt no particular sorrow for the deaths of the countless unnamed groups that had gone before.

Then, in a mere blink of the eye, considering the time-scale we have been using, it was suddenly around 1700 AD by the calendar of a different band of people, who came from far away and had guns and germs and steel tools and horses and writing and the wheel and all manner of astonishing things. It took but a moment, historically, for these supermen to extirpate the Shawnee and claim the land—which they did not in sorrow for those they'd killed, but with joy at the obvious, demonstrated superiority of their own kind. "Our God's bigger than their god!" exulted one of the new group's leaders, in a spirit far removed from pity for the land's former occupants, now extinct.

And for the next…oh…tenth-of-an-eye-blink, in the time-scale we are using, this latest group waxed greatly in power and self-confidence. Because, you see, it was obviously the *final* group to inhabit this area, which it called Grayson County, West Virginia. Clearly, it was the apex, the culmination, the Grand Capstone of History, which all previous time had been working to set proudly in place.

And the members of this group looked about them—at their own crowning position atop all those countless eons of History's long tale—and, by golly, History had made a wise decision, and they were pretty doggone proud.

And then our story begins.

Chapter 1
Real Leadership for Real Americans

Tom submerged the carburetor in a bath of parts-cleaner solution, wiped his oily hands on a bit of rag, and sank his tall, stooped frame into the workshop's rocking chair for a break. Without electricity for fans, early September in West Virginia was hot, adding to his tiredness. He'd been awakened again last night by the battery-powered intrusion alarms set to monitor his property.

It had been merely a couple of kids prowling in the darkness, easily scared off when he leaned out the window of his bedroom over the Gravely dealership and loudly racked the action on the Mossberg Model 500 twelve gauge. That gun made a truly heart-freezing sound in the darkness as it jacked a shell into the chamber. The kids were a block away and still gaining speed when he exhaled a long breath, limp with relief, and went back to bed. It was one small, non-violent victory—this time—in what he knew would be a long, long struggle, with the odds against him growing month by month, year by year— if he lasted that long.

When the batteries in his intruder alarms ran down there would be no replacements. When the gasoline in the repair shop's 55-gallon drum ran out, along with that in similar drums his neighbors had stashed, there would be no more fuel for the Gravely tractors he sold and repaired—and thus no further reason for the existence of Mountainview Gravely ("Sales and Service: Your West Virginia Hometown Source for the World's Finest Garden Tractors.")

Bone tired from the heat, his worries, and lack of sleep, Tom fished one of his last remaining packs of Dentine out of his shirt pocket and absently unwrapped a stick, trying to think.

When last night's little creeps got genuine hunger pangs, gnawing deep into their bellies, they'd no longer run at a mere threat. When the gasoline was gone, and with it his usefulness to the small town of Mountainview, there would be fewer checkup visits from Chief Barley and the Citizens Patrol to maintain security—his and the repair shop's. They'd do what they could, of course, but it was just a fact of life: their resources were limited, and in this grim new world the demands were infinite. Tom rocked slowly and pondered the likelihood that for him, as for so many millions of others, time was rapidly running out.

Like the man said, dumbfounded, when he clapped his hands and triggered an avalanche: "How could something so big be started by something so small?" In the present case, Tom reflected, his likely approaching death, and that of the people around him, and that of the larger society around them, had been triggered merely by some electrons.

"Can't get much smaller than that," he mused, chewing his gum, trying to rock the tiredness away as he sat next to his workbench.

A mere two months ago, somebody (North Korea? Iran? Al Qaeda? No one knew or at this point cared) had set off four small, primitive nukes in New York City, Washington, D.C., Chicago, and San Francisco. While the government had been paying tens of billions of tax dollars to an increasingly wealthy assortment of has-been politicians who owned the Carlisle Group's portfolio of defense contractors, for work on an ultra-high-tech Star Wars mach fifteen ballistic missile space shield, the Evildoers, it seemed, had not been decent enough to play fair; they had apparently put their nukes in four old vans—average cost $1200—and driven them into the U.S. from Mexico, mixed in with (using a daily average here) the typical traffic of about five tons of assorted dope and 15,000 illegal immigrants also crossing that border during the course of that typical day.

The U.S. government, to make clear its shock and outrage at the cowardly Evildoers' immoral use of terrorism, had immediately obliterated seven third-world countries it had suspicions about, producing an initial death toll of some five to twenty-one million peasants, depending on the estimates used.

But any hopes of teaching the natives a proper respect for Freedom, Democracy, and Decent American Values—and all the heroism of America's fighting forces abroad—proved unable to remedy the crisis. For the terrorists' primitive little nukes had been merely blasting caps to set off the real dynamite: America's economy.

Wildly overpriced for years, the American financial markets had grown ever more addicted to the cocaine of unlimited free money injected by the Greenspan Federal Reserve. In the heady, theoretical world of the stock market's Masters of the Universe, and their blowdried talking hairdos, paid to shill the rubes on the bubblevision financial shows, share prices would *always* go up—the bubble blown ever larger by the Fed's power to create unlimited sums of "money" out of thin air and pump it into the markets.

Greenspan's nerve had briefly seemed to waver in 1996, when he muttered darkly about "irrational exuberance" as frenzied speculators, bidding with essentially free money, drove the Dow up to 6000. Since it had taken from 1910 to 1968 to reach 1000 (then promptly fallen back into the 800's by 1983, when the latest advance began) the Dow's skyrocketing to 6000 in scarcely more than a decade traced a near-vertical path that fully justified alarm. But the moment of rational hesitation was swept aside as the gigantic free-money con drove the Dow further skyward to 12,000 in just the next four years! James Glassman, noted financial "expert" for *The Washington Post*, cranked out his book *Dow 36,000,* which became a huge hit—though soon cast into the shade by other "analysts" frenzied predictions of a Dow soon to hit 136,000.

The nation's prosperity bubble was (like every irrational market bubble before it) known with certainty to be solidly based on an unprecedented "new era." Why, in achieving riches for all, the Fed no longer even needed to bother physically printing the Magic Money it created out of thin air. In this new era, computers avoided any such old-fashioned nuisance by merely spewing streams of ones and zeros across data transmission lines, thereby creating unlimited amounts of money, instantly, without even the cost of paper!

Joe Lunchbucket's $50 shares in Bigcon.com sucked up some of that free money and rose to $100, then sucked up some more and went to $200. Meanwhile, Joe's $100,000 house was now "worth" $225,000—so he refinanced and put his former equity into more shares of Bigcon.com, which had blown past $500, heading for the moon. Whoever dreamed it was so easy to get rich? Why hadn't people thought of this long ago?

They had; many times. Alan Greenspan and his worshipers were proving yet again the truth of Hitler's comment about the Big Lie: just make it big enough and they will believe. Financial sophisticates, who would have scoffed at the nursery-tale notion of sorcerers spinning straw into gold, were enthralled by the *really* big idea of computers spinning…. Nothing—absolutely nothing!—into gold.

"Well," grumped a fringe handful of the hopelessly old fashioned, "maybe they can spin nothing into an abstraction called 'dollars,' but not into literal, physical *gold*. Big difference. The Confederacy printed dollars, too: see what their $20 bill is worth today, versus a Confederate $20 gold coin. If you plan on needing merely 'housing' or 'groceries' in the abstract, perhaps your abstractions called 'dollars' will suffice, temporarily. But in the long run, if you want an actual, physical 'house,' with an actual, physical portion of 'beef' on a real, genuine, 'dining room table,' you'd better have something actual and physical to trade for it. Otherwise, once people catch on to Greenspan's 'nothing-from-nothing' con, you'll discover that all those impressive abstractions called 'dollars' you think you own will no longer be worth the paper they're no longer even printed on..."

And so forth in this dismal vein would go the Lecture of Doom from the hopelessly outmoded.

"Oh, you and your long runs: in the long run, we're all dead!" wittily quipped the sophisticates as they grabbed their credit cards and headed for the shopping malls, thereby crushingly refuting the doomcryers.

Yes, Tom thought, as he went back to work, blowing off the cleaned carburetor, putting in a new jet, and replacing it on the Gravely. *Soon, we're most likely all dead – grasshoppers and ants together. Pity; the long run didn't turn out to be very long after all...*

For mixed in with the thoroughly modern sophisticates, to whom Greenspan's perpetual motion magic of economic levitation seemed perfectly reasonable, was a surprising number of lamentably unsophisticated "little people" who simply—in one analyst's words—"didn't get it."

These little people, in total, owned an awful lot of shares in their mutual funds and IRAs and company pensions and 401-Ks, and children's college funds and church and civic group endowments and so forth. Deep in the back of their minds, they were troubled and anxious. How much *was* all this paper investment stuff really worth? And how could you know for sure? In the eternal battle between greed and fear, greed had been winning for more than a decade during the greatest stock market bubble in man's history. But the pent-up fear had been growing stronger in like measure, to its own greatest level ever, awaiting the least spark to ignite it in people's minds.

When the news of the terrorist nukes hit—almost instantly followed by wildly alarmist rumor, surmise, and prediction—the little people panicked.

Urgent, "get-out-quick" selling was overtaken within an hour by frantic "get-out-at-any-price" dumping, which triggered a freefall with no bids offered at any level. The market limit mechanisms closed the markets, one after another, and there were no predictions as to re-opening dates. The NYSE, American Exchange, NASDAQ, Chicago Commodity pits, COMEX metals exchanges—all of them, right down to small, local markets, saw trading halted as the nation's economic engine seized up, lacking the lubricant of confidence about what things were "really" worth.

"That $250,000 portfolio is my entire *life savings*, for Chrissake!"

screamed Joe Lunchbucket when he finally reached his broker. "You're telling me it's *worth* maybe twenty thousand? How am I going to retire on twenty thousand dollars? I *can't* sell at that price! You got me into this: now you get me out! What am I going to do?"

In the paneled conference rooms, teams of expensively dressed experts, who had nothing but contempt for the unsophisticated little people of Joe's world, faced exactly the same problems Joe faced—though with many, many more zeros at the ends of the numbers.

"Yes, we know we're obligated for that amount. But if you demand payment, it's really quite simple: we go bankrupt and default. You'll get ten cents on the dollar, at most."

"But that's unacceptable! We have obligations of our own. If you don't honor your commitments we can't pay three of our suppliers, who'll go belly up!"

"Then take this basket of stocks as payment of the debt—at the values shown in last quarter's report."

"But they're not *worth* that amount! How can we do business when nothing's reliably worth anything anymore? How can the markets even re-open when no one could afford to sell shares for what they're *really* worth? Doing so would just unleash an ever-growing snowball of bankruptcies causing more bankruptcies. What are we going to do?"

Spokesmen vied with each other to put the "con" back in confidence. The airwaves fairly rang with a parade of dignified "experts" telling the public that the worst was over, the economy was fundamentally sound, and things were definitely looking up. But, realistically seeing the carnage ahead, no one dared set a date for re-opening the markets.

After a few days, the President himself had to be formally brought into play. Enveloped in the full dignity of the Oval Office, he managed, with only five re-takes, to tape what sounded to many like a slightly dumbed-down version of a Herbert Hoover pep talk about "Our Nation's Economic Soundness."

And still no one dared specify a date for re-opening the markets in this soon-to-be-better-than-ever economy.

Businesses closed. Some failures were involuntary, the businesses driven into bankruptcy when creditors demanded payments due. Many other companies, which still had healthy balance sheets and cash on hand, also closed because no one could buy enough of their goods or services to justify remaining open.

There were some bright spots, the President reflected, a few weeks after the nukes, as the latest meeting began to get underway in the White House Situation Room. For one, the Washington nuke had atomized the Pentagon, more than two miles away from the White House across the Potomac. The blast from the little device hadn't even cracked the White House's (bulletproof) windows, and the wind that day and the next had carried the fallout away southwards, toward Fredericksburg and Richmond.

Tough for those guys, of course, but a real blessing for himself. That cross-country, zigzag flight from one military base to another on the day of the 2001 World Trade Center bombing—remaining incommunicado, as if hiding from the nation's press and people, hour after anxious hour—had struck some as appearing just the tiniest bit panicky.

This time, with full press coverage, the President defiantly remained at his post in the White House, delivering a Rose Garden address in which he shook his fist at the Evildoers, threatened unspecified but horrible retaliation, and defied them to do their fiendish worst. With the cameras panning intermittently from his orating figure to the smoke pall still rising above the Pentagon behind him—safely distant in fact but enormously dramatic on film—that speech had been, beyond question, his finest triumph yet.

Which was better than this present crapola-shovelling session was going, he reflected sourly, glaring around the conference table to let the participants know he was not pleased.

The President's advisors sweated their Armani suit coats through and consulted their notes with ostentatious care, breathing deeply and forcing themselves to smile. The meeting was indeed not going well.

"Yes Sir, we can certainly print more money. Ha, ha—drop it out of helicopters and people will pick it up and spend it: 'Prosperity from the skies.' Yes indeed, sir—good one! Well put! But, uh, the problem, Sir, you see, is that about all we can do is just, well, *print* the money. We can't actually make it worth anything, if you see what I mean. For example, sir, suppose we distributed Monopoly money, or Confederate money, or 1920's German Weimar money, or 1980's Argentine money—well, who would accept it as payment for desirable stuff like food?

"Ha, Ha, Professor John Kenneth Galbraith! Good one, sir! But maybe not even him, I'm afraid: he may not be as dumb as he looks.

"Technically, sir, the paper we print is 'legal tender,' so people are forced, by law, to accept it. But how would we force them—assign one cop to each citizen? And what would we pay the cop with?

"You see, sir, for a long time now the U.S. dollar has not represented anything of tangible value—of actual 'worth.' It's just a piece of paper. What gives it—well, *gave* it—value is confidence that American businesses and individuals would acquire wealth. The government would then confiscate some of that wealth and use it to back, or 'give value to,' the paper dollars we print. But an economy frozen in gridlock means not much wealth is being generated; not enough wealth to seize (via taxation) means not enough backing for the paper dollars we're printing; not enough backing for the paper dollars means they've now become worth about what they – well, uh, what they *are*: pieces of paper. So to speak."

The President, who had never found economics as interesting or understandable as professional baseball, glowered at the experts sitting around the table. Someone had By God fucked up somehow, and someone was By God going to pay.

"Well back the damn things with gold or something! Get it out of the vaults and parade it around on TV and tell people each paper dollar is now worth a certain amount of the gold they can see right there with their own eyes!"

"Uh, well sir, that used to be the way it worked. But now, I'm afraid, there'd be some problems. First, we no longer have all that much gold left – in a physical sense, I mean. Of course we still have the paper receipts from the banks we loaned the gold to, which serve as their promise to repay us. But, the thing is, see, the banks are, well, broke. They're not able to repay the gold. In any case, the amount of paper dollars we've printed over the years so greatly exceeds the amount of all the gold we ever had, or ever will have, there's really not much hope of ever backing the dollar with gold."

This was not sounding at all good. The sonsabitches had really dropped him in the shit this time. He considered the possibility of firing every last one of the bastards, live, in an Oval Office address. "The President Speaks: Real Leadership For Real Americans!" – something like that, maybe. Would the yokels buy it? Hell, most of the damn yokels wouldn't even see or hear it: electric service was beginning to fail as financial gridlock squeezed off the flow of funds to and from power companies.

"Well what *do* countries do when this sort of thing happens?" he snapped. "What got us out of that goddamn Hoover Depression?"

(Although nominally a Republican, the President had never once failed to aim a ritual, crowd-pleasing kick at Hoover whenever possible—though he had never fully understood how some FBI director had brought on a Depression. And he was sure as hell not going to ask: he purely *hated* that "oh-so-superior" look people put on, and how they explained things reeeeal slowly, in little words, like he hadn't even been to Yale or anything. Stuck-up egghead bastards—who'd never in a million years have the family background to make Skull and Bones—looking down on *him*! Like this bunch around the table....)

"Well, Sir, for over a decade nothing did get us out of the Depression. People either survived it or they didn't. Then we put about 20 million men in uniform and fought the largest war in history. After the war ended in 1945 another 14 years passed, and finally—in 1959—the stock market, in inflation-adjusted terms, was back once more to where it had been in 1929. If you ignore taxes—which had gone from nearly zero for most people in 1929 to a top rate exceeding 97% by 1959. Of course, during half those 30 years, FDR made stirring speeches and posed for photographs with his cigarette-holder at a jaunty angle. I expect that helped morale. Sir."

The snotty little bastard *was* mocking him! Abruptly, the President rose, terminating the conference. As the "experts" filed out, the President allowed himself the pleasure of planning his upcoming speech. He smiled to himself. Let's just see how these smart-alecky little genius-brains like what they hear in "The President Speaks: Real Leadership for Real Americans!"

Departing, the "experts" consoled themselves by attempting to find a few faint positive notes in the gloom. At least, they reflected, the U.S. economic collapse had also brought down the economies of America's trading partners—all the other major countries on earth. There was certainly no risk now of any other major power attempting any aggression against the U.S., considering how preoccupied they all were just keeping their own citizens alive. And the U.N. – corrupt and hollow farce that it always was—had joined the League of Nations in the Dustbin of History, now that the two or three nations which funded it no longer had money to throw away.

Still, notwithstanding these faint glimmers of good news, the experts had pretty neatly set forth to the President part of the problem. With the economy grinding to a halt tax revenues dried up; and with tax revenues drying up the otherwise unbacked dollar became increasingly worthless; and as the dollar became increasingly worthless the economy slowed further toward a halt. But what the President's experts had carefully tiptoed around was the critical difference between the Great Depression and today.

In the 1930s, despite all its problems, the U.S. retained an unshakably sound foundation beneath it: a currency whose value was never in doubt. Although stocks had crashed in value, prudent investors large and small had part of their assets in bonds, and the better quality bonds went right on paying dividends—in dollars that were "as good as gold." Real estate, though producing smaller monthly rents in the Depression, still did produce rent payments—again, in dollars that were "as good as gold."

Ordinary people used gold and silver coins in daily commerce until gold was confiscated by the government in 1933. After 1933, silver was still used. There was never any question that the U.S. government's hoard of gold and silver was fully adequate to back its paper dollars. If absolute worst had come to absolute worst, in the 1930s the government could have minted its hoard of gold and silver ingots into coins and run its economy on those, without needing any paper dollars. And—most important—people knew it. Therefore, there was no panic dumping of paper dollars caused by fear they were nothing *but* paper.

Today, alas, "nothing but paper" described the U.S. dollar exactly. Even investments that continued to pay, such as rental real estate and higher quality bonds, made those payments in dollars—which were rapidly becoming worthless.

The current economic shutdown was made infinitely worse by having no value left in the paper dollar—and by having totally insufficient amounts of real money which did retain value (gold and silver) in the nation's vaults to use in re-starting the economy.

Banks (for which the FDIC actually had funds to insure about 2% of the depositors' money) failed—though they issued Official Government Notes of Assurance that "at an appropriate time" all depositors' funds would be made good "in such a manner as shall be determined by the relevant authorities." Few people had much luck trading their Official Note for a can of Spam. One citizen was hauled off to jail for using his Official Note for an act of personal hygiene, then mailing it to "The Goddamn Government, Washington, D.C."

(The FBI, which had yet to acquire a single credible lead about who had blown up four American cities, had extracted the man's DNA from his letter, scanned it against all hospital records west of the Mississippi, matched it to a skin biopsy he'd had three years earlier, and arrived at his house in the form of sixteen armor-clad SWAT team members supported by two M-113 armored personnel carriers—all within 48 hours. The many televised speeches at the FBI awards ceremony the following day were packed especially full of highflown rhetoric, for the nation was thought to need Real Heroes in its present emergency.

(But when Jack Mcgilihee, FBI Special Agent and Real Hero, had taken his $1000 meritorious bonus check to a guy he knew "with connections" who had canned goods, and attempted to get a case of pork and beans, he was dismayed at the scorn his offer unleashed.

("A whole case? Twelve cans? For a thousand bucks Federal paper? Where ya been, pal? Hey, you're a Federal guy, right? Tell you what: take your piece of paper to your fellow Feds at Fort Knox, where they got all that gold, and have them give you however much gold it's 'worth.' Then bring that back here and let's see what we got. Otherwise, I can let you have one can for your paper—but that's only for old time's sake. Look: you wanna do some real business? I can make you a sweet offer on that nine-millimeter Sig Sauer you're packing."

(The next day, Special Agent Mcgilihee had taken his $1000 check to the men's room at the West Bend Field Office. Emerging from the stall, he was disappointed it had failed to block up the toilet when flushed, so he dropped a roll of paper towels into the toilet and flushed again, this time feeling pleased with the result.

(Then Special Agent Mcgilihee filled several cardboard boxes with toilet paper, staplers, reams of bond paper, and the office coffee supplies, and loaded them along with three office swivel chairs into his FBI-issue Chevy, and left the by-now mostly deserted Field Office to begin what he described to Marge and the kids as "early retirement.")

As the U.S. dollar became increasingly worthless, government employees, civilian and military, became increasingly scarce—each one informally taking "early retirement" to care for his own family as best he could. Private sector employees did likewise, to the extent they were able.

Some plans worked better than others.

The Secretary of the Treasury, an immensely wealthy man, owned a cattle-raising *estancia* covering 700 square miles of northern Brazil, containing a palatial and well-stocked hacienda but unpopulated except by a handful of his own employees. His friend, the Vice-President, still retained enough clout throughout The Collapse to commandeer an executive jet and fix the necessary flight clearances for the trip. And the current Drug Czar heading America's campaign to "Just Say No" had close connections with Mexican Army commanders, who had been energetically and profitably just saying "How Much?" as they worked both sides of the drug-trafficking/drug-suppression caper. General Morales assured his American counterpart that enough Jet-A was stashed at a certain *narco-trafficante* airstrip in the Yucatan to refuel a Cessna Citation II—providing his own family could join the fleeing Americans at that point.

It would be a close-run thing: the 2500-foot dirt strip at the Treasury Secretary's *estancia* wouldn't handle anything bigger than a 16-passenger

Citation II. Even with minimal baggage, the pilot and his wife plus the families of the Secretary, Vice President, and Drug Czar totaled seventeen people for the jet's sixteen seats—making it impossible to take on a full fuel load because of weight limitations, therefore requiring the Yucatan refueling stop and the lies to Morales about adding his family to the overloaded jet. Nevertheless, with luck, the suddenly announced "Brazilian-American Summit Conference and Inter-Agency Working Group" gambit might succeed.

As the creaking and groaning executive jet thumped and banged heavily down the runway of Washington's Andrews Air Base, on a terrifyingly long takeoff run, the drug czar prayed mightily to his Episcopalian god for three favors: first, that takeoff speed would be reached before the end of the runway was; second, that they could somehow find the unmarked dirt strip in the Yucatan to re-fuel; and third, that the .40 caliber Smith and Wessons he and his two fellow statesmen carried in their pockets could resolve the "General Morales Problem" when that time came.

Alas, how often we pray for the wrong things. The plane was airborne with runway to spare. The airstrip in the Yucatan was at precisely the GPS coordinates they had been given. And upon landing, the Americans discovered their "General Morales Problem" (including wife, two sons, and three daughters) had already been resolved for them by six *narco-trafficantes* who had AK-47's—and bad attitudes concerning strangers.

That most definitely included gringo strangers.

"*Pigs!*" Pablo swore in a white-hot fury, a few moments after the chattering weapons fell silent and calm returned to the airstrip. "Ignorant, pig-brained spawn of sows! *Regard* this thing you have you done!"

In their enthusiasm—their AK-47s set on full-automatic—Pablo's men had sprayed the airplane so thoroughly while killing its gringo occupants the plane would obviously never fly again.

The loss deeply hurt Pablo, an enterprising young man on his way up, who only five years before had achieved a tremendous gain in status by moving from mule-back to a decrepit Toyota pickup. Visions of breaking into the *real* big-time—with an airplane, even!—died before his eyes as streams of blood, jet fuel, and hydraulic fluid dribbled from the riddled Citation onto the baked earth.

"You will *never* be more than *pigs!*" he shrieked at his now-contrite little band, as they shuffled uneasily, downcast eyes studying the accumulating puddles below the jet.

Overwhelmed by the unbearable frustration of being the one competent man in a pack of imbeciles, Pablo would have agreed wholeheartedly with an opinion so often shared by the late Vice-President, Secretary, and drug czar: decent help is impossible to find nowadays. Truly, the world is going to hell.

In time, the President himself—his own world gone all to hell—would come to echo the lament about how hard it is to find good help. In the chaotic, Saigon-evacuation-style frenzy of the U.S. Government's final hours, the President, his wife, and his closest aides were suddenly bundled into a helicopter one night and flown westward, high above the flames of a burning Washington, to one of the senior command bunkers left over from the Cold War. Like most of them, it was a concrete tomb inside a mountain, with its own well, food and other supplies for more than a year, and a tiny, handpicked detachment of elite Special Forces troops.

Some nights—and, later, occasionally for short daytime periods—the President and his wife were allowed to come up to the carefully hidden mountainside entrance of the bunker and enjoy the air within the fortified 100 square yards or so at the opening. Beyond that—and the multiple rows of razor-wire entanglements—lay the now-activated minefields. There was no question of going anywhere.

To back up the deadly seriousness of the wire, mines, and related defenses were about 200 professional troops of a definitely "no-nonsense" caliber who staffed the bunker—with sufficient food, supplies, and computer games to keep them alive for a very long time, and more than enough ordnance stockpiled to meet any battle contingency. It may not have been a great life, but it beat being dead. And the military men understood full well that the success of their sacred mission—keeping the President alive while awaiting some sort of orders from someone in their military chain of command—depended in large part on keeping the bunker secret from the subjects whose taxes had built it, at least till those subjects had died off enough to pose no remaining threat of serious attack or disease. The bunker's 200 troops, with the munitions stored, could easily kill off 2000 attackers—but what if there were 3000…? Or even just one, bearing a variant of some disease the bunker's inhabitants had not been inoculated against?

In short, the troops had no intention of allowing the President, or anyone else, to go skylarking about the countryside, offering Real Leadership for Real Americans and giving away the bunker's location.

His guardians, the President gradually came to realize, were also in practice his guards, however studiedly polite their outward manner might be.

Time slowly passed. The First Lady, a sweet Christian woman, spent more and more of her days reading her Bible. Sometimes she underlined passages she considered hopeful, and tried to bring them up in conversation with the President. The President—increasingly devoted to watching re-runs of canned sports highlights on the 72-inch TV in his own quarters—gradually accepted the fact that by being good and causing no trouble he could earn additional time in the open air at the bunker's entrance.

Perhaps it was a blessing, really, that he didn't know enough about Napoleon on Saint Helena to realize that The Widowmaker had at least had unobstructed views of the sky and the entire 360-degree horizon throughout his final years.

In the early September heat in West Virginia, lacking electricity for the fans to ventilate his repair shop, Tom resumed working, steadily and carefully, on the Gravely two-wheel "L" model tractor. The machine looked like an extremely overbuilt rototiller—heavy, solid, durable: an old-fashioned piece of farm equipment from America's old-fashioned past.

"If this doesn't need anything but the carburetor job, I can get it done before lunch," Tom estimated. "Let's hope. I need those potatoes Johnson offered for the repair, before he trades them away to someone else."

Chapter 2
Getting By

To his great relief, Tom found the Gravely ran fine without any further work. If it had needed something major, Tom would have had to run one of the shop's Gravelys he had connected to an electric generator to power his shop equipment, now that public power was out for good. The shop's Gravely produced plenty of current by turning the generator attachment, but doing so consumed precious gasoline. Increasingly in the past few days, Tom was thinking of gasoline in terms of blood: you lose it, you die.

One of Chief Barley's deputies in the Citizens' Patrol was approaching— on foot, of course. Cars were no longer used in Mountainview. There were rumors of gasoline in limitless abundance around Bayonne, New Jersey, and a few other tank-farm locations—the ones that hadn't yet been set afire accidentally by ignorant scavengers, or deliberately by vandals. But gasoline in a refinery's Bayonne, New Jersey, tank farm wasn't much use to people in Mountainview, West Virginia—now that the refinery was closed "in receivership," the trucking companies were out of business, and most people in Mountainview had no money anyone considered of any value.

At first, a few hardy souls who owned (or stole) tankers risked loading them and driving out into the countryside to exchange their gasoline for barter items, but it didn't really work out. The highways were blocked in too many places, the risk of being shot and/or roasted alive by thieves was too great, and in any case, how much in barter payments could a trucker load in his cab or strap on to the tank? Lacking gasoline and electricity, Mountainview had slid back over a hundred years in the last two months.

"Hi Tom," called the Citizens' Patrol deputy when he arrived, "How goes it?"

"Not bad. Hey, Owen, you heading toward Johnson's place? I've got his Gravely fixed if you want a ride."

"Hot Damn! These dawgs are about due for a rest!"

Tom carefully measured one cup of gasoline from his storage drum into the customer's tractor, then connected one of the new Gravely wagons from his showroom to the tractor's hitch, started the motor with a pull on the cord, and headed down the road toward Johnson's, jouncing in the wagon alongside Owen.

"Hoo Wah!" hollered Owen Paks over the engine roar, regressing from his actual twenty-four years to a goofy fifteen-year-old. "Now this, By God, is more like *perfessional* police work! Ridin' around like a pair a crimestoppin' gentleman detectives! You got the right idea, Brother Tom! How 'bout tellin' Barley to get one a these things for us in the Patrol? Think they'd hold up under serious police work?"

"The Gravely'd last about a hundred years," Tom shouted. "The gasoline to run it may last another three months or so, with luck. You see the problem?"

When he glanced at the suddenly silent Owen, all the high spirits instantly knocked out of him, Tom felt like a creep. They jounced along in the wagon. "I'm sorry," Tom wanted to say. "Jeez, Owen, for maybe the first time in days you were having a little fun, and I managed to kill it. I'm sorry." But he didn't say anything.

Johnson's place was on the opposite side of Mountainview from Tom's shop, less than a mile away. When they arrived, Johnson was so abjectly grateful to have his tractor back and running that Tom's depression was only intensified.

"Tom, I can't thank you enough for this. I have *got* to get this larger fall garden finished if we plan on eating this winter. I've *got* to! When the tractor quit on me, I…well…I…uh …"

He turned away and cleared his throat while Tom brushed some stray dirt off the tractor's fender, and Owen aimed what he hoped looked like a professionally judicious kick at one of the tires. All three men knew only too well what Johnson was saying. When the Gravely had sputtered and died in an unfinished garden, Johnson had suddenly teetered on the edge of an abyss none of them could have imagined a few months ago: hunger—possibly starvation.

"Well, I cleaned the carburetor, and it needed a new jet; and I put in a cup of gas. So with the labor and all, it works out about like the estimate," Tom said, in the awkward quiet.

"Thanks, Tom." Johnson got a bushel basket of newly dug potatoes from the shed, dumped it into the wagon, and refilled it to dump a second measure.

Then he half-filled the basket with early apples and gently poured them into the wagon. "That cover it?"

"Yeah, that's real generous. Thanks, pal. You got some gasoline stored, I guess?"

"Yep. Still got at least half a 55-gallon drum. This tractor will run forever on that much."

Detaching the wagon, Tom and Owen tied the middle of a piece of rope through the wagon tongue, so each could pull on one end. The three men stood together, half reluctant to part.

"But, you know…when the gas does run out…" Johnson said softly, almost to himself. "What do we do then? It takes well over two years to breed, foal, raise, and train a horse or mule—and you need a lot of specialized harness and implements and skills to get any use out of one anyway. And that's just before you can plow. Once the plowing's done, then you've got more months before harvesting any food. And meanwhile, the animal eats every single day. The Amish can manage it, I guess, but we sure as hell can't. What do we do?"

"It'll work out somehow," Tom offered with as much confidence as he could manage. "We may not have to go all the way back to draft animals. Let's take it step at a time."

The middle-aged Tom, tall and stooped, and young Owen, compact and muscular, walked slowly back toward the Gravely dealership, pulling the wagonload of food. Both were silent. Owen didn't need any more surprise blows to the head from their current grim reality; Tom seemed to be lost in some sort of debate with himself.

"Can you keep something quiet?"

"Yeah, Tom. Of course. What?"

"You see the problem when the last gas is gone. There's not going to be any more gasoline in our lifetime—probably not for many lifetimes. Oil drilling, shipping, refining, distributing—all that big business, heavy industry, high-tech stuff is over for a long, long time. If Mankind survives, it will take generations to rebuild a sophisticated industrial society.

"Perhaps any small remnants of survivors will have to revert all the way back to subsisting by muscle power: draft animals and brute, human sweat. That's how people survived from the Stone Age until about 1850, when, for the first time ever, mechanical power became widespread enough to begin replacing muscle power."

They walked silently for a bit, turning over in their minds the prospect of a world so primitive it lacked mechanical power, until Tom summed it up: "I'm not sure I'd really want to go on living in a world powered entirely by muscles. It wouldn't really *be* living—just surviving."

With Owen still silent, thinking, Tom continued, "But maybe, just possibly, we won't have to go all the way back to unaided muscle power. The first widely available machines to lift us up from that brute level were steam engines. They're relatively simple to make and maintain, they use coal or wood for fuel, and they just might save us.

"I've been looking into the possibility. If what I'm trying to do works, I may have something in my shop that will save a lot of lives in Mountainview over the coming years. It's that precious. It may, literally, turn out to be the most precious object in Mountainview, now and for years to come.

"But I'm going to need protection—for it and especially for the shop tools and equipment, quietly and confidentially—while I get it finished and put into service. I've approached Chief Barley about that and he felt his decision had to be no: he's responsible for trying to protect all the people of Mountainview and all their property as best he can. Playing favorites—let alone secretly— just isn't something he can do and still retain the community's trust. I understand that. In his place, maybe I'd have decided the same. But we agreed I could ask you if you'd want to help me strictly on your own time, apart from your paid hours as a Citizens' Patrol deputy."

In the early days, as the severity of the crisis dawned on people, the town of Mountainview had authorized Chief Barley's three-man police force to hire fifty deputies from among the town's 400 or so residents. They provided foot patrol around the clock, deterred any local crime, monitored the arrival of any outsiders, kept watch for fire or fire hazards (a vital security function, now that individuals were cooking with firewood and keeping containers of stored gasoline) and served as general messengers, monitors of the sick and elderly, public address news-criers, and visible reminders of organized civic authority in a world grown terribly chaotic and frightening.

For his—or, in two cases, her—weekly sixty-hour shift, each Citizens' Patrol deputy received a gallon of gas from the 2000-gallon police station tank, which he could use or barter, plus a package of slightly dubious Civil Defense food rations from a God-knew-how-old supply discovered in the police department basement, plus some sort of firearm with a few rounds of ammunition, as drawn by lot.

The police department armory had held only a dozen .357 Magnum Smith & Wesson revolvers, ten Remington 870 Model 12-gauge shotguns, and two scoped .308 Savage 110 Model long-range rifles. The remaining twenty-six weapons issued to the deputies Chief Barley had been authorized by Mountainview to purchase from its townspeople, using gasoline from the police department tank for barter. In Mountainview, where almost every family routinely kept a few shotguns and hunting rifles—of admittedly varying ages and conditions—it was not hard for the Chief to finish arming his fifty new deputies in a few minutes' barter auction on the police station steps.

The Citizens' Patrol deputies, whatever one might think of their pay in "normal times," were glad to be hired. Since wage-work in nearby larger towns had ended—and with no way to get there and back in any case—the current employment choices boiled down to working on the land—either for yourself or as hired help—or working for the handful of remaining small businesses in Mountainview, or joining the Citizens' Patrol. The Patrol's success as a morale builder and unemployment program had so far proved almost as valuable as its more official functions.

While Owen listened, Tom outlined the problems, possibilities, and strategies for the machine he had quietly been working on—and the proposed deal for Owen's moonlighting in his hours free from Patrol duty. The walk passed quickly, and once they had the wagon of food safely back to Tom's they agreed to get together the next day to take the arrangement further.

But, as matters developed, their meeting the next day had very little to do with steam power.

Chapter 3
Owen's Report

Owen was shaky and rattled-looking when he suddenly entered Tom's shop the following evening just before suppertime.

"Uh, Tom, there's this situation," he began, without even saying hello.

He paced about the shop, too jittery to sit down. Puzzled, Tom fished some Dentine out of his pocket as he waited for the deputy to proceed.

"Jeez! I don't know, Tom; I mean, I never saw nothin' like that. He, um— uh, you know, killed him. Right there. And I killed him. I never done that before. *Jesus!*"

Tom got him a glass of water, to occupy the deputy's shaking hands, and got him seated, to control the jittery pacing, and tried to get him gently headed toward the beginning of whatever it was that had hit him so badly.

Owen's story, when it finally emerged, left Tom as grim as Owen was rattled. The deputy had been walking his daily patrol at the north edge of town, routinely checking the approaches for any sign of activity. All was quiet, and when noon came he slipped off the road into some bushes alongside Sandy Run to eat his sandwiches and refill his canteen. He'd been quietly sitting there for some time, when, off to the north, he saw two figures, a man and a woman, cresting a small rise and trudging slowly along the little two-lane county road toward him.

As they drew closer, he was just about to get up and greet them when a man rode up behind them on a mule, and halted them. They were close enough by now he could hear voices, but not make out the words. Suddenly, the man got off his mule, drew a knife, and held it to the other man's throat.

"HEY! DROP THAT KNIFE!" Owen screeched in shock, jumping up and fumbling in his daypack for the old WW-II surplus .45 Colt.

All three figures were dumfounded by Owen's sudden appearance out of nowhere. The walking man suddenly jerked away from the knife man, whether as an escape attempt or merely in surprise, it was impossible to say. The knife man, equally stunned by his victim's sudden movement and Owen's sudden appearance, convulsively jerked the knife—whether deliberately across the man's throat, or merely from being startled it was impossible to say. Owen blasted away with his .45—five shots going wild but the sixth catching the knife man in the belly. Knife-man went down heavily, sitting glassy-eyed on the road, holding his hands to his gut with blood flowing out in a stream. Owen ran the few yards to the people.

Victim-man, no longer spastically chicken-jerking, was already lying quietly beside knife-man, throat cleanly slashed from ear to ear, the blood not spraying out now but merely leaking in a last, small, despairing trickle. The woman, white as death, and obviously going into shock, stood swaying aimlessly back and forth, her eyes unfocused.

Owen ran to her, put her on the road on her back with knees raised, and said "Stay like that!"

Then he double-checked that knife-man's knife was well out of his reach, and that he was too far gone—either from shock or a severed spinal cord—to use it anyway. The blood was not pulsing, but it was flowing so rapidly a major vein must have been severed. He verified that victim-man was thoroughly dead. Clearly, knife-man was rapidly joining him. An astonishingly large pool of blood spread in an expanding circle around the two.

And then Owen puked and puked and puked—hating himself for it, especially with the woman there to see, but unable to stop.

When Owen finally regained control, down on all fours on the road, with puke-slime running all over his shirt and pants, the knife man had lost consciousness and the woman had found a rock to sit on, from which she gazed into the far distance as if seeking some sign on the horizon. The mule munched contentedly on a clump of roadside weeds.

"Are you OK?" he asked shakily, trying to wipe his chin clean.

"Yes."

Her voice was so flat, so cold. Like her body was uninhabited. It sounded mechanical. It scared him so bad he almost resumed puking.

She got up and walked over to victim-man, her boots leaving horrible prints in the eight-food diameter circle of blood surrounding him on the road. She looked down at him with a sadness that forever burned itself into Owen's still-stunned brain. Removing the light windbreaker tied around her waist, she gently placed it over the man's face.

"Goodbye, my darling," she said in a whisper so low it was nearly inaudible. Then she then turned to Owen, as if to say "I'm ready."

Owen furtively glanced at the two men, one dead and the other mostly so. "We gotta get to town," he told her. "Nothin' we can do for them two. Can you get up on the mule if I help you?"

"Yes."

He cupped his hands for her foot before he realized her boot sole was bloodsoaked, then nearly started puking again when he saw the dripping mess in his cupped hands. But he swung her up onto the animal and began plodding heavily back toward town, leading the mule like some acid-dream Joseph in a nativity scene from hell, trying to clean his hands on his pant's legs.

"Chief Barley, he's got the woman at the police station," Owen concluded his story to Tom with a gulp. "I give him my statement and he wrote it all down. He says I got some vacation days due if I want to take off a while. But I don't see any point in it. He sent out to bring in the two bodies—the killer and the woman's husband—and I seen the graves being dug over to Woodside Baptist. Never found out who the knife man was; didn't have no I.D. or nothing." He gulped a great lungful of air, almost a sob. "How do they know they're Baptists?"

Tom put a hand on the young man's shoulder. "It doesn't matter, Owen. They're at peace. Everyone did all he could; especially you."

They sat silent for a bit before Owen spoke.

"Well, Tom, see: that's the thing. I can't help figuring I messed up. Maybe when I suddenly jumped up outta them weeds like that I surprised them so much—maybe, uh, I mighta caused it all. I think I mighta caused it, you know, just jumping up like that and startling them."

"No, Owen, you didn't cause it. You did exactly right. You did everything anyone could have. It sounds like you saved the woman's life. That's a wonderful thing. She's alive today because of you."

They sat silent for a moment, Owen not appearing convinced.

"Oh, the woman. That reminds me. She's still at the station with the Chief. He asked me to ask you, would you put her up. You got the whole second floor here above the shop for living space, if you'd be willing. She's a good-lookin' woman, she is, and—tell ya the truth—Chief Barley's a mite shy about takin' her in, what with the way his Betty is about other women and all. Said something about 'two women in one kitchen's beggin' for Hell.' Me an' Maybelle would put her up—I know Maybelle wouldn't mind—but, well—I just—I'm just not sure I could do it. Wasn't any of it her fault, of course. I know that. But I just couldn't live in the same house, seeing her ever day, and thinking back to, uh…. I just couldn't do it, Tom."

"Widow Stook's got that room she used to rent, but I hear she's worse than ever with the Bible Prophecy stuff—fairly runs on about it for hours and hours and no getting' her off it—so the Chief said he doubted that was the best place for somebody'd already been through what this woman has. Couldn't think of anyone else where there wasn't likely to be problems of one sort or another—or, you know, talk from the neighbors. So he asked me if I'd ask you."

"If she wants to stay here awhile I'll be glad to put her up, Owen. There's plenty of space for her to have her privacy upstairs—and I'm down here all day anyway. She'll have some peace and quiet to get herself together. Tell her if she wants to she's welcome to stay."

Chapter 4
Sophie's Two Masks

The living quarters above Mountainview Gravely were roomy enough—originally three big bedrooms, kitchen, bath, hallway and assorted closets—but things were still torn up a bit from the changes required to cope with the new conditions of the past few months. Tom sat in the shop, waiting for Chief Barley to bring the woman by, wondering who she was and how she'd react to living arrangements that would be similar in many ways to those of her grandparents.

"Well," he mused, "I guess a widow of less than four hours, who's just seen her husband's throat cut, has all kinds of adjustments to make. Using an outhouse and a woodfired cookstove are probably not among the biggest, right at this moment."

Soon, he saw the pair walking down Elm Street through the dusk toward the Gravely dealership: the middle-aged, overweight, rumpled and sweaty police chief and a tall, striking, forty-ish woman with shoulder-length brown hair beside him.

"Thank you for putting me up, Mr. Jeffson," she said when Chief Barley introduced her. Her handshake was strong and her voice quiet but accompanied by a small, refined smile. To Tom and the Chief, standing in the Gravely shop, flatfooted in dumb amazement, she appeared for all the world as calmly self-possessed as a university president's wife greeting the most junior of the new staff at the year's first faculty tea, automatically putting everyone at ease merely by exercising an aristocratic, well-bred concern for those around her.

"Yes, Ma'am. Tom. Uh ..."

His mind frantically swerved around "glad to have you here" and "pleased to meet you" and "nice to see you"—all the stock phrases so grotesquely, hideously, inappropriate in the present circumstances. He stood, sweating, mind racing in neutral, mute.

"Oh, call me Sophie, Tom—short for Sophia," she filled in so smoothly, rescuing him with such automatic, effortless grace it left him astonished. "I really appreciate your offer."

She turned to Barley and extended her hand. "Thank you again, Chief Barley, for everything you've done. No one could possibly have been more understanding. I'll see you tomorrow at the funeral?"

And with Chief Barley stammering his relieved farewells, she and Tom went up the interior stairs from the shop to the living quarters above.

The landing at the top of the stairs opened onto the bathroom, toward which Tom gestured.

"There's water available—and it's safe to drink—and the drains for the sink, tub, and toilet still work. For the bathtub we heat water on the kitchen stove. Use what water you need, just don't waste any. That 55-gallon drum up on the pedestal there makes things cramped, but it also makes possible the running water, so it's a necessary nuisance.

"On the far right," he gestured from the top of the stairs, "is my bedroom. The bathroom in front of us here has the kitchen on its right and on its left is a bedroom I converted to a den. And your bedroom's on the far left. The bed's made and I put out towels and so forth on a chair, along with an old robe of mine. Would you like a bath, or anything to eat or drink?"

"No thanks, Tom. Chief Barley fed me all I could eat at the police station, and I'll pass on that bath, for now. I'll just get a glass of water and turn in, if you don't mind."

"OK. If you need anything, give me a holler. Try to sleep as much as you can. I won't wake you early tomorrow—the funeral's not till about noon. I'll probably be downstairs in the shop. When you get up I'll make some breakfast. The kitchen stove's now a wood-burner, so just call downstairs to me when you get up and I'll show you about cooking on it. Try to get as much sleep as you can. But if you can't sleep and want to talk just give a knock on my door and we can have some tea in the den. OK?"

"Yes. Thank you, Tom, for more than I can say."

That night he lay in bed a long time in the dead-silent old house, hearing the muffled sounds of sobbing from her room, until he finally drifted off to a fitful sleep. Since turning fifty, Tom had begun to get up in the middle of the night to urinate. This night, quietly going to and from the bathroom at three a.m., he still heard her—so muffled she must have been using her pillow to avoid any sound, but faintly audible in the hush of the sleeping little village.

The next morning he rose just after sunrise, as usual, dressed, and quietly tiptoed into the kitchen. He'd hardly begun putting kindling into the woodstove when she heard him and came in from the den next door, where she'd been sitting with a book in her lap.

Outwardly she was the same tall, beautifully curved woman in her forties, with lovely shoulder-length brown hair Tom had met the previous evening. But when studied more closely she looked so awful Tom had to work to conceal his dismay. Her eyes, hollow and haunted, peered out of deep-set sockets like hopeless, fragile creatures peering up out of the bottom of a well. The black smudges around her eyes showed all the more starkly how pale the rest of her face was. She seemed almost to be swimming in slow motion, as if in a waking dream, when she entered the kitchen.

"Hi!" she chirped, in a voice so chipper the contrast nearly undid Tom altogether. "How can I help with breakfast?"

Drawing a long breath to get his own nerves under control, Tom smiled at her reassuringly and said, "I'm lighting the fire and putting some water on. It won't take five minutes before it's hot enough to fix you a bath. Let's show you how the plumbing works. By the time you're ready, this'll be hot and you can get washed up. Would you like that?"

"Oh yes, that would be wonderful! I can hardly remember the last time I had a bath. We'd been walking for days."

Quickly, Tom lit the fire in the cook stove, went to the bathroom's 55-gallon drum to fill a two-gallon water kettle, and put that on the stove. As it heated, he explained their post-Collapse circumstances.

"We've been awfully lucky, living in a town as small and out of the way as Mountainview," Tom explained, trying to emphasize the positive. "There are only about 400 people—eighty-five or so houses—in the town, and nearly all the houses are fairly old, dating back to the 1960s or much earlier, so they were almost all built to use fireplaces or wood or coal stoves for heat. Most are on acre lots, but the houses on the edges of town have cropland or pasture extending out from them. This house, which my parents built in 1946 and I inherited in 1986, is pretty typical for Mountainview. Since there's no public water or sewer here, every house has its own well and a septic tank with drainfield.

"A few weeks after the atom bombs went off, as the economy began to stall, electric power began to be sporadic. We'd have 'rolling blackouts,' but we still got power for a few hours on most days, as the grid operators tried to distribute what power they had available, as best they could.

"With the house's existing 230-volt well pump, I could fill this 55-gallon drum in about ten minutes or so—by using this hose from the bathroom sink here—whenever we were getting power. So I could keep water stored. The drain water from the tub, toilet, and sink just flows down by gravity, of course, to the septic tank and drainfield as it always did. I didn't bother re-piping anything to connect to the water storage drum: just use this garden hose, here, with the spigot, to draw water from the drum into this bucket, and then pour it into the sink or tub or whatever." He showed her the garden hose leading from the drum, with its shutoff valve.

"Yes, I get it. Running water!" she exclaimed brightly as she considered the marvels of such a treasure. "God, it's *super*! You just can't imagine how wonderful something like clean, safe, running water is."

"Life," Tom said softly to himself, lost for a moment in his own musing. "That's what it is."

Hurriedly, he resumed his businesslike tone.

"The arrangement worked ok till we finally lost electric power altogether a few weeks ago. Since then, I've had to rely on one of the Gravely 2-wheel tractors I sell, connected to the electric generator attachment Gravely makes for it, to produce power. I've needed electric service now and then anyway to run the tools in my repair shop, so while I run the tractor for that I fill this water drum too.

"Using the generator takes gas, though, and the gasoline is running out. Therefore I'd prefer not using the toilet here more than necessary. It still works fine, if you manually fill the flush tank, but it takes an awful lot of water now that we're using gasoline to pump it. I've put in an outhouse I'll show you in the backyard. At least we don't have to carry water in jerry cans from the town creek, like most people do."

"Of course! Thank God I didn't mess anything up," she exclaimed in relief. "I just, um, used it without thinking. An outhouse is fine! It'll be great!"

"Ok, run a couple gallons of water from the drum into the bucket here and set the bucket in the bathtub. I'll get the hot water from the stove. Here's the soap and shampoo. Just stand in the tub, mix the hot water with the cold, soap up, and then rinse off with the remaining water. If you misjudge and need more water heated, just holler and pass me the kettle with some more water in it, and I'll heat some more. Sound OK?"

"Sure! I'll be fine. Thanks so much for this, Tom. God, I've *never* needed a bath so desperately!"

She soaped and splashed for a considerable time, but didn't ask for any additional water. When she emerged, looking fragile and clean rather than fragile and dirty, Tom had finished making pancakes, fried eggs, and steaming mugs of tea. She gazed at the food like it was the first she'd seen in a week.

"Help yourself. Afraid I haven't got any coffee, so I made you some tea. Feel better from the bath?"

"YES!" she cried, putting food on her plate and sugar in her tea.

"Sure wish we had some bacon with this," Tom remarked wistfully as he ate. "I do miss bacon about as much as anything. We have hogs, of course, but nobody around here's cured his own bacon for a long time. Old McClintock claims he remembers how they used to do it—but some days he also claims he remembers hearing Lincoln deliver the Gettysburg Address, so I don't know. Still, you never can tell. He has his good days and his bad days, and sometimes he'll surprise you."

"Oh this is really wonderful just like it is! We'd been walking for so long, and pretty much lived on bread, plus a can of Cheese-Wiz and some cans of ravioli. This is really good!"

And so, lacking any funeral clothes but at least freshly bathed, combed, and fed, Sophie steeled herself for the brief graveside service for her husband. Tom, careful to dress in work clothes himself, walked with her the four blocks to the Woodside Baptist Church, where they found the open grave and a handful of people—most of them police department deputies led by Chief Barley.

The corpse, sewn into a clean white bed sheet for a shroud, because Sophie had nothing to barter for a coffin, was borne to the churchyard on a litter carried by six of the deputies, and interred to the accompaniment of the 23rd Psalm read by Parson Miller. The mercifully brief service was followed by equally tactful brevity on the part of Chief Barley and the others present who expressed their condolences to Sophie. In just a few minutes it was over.

In some ways, Tom thought, the most heartbreaking part of the event was the sight of Owen and Maybelle—standing as far on the fringe of the tiny group as they could, obviously feeling a need to attend but desperately hoping not to be noticed. Owen, Tom saw, seemed outwardly at least to be taking the previous day's events harder than Sophie. Tom was grateful to her when she briefly went to Owen and Maybelle and spoke what seemed comforting words to them.

It was a beautiful, blue-sky day, with the gentlest breeze carrying the scent of new-cut hay across the churchyard: the sort of day that makes a person realize how much better it is to be alive and walking on the earth rather than buried under it. Not for the first time, Tom considered how brief a moment we fireflies have to flutter about—and how, once we're dead, we're going to be dead for a long, long time. He was glad Chief Barley or someone had been thoughtful enough to see that Knife-Man's grave was in a distant corner of the graveyard, and his service had been finished before the present one began.

"It was a proper and decent burial," Tom offered as they walked home. "He'll rest in as lovely a setting as anyone could wish. At least there's that to hold on to."

"Yes. Everyone here—every person I've met—just couldn't have been more thoughtful. And the churchyard is almost out of a storybook, its setting is so beautiful. You and everyone else here have been more kind than I can say."

She spoke with a gentle, tender seriousness, not at all the raw grief of a widow who had just put her murdered husband in the earth. It was almost as if, having comforted Owen at her husband's graveside, Sophie was now devoting her attention to helping Tom over his own grief as well. They walked slowly back toward his home.

After a time, Tom broke their silence, as gently as he knew how.

"Sophia, I don't want to intrude on you. Please understand that. I will give you as much privacy as you want. But I know you are feeling grief and I know you are not outwardly expressing it. I want you to understand that it's ok to show it. You must have been through a hellacious time, even before the murder; and then that…It is ok for you to express your feelings. If you want to talk I'm here any time you'd like…"

He left off, feeling inarticulate and clumsy. They reached Mountainview Gravely and went inside.

"Thank you, Tom," she reassured him, her voice still holding the unshakable, self-possessed calm that never seemed to vary. "I appreciate that." She started up the stairs. "I think I'll lie down for a little. Sometime later will you show me what you do here in your shop?"

So Tom remained in his shop, trying to force himself to concentrate on the Gravely two-wheel tractor he was partly disassembling, and on the small steam engine he'd bought just before the Collapse—and on the possibility of combining them to, perhaps, save lives. To, perhaps, keep at least some people out of those horrible, awful, gaping, six-foot-deep-holes-in-the-dirt-for-all-eternity he'd just come away from. But he couldn't get past his bafflement about who on earth Sophie and her husband were, and how on earth they'd come to be walking toward Mountainview.

Supper was another of the bland, unappealing boiled-rice-and-beans concoctions from stored bulk foods that had become all too routine in the present time of scarcities. Tom and Sophie then tried reading a while in the den until the failing light of dusk signaled time for bed.

Self-possessed as ever, Sophie again thanked him for attending the funeral with her, said goodnight, and withdrew to her room.

Tom, entering his own room, already dreaded the suppressed, gut rending sobs of anguish he would hear throughout the night from behind her closed door. When they began—going on and on in the nighttime silence—he was not sure how much more of her public-calm/private-anguish dual personality he would be able to endure—or indeed, how much longer she herself could last in such a state without permanently going off the rails somehow.

Chapter 5
Sophie's Tale

She sounded as perky as ever the next morning, and looked even more haunted, haggard and beaten than before. Tom's increased worry about her stability led him to attempt gently steering their talk at the breakfast table.

"How'd you come to be walking toward Mountainview?" Tom asked carefully, trying to let her bring out the story in whatever way was best for her. To his surprise, she began to reply.

"We—Carl and I—my husband—were trying to get to Martinsburg, in West Virginia. We'd heard there are a lot of federal government installations there. Lots of agencies had regional offices there, which we figured are probably now the agencies' Head Offices, being fairly close to Washington, D.C., but outside the Baltimore-Washington metro area, which was apparently looted and burned out and killed off by diseases and so forth. Based on what we heard on the news—until the news stopped.

"Carl was a teacher: Lowenstein Professor of Political Science, at the Bob Dole School of Public Policy, at Stanford. He'd been to conferences in Washington several times. There may have been an offer of a Deputy Assistant Undersecretary slot in the works, before the atom bombs. It was nothing firm yet. These things go through a carefully scripted ritual of unspoken understandings before anything is formally offered. But he thought maybe he could be of some use in the emergency."

"Doing what?" Tom asked, his puzzlement making it sound blunter than he'd intended.

"Formulating policy," she answered, surprised by his failure to grasp the obvious. "His field involved the use of econometric modeling to examine correlations between America's M2 and the amount of World Bank funding available for various Third World development projects."

She caught herself, embarrassed by the jargon.

"M2's a category, or type, of dollars in circulation," she muttered apologetically.

"I've heard of it."

He sat silent, wondering what it was he must have missed.

"So your husband and you," feeling his way here, slowly and carefully, "flew from California to the East Coast…during a catastrophe unprecedented in modern history…in hopes he could formulate Federal policy…for monitoring the availability of World Bank funds…to be used in Third World development projects?"

"Well—that or some related policy area." She was hurt, defensive, interpreting his bewilderment as criticism. "But there weren't any flights available to most of the East Coast. The best we could get was one to Columbus, Ohio, with a connecting commuter hop onward to Wheeling, West Virginia. But on that hop, the captain announced in-flight that the Wheeling airport had just closed, and a lot of others, too; so we ended up landing at Clarksburg, West Virginia.

"We hoped we could arrange a charter flight, or a car or bus or something, on toward Martinsburg from there. But we couldn't get anything. It seemed that once the final chaos began it snowballed very, very rapidly. So we got a roadmap, and what supplies we could, and started walking in hopes we might be able to hitch-hike."

After thinking a moment, Tom said quietly "From Clarksburg to Martinsburg's about, ah, 200 miles or a little more. Over mountains."

"Yes; that's what we judged from the map. But we got off course. After a few days walking, we hitched a ride one evening in a National Guard truck, and they went every which way for hours and hours.

"Finally, in the middle of the night, they put us out at a crossroads, saying they were about to enter a Prohibited Zone and it was as far as we could go. I think the National Guard was as lost as we were by then. But we found the Big Dipper and the North Star, and we started walking in what seemed like a northeasterly direction. But nothing matched the map from that point on.

"Chief Barley told me this is Mountainview. I don't remember it on the map. We were pretty much just walking in hopes something would turn up, by the time we were attacked… "

She sat silent, thinking back on those few moments of horror.

"The man who tried to rob us—I don't think he was really bad, or really a thief. I don't think he'd ever done it before. He acted frightened and desperate, and didn't seem to know how to go about it. He had a kitchen knife, but he didn't need that; we'd have given him anything we had. But we didn't have any food left, and we didn't have anything else to offer. He didn't seem to believe us.

I think he was mostly just confused, more than actually bad—a victim of his environment, just as we were."

All the horror and heartache and hopelessness and dread of the past two months suddenly welled up in Tom, engulfing him in a wave of rage and despair. He looked at her, wondering how people could think the way she seemed to—which planet such people lived on.

A pair of California nitwits trying to fly to Martinsburg, West Virginia. To "formulate policy." Some half-assed yokel with a butcher knife, too dumb to successfully steal bubblegum from a two-year-old. Horrible, gruesome, pointless, death for two people—and who knew what still to come for an Owen guilt-wracked over his part in the mess. Plus this nut-case widow, who, whether she was going crazy or already there, should have stayed on whatever distant planet she came from…

Tom's hands clenched white below the breakfast table.

"You both still had the clothes you wore," he said, with deceptive, deadly quiet. "They'd have made sufficient barter goods for a few meals—especially the shoes. In addition, you'd have been a valuable commodity for rape."

He sat, trying to control himself.

"The man who attacked you was not bad, merely a victim, you believe. Let me tell you why you could not fly to the Baltimore-Washington area, or to any other major city. It's because there's almost no one still alive there. After the commercial broadcasting stations went down, our two ham operators here in Mountainview still picked up enough military and National Guard radio traffic to get a pretty clear idea of what happened.

"When the inherently worthless paper dollar was revealed to be worthless, and the economy collapsed toward a medieval barter level, and employees—military, civilian government, and private-sector—reported less and less for work they were no longer being paid for, then the electric utilities began to fail.

"As the power failed, taking with it the water and sewer systems, the millions of people in the cities—who were not 'bad,' mind you, became—as you put it—'confused victims of their environment.' They milled about slowly in circles—bewildered—like a herd of beeves in a feedlot whose owner has failed to bring them food and water.

"A few people briefly, randomly, darted this way or that for what they hoped would be a quick theft. Some tried walking out of the cities, since all the roads were by then impassable to vehicles. But after fifteen or twenty aimless miles on foot, getting nowhere, they gave that up as hopeless and drifted back to the familiarity of their homes. Also, by then many of the would-be walkers were getting sick from spoiled food and from a lack of the simplest hygiene: hand-washing in clean water.

"For the most part, though, most people just stayed put, waiting for help, milling about in passive bewilderment, too 'confused' even to dig privies, just shitting everywhere at random. So the runoff from the first little rain shower contaminated their few possible sources of drinking water.

"And then they died. They died like flies. When the waves of dysentery, typhoid, cholera and other filth-born epidemics hit, the city populations just... *died.*"

He was breathing deeply, within an inch of losing his hold on himself.

"And your husband;" he took another deep breath, "your husband, thought the most useful thing for him to do in this situation was to travel clear across the continent. To try to locate whatever was left of the federal government. So he could get a job formulating policy. To evaluate the World Bank's funding resources for Third World development projects. While—it's clear now—the population of every significant city in the U.S. was dying off. Mostly because they were—in their utter, innocent, bovine dependency on *The State* and its *Policies*—too 'confused' to dig pit privies to shit in."

Tom was by now so overwhelmed he was almost pleading with her to help him understand.

"Did your husband, in his idealistic determination to Save Mankind by Formulating Policy, ever once—just *once*—consider using a Goddamned SHOVEL?!"

"He was a brilliant teacher," she said quietly but stoutly, not about to back down. "He devoted his entire life to the public policy arena."

Tom went down to his shop. For a long time he couldn't think clearly enough to resume work on the machine he was building, and just sat in his chair.

Chapter 6
Different Values

As arranged, Owen came by the shop in mid-morning, when his midnight patrol shift was over. He had agreed to spend twenty hours a week there during his day and night off-time, helping Tom with work and providing security. Tom, who still had about a ton of the wheat, corn, beans, and rice he'd accumulated in 1999, before the Y2K computer scare proved unfounded, was to pay Owen one cup of each of those staples per week for his services. Together with what Owen earned on Citizens' Patrol, plus what Maybelle got, cooking for the half-dozen hired hands now intensively farming a nearby neighbor's truck garden, the total was enough for the couple to live on.

"Hi, Tom, how's the lady?" Owen asked as he entered the shop, too innocent to pretend a lack of curiosity.

"Crazy."

"Yeah? Well, I heard she's from California," Owen explained.

Tom said, "Husband was a big-time schoolteacher there. Must have been making a ton of dough: he held an endowed chair at Stanford University."

"Yeah? So what're they doing here?"

"Given the crisis, he felt it was important to help the federal government formulate policy."

"Why?"

Tom sighed. "Because that's what people like him do in a crisis."

"Yeah?" said Owen thoughtfully, trying to make sense of this as he idly scratched a mosquito bite. "Well, California ..." he eventually concluded. "Anyway," he offered, "sure as hell won't catch me goin' out there. Fulla queers, what I hear."

"You can't say that," Tom gently reproved him. "They're gay."

"Why?"

"Because it's considered rude. And I'm sure it would hurt Sophie's feelings if she heard you."

42

"No, I mean why are they gay? I've wondered about that. If I had some condition like that, and couldn't help it, I think I'd be sad. Or maybe angry or something. Saw some on TV a few times and they looked pretty angry—hollerin' and carryin' on like I don't know whatall. But I'm pretty sure I wouldn't be gay."

"Well, it's just a word you're supposed to use. Look, I behaved badly toward Sophie this morning when she told me about her husband. I just seem to say things I ought not. I'm sure I hurt her feelings. However crazy she and the husband were, they were also brave and well-meaning, and I oughtn't have said things I did. Go up and show her how to use the woodstove, would you—and maybe ask her if she'd like to bake some bread or something, so she'll have something to occupy her if she wants? There's a *Marlene's Magic* cookbook on the kitchen table or counter someplace, and you know where the wheat berries and hand mill and other things are. Would you sort of, you know, take charge of her for a while? And, uh, I'll be up later to apologize, okay?"

So Owen, not at all sure how this moonlighting job was going to work out, slowly climbed the stairs to undertake his first assignment.

Tom had finally settled down enough to become immersed in the Shop Manual for the 1976 "L" Model Gravely he had decided to remove the gasoline engine from. He studied the gear ratios the two-wheel tractor used with its standard 7.6 H.P. gas engine. Steam engines, he knew, have far more torque than gas engines—and develop their full torque right from the start, not needing to be rev'd up to several thousand RPM the way gas engines do. How would these differences affect the gear ratios when he put a steam engine on the Gravely in place of the gas engine it was designed for?

Puzzling the matter through, he didn't notice Owen and Sophie coming down the stairs until they were in the shop.

"I found some things to fix for your lunch, Tom," Sophie said, looking as haunted and sounding as bright and carefree as ever. She put a container on the workbench and held a box of what looked like food ingredients in her hand.

"Can I borrow Owen for a few minutes so he can show me where his house is? I thought Maybelle could help me with bread making until she has to go back to her cooking job later in the day. I'll be back this afternoon—hopefully with some decent bread for us."

"Sure, take your time, both of you. Owen, get a few hours' sleep if you feel like it, and come back to put in some time before you start your midnight Patrol shift. I'm fine here, and there's nothing much doing anyway until I get some stuff figured out."

43

When Sophie returned about five that afternoon she had a still-warm, wonderful-smelling loaf wrapped in a cloth, and Owen tagging along by her side like a devoted Newfoundland dog.

Waving the fresh bread past Tom's nose with a bit of a ballet twirl, she continued happily on upstairs to get supper ready, leaving Owen in the shop, staring up after her with awe.

"Well, she's got you hypnotized anyway," grumped Tom.

"You know," Owen replied thoughtfully, "I don't think she's a bit crazy. She was just as thoughtful as she could be to me and Maybelle both. She tole' me she really appreciated what I done during the attack—an' tole' Maybelle how lucky she was to have a husban' servin' in the Patrol. Made me 'n' Maybelle both feel pretty proud. And then them two went into the kitchen and went to chatterin' and jabberin' with each other, and I got a nap. And then Maybelle wakes me up in a few hours and they've baked bread and Maybelle says the lady showed her how to make some new thing called keesh, which is sort of whipped-up eggs—and God knows we got eggs out the wazoo right now—and it's not all that bad. Though I think it'd be better with some bacon in it. If we had some bacon. Anyway, she and Maybelle just loved each other, and I can tell you I'm pretty damn pleased by that, 'cause Maybelle's been sort of down in the dumps lately, with all the hard times we're havin.' You can tell she comes from money, all right. But, you know, she's not a bit smart-assed or anything like that. Me an' Maybelle both just think she's just as nice as can be."

"Uh huh. Got you hypnotized, all right," Tom repeated, carefully applying a small squirt of WD-40 to each of the engine-mounting bolts on the old 1976 "L" Model Gravely.

When she called downstairs that supper was ready, Tom and Owen went up to a delicious-smelling kitchen and a strangely savory dish neither had ever encountered before. It seemed to be a sort of mashed potato pie, containing pieces of canned corned beef and, of course, the ever-present eggs—this time hardboiled and chopped in with the corned beef—all in some sort of rich, aromatic gravy. With the fresh buttered bread, it made a very striking meal for people who'd become accustomed, by recent necessity, to food more along the lines of assorted forms of pottage, porridge, mush, and gruel.

"Dang!" exclaimed Owen, wolfing down another helping, "This is really good! How do you get it to have such a rich flavor? I never tasted anything quite like this. It's not...sort of...'blah.' You know what I mean?"

"I think it's the red wine," Sophia answered brightly, pleased by the reception her handiwork was receiving, and proud of her ingenuity. "I found a bottle in the cupboard and thought it might be just the missing ingredient."

"*Wine?*" asked Owen in stunned dismay. His fork froze in midair. "There's wine in this? Jeez, Sophie, I wish you'd a said. I'm a Foursquare Baptist. We don't touch no wine or alcohol of any sort. It's wrong." He sat back, stricken.

"Well, do you go to communion?"

"Course I do," he replied.

"And at communion you drink …" she prompted.

"Grape juice, of course. Welch's grape juice."

Not missing a beat, she closed the sale, "Well, there you are then. You realize the problem's the alcohol, not the grape juice. When you remove all the alcohol from wine, by evaporating it in cooking, what's left? Grape juice. Which you drink every communion."

Silently, Owen thought this over. Carefully considering it from all angles, he could see she had a point. And there was no question she was a really nice lady, and had been nice as could be to Maybelle. And there was certainly, definitely, no question this meal was delicious beyond any food he'd had in a long, long time…

"I guess you're right," he slowly admitted. "I never thought of it that way."

When Owen had gone back down to the shop after supper, to see if he could get some of the engine-mounting bolts loosened before leaving to begin his patrol shift at midnight, Tom dried while Sophie washed the dishes.

"So?" she asked, with a turn of her head and a quick little glance from the corner of her eye.

"Smooooth," Tom breathed in grudging admiration, slowly shaking his head. "You're something, you are. It sounds like he and Maybelle both would die for you. They're the most goodhearted, decent people you'll ever meet. Please don't let them down."

"I wouldn't, Tom, not for anything. I've become very fond of them. Just in the time we were together today, they've done an awful lot for me. God, I about had heart failure when he said '*wine?*' with that awful look on his face."

She gazed heavenward for a moment. "Thank you, Sweet Jesus, for saving my ignorant ass! I just never, ever *dreamed* …!"

After a moment, she asked, "Will you help me, Tom? I don't even know what I don't know about life here in Mountainview. Will you help keep me from making some terrible mistake and causing needless hurt?"

"If you'll accept my apology for the way I spoke at breakfast. Talk about ignorant: there was no excuse for my comments. I'm sorry for them."

"Then done and done." She smiled. "Can we bring our tea into the den so

I can browse through your books some more? From what I've seen so far, you're a strange one, Mr. Jeffson."

But again that night, after they'd gone to their bedrooms and he was lying in the silence waiting for sleep, he heard the faintest sounds of her muffled sobbing as it went on and on, seeming never to end.

Chapter 7
Who Might Live, and How

"For the time being," he explained to her as he served breakfast the next morning, "it's a matter of gasoline. We were very lucky. Jared's Conoco Handimart, which is our one gas station, received a tank truck delivery the day before the terrorist nukes. So it had a full 8,000 gallons in its tank. People began buying, of course, and Jared called in before noon that same day for another delivery. Chief Barley had dropped by and told him he also wanted the police department's 2000-gallon tank topped up at the same time. The rapid order placement, plus a miracle I guess, actually paid off, and in a week we got the delivery—some of the last gasoline to be delivered out this way, I understand. So we managed to enter this crisis with about as much on hand as possible.

"We're also lucky to have a good many of the most efficient users of gasoline you could ask for in our situation: Gravely two-wheel tractors. They were invented and first built right here in West Virginia, you know, by a man whose very name sums up qualities America used to have: Benjamin Franklin Gravely. During the First World War, Mr. Gravely worked out a way to put the engine from an Indian motorcycle on a garden plow. About the time his small workshop began producing the new 'Gravely Motor Plows' in quantity, the 1929 Crash and Depression hit. During the terrible years that followed, he would periodically load a half-dozen of his machines in his Studebaker car and drive as far as Florida, selling them to farm families, then return to West Virginia for another load.

"He didn't get rich, but he stayed in business. You see, the purpose of Mr. Gravely's company was to produce actual, physical products—200-lb machines that could do the work of a mule—not to produce bits of paper called 'shares' that would magically, in dot.com fashion, go up forever in value while representing nothing tangible at all.

"I've got a copy of a letter here Mr. Gravely wrote to businessmen in Charleston, West Virginia, during the Depression, soliciting their investment in his company," Tom said, showing Sophie a framed clipping he'd hung on the wall. "In it, he points out to these desperate, near-bankrupt men that 'Production is the very foundation of our existence. Without it, we are lost. Vacant lots, empty houses and idle factories do not pay dividends.'

"Production," Tom continued sourly, "big difference from our own era, in which people imagined they were going to get rich simply by holding bits of paper that magically increased in value—with no need to actually produce anything at all." He sighed.

"In building a product for his own region, Mr. Gravely did a wonderful thing for people all over the world. Within a few years, his West Virginia workshop had sales outlets in Florida and California, and there were European representatives in France, Switzerland, and Germany. In years to come, Mr. Gravely's daughter would treasure a stack of correspondence concerning her father's invention, including letters from Puerto Rico, Palestine, Venezuela, The Netherlands, Belgium, Kenya, Hungary, Turkey, El Salvador, Iceland, Guatemala, and many other faraway places. As she said, 'Papa would have been happy to know that the Gravely tractor is giving people work.'

"For our conditions," Tom explained, "small- to medium-sized fields, abundant labor supply, and widespread, decentralized ownership of lands and equipment—the Gravely tractor is about the most efficient machine of its kind ever made. In a 50,000-acre Kansas wheat field it'd be uselessly inadequate; or in a half-acre backyard garden it'd be needlessly excessive. But for the two-to-fifty-acre fields we have here, it's perfect. You've heard the expression about the typical pioneer homestead being 'Forty acres and a mule?' Well, the Gravely is the ideal, mechanical super-mule for that size operation—and it beats a muscle-powered mule as much as a gas chainsaw beats the muscle-powered 'Armstrong' variety for felling trees and cutting cords of firewood.

"Unless you want some more breakfast, come down to the shop. I'll show you how the device that helped pull countless small farm families through the Depression is now the best hope you've got for staying alive in today's new world."

They went downstairs to the nearly bare showroom, where Tom pointed to a shiny new Pro model two-wheel tractor awaiting sale. It was the first time Sophie had actually paid any attention to the machines, either in the shop or the showroom, and she studied it with interest.

"It's a rototiller, isn't it?" she asked, faintly disappointed after his previous buildup.

"Yes, for a start. You can see these blades, called tines, which turn beneath the tractor as it moves forward, churning up the soil. You can break up sod that way, if you're turning a pasture into a tilled field, for example; or you can rototill to chop up weeds, aerate the soil, and loosen it to prepare it for planting. Lots of other companies make rototillers but the Gravely is by far the heaviest, most indestructible, most capable – and, alas, most expensive. I had a hard time selling them before The Collapse because they just plain cost too much. People wanted them, but wouldn't spend the money." He shrugged.

"Oh well, the bright side is: nothing's so bad it can't get worse. Used to be hard to sell them, now it's impossible. They're worth even more today than they were—and people have even less to trade for them. So I'll do with this new one what I'm already doing with the rest of my new machines: rent it out for whatever I can get on a share-crop basis until the last of the gasoline's gone. Then I'll take them all back and basically eat the several thousand dollar loss on each one.

"But what I wanted to show you is that rototilling is just the beginning of a world of uses for the Gravely. The machine's many other functions make it more properly called a two-wheel tractor than simply a rototiller. The number and variety of attachments available for this machine make it by far the most adaptable power source for small farms ever manufactured."

Taking a leaflet from a rack of sales materials, he showed her a list of accessories and attachments designed for Gravely two-wheel tractors.

1. Aerator, soil
2. Axels, extended
3. Back-hoe
4. Barrow, power
5. Blade, scraper
6. Blower, leaf
7. Brush, power
8. Car pusher
9. Cart, hauling (front & rear mount)
10. Chains, tire
11. Cultivators, 5 & 7 tooth
12. Cultivator, rotary
13. Digger, post hole
14. Distributor, fertilizer
15. Fogger
16. Furrower

17. Generator, electric
18. Harrow, disc
19. Harrow, peg tooth
20. Hitch, rear
21. Leafaway (mulcher)
22. Mower, 30" rotary
23. Mower, 50" rotary
24. Mower-Mulcher, rotary
25. Mowers, reel, gang-type
26. Planter drill
27. Plow, rotary (dirt)
28. Power take off (PTO)
29. Pump, water
30. Rake, hay
31. Roller, lawn (water-filled)
32. Saw, chain-type
33. Saw, circular
34. Scoop, utility
35. Seeder-Spreader
36. Shredder, compost
37. Sickle Mower
38. Snowblades, V-type & straight
39. Snowblower
40. Splitter, log
41. Sprayer
42. Starter, electric
43. Sulky, riding
44. Sweeper, lawn
45. Trenchdigger
46. Wheels, dual
47. Wheels, gear reduction

"I'm not sure what half these things are," she said, reading down the list, "but even I can see this machine will do all sorts of things people need done."

"Yes. And the agricultural jobs it will do—about anything you'd need done to grow and harvest crops on small or medium acreages—are almost secondary in some respects to all the non-agricultural things it will do. Running the generator, for example, allows us to use the shop equipment here—lathes, drills, welders, grinders, etc.—all of which require 115 or 230 volt electric current. So we can build and repair all sorts of other equipment we need. And, of course, pump water to the house electrically instead of pumping it manually or carrying it from the creek.

"The Gravely's chain saw attachment can rapidly cut huge amounts of fire wood—our only heating and cooking fuel now—and the log splitter attachment will easily reduce the wood to kitchen-stove size. The circular saw will cut the masses of fence-posts we'll need to keep our animals out of our tilled fields, and the posthole digger will make rapid fence construction possible. The circular saw will also mill tree trunks into the rough lumber we're going to need for repairs and new construction.

"The cart will transport material—firewood, manure, fence posts, building stone, harvested crops—far faster than we could move such things using muscle power. The riding sulky will transport riders at a horseback pace—without needing to be fed, watered, housed, and groomed daily, whether used or not. The geared-down dual wheels, with chains, make the Gravely into a log-skidder capable of dragging heavy sections of tree trunk out of the surrounding forest, to where we can work with them.

"The Gravely will dig trenches to bury waterlines and prevent them freezing, it will plow dirt to make banks or berms or irrigation ditches, and it will plow or blow snow to keep our town sidewalks passable in winter. It will pump irrigation water for our fields from the nearby creek, and blow air for the old fashioned winnowing we'll have to do to separate grain from chaff when we harvest crops.

"The Gravely, with it's myriad attachments, will do as much as any machine could to make it possible – just possible—that with an enormous amount of work and a lot of deprivation we might be able to keep ourselves alive here in Mountainview. And maybe – just maybe—eventually reach a point, years down the road, where we're doing more than just keeping ourselves alive—where we're actually starting to rebuild a living standard that offers more than endless toil and a barely continued existence on the thinnest of margins."

He led her to the old L Model Gravely he and Owen were working on, and then beyond it to the steam engine on the shop floor.

"But, see, Sophie, we're never going to reach that happy day—in fact, we're none of us likely to be here a year from now—if we depend on Gravelys using the gas engines they're equipped with. Our gasoline is running out. As little as a Gravely burns, and using nothing but them, we've still got only a few months' gas left. At that point, we either have the first steam powered Gravely up and running, or we revert to the muscle-powered, pre-mechanical life people lived throughout human history—from hunter-gatherer times until about 1850.

"I doubt we'd make it without mechanical power to help us: we're too soft, we have too little in the way of primitive skills, and our expectations of life would not allow us to revert that far and still go on living. Most of us—I for one—would just say The Hell With It and begin a brief, apathetic decline if we had to re-enter such a primitive age. With a steam powered Gravely, though, we have enough wood fuel to run it forever, and we could use it as an electric power source for the shop tools here to make possible the building of more steam engines to put on more Gravelys. Eventually, we might be able to work our way out of our current desperate situation."

She thought over what he'd said. "Isn't there a possibility of receiving help from someplace?"

"Doesn't look very likely. In theory, miracles could always happen, I guess, but I doubt it very much. I expect there are various isolated military units of one sort or another, holed up in forts or bunkers somewhere, living on stored rations. But I doubt if they're likely to have the skills, tools, or inclination to produce their own food and other necessities once their stockpiles run out. In any case, helping us in Mountainview is certainly not going to head their list of priorities.

"In the early days of The Collapse some Mountainview residents left here, trying to join relatives elsewhere in the country. Without exception, they never reappeared and we never heard anything from them. OK: reasonable enough for those traveling to some distant point. But even people who just went to Grayson, the county seat? Twenty-five miles away? We simply never heard from them again. It was spooky, all right. How could they just…disappear? We'll figure it out eventually, I suppose; but in the meantime we've had more pressing concerns just keeping ourselves alive.

"We did hear enough over the radio—from commercial broadcasts then from military traffic after the commercial stations went down—to know that virtually all people who lived in communities larger than small towns are, to be blunt, dead. When the economy collapsed, and the no-longer-paid workers who had provided social order and public services quit, and the power, water, and sanitation failed, it was astonishing how quickly social chaos, hunger, and—most of all—disease from polluted drinking water killed off the urban populations.

"At the other end of the spectrum from urban concentrations is the tiny handful of people who were still living on farms in completely rural areas. If they haven't yet died, they soon will. A family in Kansas or Wyoming, for example, in their farmhouse, surrounded by a thousand square miles of gorgeous, fertile wheat fields, can't possibly make it. Their machinery is all huge, diesel-powered stuff for which there's no fuel. The only thing they're set up to grow is corn or wheat or some other single crop, which is not nearly enough to live on; and they've no way to barter their surplus for all the other stuff they need. Perhaps most important, there isn't enough adjoining timber to furnish adequate firewood for very long—therefore no cooking or heating. And one farm family, or a few grouped together in a single house, won't have enough able bodies to perform the labor necessary for survival, or to defend themselves against random attacks by looters or the merely hungry.

"It looks pretty clear that the people still alive—at least those with any chance of being alive six months or a year from now—are those in tiny towns, small enough to support themselves from crops and animals raised on truck-garden-sized acreages immediately surrounding the town itself, yet large enough to furnish sufficient manpower for cultivation, other labor needs, and defense. The small towns in question will have to be in areas with reasonably moderate climate, adequate rainfall for farming, and—extremely important—abundant timber. Wood is vital for more than just energy. After all, we're leaving the age of metals and plastics, slipping back to the time when wood was the all-purpose material for whatever you needed to make. As for energy, not many locations anymore have useable deposits of coal lying on or near the surface to be picked up. And primitive mining operations, even if they could meet a group's energy needs, still wouldn't produce the wood needed for building and countless other uses if the area lacked abundant forest.

"Finally, I think the communities that survive will be ones—like Mountainview—with limited accessibility. Any community too easy to get to will have to spend too much of its resources defending itself, whether from armed attack or merely from hungry and desperate freeloaders, to survive.

"You may have noticed from the map, when you set out to walk, that eastern West Virginia consists of countless mountain ridges paralleling each other in a roughly north/south direction."

He placed his left hand on the workbench, fingers slightly separated to indicate the parallel ridges and valleys between them.

"The 'mountains,' so-called, are only two or three thousand feet high; but they are very, very steep and rugged. You couldn't ride a horse or mule across most of them, up one side and down the other, because they're just too steep and too thickly forested. Realistically, the only travel in these parts is along whatever valley you're in, until you reach a 'gap'—what the New Englanders call a 'notch'—that is a crossover point into an adjacent valley.

"Mountainview is almost at the extreme south, or 'dead end' of our valley. There's only a cluster of three or four Mennonite families—maybe thirty people total—living south of us at the 'dead end' of the valley; so we wont have any problems coming from that direction. Any significant number of outsiders could approach us only as you did: down County Route 12 from the north—and even that's not likely, as far off any major highways as we are. So that bit of luck has helped us stay alive.

"Aside from small communities like Mountainview scattered across the country, I think there may also be a tiny handful of 'mountain men' who will survive in the wild by trapping, hunting, and gathering: latter-day Jim Bridger types, who successfully revert to the level of the Indians in Bridger's time. But keep in mind, even Bridger traded his furs yearly for the artifacts of civilization—powder and lead, knives and axes, traps and fish hooks, etcetera. Any 'mountain men' from now on would eventually revert permanently back to the level of the aboriginal Indians—a Stone Age people without metal artifacts, writing, or the wheel. Ug.

"So, no, we're not going to be rescued by anyone from outside. With luck, we're sufficiently numerous, well-armed, and organized to defeat any likely level of small-scale attack. And I think we have a diverse enough need for a range of skills and abilities that we can incorporate small numbers of people who want to peacefully join us, and offer them work sufficient for them to pay their way. But, bottom line: I think it's going to be up to us. Rescue doesn't seem to be in the cards. Our rescue, if it is that, is waiting right there," and he pointed to the steam engine, sitting rather forlornly by itself on the workshop's concrete floor.

As she went back upstairs to start lunch, looking more somber and thoughtful than he'd previously seen her, he knelt to continue work on the old 1976 L Model he and Owen were removing the engine from.

Well. At least I managed to avoid any comment about our rescue depending on a properly formulated policy for monitoring M2 levels and their impact on the World Bank's resources, he thought sourly, reaching for a 5/8-inch socket.

Chapter 8

The Attack

But just after noon, Tom's work was interrupted when Chief Barley arrived at the shop carrying several clamp-on reflector lights and some electrical extension cords.

"Hi, Tom. Got a moment?"

"Hey, Chief. Have a seat. Anything beats working."

"This may not."

Looking more closely, Tom could see Barley was tense, scowling in an attempt to conceal his worry.

"Phil Black had patrol duty at the north edge of town last night, out where Route 12 enters Mountainview," Barley stated.

The Chief was silent for a moment. Both men thought back to the events at that location only two days ago, leaving a pair of deaths, a widow, and a still-shaken deputy in their wake.

"Shit!" Barley vented his current anxiety, then took a deep breath. "Phil reported in to the Station this morning, when his shift was up, and he had two observations from last night. Maybe. The wind was light and fluky, and one time when it shifted momentarily he *thought* he heard a horse whinny. Phil's a good man. He's not out on patrol with his thumb up his ass and his mind in Arizona, like some of 'em. He knew the only horse we've got here is Jenson's old gelding, over the other side of town. Couldn't have been his.

"So he spends the rest of his patrol right where he is, waiting quietly, and an hour or so later, with another momentary wind shift, he's pretty sure he can smell wood smoke, coming from beyond the north edge of town. It was just the least little whiff—and only for an instant before the wind shifted again. He can't be positive he smelled it, but he thinks so. And I think Phil's pretty dependable.

"So we have to consider there may be some person or persons, probably horse-mounted, approaching us along Route 12 and taking care to stay hidden.

He or they apparently camped a ways out of town last night. My guess is they're moving only in darkness, and plan to enter us tonight. So I'd like to have our welcome arranged before nightfall."

Briefly, the two men worked out Tom's assignment, then Barley went back to the Station to issue instructions to his deputies.

Tom made sure there was gas in his remaining brand-new two-wheel tractor he'd just been showing to Sophia. It was a deluxe Pro Model with electric start, and Tom tried it a couple of times in the showroom to make sure it started easily. Satisfied, he hitched it to a cart and put the Chief's lights and extension cords into the cart, along with several more clamp-on reflector lights and extension cords from his shop. Then he hitched the Gravely generator accessory on behind the cart, started up, and trundled off toward Rt. 12 at the edge of town.

Once there, he positioned the Gravely behind some brush in the bar ditch, so it was well hidden from the little two-lane blacktop county road. He moved the wagon aside, connected the generator, and ran his extension cords along the ditch at the roadside. He plugged in all twelve of his assorted lights, clipping them to available brush and branches so the shiny reflectors would illuminate about a forty-foot section of the road. As he worked, deputies began quietly arriving in twos and threes, taking up positions in the roadside ditch behind the lights, piling up a few rocks or branches in front of themselves for cover in spots where there was none naturally.

There was no noise or confusion, no jive-assing braggadocio among the men, Tom observed with satisfaction, simply a quiet, grim determination to do well whatever they would soon need to do—however gruesome it might be.

The Chief arrived as dusk began to fall, inspected each man's position and weapon, approving them with a quiet word or nod or pat on the back, and then made his way to Tom at the Gravely.

"Whoever they are, they're not likely to get off the road I figure," he whispered to Tom. "That would mean crossing the roadside ditch and then slogging around through soft, plowed fields to approach town from some other direction. I've got men posted all round the edge of town, just in case, but I expect this road's going to be the way they come. Let's hope it's good and dark before they try it, so we get the maximum value from these lights."

And then they quietly waited. Soon, there was all the darkness the Chief had hoped for, and then some. The faintest sliver of a new moon didn't provide light enough to see a hand in front of one's face. Silently waiting in the blackness, Tom felt certain time had come to a complete standstill, even though his watch showed only two hours since full dark had fallen.

Finally, they heard sounds from the road, distant and faint but coming their way. There was a quiet plod of what must have been a very heavy horse, and the lighter hooves of some smaller animal or animals. Then, most peculiar, Tom barely saw the faintest possible glimmer of light. It floated slowly down the center of the road, hanging in mid-air a couple of feet above the blacktop, its creepy silence enough to give anyone the bejeebers. Tom could sense the man on each side of him moving his weapon's safety to "off."

When Chief Barley judged that whatever it was had entered the killing zone, he tapped Tom on the arm. Tom turned the key on the Gravely. As the motor suddenly roared into life, he clutched in the generator. Instantly, the road was lit up as if a magnesium flare had gone off.

"HALT! STOP WHERE YOU ARE!" shouted Chief Barley.

It was hard to know which side was more dumbfounded, but Tom felt an intense pity for the group now exposed on the road. Suddenly caught exposed and unaware in brilliant light, knowing that armed men were unseen but obvious behind the blinding dazzle, the family of travelers from the 18th century exhibited an amazingly calm bravery that moved Tom deeply.

"Friend, thee are welcome to our goods," said a bearded old man from the seat of what looked like a Conestoga wagon. "We ask thee to spare us our lives."

His voice held what seemed like infinite disappointment, rather than any shock or fear.

"It's Amish!" the Chief cried, his voice nearly cracking with relief. "Hold your fire! Stay in your positions! Safe your weapons!"

"Sir, we're not after your goods. We were afraid we were being attacked. I apologize for the scare."

"We are not affrighted," the old bearded one softly replied, "for we attack no one." The logic of this escaped Tom, though it seemed obvious to the old man.

"The English..." muttered the old one, with what seemed a deep despair. "With all thy guns and...and...'*Devices*' ..." (His tone made the word into an epithet.) "Will not even the recent events—of guns and yet far worse—turn thee from thy weapons? Ever?" He spoke in bitter sadness, obviously expecting no answer.

During this interchange, Tom was able to make sense of the party on the road. At its head, a boy of perhaps ten or twelve carried a flashlight with a handkerchief over its lens to block all but the faintest glimmer, just enough, when two feet or so directly above the road's dashed centerline, to pick that out and thereby stay in the middle. About ten feet behind the child, walking in total blackness but bearing on the tiny dot of the flashlight, were two gigantic farm boys with a huge draft horse between them, which they guided holding its bridle on either side. Each young giant carried a medieval-looking quarterstaff fully three inches thick and six feet long. The horse pulled a Conestoga-like covered wagon, rolling quietly on its hard rubber tires, with the bearded old man in the seat. Next to him sat a young woman. From the wagon's tailgate another young woman and two small children peered, their faces showing a mixture of fright and curiosity. Behind the wagon walked a milk cow and a young heifer, their halter ropes tied to the wagon's tailgate. On an unobstructed road, the entire convoy could move in total darkness, using only the faintest glow from the lead-boy to keep to the centerline.

"Point the lights off to the side so we can gather some firewood," the Chief instructed Tom. "Men, gather some wood and light a fire off this side of the road. Then we'll shut down the Gravely to save gas."

It took only moments until a fire provided light enough to see by, and Tom shut off the Gravely.

The instant the engine's racket and the brilliant electric lights' glare suddenly ceased—in a disorienting mere split-second—things seemed to slip back 300 years. Leaving the 21st century with a turn of the Gravely's ignition key, the group seemed to enter the 18th—sitting near the wagon around a nighttime campfire, to parlay with these travelers who dressed in dark blue broadcloth trousers or long dresses, and spoke strangely.

"Jacob, unharness the horse and stake it in yonder grass, then join us. Joshua, tend likewise to the kine; then come as well."

The old man climbed down from the wagon seat and went to the fire Barley's men were lighting nearby, extending his hand to the Chief. The woman, unbidden, left the wagon seat and entered the wagon to join the other woman and children inside, from where they peered out at the men.

"Welcome to Mountainview," Barley said, extending his hand. "I'm Jack Barley, police chief here. Again, I'm sorry for the misunderstanding. Would you like to come on into town? You must have been on the road a good while."

"Many thanks, but no; this place will serve for tonight. If we are to be allowed, we are pressed to continue on our way. I felt keenly, moments ago, a great woefulness believing we were struck down so close to our journey's end. God be praised that you are decent persons. He has kept us safe in His hands, even when I deserved it not, for I would despair. He is patient and merciful beyond my understanding. My name is Caleb Yoder. Know thou if persons named Yoost be living down this road at some small distance?"

"Yes indeed. There are three or four families of Amish at the end of this road, about eleven miles from here. Their houses are grouped fairly close together near the road's end, in a sort of hub, and their lands fan out from that center. I assume you're joining them, being Amish?"

"Thank you, Blessed God, for directing us!" Caleb said softly to his Creator. "Yes, we seek to join them. We are come from near Dayton, Virginia. My sister's husband, Amon, is of the Yoosts down this road. When the Troubles came, he sent us a map and an invitation to the safety of their location. We made what haste we could. Dayton and the surrounding area is by now, I'm sure, all taken by the great dying. We left just in time."

The pair of young giants, having staked out the animals, arrived in the circle of firelight.

"My sons, Jacob and Joshua," said Caleb simply. "This good man is Chief Barley of the police here. We owe him and his men a great debt."

As the men introduced themselves, the Chief took Tom aside and said, "I'd like to go with Owen and the Gravely back to your place and leave the lights and generator there. Owen can drop me off at the station so I can pass the word to the rest of the patrol units to resume their normal deployments. Can you have Owen pull the cart around town, picking up any supplies we can spare for these folks? We couldn't ask for safer or better people to have down the road from us. I think it'd be worth our while to help them, to the extent we can.

"But, look, Tom—to help our own people see their way clear to donating items of value, at such short notice, could we possibly offer any guarantee they're not just throwing their goods away? Until we can get the matter talked over and explained to them so they feel comfortable about it?"

"Yes, I think that's a good idea, Chief," Tom replied. "How about if I have Owen keep a list of each donation and donor. I'll pledge staples—wheat, corn, beans, or rice—from the Y2K supplies I have left, to guarantee each person's donation. At the end of a week, anyone who has second thoughts about donating, and wishes he hadn't done so, can come to me and get a fair-value repayment for his donation from my supply of staples."

Tom and the Chief explained the plan to Owen and the three returned to the circle around the fire where the Chief outlined it to the entire group. Soon Owen was racketing back to town with the Gravely, using for a headlight the single 12-volt bulb in a clamp-on reflector Tom had jury-rigged, with its leads clipped to the battery terminal by alligator clips. Along with the generator,

Owen towed the cart, now containing the Chief and most of the deputies, who were more than ready to turn in for the night. Tom returned to the smaller circle remaining around the fire.

Chapter 9
Faith

"As the Chief explained," Tom said to Caleb and his two sons, "you've only about eleven miles to go: four hours walk in daylight tomorrow. I think you'll be reasonably safe once you reach the Yoosts. They're at the dead end of the valley. This road's the only access, and we keep a pretty close eye out for anyone who travels it. We want to help you because we think eventually you might help us too. But tell me—how did you make it all this way? Dayton, Virginia, must be over a hundred miles from here."

"Aye, well over a hundred miles, the roundabout way we came, through the George Washington and the Monongahela National Forests," replied Caleb Yoder. "We hid carefully each day, traveling by night. Because conditions at our home were becoming so unsafe, we had to set out before we desired to— before the waning moon had grown as dark as we wanted. But God sent us a steady rain the first three nights, which gave us darkness and kept people indoors. We've been on the road nine days now, and again time was growing short, for we wished to arrive before the new moon grows too bright to hide us."

Tom thought of these men, women, and children walking the pitch-black roads in the first three nights of continuous rain, hauling everything they now owned, toward a hoped-for destination none had ever seen.

"You just left your property near Dayton? Traveling all this way by night? On the strength of a map your sister's husband sent you?"

"We have done so before. If it be God's will, we will do so again," Caleb replied simply, dismissing that issue.

"Before? When?"

"Seventeen-oh-three. My ancestors were farmers in a region near what is now the Swiss/Austrian border. Our religion was not acceptable to the people there, and they killed many of us. My ancestors loaded what they could in a handcart and fled by night, hiding during the daytime. They walked until they reached the port of Bremen, where they had heard they might work their passage to America, to live and worship in safety."

Tom's lifelong dispute with what he suspected was a nonexistent God (or, far worse, a bored and indifferent one) deepened a further notch into a harder bitterness as he heard Caleb's tale.

"They arrived in Philadelphia," Caleb continued, "and walked westward to the Reading, Pennsylvania, area where they found land to clear, and built homes and barns, and began farming again.

"In 1778 the Revolutionary War, which had previously been fought at some distance, swept through their area. Their neighbors—both Tory and Revolutionist—suspended their enthusiastic killing of each other long enough to agree on one thing: my ancestors' refusal to fight for either side justified killing them. So once again we left what we could not carry, and slipped away at night, hiding during the day.

"This time the direction was south, to what is now the area around Dayton, Virginia, where we have lived until this day with but two interruptions. In 1860, the conscription gangs rounding up cannon fodder for the Confederacy swept through the area and our young men had to flee their homes to live in hiding in the forests to the west. Then, in 1864, the Union troops swept down the Shenandoah Valley, stealing anything they could and burning all they could not, so our women and children had to join our men in the forests. They were hard times. But those who remained alive returned to our lands after the war, rebuilt the burned buildings, reclaimed the grown-over fields, and began anew.

"So this," he gestured at the wagon with its women, children, and few pitiful possessions, "is nothing new for us. God has His plan."

He fell silent a minute, then said "But, friend, sometimes I cannot understand the need in His plan for weapons, and armies, and men fighting other men like savage beasts in a pit, too blind to see that we could all live together in a peaceable kingdom."

"He finds it entertaining." Tom's bitterness briefly escaped control. "It amuses Him to watch—until it bores Him and He loses interest. At least you have the satisfaction of shaming Him by your own decency. Your pacifist bravery in an armed world illustrates His contrasting bloody vileness better than anything else ever could."

"Bravery!" said Caleb with a small chuckle. "We have no need for bravery. We have trust instead—trust that He will use us in His plan and bring us home to Him when we have served. Without such trust, friend, I would truly feel alone and hopeless. Then indeed would I need a great deal of bravery just to arise each day."

Strangely, Tom felt he could communicate with this old man from the 18th century, whose people even long before that time had been outcasts and oddballs, more fully than with anyone he knew in today's world.

"For years I've felt an admiration for the Amish and what they've achieved," he admitted. "A simple, peaceful life, centered around things of genuine value, rather than frittered away desperately buying each new bit of plastic rubbish advertised on television; a society without crime or drugs or broken homes; with no throwaway children, no abandoned wives, no husbands destroyed totally by the maneuverings of slimeball divorce lawyers; a society with neither the obscenely rich nor the abjectly poor—I've craved such a world for as long as I can remember."

Tom grinned at his own folly. "Of course, not believing in the religious stuff would present a bit of an obstacle to joining you—even if the Amish accepted converts, which I understand they don't."

Caleb shared Tom's wry grin. "The 'religious stuff,' as thee puts it, presents a bit of an obstacle to me too, at times—and to all of us, in our weaker hours. We simply carry on, believing faith will return to us when it suits His plan. But as for accepting converts, thou mistakes us, friend. Most Amish indeed discourage conversion, but we are not Amish. I and my sons and their wives and children are Mennonites. The Yoosts, whom we seek to join, are Hutterites, though admittedly one or two among them are former Amish who became Hutterian Brethren years ago.

"When my sister left our Mennonite community to marry Amon Yoost of the Hutterites, we were distressed almost beyond telling. Over and over, we asked each other in tears how God could have wanted such a thing. And now, you see, we appear to be receiving His answer. My children and their children, and theirs in turn, have received a chance to escape the great dying of our old home near Dayton—to join my sister here with the Yoosts in a place of safety."

They sat silent for a moment.

"Only trust, friend," said the old man softly, "only trust."

"I admire that quality in you," Tom confessed, "though I could never share it. Traveling unarmed, over a hundred miles, in these times—call it bravery or trust, as you will, it still leaves me astonished. Wasn't there any point where you were seen...when you feared attack?"

"Most people—those still left—lock themselves securely indoors when night falls, and venture not out until first light, so we seldom encountered anyone while traveling in darkness. We were seen a few times during daylight, when sufficient concealment was not available, but we were not molested.

Perhaps any persons who might have been tempted mistook the walking staffs of Jacob and Joshua for weapons of some sort," the old man confessed with a twinkle in his eye.

Tom looked at the pair of giants in their early twenties—each fully six and a half feet tall, each close upon 300 pounds of bone and muscle, each clutching a hardwood stave at least three inches thick and six feet long.

"Yes," he said with a smile, "I can understand someone making that mistake."

"God, we hope, does not hold against us the misunderstandings of others," the old one concluded.

In turns, the men slept the remainder of the night around the fire, giving the women and children in the wagon their safest rest of the journey.

Shortly after daybreak Owen appeared, the racketing Gravely pulling a fully loaded cart. He presented the list of donations and donors to Tom, with a carbon copy he'd made.

"We want to help you simply as a matter of good business," Tom repeated to Caleb, giving him the carbon copy of the donations list. "These are things we can spare. We hope at some time you might consider them as barter, rather than simply gifts, and reciprocate in the future with items you can spare. In that way, we help each other."

"You are kind and generous," Caleb replied to the Mountainview people who'd come to see them off. "I know already of one item that might serve as partial repayment, if you would want it. In his letter inviting us to join them, Amon Yoost mentioned he and my sister had a young stallion that concerned them. It has a fine bloodline, and strikes them as well conformed and promising, so they are loath to geld it. But as much as they would like to keep it intact for breeding, it's becoming too difficult and dangerous to have anywhere near their mares used daily for work. Nor do they want to keep it at some far distance, where it might more easily be stolen. If you have no mares, would you wish to have the horse, use it yourselves, and receive the income from stud fees when we want our mares bred? Breeding stock, in the days to come, may prove to be of some value."

This proposal struck both sides as advantageous, and agreement was reached that someone from Mountainview would go to the Yoosts that morning to fetch back the horse. Then things hit a snag.

"I know our beliefs are not those of you English," Caleb explained with hesitation, "but it would not be proper for me to bring into our new home any person carrying weapons. Our history and our beliefs make this an important matter for us. Will any coming with us to get the horse agree to leave their guns here, among you who accept such things?"

The men from Mountainview thought about the eleven-mile walk to the Yoosts, unarmed. Then the same distance back—leading a highly valuable animal—even more nakedly unarmed. Their eyes darted, against their will, to the eight foot diameter human bloodstain on the asphalt not far from Yoder's wagon. They shifted their feet uneasily and fell to silently studying the ground, each waiting for someone else to do something.

"I'll agree to that," said Owen. "Won't need nobody but me to fetch that horse. Here, Tom, you hold this." And he fished the old .45 Colt from his pack and handed it to Tom.

And so they began loading the items from the Gravely cart into Yoder's wagon. There was a stack of clothing and blankets, cinched tight with rope to make the bundle as small as possible. A mixed assortment of goods that would not long ago have been flea market items, but were now valuables, followed the textiles into the wagon. Johnson had contributed a fifty-pound sack of cracked corn, which they opened. They gave about four cups of it to the huge Belgian mare in her feed bucket, gave two cups to the milk cow and one to the heifer, and then divided a cup between the chicken coops and rabbit coops in the wagon. Closing the sack and re-tying its neck with twine, Joshua picked up the remaining 48 pounds or so with one hand and gently placed it in the wagon.

"Daisy, our Belgian," he said to Owen with a gentle smile, "really appreciates the kindness of this corn. She's been mostly on grass the past several days and needs grain. I'm glad you'll be coming with us, Owen. Last night I saw you operate that tractor. For a day's plowing it would be a lot noisier than Daisy—but it must be very convenient in some ways too. Maybe sometime you could show me its operation?"

"Sure, I'd be glad to. But, uh, is that ok? I mean, you know, aren't you forbidden to use machinery in place of draft animals?"

"Not really. We believe there's nothing wrong with tractors, or cars, or electricity or such things—in themselves. But we believe we should have as little dependence as possible on outsiders, who may not share our values. Using tractors would place our livelihood, even our lives, in the grip of many people we do not know, in places far away—people who drill for oil and refine it into tractor fuel and transport it to us. We would not feel secure, doing so. Owning cars would require that we join all you English, paying taxes to a huge government that would use the money for building weapons and funding other programs we feel are morally wrong. Connecting ourselves to the electric system would likewise mean joining with all the other people connected – joining with our money, our lives, eventually our values—to people we should not join, but instead strive to set an example for. Our path, we believe, is to try to demonstrate a better alternative, not join the world on the path the world has chosen."

"Well," Owen muttered, turning this over in his mind, "considering how things have turned out, maybe people could use an example of some different way. Couldn't hardly end up much worse, I guess…"

Then he perked up. "I had Brother Stainfuss—he's preacher at Foursquare Baptist, where me and Maybelle, my wife, go—look for stuff you folks might want. And he found that *Atlas of the Bible Lands* there. It's got maps from back in olden times showing the route the Israelites took out of Egypt, and Saint Paul's journeys and so forth, plus color pictures of Bible characters the way they was supposed to look back then—all that kind of stuff. And he got a stack of blank paper and a tin can full of crayons from the Sunday school, where Sister Skitch is gonna have a full-blown attack come Sunday when she finds out. Anyway, she ain't the only one gonna get their bowels in an uproar. Maybelle, see, cooks for this farm crew a few houses down from ours. And those four pies, from the year's first apples, was supposed to be for that crew's lunch today. Trust me: you and me don't wanta be around here when that bunch finds out they got no dessert."

Filled with the warm joy of skipping out on a mess left for others to clean up, Jacob, Joshua, and Owen enjoyed picturing themselves as co-conspirators, getting one back against the grownups, while the final items were transferred to Yoder's wagon, and the group got under way.

"Tell Maybelle I'll be back when it's safe to come back," hollered Owen with delight to one of the men returning to Mountainview.

Chapter 10
Will Engage in Interpersonal Communication for Food or Sex

"You know that empty storefront on Main? A block toward Owen and Maybelle's house from here?" Sophia asked Tom one morning at breakfast.

Each night she was spending less time crying in her bedroom. This morning she looked more rested and alive than Tom had ever seen her. In addition, her bread-baking was becoming more successful with every day's experience. This morning's contribution to their routine fried eggs made a breakfast tastier than any Tom had had in weeks.

"Wow, this bread's good!" he exclaimed, looking up at her from his chair as she groped for a new jar of honey high above her on the pantry's top shelf.

Finding it at last, clutching the honey above her head in triumph, she executed an astonishingly expert bump and grind, twirled and placed the honey on the table, drew up her chair, and sat down.

"Ta-da!" she announced, passing him the honey.

Tom's jaw dropped, and he sat there, gaping.

"Glad you like it. Here," she said demurely, handing him the honey for his fresh bread.

"By God, I *do* like it!" said the dumbfounded Tom. "The food's right good too! Where on *earth* did you learn that sort of a move?"

"Oh, that." She dismissed the matter with a casual wave of her hand. "So, anyway, Tom, what's the deal with that vacant storefront on Main?"

Way behind whatever was happening, Tom could only sit for a moment, staring and remembering the sight he'd just seen—if he *had* seen it, and wasn't going nutso and dreaming things. He finally pulled himself together.

"The storefront. Yeah. Used to be Gump's Five and Dime. Went broke a few years ago, and old Gump hasn't had any takers for the building, what I hear. Too bad; I'm sure he and Evaline could use whatever they could sell or rent it for. Why?"

"Well, as grateful as I am to you for putting me up here, Tom, I obviously have to find something to do to pay my way. I was thinking about that empty storefront. From what I've seen, you don't have any clubs here in Mountainview. What would you think about my starting one in the empty storefront? If the Gumps would help rehab the building I'd pay that back as part of each month's rent out of my cash-flow, so maybe I could get started without any major cash investment of my own up front."

"Clubs?" Tom was getting more completely lost by the minute. "We have clubs here. The 4-H is still going, and I think the Garden Ladies, and maybe the Kiwanis, but I'm not sure. But we got clubs...."

"No, silly, I mean '*clubs*' – like nightspots. Granted, Mountainview's not very large, but I think maybe the same club could be several-in-one by serving different functions on different nights of the week.

"For example, let's assume it's closed Sunday and Monday nights ..." she began.

"A very safe assumption," Tom interjected. "Now extend that safe beginning for five more nights and we'll be on solid ground."

"No, no. Really, Tom, I've been thinking about this. Let's say on Tuesday nights the club's a singles spot—mix 'n' mingle with hors d'oeuvres and a glass of wine, that sort of thing. Wednesday nights are 'Cigar Nights' with a Gentleman's Club atmosphere—drinks and some entertainment. Thursdays are Bohemian Coffeehouse nights—cool jazz or poetry readings, coffee, and lots of talk. And Fridays and Saturdays are just plain supper-club evenings for anyone who wants to get out of the house and have a decent meal in a convivial atmosphere."

She was so clearly carried away by the excitement of her grand design that Tom hated to allow reality into the picture. But this...this—he remembered the sight of that bump-and-grind moments ago—this astonishing woman from some far distant planet had to be protected from herself.

"Sophia," Tom began patiently, as if to a child, "we have 'singles clubs' here. In Mountainview we call them 'churches.' That's where young people go to mix 'n' mingle—which they do with a pig-in-blanket and a glass of Kool-Aid, by the way.

"Moving—rapidly—on to Wednesday night's agenda, I'm not even going to imagine the nature of any 'entertainment' provided for Gentlemen's Night. We do not have 'Gentlemen' in Mountainview; and they would *absolutely* not be 'entertained' in any establishment on Main Street. Or any other street, for that matter. And anyway, what was that, uh, that uh—you know, uh, just a moment ago. What was that all about?"

"Oh now, Tom. Surely you're not going to go all scandalized and Victorian on me. I was just considering some means of paying my way here, given my situation: no capital and only what skills I already have. I financed my Master's in Sociology by dancing in a go-go club. It was super pay for short hours of easy work: I couldn't have come anywhere near such a fantastic deal in any other job. The Gentleman's Club night would simply involve serving drinks and having a go-go dancer on a platform in one corner. For Heaven's sakes, Tom—I'm not talking about some den of vice and degradation!"

"Oh, *well* then," Tom responded, sarcasm-level set on High. "Moving right along from running a perfectly respectable strip joint on Wednesdays we get to our Bohemian, commie/anarchist, beatnik-subversive theme for Thursdays, when people read...*poetry.*"

Tom paused. "I'm not sure which would more deeply horrify people here in Mountainview, Sophie: having a strip joint on Main Street or, *publicly* reading actual, artistic-type, *poetry*. Out loud. It's just not done. Never has been. Never will be. Forget it.

"As for something refreshingly sane and normal, like your Friday and Saturday night idea, when people simply go out for a bite to eat, it's been tried. The Burger Den used to stay open till six-thirty on summer evenings, but it closed down. Folks can fix their own food.

"Look, Sophie, this is Mountainview, not Berkley or Palo Alto." He felt bad, but someone had to inject a trace of reality into her fantasy world. "There are things that just aren't done here."

"Yeah. Never have been; never will be." She took the bursting of her bubble glumly but calmly. "Well, back to the drawing board."

She sat silent for a minute, chewing her bread and honey, sipping her tea.

"But," she resumed after some thought, with what Tom detected as an ominous undertone in her voice, "you do not need to play the bumpkin with me, Mr. Jeffson. I have scanned the titles in your library. Do you really suppose I buy your role as the simple-but-honest rototiller mechanic, happily whistling all the livelong day in his small-town workshop, contentedly fixing his machines?"

"I also sell them," Tom replied with all the gravity he could muster. "I am, in my own way, a capitalist—much like Bill Gates, for example. Though I will admit to some differences in our net worth."

"Well why aren't you married?"

The damned woman never failed to hit him from some unexpected direction. Stalling for time, he turned to her, placing his hand on his heart, and announced soberly, "Madam: I sell, buy, and repair Gravelys. For those of us sworn to that calling, the Gravely is our bride. There would be room for none other."

Slowly, with the elegance that comes only from generations of the finest breeding, she silently rolled her eyes and raised a single middle finger.

"Then let's put it this way," she proposed, "if I show you mine, will you show me yours? It's high time we found out about each other's past. Not to mention the possibility of bacon …"

Throughout the 1960s, Tom had never been the least bit tempted by drugs. The swirling, goofy, craziness of this conversation reminded him of why.

"Bacon?"

"Oh, stuff Maybelle and I found in an old housekeeping manual she dug up. Curing bacon's apparently not difficult at all. Well—how hard could it have been? Millions of frontier wives without a day of schooling routinely did it every year when they slaughtered pigs each fall. No big deal."

She paused a beat, then beamed him the look an Armenian rug-merchant might direct toward a tourist who had blundered into his part of the bazaar. "*If you know how to do it, of course …*"

She sat quietly.

"Bacon," he repeated.

Like a man swirling down into the abyss, Tom clutched at this simple, physical fact.

Sophia nodded casually, slightly bored, raising—coincidentally—another piece of the latest delicious bread to her mouth.

"What do you want to know?"

She smiled at how easy it was. Men. You really had to feel sorry for them. "Everything."

"My father's parents came here in the late 1800s to farm," Tom began. "They were probably drawn by the give-away land prices throughout the conquered, crushed, and still nearly starving South—which West Virginia was very much a part of, despite Lincoln's legal hanky-panky to make it a different state than Virginia.

"My father was a late child, his parents' only one to survive, born in 1919. By the time he graduated from the local high school, in 1937, he knew he had no intention of trying to scratch a marginal living out of a few acres of corn, some cattle, and occasional clear-cutting of timber, the way his parents had. But he stuck with it until he entered the Army Air Corps, where he spent three and a half years as a waist-gunner on B-17's. His parents died during the war years, leaving him the farm.

"Within two months of returning here from Europe in mid-1945, using what he'd saved from his military pay, he bought an option on the Gravely sales and service franchise for this area. Then he sold his inherited farm acreage and used the money to buy this town lot. He contracted to have this house built on it, with the Gravely dealership on the ground floor. In 1946 the house was finished and the dealership was starting to make money, so he telephoned a young woman he'd seen exhibiting a quilt at the previous month's Grayson County Fair. When he asked her out for a hamburger and movie she declined. She'd been in the WACs during the last few months of the war, and was currently attending college on the GI Bill to become a schoolteacher.

"My father, who smoked a pipe and was never ruffled or uncertain a single day of his life, calmly assured her she was doing a wise thing, and asked if he might write to her, then call again when she returned, as he figured he would marry her.

"Eighteen months later, she returned to teach school at Grayson, the county seat. That week my father drove over to see her. In two months they were married, and within a year I was born.

"By the time I reached high school, I'd had it up to here with the charming, Norman Rockwell quaintness of Mayberry, RFD. I couldn't wait to go to college—actually, just to *go*. Anywhere.

"The University of Maryland, in College Park, fit my requirements perfectly. It was a huge state college, amazingly cheap in those days, with no academic pretensions whatever, fanatically devoted to beer and football as harmless outlets for its students' energies. Equally important, it was located on the edge of Washington, D.C., which we'd visited for my high school senior class trip, and where I'd glimpsed a whole wide world of museums I intended to make the center of my own energies.

"With no need for more than the barest pretense of schoolwork, I divided my time between reading *The Washington Post, the New Yorker, Mother Earth News,* and *The American Rifleman* in the university library, and studying the many Smithsonian and other museums in D.C. These activities were free, and I did almost nothing else, so I hardly ever needed any money from home. I suspect my parents were a bit worried about this, and may have wondered if I was dealing drugs.

"My businessman father, rightly, would have doubted I was sufficiently skilled in business to make a go of it. A typically sheltered product of the middle class, I had reached adulthood without once having the faintest trace of any experience at actually selling something for profit—the quaint old concept called 'capitalism'—still sentimentally revered in theory but long since discarded in practice by respectable corporate-bureaucratic America. To actually gain my first experience as a capitalist, I had to get involved with some devoutly anti-capitalist people, who fancied themselves on the Cutting Edge, but were actually old fashioned enough for the term 'capitalist' still to have meaning. But that's getting ahead of my story.

"Since I had no particular academic interests—or abilities, for that matter—I majored in English. In four years, I had a completely meaningless and useless degree and a rather good education, gleaned from reading at the library, studying the exhibits in countless miles of museum walking, and looking carefully around me at the functioning of Our Nation's Capitol.

"It was desperately important at the time, the late 1960s, for the sons of blue-collar families to go to Vietnam, where they could patriotically have their arms or legs blown off for 'freedom' in some shit-filled rice paddy—and for the sons of white collar families to go to the Washington Mall or Pentagon, where they could patriotically have their head split open for 'freedom' by a club-swinging cop at a protest. I had, and have, equal contempt for the stupidity of both groups. If either bunch were willing to *look*, to *see*, how our government really behaves—the sordid, slimy squalor with which it actually goes about its daily sausage making—they would comprehend the silliness of risking anything to either support or oppose it.

"Like a pile of dog shit on the sidewalk, the government's just 'there,' just a natural (if regrettable) fact of life, alas. If you have any sense at all, it's something you merely walk around and ignore, getting on with your affairs. Devoting energy to either loving it or loathing it marks you as someone with too much time on his hands and too little to do in life.

"By graduation time, after three and a half years of immersion in the era's 'Love-It-Or-Leave-It' religious wars, I was weary of the college scene. But reality whispered to me that grad school would continue my draft deferment. So I got a graduate assistantship and spent the next eighteen months scribbling B+ on illiterate freshman themes, while finishing my own M.A. By then the draft was ended and it was safe to come out of hiding.

"But I was faced with a dilemma: either get a job and go to work, or join the government. Like many a country lass of doubtful virtue, on her own in the big city, I foolishly chose the easy money. Entering the federal Medicare bureaucracy as a GS-7, I rose rapidly to GS-12—roughly the civilian equivalent to a light Colonel on the military side.

"My job was to help design and conduct 'studies' intended to prove things important politicians or interest groups wanted proved about Medicare.

"For example, the Slee-Zee Wheelchair Company might consider it wise for Medicare to greatly increase its purchases of the overpriced wheelchairs the company sold. After appropriate campaign contributions to a Congressional Committee Chairman or Ranking Member—the Honorable Ponsonby 'Butch' Pierpointe IV, for example—that Honorable Member would write to us Medicare bureaucrats outlining his dismay about the current crisis, and expressing the urgent need for Medicare to buy additional wheelchairs. Could we not help clarify this critical issue, he would ask us, by conducting a study of the matter?

"Indeed we could. Particularly for our good friend the Honorable Member, who voted each year on our agency's budget request. My job was to help make sure we designed and conducted the study so it would prove what it was supposed to. We screwed up now and then, of course, but if a study showed any untoward results we simply cancelled it and reworked the design. Took as many as three tries, on some occasions, but we never failed.

"Once our objective study, conducted by 'experts,' proved its point everybody got something. The Slee-Zee Company sold wheelchairs by the carload. With a mere 10% of the take, it could generously compensate the Honorable Member for bearing the many sacrifices his devotion to Public Service entailed. We bureaucrats got regular pay raises and bonuses. Thousands of spry but puzzled old folks received unwanted wheelchairs to store in the garage and trip over. And the ignorant sheeple footing the bill for all this, the taxpayers, got what they craved too – and got it good and hard.

"Everyone was happy. Except me—out of step as usual. I lived in a state of continuous mild nausea. I believed I should walk around the dog shit on the sidewalk, known as government, and get on with my life. Yet here I was rolling in it—however well paid to do so. You asked why I'm not married. Do I sound like the sort of Ken many Barbies would give up a day at the mall for?

"After fourteen years, with the daily nausea beginning to slide frighteningly down into serious depression, I'd finally had enough. If the Establishment and its government did not have The Answer, maybe the opposing side would.

"I quit the Feds and joined a group of hippies living in an old farmhouse on 124 acres in southern Virginia. When they were too short of money to buy dope—and therefore temporarily not stoned—they handcrafted very lovely oak lawn furniture. As the most 'respectable-looking' member, my job was to load up their old Ford Econoline van full of products and drive from one arts and crafts show to another, selling them.

"The humor did not escape me. Amid the happy throng of yuppie shoppers at an artsy-craftsy show—all that mass of accountants and engineers and urban planners and so-called 'business' people, enjoying their day away from their tiny little corporate-bureaucratic niches in vast organizations—all that mass of cubicle-dwelling Dilbert-People—I was very often the only actual, outright, hands-on *capitalist* in the entire crowd. And there I was, earnestly retailing for a profit various items we had actually made—to support a commune-full of hippies who lived for the overthrow of the capitalist system. God works in mysterious ways.

"At various times I ranged from Maine to Florida, and as far west as Chicago and Dallas, living the 'carnie' life, selling hippie crafts and sleeping in the van. Lo and behold, I was actually good at the job, bringing in sufficient wads of money to cause intense heartburn and soul-searching among the devoutly anti-materialist hippies. That was fun, of course, and the 'carnie' life itself was fun too—though only for a limited time and only while I was still fairly young. Mostly, it was just a real relief to pass my time harmlessly jerking off for a change, instead of devoting forty hours a week to actively damaging my country. So call me a flaming patriot.

"My mother died in 1985, and my father followed eighteen months later, leaving me this house and the Gravely dealership. Toward the end, as my father had aged, the business had fallen off, but it was still here. I'd invested a good bit of my government pay while I was earning it, which had further compounded during my six years roaming the country in a van, so I had enough income to get by on. I moved here and took over the Gravely business and have enjoyed life ever since. The machines are so simple and rugged even I can fix the few things that go wrong with them. And once in a while someone would get an inheritance or some other windfall and actually buy one.

"The little public library, twenty-five miles away at Grayson, the county seat, would get me any book from any public library anywhere in the U.S., free, via Interlibrary Loan. And once the internet got up and running, I could receive all the news, music, and research access anyone could ever want, also for nearly free. Life was good.

"I knew the government—by overwhelming popular demand, let me stress—was promoting an unsustainable economic bubble, while debauching the currency, while making promises of middle class welfare handouts it could not possibly keep, while creating millions of fanatical enemies by its incessant foreign adventures, while steadily increasing the contempt felt by the more educated citizenry who observed its blatant incompetence and corruption. And I knew matters could not continue forever in that direction.

"So I bought over a ton of staples—grains and other dry foods—in six-gallon buckets, along with related supplies, and went harmlessly about my life here, fixing garden tractors and waiting. I had no impulse to 'save people' by converting them to any end-of-the-world beliefs. I did what I could for me: their problems were their business.

"It didn't take a genius to foresee events. If you consistently run across a busy road without checking for traffic, I can foresee what's going to happen: you'll get hit. No, I can't tell you on which day or hour; or whether by a car, truck, or van; or what the vehicle's color will be—but what I *can* tell you is what matters: you're going to get hit. Anybody willing to look could easily have foreseen the future events that mattered: quibbling over details was merely an excuse for refusing to look."

Tom pointed to a piece of machinery sitting rather forlornly on the workshop floor. "Still, the steam engine that may save us was to some extent an unforeseen lucky fluke. Since elementary school, I've always been interested in small engines. By the time I was in high school my collection included various small two and four-stroke gas engines with sparkplug ignition, a glow-plug two stroke, a diesel, some electric motors I'd made, rocket motors, and a toy-sized working steam engine. The more I thought about what seemed to lie ahead, the more convinced I was that an end to refined petroleum products, mostly gasoline and diesel, was a principal threat to hopes for long term, civilized survival. The only fuels sufficiently abundant, renewable, and low-tech to provide mechanical power in a post-petroleum world are coal and wood; and the only mechanical power source simple enough to build and maintain in a low-tech world is the old fashioned, slow speed, reciprocating steam engine.

"Let me tell you—their engine may be old fashioned, but by golly the 'Steamies' are not: the internet's packed with forums and websites devoted to every conceivable aspect of steam power. After months of research, I finally decided to buy a single-cylinder 4 HP engine and boiler from the Reliable Steam Engine Company. I'd found them on the internet and chose them because, unlike most of the many steam engine builders, they offered the option of buying a completed, working engine instead of a set of castings that would have required considerable machining before being assembled into an engine. Because of differences in calculating horsepower ratings, Reliable's 4 HP steam engine looks like the closest in actual power output to the Gravely's original 7.6 HP gasoline engine.

"The engine and boiler arrived here just three weeks before the nukes hit. I immediately phoned and ordered four more on the day of the nukes, but I never received them, so it looks like what we have is what we've got. Pity. I'll get the one we have mounted on a Gravely and test it to see if the idea's workable. If so, one major use for that prototype will be to run the generator to power the electric shop tools here. Then I can try to build additional steam engines using pistons, cylinders, crankcase assemblies, and other parts from various small gas engines. Might work, might not, but it's about the best hope we've got."

He thought a bit.

"Now that the waiting's over, it turns out there's not much satisfaction after all in saying 'I told you so!' As I'd accurately assumed, the most obvious and inescapable characteristic of post-Collapse life is utter, mind-rotting boredom. The bland food's boring; the shortage of news, music, and books is boring; the impossibility of travel is boring; the darkness at sundown every evening is boring. The dreary daily drudgery of life, now that we're back in the 1800s, is—in a word—*boring*. I suspect that many 'survivalists' all across the county, holed up in fortified retreats, with their exciting Rambo fantasies and stockpiles of 'beans and bullets,' are going to literally die of boredom. After a certain point, just keeping on keeping on will simply become more bother than it's worth.

"Apart from boredom, I mostly feel a sense of disgust. All those heaps of rotting carrion in what used to be the nation's cities: those piles of dead-and-useless beeves who died bewildered in the urban stockyards because their government owners failed to feed and water them.... Just a very deep disgust, really: at the sight, the smell, the stupid senselessness of it all. Humans may survive—I guess I'll join others to do what I can, at least until I've had enough and say 'the hell with it'—but I'm not convinced they really deserve to.

"So. That's my poor excuse for breathing air and taking up space; what's yours?"

She spent a few moments silently reflecting. Then Sophie said briskly "Well. I can see the basic outlines of what needs doing here."

"Jesus..." sighed Tom. "Just go make some bacon."

But other matters were to occupy Sophie's attention first.

Chapter 11
Nothing but a Scratch

Maybelle arrived at the Gravely shop just after noon, in obvious distress. "Hi, Tom. Is Sophie here?"

"Sure is, Maybelle; she's upstairs. Is something wrong?"

"I'm afraid so. Tim Baker's looking in a bad way. He's that kid in the farm crew I cook for: just fourteen or so, but big and strong enough to do most of a man's work. His leg's infected, and it's got us scared. When he didn't come to work for the second day I went over to the Bakers' to check, and he's in bed there. Since Owen's still away at the Amish to get that horse, I had Doc Billings come over and look. Doc checked it and right away asked if I knew anyone who might help him. So I told him I'd see if Sophie would. She's awful smart, you know."

As Maybelle hurried upstairs to get Sophia, Tom reflected on how strongly and favorably Sophia had already impressed Owen and Maybelle. But medical abilities? He hadn't heard Sophia mention any skills or experience in that area. It sure would be a godsend, though.

Mountainview was far too small to have a doctor. There was one RN: old Miz Parnell. Technically, having her on the payroll had met the state requirement that Mountainview Elementary, the town's only public school, have an RN available. But poor old Miz Parnell, who was undeniably goodhearted and fond of kids, was no one's idea of a medical genius—even if she'd still remembered much of what little she'd learned as a C student, fifty-five years ago in a long-since-terminated evening nursing program run by a little country "hospital" which had lost its accreditation and folded decades past. She was sweet to the school children, and managed to keep their immunization records in fairly good alphabetical order in three large filing cabinets—but that was about the extent of Nurse Parnell's current medical abilities.

Two of the town's volunteer firemen had taken a basic first aid course at the local community college one weekend a few years ago. They both still remembered the course's Three Main Points: don't move the victim unless absolutely necessary, keep him warm, and summon medical assistance without delay. Beyond that, their own memories had grown a bit hazy as to the finer technical details.

But Mountainview did have a qualified, thoroughly competent young veterinarian, just four years out of vet school. Equally important, Doc Billings had a fairly adequate inventory of veterinary equipment and pharmaceuticals for his little one-man general vet practice.

"Tom, Maybelle and I are going to check on the Baker boy. I've left you some sandwiches in case I'm late getting back. I've borrowed the *Veterinary Merck Manual* from your library but I couldn't find the standard human *Merck*. Would you have one anywhere—or a *Physicians' Desk Reference* maybe?"

"No, I'm sorry. Doc Billings will certainly have the *Vet Merck* also. You could check in the fire department office, back of the police station. Even if they don't have a copy of the *PDR* they might at least have some useful first aid manuals. Good luck—let me know if I can do anything?"

"We will. I'll be back when I get back."

At the Baker home, three houses down from Owen and Maybelle's, Sophie nearly panicked when she and Maybelle walked in the door and she took one sniff. Doc Billings was issuing a series of directions to Tim Baker's trembling mother and father—partly, Sophia sensed, to keep them occupied.

"It's good to meet you, Sophie. I'm going to go back to my clinic for a few minutes to get some things. Maybelle, would you go check in the police station and fire department? If they have a *PDR* or any other medical material that looks like it might be useful, bring it here. Also, on your way, ask old Judge Parker if he has any human-medicine books of any sort. I can't think of anyone else who'd be likely to, but see if he can think of anyone.

"Sophie, I've told Mr. and Mrs. Baker I want them to mix two cups of Clorox with a gallon of water, then clean out their pump-up garden sprayer and put the solution in it. Spray a fine mist all over the living room here: ceiling, walls, curtains, floor, carpet—everything. Mix up more solution if you need it. Then put this plastic dropcloth sheeting on the floor here, and mist it with the Clorox solution too. Then scrub every part of that big kitchen table with solution and bring the table in here to the middle of the room and put it on the plastic sheeting. Set that card table up next to the dining table and mist the card table with Clorox solution too. Then tear up some old sheets into pieces about a foot wide and three feet or so long, and put them in a big pot of water to boil for thirty minutes along with some kitchen tongs. Meanwhile, scrub some cookie sheets with the Clorox solution. After thirty minutes, fish out the tongs with a fork or something, and when they're cool enough to handle use them to fish out the cloth strips. Put the cloths on the cookie sheets in a low oven till they're dry."

He looked out the window, judging the light in the early afternoon sky, thinking a moment.

"Maybelle," he added, "after you get back here with any medical books you can round up, go back to Tom's and ask him if he has a charged car battery and a couple of 12-volt lights he could bring over in a few hours. Otherwise, we may need him to run a Gravely with a generator for lights, despite the noise. Either way, ask him to be here an hour or so before dusk."

After a quick glance toward Maybelle, Sophie, and Mr. and Mrs. Baker in case of questions, Doc Billings strode quickly out the door heading for his own home and vet clinic a few blocks away.

Mrs. Baker, utterly distraught, clutched desperately at Sophie's arm and cried, "It was nothing but a scratch! It was just a scratch! It was just a scratch!"

The poor, frantic woman pleaded with Sophie for absolution, for hope, for strength—for anything Sophie had to offer.

Sophie took her in her arms, enfolding the weeping mother with a fiercely strong bear hug.

"I know. Things are so different now. No one could have known what might happen. You've done just fine to get Doc here, and Maybelle and me. We're going to do fine. You'll see. Tim's going to be fine. Meanwhile, we've got some work to do. Will you help us with that?"

Etta Baker gulped and nodded, blowing her nose. Sophie gave her a quick glance of appraisal and then several brisk pats on the back—firm enough to be just shy of outright blows.

"Good. Now let's get a container and mix two cups of Clorox with a gallon of water."

Once Sophie was confident Etta Baker had the proper Clorox sterilizing solution made, and was cleaning the garden sprayer properly, she glanced briefly at the boy in the adjoining ground floor room. They'd put a cot there in the parlor for him, and he lay sweating in feverish semi-consciousness. His leg left no doubt as to the frightening smell Sophie had noticed on entering the house. Whether it was some rampant strep infection, 'blood poisoning,' gangrene, or whatever, Sophie had no idea. But the leg, puffy and discolored in streaks below the knee, looked and smelled awfully far gone for anything short of first rate hospital care.

"He just had a scratch," said Alvin Baker softly, coming up behind Sophie. "He came home from work three days ago with a scratch on his calf a couple of inches long where he'd brushed against some barbed wire. It was the sort of thing you dab some iodine on and in three days it's gone. We didn't even put a Band-Aid on it—it was that minor."

The man seemed to be pleading with Sophie for her to make sense of the incomprehensible: his son lying there dying from a scratch too insignificant for a Band-Aid.

"He's going to be all right," she told the bewildered father, steering him back into the living room. "Doc's fully capable of fixing him up. You'll see. Will you help me scrub the kitchen table?"

Etta was finishing her thorough spraying of the living room with Clorox solution. When she was done, she joined her husband and Sophie in the kitchen and scrubbed the heavy wooden table with solution. The three of them heaved the table into the living room, placing it on the plastic sheeting, then set up and sprayed the card table alongside it. Sophie had Alvin go get three old cotton sheets, and had him sit in the kitchen tearing them into pieces while the large pot of water heated on the stove.

The man seemed aimless, as if overwhelmed by his task. Periodically, Sophie would check on him and gently get him started again if she found him just sitting idly in his chair.

"What're we going to do?" he asked her each time she appeared.

"We're going to fix Tim up good as new," she confidently assured him each time.

The room and table were finished and the pieces of boiled sheet drying in the oven by the time Maybelle returned. She'd had little success: a couple of intermediate first-aid manuals but no leads on any other medical books. Tom was alerted and ready to provide light when required.

Doc Billings returned with a large leather satchel of tools, medicines, and a couple of books. He took Sophie into the adjoining room where Tim lay, closing the door behind them with the others outside. He looked shrewdly at Sophie, gauging her replies to his questions, speaking too softly for Tim to hear.

"What do you assume we're going to do?"

"Amputate the leg," she replied evenly.

"Ever done anything medical before?"

"Nope."

"Blood. What's venous and arterial?"

"Venous is bluish and flows; arterial is reddish and spurts."

"Faint when you see it?"

"No."

"With what we've got here, what's the best way we can stop bleeding?"

"Direct pressure with a cloth. Maybe you can cauterize larger vessels with a hot iron?"

"Right. You'll be fine. Hey—just washing your hands puts you head and shoulders above the world's most eminent surgeons from 200 years ago."

He smiled reassuringly.

"Now; I can't give him a general anesthetic. I don't know the human dosages for my animal drugs—and they don't always act the same in humans anyway. But I have a local anesthetic I can use. I'll give him several shots before we begin. Watch how I do it. Mainly, be sure to hold the syringe upright and gently press the plunger to make sure any air is expelled before injecting the fluid. We don't want to inject any air into him. I'll tell you when and where to inject if I need you to do it midway through.

"Your main job will be to reduce bleeding by applying pressure with a piece of cloth. You'll quickly see where and when. Don't worry if the bleeding continues; it will. But you can slow it enough to make all the difference. I'll give you some Styptic powder to apply, also. It helps the blood to clot. I will have to cauterize heavier bleeders by using a hot iron. Be sure not to inhale when I do: the smell might make you sick. The heaviest bleeders I can tie off.

"For many people, the initial incision is especially upsetting to see. I'll tell you beforehand and I want you to briefly look away. I'll tell you when to look back again. You'll find once that's done the rest won't be so upsetting, except for the sound when I saw the bone. At that time, talk to yourself—count out loud, for example, or recite the alphabet—to cover the noise. We don't need any goddamm heroes here, understand? If you faint or puke that's not going to help things much. So use these little tricks to keep yourself functional. You'll do fine. Any questions?"

"No. I'm ok."

Christ, thought the vet, observing her attentively, *if she ain't a cool one. No shallow breathing, no paleness, no tremors of the extremities... I've by God lucked into a Live One here. Since I'm now apparently the entire Mountainview Trauma Center, she just might come in handy.*

"I'm going to speak with Mr. and Mrs. Baker for a moment. While I do, you go in the kitchen or pantry and see if you can find a couple of opaque plastic bags large enough to contain a leg from the knee down. If you find any, just quietly put them under the table where we'll be working; no need for anyone else to notice them. All set?"

"Yep."

Tom had arrived with a 12-volt Gravely starter battery he kept on a solar charger, plus two clip-on reflector lights and wires with alligator clamps to run to the battery's terminals. He helped Doc and Sophie and Maybelle carry the semi-conscious Tim on his cot into the prepared room and place him on the clean table. Doc stepped into the kitchen and asked Mr. and Mrs. Baker to come with him upstairs to their bedroom.

When he came back downstairs alone in a few minutes they were all hit hard by the sounds of crying from the upper story—especially, for some reason, by the barely audible sounds from the father, mixed with prayer. Sophie had found some black plastic garbage bags under the kitchen sink, taken two, and casually put them on the floor below Tim as he lay on the prepared table. Doc placed a couple of knitting-needle-sized metal rods in the flame of the kitchen stove to heat for use in cauterizing, and brought the cookie sheets heaped with sterilized cloths into the living room. He ushered Tom and Maybelle out and closed the doors, suggesting they might want to check on Mr. and Mrs. Baker upstairs.

"Tim? Can you understand me? We're going to make you better," he said gently to the semi-conscious boy, watching him closely. He got ambiguous eye movements but no coherent verbal response. Taking the left wrist, Doc counted the boy's pulse: fifty pulses in a half-minute. He slipped the metal expansion band of his wristwatch off and gave it to Sophia to put on.

"In a moment, while I'm washing up, you can practice counting his pulse. Hold his left wrist firmly like this," he showed her, "and count how many pulses in thirty seconds by the sweep second hand, then double that number for beats per minute. Whenever you've got time during the operation, count his pulse again and call out the numbers to me, along with the current time. Blood pressure would be nice to monitor, too, but frankly there's not a whole lot we could do about it anyway, so we'll let that go."

He rolled Tim over face down, filled a syringe with local anesthetic, swabbed the base of Tim's spine with alcohol, and carefully inserted the needle, injecting a spinal block anesthesia, then replaced him on his back.

Doc then removed a couple of polypropylene animal restraint straps from his bag. Each was two inches wide by about six feet long, with a "double D-ring" at one end similar to the sort used on motorcycle helmet chin straps. Passing the first strap over Tim's chest, he brought it down under the armpits, beneath the table, and cinched it snugly with the double D-ring. Using the other strap, he secured Tim's good leg to the table, midway between crotch and knee. Then he went to the kitchen next door and washed his hands with antibacterial soap, letting them air dry.

When he returned, Sophie said, "One hundred and ten per minute; time is 4:17"

"Good. Now go wash your hands thoroughly, up to the elbows, with that liquid soap on the kitchen sink. Don't dry them afterwards."

While she washed, he took a packaged sterile cloth drape from his satchel, removed it from the packaging, and unfolded it to cover the card table. Then he began laying out his tools, removing the sterile cloth wrap from each tool and placing the sterile cloths together in a pile, for use as pressure pads if needed. Tearing open a gauze pack, he soaked the sterile gauze with Betadine antiseptic and scrubbed Tim's bad leg from crotch to calf with the brownish fluid.

When Sophie returned from the kitchen, he told her, "Take one of the boiled cloths, soak it with this Betadine, and scrub your hands up to the elbows. I don't have many packs of sterile gloves, and they're going to be so precious I'll only use a set myself. If you see something that needs doing in the open wound just tell me and point, and I'll do it, instead of you touching the open wound. OK? When you're applying pressure, keep the sterile cloth pad between your fingers and the wound. Now watch how I fill the syringe with local anesthetic—like this—and expel the air—like this—and inject around the incision site—like this. Got it?"

"Yes."

"Fine." He injected the anesthetic at a half-dozen points all around Tim's leg just above the knee, re-filling the syringe every three or four injections. That done, he examined the textbook on the card table, which he'd propped open to a plate illustrating the human nervous system.

He kept looking back and forth from the book to Tim's leg, fixing in his mind the routing of the major human nerves and blood vessels involved.

"*Gray's Anatomy* for Chrissakes! 1859—First Edition Facsimile reprint. Handsome binding, though, isn't it? My grandmother never understood vets receive doctorates too: she always thought anyone who was a doctor must be a real doctor, so she gave me this when I graduated."

Sophie's heart went out to him—so unfairly thrown into this situation, with such inadequate resources, expected to do the impossible using miraculous, rather than medical, means.

"One hundred and twelve pulse. Time is 4:38," she said loudly, as deliberately hard and callous as possible, willing him every ounce of gritty determination she possessed. It was not a moment when might-have-been's or human compassion would be helpful—for her, for Doc, or least of all for Tim.

He gently pricked the skin in various places with the scalpel tip, closely observing Tim's lack of response. Then he tightened the tourniquet on Tim's thigh.

"Give me pulse and time. Look away for a moment."

He jotted the pulse and time figures on a pad, noted "Start" next to them, and began the incision.

As the amputation progressed, he occasionally stopped cutting and took over maintaining pressure on the cloth pads to reduce bleeding, while she dashed to the kitchen to get a hot iron from the stove. She quickly developed the ability to apply pressure with one hand while taking pulses with the other while intently searching for bleeders and then making sure he was aware of them. At one point, he flipped the textbook to another place he'd marked— Skeletal, Lower Extremity – for a moment's final check of that illustration.

"Talk nice and loud," he told her, picking up the bone saw.

Taking Tim's wrist and fixing her eyes on Doc's bulky watch on her own wrist, Sophie said "THIS PATIENT'S PULSE IS NOW! COUNTING! ONE! TWO! THREE! FOUR! FIVE!..."

It took surprisingly few strokes with the saw. Midway through, Doc darted a split-second glance at Sophie to assess her. Reassured, he said, "Good. Can you hold the leg up here for me—like this?"

Then, "Good. Get another iron from the stove. Quick." He dropped the severed leg on the floor and idly poked it under the table with his foot so as not to trip on it, working as rapidly as possible to tie off the largest blood vessels, cauterize the medium sized ones, and apply pressure and Styptic powder to the smallest ones. The workload would have kept three or four skilled people very busy, Sophie noted.

Finally, the pace slowed a bit, and he had time to explain as he pored intently over the exposed stump.

"Before I fold the soft tissue flap over the stump and suture it in place, we want to make sure we've got as much bleeding stopped as possible. Use all five or six hands if you need to: maintain pressure on the smallest bleeders, while blotting up blood so we can see what's what, and sing out if you locate any larger bleeders we still need to cauterize. Also, when you can, give me another pulse and time. I'm going to release the tourniquet."

When she did so, he jotted the pulse and time on the paper beneath the "Start" figures he'd previously noted.

Together, they scrutinized every millimeter of the stump: blotting and watching, applying pressure, cauterizing when pressure didn't work, blotting and watching again, re-applying pressure, re-cauterizing where necessary, more blotting and watching. It seemed unending. Sophie felt she was loosing her sharpness of vision. Her back and neck muscles, knotted like iron, were killing her. For the first time, she seriously wondered how much longer she could last. Doc, she could see, was just as physically exhausted—and under far more intellectual and emotional stress. That kept her going: she was *damned* if she'd quit first, when he'd done the most work.

For what seemed like the hundredth time, she called out the numbers.

"One-twenty-five pulse. Time is 5:19."

"OK," Doc said softly, jotting the numbers down on the sheet below the others, "let's close him up."

He sutured the soft tissue flap most of the way around the stump, leaving only a small gap unclosed, with an inch of wicking inside the wound and protruding outside the wound to promote drainage. He double-checked his computations for dosages of the veterinary antibiotics he had available, and loaded the syringe for local, intra-muscular injections, then for an intra-venous. Those given, he called for a final pulse and time and jotted those numbers on his pad, then loosened the restraining straps slightly around Tim's chest and good leg.

"Done," he said with an exhausted smile at Sophie. "Thank you. Couldn't have done it without you, you know."

"Yeah, right, Doctor DeBakey. Save that for the little blonde piece who normally does O.R. and pants for your every attention. Now go in the kitchen and get some tea or coffee—if these God-fearing people don't have anything stronger."

She pushed him into the kitchen where he slumped into a chair, collecting himself.

She closed the door to the kitchen, then opened the other living room door and called up the stairs to where Tom and Maybelle were sitting with Tim's parents.

"All done!" she called brightly. "Can we have something refreshing for Doc and me? I'll be out in a moment." Then she shut that door, too.

Working quickly, she put the severed leg in a plastic bag and dumped the heap of bloody cloths in with it. Then she pulled up the bloody plastic sheeting from around the table and wadded that into the other garbage bag. She bundled the bloody medical implements into a clean cloth, and placed them with the closed anatomy text on the card table, which she pulled into a corner of the room. Lastly, she gave a final swipe to the kitchen table to remove the worst of the gore. She draped Tim's lower half with a sterile cloth. Though it did not conceal the absence of a leg, it mercifully covered the bloodstained table and blood-soaked wadding which bandaged the stump.

Tom knocked softly on the living room door.

"Sophia? You OK in there?"

She opened the living room door into the front hall, then opened the front door and set the two bulky garbage bags on the porch outside the house, then closed the front door.

"Yes, fine. If Mr. and Mrs. Baker would like to, they can see Tim. Tell them he's not conscious, though, and if they'd like to wait that would be OK. Tell them it went well. Doc's very hopeful."

Then she went through into the kitchen and took a chair. Maybelle handed her a steaming mug of coffee. Tom ushered the Baker parents down the stairs and into the living room, where they stood together, weeping silently in mixed relief and dread as they looked at their son on the table, gently stroking his forehead and cheeks. Then Tom guided them into the kitchen, where Maybelle gave them coffee and Doc explained there were good grounds for hope that Tim would "be okay" as he put it.

In silence, Tom considered bitterly just how "okay" the life of a one-legged fourteen-year-old in Mountainview's new world of the 1800s would be, and wanted to smash his fist through a wall.

After a few minutes, Doc quietly took Sophia away from the group in the kitchen and spoke to her in the living room. With a small wave of the hand, he gestured toward the draped young boy and the cleaned-up room.

"Thank you. I mean it. You're an amazing person. I was awfully tired there for a few minutes. There's nothing more we can do here today: if he starts to fail we don't have any equipment to save him. Go on home and get some sleep. And, uh, if you'd join me back here tomorrow morning around nine to look in on him I'd be pleased and honored."

"I'd be glad to, Doc. You're downright impressive—what you managed here today."

Maybelle agreed to stay at the Bakers, spelling each of them in turn so someone could sit in the room with Tim. There was nothing else anyone could do.

Chapter 12
Bolshevism, Fairness, Stupidity, and God

Tom and Sophia walked the few blocks back to the Gravely dealership and home, carrying the two black garbage bags for backyard burial. Each was lost in thought.

Later, as they were fixing supper, he said, "You continue to amaze me. You've had no medical training, yet you did things today most people could not have done without becoming physically or emotionally incapacitated. And you did so while still under enormous stress from your own recent horrors. You're truly amazing."

"Oh for heaven sakes, Tom—when something needs doing, you just put your mind to it and do it. Don't get all worked up over 'heroes.' Someone wisely pointed out that behavior perceived as 'heroic' is far from being desirable. Rather, instances of 'heroism' simply illustrate failures in what should have been smoothly and routinely functioning social systems. With the correct public policies in place, there's not the slightest need—or room—for any antique nonsense involving 'heroes.'

"In this instance, for example," her tone took on an ominous, steely quiet, "Mountainview has had *over two months* to formulate and implement public policy for medical care. And what have people done in all that time? BUGGERIN' FUCKALL! So a young veterinarian was dumped headfirst and alone into a situation he should never have had to face without careful planning, organization, and support. It's *disgraceful*!

"By God, there are going to be some changes here. Doc's going to receive public funding to provide his income, and public funding for whatever facilities, equipment, supplies, and trained assistants it's possible to provide. This community will have the best publicly supported health care services achievable. And it's NOT going to be done by bartering sacks of potatoes for leg amputations, performed by a vet who hasn't been given time to learn human anatomy, assisted by any casual drop-in who doesn't faint at the sight of blood! It's *outrageous*! And as of right now, it's By God going to change!"

"Umm," Tom began fearfully. If this was going where he thought it was going, in Sophia's current state he was a dead man. "Umm… when you say, uh 'public' funding for …"

"SOCIALIZED MEDICINE, Mr. Jeffson! Communistic, Big Government, Welfare State, Tax-Funded Socialized Medicine! Which—I am very damn well aware—is not done here, and never has been, and never will be. Well, we'll just By God *see*!"

"Oh Jesus," Tom sighed softly, "Oh Lord …"

"Not to mention the gasoline!"

All the gasoline in the world would not have the inflammatory potential of socialized medicine in Mountainview. With a fool's optimism, Tom eagerly grabbed at this new tangent. "Gasoline?" he said, encouragingly.

"Who has it, and how much, and where?"

"Well…. uh, people who stored it have whatever's left from what they stored. Some folks filled a 55-gallon drum or two. Most had a few five-gallon cans, plus what was in their cars and trucks. I guess there are people who don't have any, by now.

"The police department has a 2000 gallon tank, I believe, and they had it filled at the start of The Collapse. So they've got whatever's in there now.

"And there's Jared's Conoco Handimart, our one gas station. I think he has an 8000 gallon tank, and he also got it filled at the start of The Collapse. So there's whatever's left in it."

"Which he *sells*," she virtually spat out the word, "I assume?"

"Yeah, sure."

"At whatever price the traffic will bear!" Her triumph at having proved her point was moderated only by her disgust at the point she'd just proved.

"Well, yeah…" Tom took a moment to catch up. "Oh! Yeah! It's expensive all right. Last I heard, a gallon was going for ninety-five pounds of potatoes."

"And it's aaaalllll this 'Jared' fellow's personal gasoline, isn't it? All 8000 gallons, or whatever. To sell for however much he wants to charge for it. To people who have no other place to obtain it—and who *must* have it to grow their food until your steam engine gets working. Who *must*, in other words, pay any price he chooses to demand."

She laid it out slowly, so even Tom could grasp what obviously had to be done.

"Well, yeah. It's his gasoline. I mean, he bought it and it's in his tank at his station. And he trades it to people for high value. That's because its value is very high."

Sophia fought hard for the necessary patience, instructing her frustratingly slow pupil.

"In this crisis," she drew him the apparently necessary picture, "gasoline's a vital, life-or-death resource for the entire community. It should be managed accordingly. If Jared can see the necessity of that, fine; I'd be the first to applaud him. But if he refuses, it ought to be seized by the community for the good of the community. Chief Barley's police department should assume custody of that gasoline for the general wellbeing of us all."

"But legally it's Jared's property. What if he doesn't want his property seized?"

"Just enact a new Town Ordinance or something altering the law for the duration of the emergency. Then seize it legally. At bayonet-point, if necessary," she added, calling up that bit of dramatic emphasis from some long-ago campus speech.

"Far as I know, Chief Barley's deputies don't have any bayonets. Widow Stook's husband, Charley, had one on a captured Mauser he brought home from WW-II. But that's the only bayonet I know of around here.

"Anyway, they probably wouldn't need 'em: Jared sells gas to the police department whenever they want. And he actually couldn't charge any price he felt like. In the first place, when he trades gas to the police department, Chief Barley has to agree the price is fair in light of its current value and our current circumstances, or there's no trade. If Jared's demands were persistently unreasonable, I suspect you might see the round-the-clock Citizens Patrol now guarding Jared's Conoco station cut back a bit …

"You see, Sophia, this is a small town. We all live here together. No one has the power to simply charge whatever he wants or do whatever he pleases. If Jared tried to charge unacceptable prices to individuals for the gasoline they need, then there wouldn't be any trades. Jared and Elise don't have any land: where would they get the food they need for themselves and Stewart, their handicapped teenage boy? Not by working for it on someone else's land—not if they'd tried to screw people by charging them unreasonable prices."

She fell quiet, but she wasn't sold, by a long shot.

"What about people who lack sufficient land, or land of sufficient quality, to grow enough to meet Jared's obviously extortionate price? They're just supposed to do without?"

"Yep. Use a shovel and hoe. If Farmer Bountiful can produce enough food to break even, despite a high gas price, but Farmer Hardscrabble can't, who do you want getting that scarce gasoline: the more productive or less productive food producer?"

"So Scrabble, who maybe didn't *inherit* prime acreage," she spat out the epithet, "should just go hungry?" Her eyes blazed.

"Well, better him than Bountiful. Hungry men don't work well, and we're going to need every last bit of food we can produce. If Bountiful is best able to produce it, I say keep him fed. I say that from naked self-interest, by the way: I don't own any farmland. Therefore I'll be living on whatever food people like Bountiful can grow to trade me. If Scrabble can't grow much, then he's also living at least partly on what Bountiful can grow. God bless Bountiful. Let's hope the market is left free to work as it should, allocating gasoline and other scarce resources to the places they can provide the greatest possible return."

That did quiet her, but only briefly.

"Well, I'm not against maximizing efficiency. But unlike you I don't dismiss all other considerations. I care deeply about whether the system is not merely efficient but also humane and fair. We're human beings, not animals: we have to display higher qualities in our lives."

"No we don't," he replied. "We *do* have to have enough food—we *don't* have to be humane, fair, kind, or loving. The first is a 'must-have,' or we die. The second is a 'nice-to-have,' to the extent feasible. We *are* animals. Granted, we *may* be humans too—if possible, as circumstances permit, to the extent we're able – but if we don't meet the needs of basic animal survival we damn sure won't be around to work on our 'nicer' qualities.

"We're not going to have the well-fed luxury of seeing to it all the people in Mountainview receive treatment that's 'fair.' It's not 'fair' for those of us who didn't cause it to be in this screwed-up mess in the first place. It wasn't 'fair' for Tim to lose his leg from an infection that would easily have been cured in a routine thirty-minute visit to any clinic or doctor's office—if there were one. It's not 'fair' that we've slipped back 200 years and no longer have such care—so all of us must pay an indescribable price for an economic and social Collapse brought on by the stupidity and amorality of only some.

"People throughout the nation have died like flies, or been savagely punished if still alive, as a consequence of stupid policies they stupidly demanded from the politicians they stupidly elected. They're dying because of the consequences, economic and otherwise, of their own stupidity. OK, I admit: for the most part their stupidity is something they can't help. I acknowledge that. But it doesn't reduce my fury.

"The voters were a pack of two-year-olds, democratically allowed the freedom to do as they chose. And they chose, as two year olds will, to play in the street. Now they've been hit by cars—and are dead or dying or in terrible pain. If you're so almighty worked up over 'fairness' take it up with whatever Cosmic Grand Poobah ordained a world in which two year olds are permitted to play in the street. In which voters are permitted to elect whichever cunning sociopath will promise them the gaudiest array of Magic Programs guaranteeing something for nothing. Go pester some Cosmic Grand Wazoo with your demands for 'fairness,' but don't bother me with them.

"I told you earlier: I'll do what I can to assist human survival—at least till I've had enough and say 'the hell with it.' But don't expect me to believe this ignorant human species really deserves to survive. That question, along with the 'fairness' you're so concerned about, is way above my pay grade. I flipped a finger to the world years ago and came here to Mountainview, to retire amidst books and music and the lazy peace and quiet of a life where nothing more exciting than an occasional Gravely sale would occur. I haven't been granted even that harmless, minimal request—as you might point out to the Great One when you address your 'fairness' complaints to Him.

"And, you might mention to Him in passing, I am pretty Goddamn pissed about how 'unfair' it is that ants like myself, who did nothing to bring on our current Collapse, get to suffer right along with the grasshoppers whose childishness and stupidity did bring it on. As far as your need for 'fairness' is concerned: go tell it on the mountain; take it to the Lord in prayer; chat with the chaplain; write your Congressman; vote for the party of your choice—but don't bother me any more with your 'fairness.' I no longer give a rat's ass."

She looked at him a long moment, then said "Yes you do. You're human."

Then she was silent another moment.

"Tom, when Etta Baker and I were scrubbing the kitchen table we would soon use for cutting her son's leg off, you know one of the things that was foremost on her mind? I'll tell you. She was at great pains to assure me she and Alvin had sufficient furniture and rugs and silverware and linens and other household items of value to cover whatever *fee* I was going to charge for helping cut off her son's leg. That's *outrageous*! Payment for such things should simply *not* be a factor."

Tom had had enough. "Typical Goddamn woman!" he exploded. "You're so in love with Moral Outrage you're too damn dumb to even know what to be outraged about. The woman was assuring you she was not dependant on charity! She could pay her bills! That's outrageous? Only by the sick, warped, loathsome standards of a California Lefty. As much as you love feeling Morally Outraged, at least have sense enough to look around and realize what there is to be outraged *about.*

"For starters, I'd suggest being outraged about people who *didn't* pay their bills; who never intended to; who never saw any need for such square, old-fashioned foolishness. So-called 'citizens,' for example, who lived their entire working lives without saving a dime for the expenses they knew they'd incur in old age—merely figuring 'that's the Government's problem.' Voters, for example, who genuinely saw nothing whatsoever wrong about borrowing trillions of dollars from their children, grandchildren, great-grandchildren and untold subsequent generations—to give themselves 'free' government benefits their offspring would pay for until the end of time. With interest.

"You might also try a little Moral Outrage about the behavior of politicians, who pandered to those peoples' despicable morality by adopting an equally despicable morality of their own. When the voters *demanded* freebie government giveaways, far beyond the ability of any government to honestly finance them, the politicians satisfied the voters by enacting the giveaway programs anyway, and *dis*honestly financing them. By using inflation, for example: the deliberate debasing of the nation's money until, as we've seen, it became worthless. Thereby causing all the ensuing tragedy of The Collapse we're now living though—or not living through, in the case of many, many millions.

"Were you really so drunkenly besotted with your ideology of 'free' government handouts you truly couldn't understand that nothing is free? Did you really think there'd never be any consequences for such childish irresponsibility? Ever? Or—as members of the Public Policy-Making Elite— did you just cunningly figure the consequences could be put off until *you* were out of office? Then, of course, the house of cards you'd helped build a few stories higher would collapse during some later political slimewad's term—and be all his fault.

"Look around you at the mess you and your sort, pandering to the ignorance of the childish masses, has put us in. And keep in mind *we're* the lucky ones: we're still living! And don't you even *think* about discussing 'fairness' with me—as long as you and any of your kind are still alive."

The violence of Tom's pent-up rage truly frightened her. But her dismay went much deeper than that. For Sophia was an intelligent woman from an old and wealthy California family which had long ago accepted its deep moral obligation to help the less fortunate. Her intelligence made ideas centrally important to her. Being reared in a family deeply devoted to *noblesse oblige* had given her an unwavering moral compass, pointing always toward more government help for the less fortunate. And in the rarified culture of her childhood at Berkeley—where both her parents taught—then at Palo Alto, where her husband had taught, she had never—not once—been subjected to such utterly wrong ideas and such unjustified moral condemnation as Tom had directed at her.

She—in the intellectually Gifted and Talented group since her Montessori pre-school days, universally admired subsequently by her peers for the courage and correctness of her Progressive views—had just been called both stupid and morally vicious: the two gravest charges imaginable against someone from her world. That familiar world—where "diversity" meant including a liberal woman, liberal Black, liberal gay, liberal Hispanic, and liberal Aleut-or-Pacific-Islander on any symposium panel, to balance the liberal white males—had suddenly been turned upside down. She was dumbfounded and frightened in equal measure, alone in this heart of darkness, somewhere in the primitive depths of Flyover Country, where all the normal certainties had gone haywire.

She said quietly, "We tried to do what we thought was right. We did the best we could. Yes, we made some mistakes. But they were honest mistakes. We meant well."

"Ah! OK then! Fine! No problem! As long as you *meant* well …"

But Tom's rage had spent itself, leaving only a deep, empty chasm of despair.

Chapter 13

Socialist Livestock; Capitalist Entrepreneurs; *"People..."*

But Creeping Socialism, however unlikely the scenario, came creeping into Mountainview in broad daylight, right up Rt. 12 South from the direction of the Mennonite community (which people persisted in calling "Amish") in the innocent-seeming person of Owen Paks leading a young Belgian stallion.

"Ain't he *something*!" Owen exclaimed over and over to everyone he met as he led the horse into town, up Main Street, and over to Johnson's place on the edge of Mountainview, where arrangements had been made for temporary boarding. "Damn—This here is one fine piece a horseflesh! Look at that confirmation!" he urged, getting his new word almost right.

"If I'd known Maybelle was expecting, I'd have given him some cigars to hand out," Tom muttered to Chief Barley in the shop the next day, no more sourly than usual—but no less so, either.

Barley chuckled. "Well, hell, Tom. It is a beautiful-looking horse. By God, the fucker's *huge,* isn't it? And they tell me it's still so young it's not really trained yet—not even full-grown. Damn!" He shook his head admiringly.

"Anyhow, that's what I wanted to get your ideas on."

The Police Chief, no innocent when it came to small town political realities, had long made it a practice to informally chat about major decisions with Tom and a few other citizens before making the decisions. Better a quiet change of course before taking some position than an embarrassing public pullback after an untenable decision had been formally announced.

Tom returned to his work, machining a mounting flange for the steam engine, and recalled the sight of the Owen Paks horse parade as it had made its way up and down most of the town's dozen or so streets, drawing a crowd of kids and idlers in its wake, proceeding along Main past the Gravely dealership.

"Uh," he grunted noncommittally.

"You know," the Chief began, "having the Department own that mule from the thief Owen shot has worked out right well."

Tom had given the matter little thought, but knew Barley had decided to claim police department ownership of the mule Owen led into town with the stunned Sophie astride it when her husband had been killed. Police department ownership seemed reasonable, considering the mule as an item seized by a police deputy from a criminal during commission of a crime.

"We've rented it out to Bill Etter, who you've probably seen using it to haul water. He didn't have anything to pay rent with up front, or pay to have the Scouse brothers make him a water cart, so the department agreed to cover that and take twenty percent of what he gets in trade for his water, as he gets paid. Those bastard Scouse brothers were happy to cut the back end off one of their junk pickups and weld some shafts on it for a mule, then put a 200 gallon tank in the bed. They wanted an ongoing fifty percent share of the profits, too— from now till forever. But I had a little chat with them about this 'n' that, and they decided they'd be happy to have twenty-five gallons of gas from the police tank instead, as a one-time payment.

"So now Etter's got a self-supporting business, running a very useful service. Instead of near every family in the whole damn town sending someone to the creek daily to carry water, now people can buy their water delivered to the door, if they've a mind. Especially for the old or sick, it's a real blessing. And once winter comes...

"Plus, it's been a good deal for the department. Our twenty percent of Etter's profit, even though it's in wheat, corn, potatoes, silver coins, cut firewood, used shoes—every damn thing you can think of—is starting to accumulate. And let me tell you, it helps our own budget a whole hell of a lot.

"And that's where this latest new baby of Owen's comes in. It looks to me like that horse is the whole town's property. After all, we took up that town-wide collection to help those poor people, and they responded with the gift of the horse, so I figure it's owned by the whole town.

"Anyway," he pointed out, with the realism of a small town police chief, "how's any single person going to feed the damn thing all by himself? Fucker's big as an elephant—and probably eats twice as much."

"Got that right," Tom was willing to admit.

"So here's what I was thinking. With the mule, if the department also owns that new beast, and maintains it, trains it, et cetera—and collects any income from renting its labor, or for stud fees or whatever—then that leaves only one other work animal here in Mountainview: Jensen's old gelding. Now I happen to know Jenson would be willing to let it go. He only had it for his grandkids to ride when they visited in summertime, and to tell you the truth I think it kind of reminds him of those grandkids more than he'd like. Never did get word from Atlanta about Mae or any of them after The Collapse.

"Anyway, what would you think if the Department bought the gelding from Jensen, and maintained it together with the mule and this new Belgian colt, and assigned a deputy full-time to horse duty?"

"*Unarmed* horse duty, maybe?" Tom glanced shrewdly at the Chief.

The Chief returned the glance, his assessment of Tom confirmed. Sour as the old bugger was most of the time these days, he was still smart as ever.

"Yep. Owen's a good man, Tom; I'd hate to lose him. He's been in to see me twice now: first time, a few days after he killed that man; and again this morning now that he's back from the Amish. He doesn't want to carry a gun any more. I expect he'd quit before he'd carry one.

"He's a good man. Was anyone else willing to go with the Amish to get that half-trained horse, then lead it back here eleven miles, since it's not saddle-broke yet, walking all that way unarmed? With something that valuable at the end of a halter rope? I think a position of 'Special Deputy, Equine Unit, Unarmed' might be a hell of a good idea for the department, for Owen, and for the whole town. What're your thoughts?"

"I'd agree," said Tom. "Owen's too good for the department to needlessly lose. The deal you've come up with will be good for him, for the department, and for Mountainview at large. I'll support it."

Then he added, "But dammit: it's unreasonable. Look, Chief, like it or not, we're going to stay alive—and those pacifist 'Amish' are going to stay alive, and Owen's going to stay alive—only so long as we have the guns and the willingness to kill anyone who would rob us. Not one day longer. What moral difference does it make whether you use a gun yourself to stay alive, or allow someone else to use it on your behalf to keep you alive?"

The Chief, who had a lot more to do than ponder philosophical inconsistencies, made haste to agree with Tom's point and prepare his departure, mission accomplished. Sour old bastard must be going round the bend, fretting over abstract crap like that. Let the sumbitch try running the police for a day, and see how much free time he had for playing Socrates.

"Good point! Damn if I know how anyone could make that case, Tom. Like you say, it's unreasonable. But—there you go: *people* ..." He shrugged a tolerant, forgiving shrug as he clapped Tom on the back in farewell.

Maybe that California woman can straighten him out, Barley speculated, as he walked back toward the station. Be a shame if the old fart went completely off the rails before he got that steam engine thing working. *If* it ever worked. Which Barley had some doubts about. But you had to cover all angles. Maybe he'd see that California woman, and sort of gently work her around to understanding the desirability of Tom's staying functional until the steam engine either worked or didn't. Hell, have her talk philosophy or some damn thing with him, if that's what he wants.

Personally (here the chief's thoughts wandered a bit from strictly professional matters) what *he'd* want from that good-looking broad would not include philosophy. But Tom was probably too wrapped up in analyzing 'moral inconsistencies' to make his move ...

Ah, well, Barley sighed to himself with a tolerant shrug: *People. What can you do?*

First thing next morning, Owen burst into the Gravely shop at full gallop.

"Hey, Tom, didja hear? The Chief's gonna create a whole new Special Deputy position! I'm gonna be a 'Special Deputy, Equine Unit, Unarmed.' He said I'll devote full time to care for and train the Belgian colt, plus the mule, plus that gelding the Department's buying from Jensen! Is that great, or what?"

"Wonderful, Owen! They're lucky to have the right man for the job," Tom congratulated him.

Two hours later, Jensen dropped by to have Tom weld a broken snaffle. He confided he was including it as a "sweetener" in an upcoming deal for the police department to buy that old gelding he'd been trying to get rid of forever. Confidentially, he told Tom, he was overjoyed at his good fortune.

"Terrific!" Tom said, hearing the man's news. "I'm glad the deal worked out."

Just before noon, Sophie returned from a bread-baking visit to Maybelle's.

"Did you hear, Tom? About Chief Barley's new policy? I'll confess I underestimated that man. It was a little hard to decipher what Maybelle said, but the upshot seems to be the Chief's decided that ownership of all Mountainview's draft animals will be held in common by the police department—on behalf of *all* the townspeople! Owen's to be in charge, he told Maybelle. I just *knew* there could be a start to creating public policy for social progress here!"

And on and on she went. She was so innocently genuine in her excitement, so overflowing with newfound hope for the triumph of moral rightness—and so excruciatingly well-bred—that a gloating I-told-you-so never even crossed her mind.

Tom wanted to kick her. But he confined himself to saying, "Hey, that sounds great, Sophia! It'll be just the thing for Owen. What this town's really needed for a long time is for the police department to have its own cavalry unit." He took long, slow breaths.

When he came downstairs to the shop after lunch, he found the Scouse brothers, Jimson and Jackson, lounging in the doorway awaiting him.

In her day, the twins' mother, Etta Biggen, had been the subject of more shocked gossip than any other half-dozen Mountainview residents combined. Some nine months or so before the twins' birth, two of her particularly favored gentlemen callers—among scandalously many—had been Jim Pike and Jack Braley. Her choice of names for the resulting litter did nothing to improve her standing among the town's respectable people—nor did reports that she and the boys were wont to laugh out loud about the matter.

The twins had inherited her pigsty shack at the edge of town, and "improved" it by accumulating the raunchiest assortment of eyesore trash imaginable. Old toilets were dumped among broken bedsprings. Rusting 55-gallon drums were piled in heaps of tangled barbed wire and cement block, mixed with equally tangled messes of electrical wire. Broken TV sets, old car batteries, and a disintegrating sofa made an impressive mound on one side of their front yard—matched on the other side by an array of the sorriest-looking junk vehicles anyone had ever seen. Even as *junk,* these junk vehicles were absolute bottom quality.

In short, the Scouse brothers had struck it rich beyond their wildest dreams. Following The Collapse, they were the ones who had what people needed. Whether it was lead for bullets, melted from the wheel-balancing weights off scrap car wheels, or copper melted out of wires, or copper wires themselves, or any imaginable bits of this and that which were indispensable for building and repairing anything under the sun: the Scouse brothers were usually where you had to go to get it. And they knew it.

In truth, they were probably no worse thieves than, say, J.P. Morgan, or Lyndon Johnson, or Ken Lay. But they smelled a whole lot worse, and they shaved less often, and they were probably more open about relishing the recent ill wind that had blown them such good fortune.

For years, Barley had been on their case to clean up their garbage dump, and for years they had been devoutly promising to do so. After endless wrangling, agreement had finally been reached for them to construct a tall board fence, to screen off their pigsty from the eyes of civilized people. The fence proved to be a work-in-progress—if its glacial pace of construction could honestly be considered progress. Every time the heat from Chief Barley grew especially intense, the Scouse brothers made a great show of nailing more boards up along the fence's projected path. But every time the heat let up, the work did too—and rotting boards from previous bursts of energy began falling off the old end of the fence, even as new ones were sporadically nailed up at the new end.

Tom knew he could ruin Chief Barley's entire day, any time he chose, by simply saying "the fence."

"Ja hear the news?" leered one of the brothers. Tom never knew which was which, and secretly suspected them of swapping names at random intervals.

"What news?"

"He ain't heard the news," one of them confided to the other, out of the corner of his mouth.

"Horse carts," the other one explained. "Town's gonna go horse carts in a big way. Need a bunch of 'em; different kinds. Po-lice gonna have three horses they rent out. Ja hear that? In't it *great?*"

"I had heard something of the sort." Tom breathed very deeply, very slowly.

"Well, we gotta cut the back ends outta some pickups, and weld some shafts on 'em for horses to pull. How about borryin' us your generator for a little while so's we can use our electric cutter and arc welder? Save usin' up our bottled gasses on a lotta heavy work like that. We'll pay ya back later, promise."

Pay me back later? Do I look that stupid, Tom thought to himself. He considered his own work he had waiting, mentally prioritizing it.

"I'll bring the generator over and stay with it all day for three days total, taking it home with me each night. I'll provide the gasoline and I'll run it. It will cost you whatever price you work out with Chief Barley, on his signed agreement. We can do it when you've reached a deal with Barley."

The brothers halfheartedly attempted portraying the grievous hurt of injured innocence that their own promise to pay was not good enough. They generously offered to relieve Tom of the nuisance of coming over himself: he could just "borry them" the generator and they'd promise to use it carefully and return it when agreed. They affected shock, and expressed considerable personal pain, that he did not seem entirely to trust them. Finally—leaning in close, one on either side of him—and speaking quietly out of the corner of their mouths, they pointed out to Tom that this cart-making scam could be a really Good Thing. They might be willing to let him have a piece of it...if he was willing to play ball…if he knew what they meant.

But Tom's icy silence, and something about his look, cut short the brothers' attempts to negotiate. They soon accepted his terms and were on their way.

"Somethin's eatin' him," one confided to the other from the corner of his mouth as they left the shop. "He don't act pleased about this whole horse-cart business."

"Yup," responded the other. "Ja ever see that broad's livin' with him now? *Damn!* That's somethin' *fine*! He pro'lly ain't getting' any. Got his shorts in a twist."

"Well," replied the more realistic of the twins, Jimson—or possibly Jackson—"she's there all night. Why don't he just *jump* her?"

"*Aaah,*" explained the more sophisticated of the twins, Jackson—or possibly Jimson—"That sorta people…what can you do?"

Chapter 14
Commerce: Fairly or Not, Some 5000 Years of Progress Is Re-achieved

The Scouse brothers were far from the only Mountainview inhabitants whose financial circumstances and practices had changed, suddenly and forever, with The Collapse. In this new world, paper was valuable for writing if it was blank; but it had almost no value except as fire-starter if it was printed over with dead politicians' pictures, ornately designed numbers, and serious-sounding legalistic crap.

Initially, having no money of accepted worth, people used direct barter for transactions. But, as their ancestors had discovered 5000 years earlier, that was a terribly clumsy system. If I have rabbits for sale and need size ten shoes, and you have size ten shoes for sale but need gasoline, not food, our barter deal runs aground. Trying to find exactly the right third party—who wants my rabbits and will trade gasoline for them, which I can then deliver to you in exchange for your shoes—quickly becomes a hopelessly complex muddle. A widely accepted "common denominator" item, called "currency"—or perhaps a small number of such items—was obviously needed.

At first, potatoes were widely accepted as a form of currency, until people began to worry about spoilage. Grains became a more desirable currency because they were a bit less bulky and the spoilage risk was reduced, though by no means eliminated. But Mountainview had not been producing much grain except some corn for local Tyson chicken raisers. It had been clearly impossible to compete with multi-square-mile Kansas and Nebraska wheat fields, so wheat had not been planted in the Mountainview area for nearly a century. But people needed, and could store, only so much corn; it became less and less used for currency as more and more people began to reach that point.

As time passed, corn was sought mainly by people who had small animal operations: chickens, ducks, rabbits, sheep, goats, and pigs. Initially, many of these "small animal operations" were indeed about as small as it was possible to be: some people had one single animal—a pet duck, or a rabbit, or whatever. They found a neighbor with one or more of the opposite sex and began to breed the stock, constructing pens or cages in their garage.

The small animal enterprises were clearly going to be profitable, because without refrigeration people needed meat in small enough quantities to consume before it spoiled. But accepting more and more corn as payment left the animal producers facing the spoilage risk: the more corn they had in storage, the more difficult it was to keep it free of mildew and rodents.

Gradually, people began doing once again what they had first done 5000 years ago—and had done and re-done throughout the centuries countless times since, after each and every failure in the long history of Man's doomed attempts at using something without value—paper—to *represent* something *with* value: "money." People gradually came to see that gold, and especially silver, were substances they could agree on as having an intrinsic, innate, value. Gold and silver were not paper certificates claiming to represent wealth: they *were* wealth.

This consensus was not reached quickly—and indeed it never became a unanimous view. For a long time, some people continued to prefer goods such as ammunition or salt or gasoline to gold or silver. But this was no serious problem, because once gold and silver achieved fairly widespread acceptance it became easy to satisfy a barter demand for ammunition, or whatever, simply by purchasing that item from any seller willing to accept gold or silver, then using it to conclude the barter deal.

There were countless hours of wrangling and opinionating as to why gold and silver, of all substances, should be generally accepted as valuable.

"You can't eat 'em," maintained some people.

"No; but they won't mildew, burn, sprout, rust, dissolve, or get rat-and-roach infested, either," pointed out others. "And it's a lot easier to carry three ounces of assorted silver coins than 250 pounds of wheat—especially if you're shopping at ten widely scattered houses to buy an overcoat, four candles, a dozen eggs, and a pair of breeding-age rabbits."

Many arguments were advanced citing the facts that gold and silver were safe against fire, rust, spoilage, and being eaten by pests. In addition to their safety in storage, they were compact enough to make transport and storage convenient. Also, gold and silver could be divided and sub-divided almost without limit, into as small a unit as desired, yet the sub-units would retain 100% pro rata value of the original: four quarters of a piece of gold or silver each being worth 25% of the original piece, or eight equal bits of the original metal each being worth 12.5% of the original's value. This was a handy feature not shared by, say, one leg of a draft horse, or the left side of a garden cultivator, or seven-tenths of a kerosene lamp.

An additional plus for gold and silver were their universal, one-size-fits-all, characteristic. Ammunition might be very handy in the right caliber, but 20–gauge shotgun shells were not too useful if you had a .30 caliber rifle; nor were size ten boots ideal if you wore a size twelve; nor diesel fuel if you had a gasoline engine. Gold and silver in any form, though, could eventually be exchanged for anything: you didn't need to have a particular size, type, or model of gold or silver coin to make a trade. Indeed, except for the convenience of having its weight and purity stamped on it, precious metal did not even need to be in coin form at all: gold was gold and silver was silver—be it in the form of discs, bars, bits of jewelry, or any random size and shape lumps whatever.

In the end, after all the arguments pro and con were carefully weighed, most people agreed gold and silver were reliable stores of value because—well—because since civilization began, some 5000 years ago, people always had. At bottom, it was as simple, or mystical, or inexplicable, as that.

There was a shortage of gold and silver in Mountainview, of course—but not as severe a shortage as one might at first have imagined. For starters, Mountainview was a tiny, conservative hamlet in West Virginia. Its residents tended to be older people with simpler ways. They did not, as a rule, invest heavily in convertible debentures, interest rate arbitrage, "naked shorts" on cocoa futures, or "puts" on the NASDAQ. Instead, they tended to accumulate firewood, quilts and rag rugs, peach preserves, and case after excessive case of endless, damnable, unstoppable, home-canned tomatoes. People like that also tended to accumulate the occasional silver coin every now and then—and sometimes even a few gold ones.

Numerous middle aged Mountainview residents had saved some coffee cans full of 90% silver coins after 1964, when LBJ decided to pay for the twin triumphs of his War on Poverty and War on Vietnam by debasing the nation's coinage from 90% silver to pot-metal tokens. From just a few years before that, several of the old-timers remembered going into the Grayson County Bank regularly once a month with their father, handing the teller a crumpled, sweaty wad of paper ones accumulated from their chore-money, and receiving equivalent silver dollars to stash in their piggy banks.

"A silver dollar," they would explain, "cost exactly as much in paper back then as it had stamped on it: One Dollar." And the old-timers would cackle at how simpleminded some damn fool bank teller in Grayson had been, giving them a hefty chunk of real silver for a piece of paper. Since a silver dollar soon became worth ten or more paper ones—years before the paper ones became worthless altogether—at least two generations of Mountainview folk had enjoyed putting this move on those "stuck-up city boys" in the huge (pop. 4362) city of Grayson.

Other people, too young to have personal experience of honest U.S. coinage in circulation, had been occasionally buying one ounce U.S. Silver Eagles or other silver coins to stash in their sock drawer for a rainy day. And in addition to coins, which are minted by the government, there were many other pieces called "rounds," which are essentially the same as coins but minted by private refiners instead of governments.

Over the years, private refiners had issued an amazing variety of one ounce silver rounds in collectible sets to commemorate any conceivable subject: NASCAR drivers, signs of the zodiac, noteworthy firearms, baseball players, military triumphs, large game animals, WWII fighter planes, official state trees, famous sailing ships...There seemed no limit to the range of excuses for minting one ounce silver rounds—each one a permanent, imperishable store of value, costing about the price of a pizza. Many young men in Mountainview, not interested in the IPO's of telecom hustles (or even aware such Great Deals existed) bought silver coins or rounds now and then as they could, and put them aside.

It was what their people had always done. They knew those fast-talkers in big cities far away were invariably up to some sort of financial hanky-panky, so they liked having some of their money where they could keep an eye on it. Their parents or grandparents had terrible tales of losses and resulting hardship from the bank failures of the 1930s. And *their* grandparents had told of far, far worse: memories ran deep in the only part of the U.S. ever to have been conquered, crushed, looted, and occupied by an invading army—to have its paper dollars made totally worthless, and its population's widespread physical hunger prolonged for more than a generation. That kind of experience marks a people, often in ways they themselves may not consciously see.

Just as it was nothing new for the "Amish" from Dayton, Virginia, to flee their homes by night and travel again toward safety, so it was nothing new for the rural folk of Mountainview, West Virginia, to cope with yet another collapse of a fraudulent paper currency. Given the collapse of paper "Continentals" during the Revolution, and the collapse of Confederate paper dollars in the Civil War, this latest collapse made the third time the same thing had happened—if you ignored the long term debasement of the U.S. dollar's value under the Federal Reserve System. From the FED's founding in 1913 until 2004, that ninety-year period had seen the paper dollar's value reduced by 97%—technically not quite a fourth instance of total collapse.

The simple, old-fashioned ways of people in Mountainview proved invaluable after this latest Collapse. In total, they had enough gold and silver, retrieved quietly piece by piece out of many a sock drawer and family keepsake collection, to make possible a transition from the direct barter economy of the Dark Ages into a workable, if rudimentary, money economy from the early capitalist Renaissance. The transition wasn't completed overnight, and certainly wasn't "fair" or pretty to look at. But the first step back toward full civilization was achieved: there was enough gold and silver—now having many times its pre-Collapse value—to bypass wampum, giant stone wheels, tobacco, cattle, and similar primitive forerunners of precious metal currency.

Any upheaval produces winners and losers, and the latest Collapse was no exception. The Scouse brothers' garbage pile/junkyard made them (by current standards) rich men within a month. Several of Mountainview's upper crust, living very well indeed on generous military or civilian pensions, suddenly became destitute. Small landowners, who had been gradually going broke for years because their small-scale farming or stock-raising was not competitive with huge, corporate agro-business, were suddenly wealthy. Provident, responsible people who had lived frugally all their lives, carefully accumulating holdings of the safest, most conservative investments available, saw their portfolios of sound public utilities, the bluest of corporate blue-chips, and "absolutely secure" U.S. Treasuries become worthless. The totally careless indifference of fate, its brutal, random whimsy in bestowing unearned windfall fortunes on some while destroying the hard-earned fortunes of others— completely without regard to any claim of reason or fairness—made clear how much of life is beyond Man's control or understanding.

Old Miz Strewk, who had spent 45 years slowly but steadily henpecking her Poor Arthur into his grave, finally reaped the consequences of her behavior: she became one of the richest people in Mountainview.

Poor Arthur, who was not permitted to be out late of an evening, had achieved his only escape from the rusty-nail voice of his beloved while hiding in his den, quietly working on his coin collection. Had it been a stamp collection, containing tens of millions of dollars worth of the most extreme rarities, it would have been worthless in post-Collapse Mountainview, leaving Miz Strewk destitute. Had it been an art collection, featuring the most exquisite works of Rembrandt or Van Gough, it would have been nearly worthless in post-Collapse Mountainview, leaving Miz Strewk nearly destitute. Had it been a coin collection of the most priceless early Byzantine or Chinese bronze pieces, it would have been worthless, leaving Miz Strewk destitute.

But whether by destiny or random chance, Poor Arthur had been deeply in love with…dimes. He collected dimes from every year, dimes from every mint, dimes of nearly every grade, dimes acquired in places he had been, dimes received as change from important purchases he had made, dimes of every possible category. And for every category he could, Poor Arthur had at least several "backup dimes," not quite good enough to make it into his official collection, but held in reserve or for possible future trades. Poor Arthur had an awful lot of dimes.

And those were just the ones involved in his collection. To *get* those, he bought "unsearched full bags" of what are called "junk silver dimes" from coin dealers—that is, random, pre-1965 dimes minted from 90% silver, not screened for dates, mint marks, etc.—in quantities of $1000 total face value, making up what was called a "full bag." It requires 10,000 dimes (or 4000 quarters, or 2000 halves) to make up the $1000 face value of a "full bag," which the post office delivers in a cube-shaped cardboard box about the size and weight of a bowling ball. The coin dealer—selling dimes, quarters, or halves merely by weight of their silver content (any circulated 90% silver coins totaling $1000 face value will contain about 715 ounces of pure silver) doesn't care which coin you buy. Poor Arthur specified dimes because he loved dimes, and he got full bags, instead of half-bags, quarter-bags, or even individual coins, because the standard full bag was the least expensive way to buy silver coins.

As luck or destiny would have it, before his fatal coronary Poor Arthur had just taken delivery of a bag, 10,000 dimes, through which he intended to spend many quiet hours carefully sorting in hopes of finding one, or possibly even two, worthy of being added to his collection. In the upheaval of his sudden death, the bag of dimes was put aside to be dealt with later—but never was.

Aside from dimes, the few remaining items in his collection were long-forgotten leftovers from the earliest days of Poor Arthur's interest in coins: a handful of pieces he'd acquired but then lost interest in when seized by the allure of dimes. These long-neglected items, a mere dozen all told, happened to be $20 U.S. gold coins, known as "Double Eagles." When he got them he was just out of night school, where he'd taken a drafting course, and working for Apex Industries in Baltimore. That was in 1931, 1932, and early 1933.

At that time (things were so simple back then!) a $20 gold piece cost—$20. You would just hand any merchant or bank teller a paper $20 bill and he was happy (if foolish) to return you the "same" $20 in gold—which the dollar was then "as good as." A thrifty lad, Poor Arthur did exactly this every few months when able, and put his gold coins aside.

Then disaster struck. On April 5, 1933, Roosevelt confiscated the nation's gold. Fines up to $10,000 and prison sentences up to 10 years were sternly threatened against holders of what, on April 4, had been perfectly legal coins issued by the U.S. mint. Poor Arthur panicked. Always the mildest, most inoffensive and law-abiding of men, he somehow got it into his head that the government would hound him to the ends of the earth and throw him in prison for having had such coins. Trembling, he stuffed them deep into the furthest recesses of his closet, and prayed J. Edgar Hoover's G-Men, who he saw in the Movietone Newsreels every week, would not search the entire nation house-to-house until they found him.

They didn't. Years passed, and eventually Poor Arthur seldom thought any more about his hairbreadth escape from the penitentiary. By the time gold ownership was re-legalized in 1975 he was sixty-four, had been caught up forever by the allure of dimes, and had no interest in the abandoned relics of his wild, criminal youth.

After Poor Arthur (with a look of gratitude, some people maliciously said) passed to his eternal reward in 2003, it was not long before The Collapse provided his beloved with her own reward right here on earth. Once The Collapse began, within two months she had become one of the richest people in Mountainview. Old Miz Strewk had about a hundred pounds of 90% silver dimes—plus a fair percentage of all the gold in town.

Gradually, to Sophia's intense disapproval, Old Miz Strewk became what is called a "banker": she allowed people the temporary use of her coins (to buy materials for starting or expanding a business, for example) upon payment of a fee; just as Tom rented the use of his Gravelys (to produce a corn crop, for example) upon payment of a fee; and Chief Barley's police department rented the use of its mule (to haul water) in return for a fee.

After its brief, initial slide back into a primitive barter economy from the Dark Ages, Mountainview began reemerging into the vastly more civilized conditions of the Renaissance and that era's early capitalism. The progress was made possible because the community had a stock of widely accepted money—gold and silver—and a person willing to allow others the temporary use of that money upon payment of a rental fee, called "interest."

In no case did anyone *have* to rent the relevant item—a handful of coins for business purposes, or a Gravely for growing crops, or a mule for hauling water. People could still do business by hauling hundred-pound bags of corn or potatoes back and forth. But renting the use of a handful of dimes was more efficient and convenient. They could still farm with a shovel and hoe instead of a mechanical tractor. But renting the use of a Gravely was more efficient and convenient. They could still hike to the creek for buckets of water each day. But paying Bill Etter and his rented mule to deliver it was more efficient and convenient.

As Mountainview gradually began rebuilding a capitalist economy, the availability of a trustworthy form of money made possible an increased division of labor. To a greater and greater extent, people produced mainly the thing they produced best, then used convenient silver coins to buy other necessities from other people who could produce those other things better.

Someone who became an expert at repairing shoes could best spend his time doing that, instead of hiking to the creek and back for water each day. He benefitted by repairing more shoes, other people benefitted by having better-fixed shoes than they could have done for themselves, Bill Etter benefitted from the payments of yet another customer for his home-delivered water, the police department benefitted from its increased income from Etter's rented mule, and the town at large benefitted from a better-funded police department. And the shoe repairman, receiving more dimes for his services than he needed to spend right away, occasionally sent a few of his extra dimes over to Miz Strewk, who loaned them out to other people and gave him part of the interest she charged.

"Over time," the cobbler would think to himself, "the amount of spare money I'm able to send to Miz Strewk, plus my share of what she charges others for the use of that money, should be enough to pay my bills when I get too old to repair shoes any more. But unlike dubious 'savings' in a paper currency, whose value is based purely on faith, I will have my savings in a substance man has prized continuously since the dawn of civilization: precious metal. I will know that an ounce of silver or an ounce of gold will forever be worth exactly that much. Such savings will be far more dependable than the previous system of staking my hopes for security in old age on a vague abstraction such as paper 'dollars,' which are worth...what, exactly?

In 1970, the shoemaker might reflect, with the price of gold at $35 an ounce, one 'dollar' was worth, obviously, 1/35th of an ounce of gold. A mere ten years later, in 1980, with gold at $800 an ounce, that 'dollar' was worth merely 1/800th of an ounce of gold! Oh hapless retiree, whose security rested on the value of such carefully saved but whimsical 'dollars'!

What had changed between 1970 and 1980 was not the value of gold, which has remained nearly constant throughout history. One ounce of gold would buy a toga for a Roman 2000 years ago, and the same one ounce of gold would buy a man's business suit right up until our own era's Collapse.

As old-timers in Mountainview knew from their own parents' experience, a U.S. $20 gold piece, or "Double Eagle," was the standard price for a fattened, market-ready beef in the early years of the 20th century. The same gold piece (now worth over 600 paper 'dollars') would still buy a whole market-ready beef a hundred years later, in the early 21st century—by which time 20 'dollars' in paper would buy perhaps three or four little plastic-wrapped packages of meat at a grocery. What had changed was not the value of the gold coin but the value of slips of paper called 'dollars.'

With my future security at stake, the cobbler in today's Mountainview might reflect, let me put aside my savings in something *stable*—not bits of paper that can become worth anything or nothing from year to year, as the whims of politicians and the vagaries of fate may decree!

But not everyone agreed with this reasoning. Sophia, for one, passionately believed the shoemaker's real security should lie not in his own thrifty accumulation of gold or silver coins over the years, but rather in the promise that his surrounding community would, when he became old, support him out of the community's income at that future date. He should depend not on a personally achieved security, requiring his own thrift and provident behavior, but upon a politically achieved—i.e. a *social* security—in which he trusted his fate to whatever the economic conditions and the popular voting choices might hold in store for him many decades in the future.

Many people in Mountainview, constitutionally unable to save one coin at a time, year in, year out, amid the countless temptations of daily life, were only too eager to jump at promises of security that did not place such an onerous burden of prudence and self-control on them. They were…weak? dishonest? childlike? foolish? Perhaps one could say—most accurately as well as most forgivingly—that they were just…*people.* Just ordinary, average, run-of-the-mill little people: small in their vision, simple in their ways, stoic in bearing the hardships their stupidity made it certain they would bear.

They could simply have been *told* to save for their own future—*ordered* to do so, in no uncertain terms—by those with more maturity and self-control than they themselves had been granted. And given a clear command, they would mostly have obeyed. By and large, they wanted to do the right thing, and be praised for it—to please those in the community they looked up to. But some of their natural leaders, who should have backed up such an order with one, unified voice, instead "felt the little people's pain" at life's daily denials of small pleasure—the coin put aside for tomorrow, rather than enjoyed today—and forgivingly told them not to worry: *social* security would provide for them when personal prudence did not.

Sophie, for example, who herself displayed an intense awareness of the future, and powers of self-control stronger than tempered steel, urged neither of these qualities on the weaker people who looked up to her for guidance. She deeply rejected such necessary characteristics of capitalist life.

The tragedy of people like Sophie, and the foolish, self-destructive counsel with which they had misled the ordinary people, Tom gradually came to see, bore out the truth of the observation that Man's sins will be repaid not only against him but against his posterity, even unto the fourth generation. Tom's vehement objections to Sophie's values intensified, if anything, as he learned more about her background. But as he came to understand the origins of her values, he acquired an increased appreciation of how today's errors and tragedies are, so often, the inevitable outcome of yesterday's.

Sophia's immensely wealthy family had obtained its wealth in the 1880s by importing shiploads of half-starved Chinese coolies into California and using them on blasting jobs white men, even the Irish, were not willing to do. If a railroad bridge or tunnel or building site or roadway needed rock blasted, the coolies were given drills to bore holes, blasting powder to tamp into them, and fuses to place in the powder and light. The fuses—cheapest-available— burned at unreliable speeds, so attrition among the coolies who couldn't escape in time was staggering. But upon payment of a $3.00 "goodwill fee" to the village headman from a dead coolie's village, and a cursory cleanup of scattered body parts, construction resumed without delay: the profit being made by Sophia's ancestors was stupendous, and there were always plenty more coolies where the previous batch had come from.

Sophia had grown up in a very wealthy family which had very good reasons to have spent its past hundred years entertaining serious doubts about the wonders of the capitalist system. Her blind, passionate loathing of "Mean-Spiritedness" and her equally passionate devotion to "Fairness"—at whatever price in terms of ridiculousness, or even long-term catastrophe for the very people she was trying so hard to help—was an obsession Tom became increasingly able to understand. Our best qualities, no less than our worst ones, tie us eternally to our past.

But Sophie was not the only person dismayed by the lack of fairness economic fate had visited on Mountainview's post-Collapse economy.

Numismatic value—the value collectors placed on rare coins simply because of their prettiness and their rarity—became a thing of the past after The Collapse. As far as most people were concerned, struggling to survive in this hard new world, silver was silver, gold was gold, and an ounce was an ounce was an ounce: rare dates, mint marks, and PCGS coin-grading certificates be damned. Therefore, some of the rarer dimes and all the gold Double Eagles Miz Strewk had inherited, were reduced to simply the value of their metal content, losing their previously greater numismatic value. This meant, overall, that the coins Poor Arthur left to his beloved increased in real value merely hundreds of times over, rather than thousands.

In character to the very end, Miz Strewk spent her final three years on earth bitterly complaining to anyone she could buttonhole that life was unfair— outrageously, bitterly, indecently, mean-spiritedly UNFAIR!

Chapter 15
Meals with a Hidden Agenda; Woodcutting; Failure and Success at Bonding

"You know that vacant storefront we talked about?" Sophia began a few days later at breakfast.

"The one just perfect for a strip joint, singles bar, and anarchist poetry coffeehouse?"

"Uh…well…I've been thinking a bit more about that."

To prepare himself for the latest harebrained scheme, Tom ate another slice of the exceptionally tasty bread. He had to admit, Sophia and Maybelle together were turning out not just breads but all kinds of other foods that were far more delicious than he'd thought possible with such limited a range of ingredients.

"What would you think about using the place—just occasionally, maybe once a week—to put on an interesting dinner?"

"Hmmm," Tom said with grave thoughtfulness, as if he gave a damn.

"For example, if we can get Mr. and Mrs. Gump to approve some minor remodeling, so we can cook and serve food there, we might offer a 'Greek Feast' some Saturday afternoon. We'd charge each attendee maybe thirty cents silver, pay five of that to the Gumps, and use the rest for ingredients, et cetera. We'd serve a Greek meal: lamb or goat, rice, flat bread, hummus and tabouli, stuffed grape leaves—that sort of thing. I'm pretty sure we can scrounge up the ingredients for those dishes, or near enough to fake it."

"Hmmm!" Tom gave the matter the weighty thought it suddenly deserved, *Lamb! Rice!* Then he came back down to earth. "We?"

"Maybelle and I. She knows everybody in Mountainview: who's got what food hidden away, and how much they're likely to charge for it, and how to

112

dicker with them. Besides, she's an excellent basic cook, and really quick to pick up on anything she hasn't yet been exposed to. And, finally, Maybelle could promote the affair among the people here far more successfully than I ever could."

"True. But haven't you taken on medical care activities full time, helping Doc and so forth?"

"Not really; Doc says Tim's leg is healing. Barring something unexpected, he should live. I'm just filling in helping Doc until there's someone else ready to do it. In fact, maybe I can hasten the medical training process, and a lot of other training-and-recruitment processes, if the thing I'm planning works out..." She paused, hesitant to explain further.

"Well, anyway, back to the Greek food idea," Tom said. "Hmm..." He was intrigued now, despite himself, calculating.

"I don't know how much you'd pocket after expenses. Ahh, thirty cents silver a head...? I guess some would pay that. Lamb and rice, huh? Wow! I don't know if you'd make anything or not, expensive as ingredients are. Wonder if charging forty cents would price you out of the market? Probably. Maybe start with a thirty-cent introductory price, hope you don't lose too much on it, then see if you can work up to two-meals-for-seventy-cents at a later date. Jeez, I just don't know...Small business startups are nightmares, always, every last one, without exception. What you'd make on it I just can't figure...Hell, for all I know you might make a killing: starting a small business, there's just no earthly way to predict. I assume what's in the house here—plus what Maybelle's got—would provide sufficient cookware, dishes, tablecloths, napkins, etc. But you would still have some expenses for consumable supplies—stove wood, dishwashing soap...Still, your main costs would be the food ingredients and rent..."

"Well, yes," she urged him along, trying hard to conceal her impatience that he'd completely missed the point and wandered off into some sort of financial trivia, "There's all that to consider, of course. But what do you *think* of the *idea* of presenting to the whole community (well, to anyone who'd come) a full afternoon/evening program centered around the theme of *Greece?*"

She struggled to make it even clearer.

"They were, in many ways, the originators of Western Civilization. Democracy, politics, comic and tragic drama, mathematics, sculpture, architecture, poetry—the paths taken by the ancient Greeks in those areas make us Westerners today, as opposed to Orientals or Native Americans or Africans or whatever. Who we are and how we think are determined in so many ways by who the Greeks were and how they thought. Obviously, that's far too much to go into in one evening, but still…the basics …"

She lamely drifted to a halt.

"Oh yeah. Greek civilization. Yeah, it's interesting. I mean, Jeez, think about those old farts: they got no toilet paper and no way to combat the body lice that covered them from birth till death—and they're spending their time working out the most incredibly elegant proofs of abstract mathematical theorems. Jeez. Wouldn't you think they'd have sort of concentrated, you know, on first things first?"

He shook his head, baffled but genuinely intrigued by the matter. "Stinkin' and scratchin'—and thinking about the square of the hypotenuse of a right triangle …"

"That's not the *point!*" She fought back tears of frustration. She had thought it all over, so carefully. And first he got off the subject onto some sort of financial trivia; and now he was on lice and toilet paper …

It was either scream or breathe very slowly and deeply. With every last ounce of will, she managed the second option.

"The *point,*" she said—very, very slowly, under complete control— "is to arrange an attractive setting—a meal—which could serve as a non-threatening activity *leading* to opportunities for… for…"

But her nerve failed her at the critical moment. The project was so desperately important to her. She simply couldn't bear the risk of setting it all out bluntly—and perhaps seeing it fail. She couldn't.

Tom could clearly see that for whatever reason the crazy woman had worked herself into a state of some sort. No figuring people like that. He cast about for some words that might alleviate her problem, whatever it was.

"Well, tell you one thing: if you could get the ingredients I bet you'd sure make a hell of a hit with baklava. Man, I love that stuff! I bet folks here would go nuts over it."

"Baklava." Her voice was small and faint. "I will keep that in mind, Tom. Thank you."

She'd sounded so forlorn and defeated, Tom mused as he went downstairs to the shop. Like she'd failed to get something across, maybe? Who could say. Maybe she didn't like baklava? Aha! Maybe she *did* like baklava—really, really liked it. And she couldn't get the necessary ingredients from the limited supplies available here. And that really hit her hard. She *really* wanted to be able to make baklava so bad…Well, hell, he liked it too. Man, what he wouldn't give for a ton of baklava now. But, Jeez, to let it get to you as badly as she had…! Some people had no clear grasp of reality.

But he had no time for trivia. Mounting a steam engine on the L Model Gravely was fiendishly difficult. The complexities of just physically attaching all the steam equipment to the tractor frame, for one thing, were nightmarish. In addition to the engine itself, there was the firebox and boiler assembly to mount, and the steam delivery line to run from the boiler to the engine's single cylinder—all of which had to be done with regard to accessibility for lubrication and maintenance, filling the boiler with water and monitoring the water level, fueling the firebox and removing wood ash, avoiding excessive heat too near the operator, and so forth. Not to mention the need for the maximum feasible strength at every mounting point. In addition to the complexities of transmitting the power from engine to tractor, using a totally different engine than the tractor was meant for.

And, infinitely compounding the frustration, was the need to do all this—design, fabrication, machining, welding, etc.—within the limits of the machine tools Tom had in his shop, and the spare parts and metal stock he had available or could obtain. Time and again, Tom clinched his fists in frustration, recalling just the perfect tool he'd seen advertised for sale, but decided not to buy because "I could always get it later if I really needed it."

So a necessary process that could have been done quickly and simply now had to be done the roundabout, long and hard way. Time and again he kicked himself because he lacked some common part, or even metal stock to make it from, which he could formerly have obtained for nearly nothing. So, lacking that part, he had to re-engineer his way around it, devising some substitute.

And, always, he had the nearly unbearable frustration of his own limitations. He sold garden tractors, for Chrissake, and fixed them, when necessary, by removing broken parts and replacing those with identical new ones! That's all! He was not a post-graduate metallurgist, or tool-and-die maker, or mechanical engineer, or certified welder, or skilled machinist—all of which, and more, was necessary for this impossible task he had stupidly undertaken. On some twelve-hour days, the grand total of his progress was one, precisely drilled hole—achieved at the price of such seething, raging frustration Tom was ready to chuck the entire project.

He was kept going, more than anything, by the one undeniably hopeful bit of success achieved so far. After testing the little 4 HP Reliable steam engine he'd bought, to be sure it operated normally, he'd jury-rigged a mounting frame for it with a V-belt running to one of the generators he sold as Gravely accessories. Sure enough, he now had a working, steam powered electric generator. With it, by carefully imposing only one load at a time, he could power his electric welder and shop equipment, all of which took either 115 or 230 volts, and his water well pump, which took 230—and even some electric lights plugged in at the day's end, to catch the last, fading power when the fire was allowed to die in the firebox and the boiler's steam pressure slowly subsided.

Being able to produce electrical power without using gasoline had important secondary benefits, too. Tom undertook a serious battery-scavenging campaign, obtaining by gift or barter eventually over a hundred batteries from cars, trucks, riding mowers, farm machines, and any other sources available. Arraying them in long rows across the floor of his now-idle showroom, he took great care to keep each one fully charged, using the steam powered generator as necessary, typically every week or two. Maintained in that fashion, he knew, a lead-acid battery can last a decade.

The ability to generate electricity without using gasoline gave Tom's larger project a vastly extended lifetime. *Surely,* he thought, *as long as there's firewood to burn, I can just keep trying here with the shop tools I've got – and eventually get that steam engine mounted and working on a Gravely. If I don't go berserk first.*

Owen came by the shop to help when he could, but that was less with every passing day because of his new equine responsibilities. Invincible, as the Chief had agreed to name the Belgian colt, had been trained by the Amish to lead on a bridle, but had not yet been saddle-broke. During the four days Owen had spent with the Amish, they had showed him a first step in saddle-breaking: accustoming the horse to an object on its back. They had sewn a pair of oversized pack-bags from heavy canvass, and gentled the colt to carrying them while led. Once that was achieved, the Amish had placed in one of the bags an old draft-horse collar, badly worn but still usable for a while. In the other bag, to balance the weight, they had put a small piece from a salt-lick, some corn-and-oats feed mix, a quantity of good hay, and four huge horseshoes, for use when Invincible outgrew his present ones. Around and around the Amish community's pasture, hour after hour, Owen patiently led the horse, learning to perform his own function even as Invincible was learning his.

Upon his return to Mountainview, Owen had begun training Invincible to wear the big, padded-leather draft collar. He was preparing the horse to be harnessed to an object, so he could train it to pull. There were plenty of perfect objects at hand: tree trunks were strewn all around the town's outlying woodlots, lying where they had been felled, awaiting transport to town where it would be more convenient to cut them up for firewood or lumber. Owen planned to start with ridiculously small trunks, to accustom the horse to the task, then gradually move up to weights more in keeping with the young giant's true strength.

Chief Barley obtained from Jared's Conoco station a pair of 5/8-inch chains fifteen feet long, formerly used for vehicle towing, now to be used as traces. Owen attached one end of each trace to the hames, or projections on Invincible's collar, and led the other end back to a small tree trunk, to which he secured it. After some patient encouragement and nibbles of carrot treats, Invincible began to get the idea, and followed Owen as the excited young man proudly walked beside his monster draft horse, leading him this way and that.

"He loves learnin' how to do it! I can tell he loves it!" Owen exulted, thrilled beyond description at this working bond between man and beast.

"I'm figurin' out stuff Invincible can't think of—and Invincible's usin' more muscles than ten of me would have—and *together* we're doin' more than we could do separately in a hunnerd years!"

For both these creatures of God, a whole new world had suddenly opened up. One after another, with increasing dexterity each time, they dragged larger and larger tree trunks this way and that, up and down the training area, around stumps and other obstacles. "We can actually *do it!*" they exulted in unison, each in his own way.

When a human succeeds in forming a working bond with another species—almost any other species, doing almost any sort of work—something happens to both. The terrible sense of "alone-ness" we feel in a world lacking any other creatures like us dissolves a bit, and we can enjoy a newfound comradeship with another, across what was formerly an impassable abyss. There can be no doubt the animal feels something similar: one sees it beyond question in the self-important way any animal mastering a new skill carries itself, displaying a visible sense of pride in its accomplishment, an unmistakable delight in pleasing the master who devotes his time and love and attention to training the animal.

Owen and Invincible hauled tree trunks, one after the other, from outlying woodlots to convenient stockpiles at the edge of town. They did it—in the first flush of their delight at mastering the skill—for the pure, thrilling, physical and mental *joy* of working together.

Woodcutters, now the second largest labor category in Mountainview, after farm workers, had used chainsaws to fell selected trees in the forests adjoining the town and then to buck off the limbs for immediate use as firewood, leaving the tree trunks where they lay. In some cases, a woodlot owner had sons of an age to work, and they cut their own trees on their own land without any need for hired labor. In other cases, if a landowner was not able to work, and lacked appropriate sons or close relatives, he hired other men to cut his trees, either for wages in coin or for a percentage of the wood.

Woodlot owners understood full well that their land and its timber would be the source of their income for food and other necessities—not just for this year but for all the remaining years they and their descendants lived. They chose very carefully which individual trees to cut, with a far more direct and personal concern than some Weyerhauser or Georgia-Pacific executive would have felt, sitting at a desk in his forty-fifth-floor office, 1500 miles away.

Some trees were obviously to be culled for firewood, to thin out crowded stands and allow straighter, more valuable lumber trees to thrive. Some lovely old mature trees were cut for firewood, lumber, or both, before advancing age, disease and insects, or storms could damage them. Some trees on the edges of clearings were cut to expand grazing pastures or tilled fields.

In Mountainview's current circumstances there was a huge demand for cook-stove wood and fireplace or furnace wood—soon to be increased, Tom hoped, by a growing demand for steam engine boiler fuel. But West Virginia's fertile valleys and steep hillsides had, from time immemorial, produced timber in amazing abundance. Given Mountainview's small population, and with reasonably intelligent timber management practices, there should be no lack of accessible firewood or lumber for many generations, if ever.

In the much nearer future, by the time the available chainsaws no longer worked, because there was no longer any oil and gas to run them, Tom prayed his steam-powered Gravely would be ready, with its firewood-cutting, wood-splitting, and lumber-sawing attachments. If not, he mused, people were going to learn some bitter lessons about the amount of sheer, brutal, backbreaking, human toil required to fell, buck, and split trees using nothing but saws, axes, wedges—and brute, human muscle.

"May humans never again be dragged back to that level of slave-existence," he beseeched the God he didn't believe in, as he doggedly worked through one problem after another on his steam powered Gravely.

Chapter 16
Steam and Justice in the New World

"Got a minute?"

Barley didn't make it a habit to come by the Gravely shop out of idleness, so of course Tom left off metalworking and cursing—lately doing more of the latter than the former, it seemed – and waved the Chief to a chair beside his own rocker.

"Hey, Chief. If you got the money I got the time. *Nobody's* got a planetary gearbox the right size. So I've got to think up some decent alternative—unless I lose hope and settle for some crappy belt drive with pulleys. Which I can always do, but, Jeeze—it's sure a second-rate comedown from a decent gear transmission."

"Why?"

"Ah Hell. For a hundred reasons," said a tired and disgusted Tom. "Belts stretch with wear and have to be readjusted. They wear out. We can't make rubberized V-belts, which would be best, so we'd have to use flat leather belts, and they'll tend to slip under load. And stretch. And wear out. The most primitive horseless carriages used them for drive belts. One of the first and biggest improvements in automobile technology was the leap to an infinitely better way to transmit the engine's power: gears meshing in a gearbox. But making our own sets of gears—the metallurgy, forging, machining, all that sort of thing—stuff that was fairly common technology by the 1880s—is way beyond our capabilities here. Won't always be, I hope. But it sure is for now, and the foreseeable future."

Tom sat in silent dejection for a time. Then he sighed and quoted a poem he'd been using more and more often, as his frustration level increased daily in the Gravely shop: "Here we sit, brokenhearted / Tried to shit, only farted."

Barley chuckled in knowing sympathy. Truth be told, he too had an ample supply of reasons for gloom and frustration.

"Well, tell me this, Tom: what's the big deal about putting a steam engine on a Gravely? I mean, look, you've got the steam engine hooked up to that generator. It runs. You can make electric power from now till the cows come home. And you could just as well hook it up to a saw or a water pump or whatever. People used stationary engines all over small farms back a hundred years ago."

"True," Tom acknowledged, "and if we have to do that, then that's what we'll have to do. But it's a terribly poor second choice to putting the steam engine on a Gravely. For one thing, a stationary engine wouldn't serve most agricultural needs—plowing, cultivating, harvesting: stuff that requires a self-propelled tractor. Many other tasks, too, require the machine be self-propelled: hauling stuff in a cart, plowing snow or dirt, trench-digging, dragging home tree trunks. Even stationary jobs require the machine to get to and from the job site: vastly easier if the machine will move itself there and back.

"Also, the Gravely's designed to quickly accommodate a huge array of attachments—very many of which we've got here, I'm happy to say—usually just by bolting the desired attachment onto the tractor's front end with four bolts. Shazam: Quick and easy! To jury-rig a stationary steam engine onto each and every one of those Gravely attachments individually would be far more trouble than having the engine permanently on the Gravely, then just connecting the attachment desired."

"Yeah, I can see your point. But, look, if trying to mount the steam engine on a Gravely is such a headache, couldn't you stick with the existing gas engine and modify that some way to make it usable after our gasoline's gone?"

"Short term, yes, sort of—but long term, no. It is true we could distill alcohol—that's not hard—and convert a gasoline engine to use it. We could also heat wood in an enclosed container, trap the flammable gasses given off, and use those gasses to run a gasoline engine—rather like propane is sometimes used. Both alcohol and wood-gas have been tried, although with very marginal success, for example by farmers in occupied France in WW-II, when the Germans had all the gasoline. But in both cases, the engine's power is so greatly reduced—by fifty percent or more—that a Gravely's little engine wouldn't be worth much. Also, long-term, with any gasoline engine there's the spark plug issue: they wear out, we can't make 'em, and a gasoline engine won't run without 'em."

"I see. So gasoline's not the only limiting factor for using gasoline engines. But diesels don't have spark plugs. And I even heard somewhere they can be made to run on just about any liquid that will burn. Wouldn't converting a Gravely to diesel power be simpler than to steam?"

"Yes. And you're right, diesels can be made to burn several liquids we could produce here—alcohol or animal fats or vegetable oils, or a mixture of those, for example. But diesels, especially small, high speed ones, operate at hellishly high pressures and temperatures. They require really superb, high-tech lubricating oils—much better oils than gasoline engines, even. And there's no way we're going to be able to refine petroleum to produce those high-tech oils, not for generations to come."

"You've thought it all through, haven't you?" Barley considered. "So steam looks like about the only possibility...But as far as lubricating oil goes, what are you going to use in the steam engine, once we run out of what we've got?"

"Ah, there we've caught a break," Tom explained, happy to have at least one small bit of good news to report for a change.

"Steam engines operate at slow speeds and low pressures—say, a tenth of this gas engine's speed: 260 instead of 2600 RPM." He pointed at the 7.6 HP Gravely gas engine. "And even a much smaller fraction of its internal pressures—only a few percent of the pressure produced in that cylinder when a gasoline/air mixture explodes. The slow speed and low pressure make lubricating a steam engine vastly easier than any other type. So we'll use what the original steam engines as far back as the 1780s used: rendered beef tallow. Back then, folks used the same stuff as an ingredient in soap, by the way, so we'll need it in any case.

"The tallow won't provide any corrosion protection. However, adding even a tiny bit of our existing supply of petroleum-based oils to the tallow will accomplish that. We've salvaged enough used oil from all of Mountainview's vehicles, plus the new stock we had on hand, to carry us for years.

"True, even using just the small amounts necessary as an additive will mean our supply of modern refined oil will run out eventually. But we won't need modern, refined petroleum products even then. There are sufficient natural petroleum 'seeps' throughout the Pennsylvania/West Virginia/Ohio area for us to obtain crude oil we can use, years from now, after our refined oils are all gone. Those petroleum 'seeps,' as fate would have it, are in many cases the very same ones people tapped 150 or more years ago for exactly the same purpose: to lubricate the steam engines they were running back then."

Tom fell silent a moment, considering.

"If I can get it working, Chief, I think a steam-powered Gravely will go on working for a long, long time. We're not going to run out of firewood, beef tallow, or crude petroleum from natural 'seeps' anytime soon. And these slow-turning, low pressure steam engines don't mechanically wear out for many decades. Until The Collapse a few months ago, there used to be frequent gatherings of steam enthusiasts all over the country, where they routinely ran engines considerably more than a hundred years old—many of which had been in continuous service for most of that time. They're intentionally over-designed and overbuilt, and they just don't wear out, any more than Gravelys do."

"Well, let's hope you can get it up and running." The Chief seemed lost in quiet thought for a moment, before returning to the present. "Now that it looks like Owen's going to be pretty busy with his horse duties, I'll just informally have the rest of the Citizens' Patrol deputies cover your shop here a little more tightly than they have been. With fairly constant but irregular 'drop-by's' from the deputies, I think things should stay pretty secure till your project gets finished.

"But—tell ya the truth—a steam-powered Gravely's pretty long-range for me. Each day, seems like I'm just trying to somehow make it to the end of the day. What I came by for, was to see if we could use a plain old standard-issue Gravely to pull a cart up to a shack a few miles east of town. We might have a kind of a situation. Hard to tell."

"Sure Chief, when do you want it?"

"How about now? Also, do you have some old feed sacks and scrap parts and an old piece of tarp to throw in the cart? And—uh—if you're free, and you can come along that'd be nice. May just be a waste-of-time nuisance…or it may be unpleasant. I don't want to pressure you."

"Hell, I'm game, Chief. Let me hook up the cart. There's some trash and a piece of tarp over there you can have. What's going on?"

It took only a few minutes for Tom to fully gas up a Gravely from his showroom floor, attach the cart, and put in the junk the Chief had asked for. Then he jotted a note to Sophie saying he'd be back when he got back, and in short order he and Barley were jolting down Main toward the police station, where, Barley indicated, they were to pick up something.

At the Station, Barley had Tom pull into the garage instead of merely stopping at the curb. In the enclosed garage was Dick Peters, Barley's right-hand man. He was holding a canteen, two MRE food packs, and a Savage 24F-12 combination. That was a weapon Tom had long coveted, having a rifle barrel on top and shotgun barrel below. Both barrels had been available in a range of calibers and gauges, Tom knew, but the weapon in Dick's hands appeared to combine a .30-.30 rifle and a 12–gauge shotgun.

Carefully wrapping his weapon in a blanket, to protect it, Dick placed it in the cart. Then he placed a similarly wrapped little Smith and Wesson .38 snub nosed revolver next to it in the cart, climbed in himself, and lay down. As Tom watched in astonishment, the Chief covered him with the old tarp, piled on assorted bits of junk to make sure a human form was not recognizable, and then turned to Tom with a thumbs-up and a grim smile.

"Okay." He checked his watch. "We should get there about dusk. Let's go. I'll direct you. I'll fill you in on our way there."

"Jeez, Chief. I'd hope so," Tom wryly replied.

As they jounced and jolted along a dirt track, heading east out of town, Barley explained things to Tom—sort of.

"This may be a wild goose chase. May not be. Night before last, the deputy on Citizen's Patrol out at this edge of town heard a gunshot. Last night, a certain fellow who comes into town quietly now and then never showed up."

The Chief, torn between his desire to keep confidential matters confidential, versus the need to inform Tom of their mission, debated with himself in silence for a moment.

Finally, he asked Tom, "Know much about Sam Stone?"

"The Crazy? Oh, is that where we're headed? No, not much; just that he lives in some shack on the mountainside out this way. Supposed to be a Vietnam vet. Came home all screwed up in the head, and lives out in the woods in a cabin by himself. I haven't actually seen him in years. Jeez, he must be, what—in his late fifties by now? Rumor was, when he first came back, all those years ago, that he'd been some kind of war hero. Well, you know how it is with people—talk gets started ...

"But no, don't know much about him. Never seen his shack. What's the big deal about hearing a gunshot? Maybe he got a deer or something. You enforcing the game laws now?"

Tom was obviously kidding, knowing full well how silly that idea was, but the Chief wasn't in a kidding mood. He just somberly chewed over his own thoughts.

Finally, he said, "It's just—well—last night he should have slipped into town. It was full moon. See, Tom, what Sam does is make moonshine and various wines. He delivers to his regulars in town every full moon. Has an old pack frame that he loads with God knows how many mason jars of hooch, each one carefully wrapped to prevent noise. He's getting on in years but he's still strong as an ox. Hikes down this trail from his shack to the town in the moonlight, makes his deliveries and gets payment, then back up the trail and gone, long before dawn. Didn't you know that?"

"Well...maybe I might have heard a rumor. But I don't make it my business to cause legal problems for anyone."

"Oh, for Chrissakes, Tom! I'm not about to hassle him over moonshining! If he can make decent hooch, and sell it to them that wants it, good for him. I've known about it for years. But now, I'm afraid...I think...maybe something's gone wrong." He sighed. "We'll soon see. When we get there, give no indication Dick's in the cart with a gun. Just follow my directions."

After the Gravely had pulled the cart four miles from town, along an intermittent, hardly visible deer path running steeply up the slope of the heavily forested mountain, then down several sharp ravines and back up again, they neared Sam Stone's cabin. But before they saw any problem they smelled it: putrefaction. Then they heard it: a cloud of blueflies buzzing loudly over the heap in the shack's doorway. Then they saw it, the corpse itself.

"Shit," Barley said when he recognized it as Sam's.

"Well, nothing to do about it now," he added, speaking loudly. "It's too late to get back to town with it before night. We'll sleep here and haul it back first thing in the morning."

He gingerly rolled the corpse over with a tug at its shirtsleeve.

"Bob was right about hearing a shot. Well, *fuck*. Tom, why don't you start a little fire over there upwind," the Chief pointed, "I'll just see if there's anything we ought to take down with us for the burying."

Thoroughly baffled, Tom did as told, going around to the back side of the cabin and starting a small campfire where Barley had directed, while at the doorway side of the shack the Chief went through into the pitifully small single room. By the time the fire was going, the Chief re-emerged from the doorway, carrying a small sack of personal effects and a crutch, which he placed on the ground beside the corpse. They pulled the Gravely and cart up beside it also, ready to load up in the morning.

Then the two men went around to the shack's far side and lay on the ground beside the campfire in the dimming light. Barley placed a water bottle between them, and handed Tom an MRE. They ate and drank quietly beside the fire, and before much longer began to grow drowsy in the gathering darkness. For Tom, the bizarre unreality of this whole business was more than he could cope with—sleep was the only sensible option he had.

Just before dawn they awoke.

"Well, let's get it done," the Chief directed.

They checked that their fire was out, then started around the cabin when Tom paused and sniffed.

"That's funny. Our fire's out, but I thought I just faintly smelled wood smoke."

"You didn't smell anything," Chief Barley told him very definitely, in no uncertain tone. "Help me with the body."

More baffled than ever, Tom silently continued on around the shack to where the corpse lay beside the Gravely cart. Taking it by the clothing, in an attempt to lessen their distaste for touching the body itself, they swung it up into the cart, then covered it with the old piece of tarp. Then they added the crutch and sack of personal belongings, which Barley also placed under the tarp. With a pull on the starter cord, the Gravely roared into life, the two men got into the cart, and Tom swung the Gravely round and headed back toward town.

"I guess I'm not supposed to ask where Dick Peters disappeared to during the night, or anything else about what the flaming hell is going on," Tom commented acidly to the police chief during the ride.

"I expect you've guessed some of it by now," Barley replied. "I should have done more to make it clear to poor old Sam that his moonshining was ok and he could come into town, where he'd have been safer. Nowadays, a working still and its products are too valuable to be hidden away and guarded by a single person."

There was silence for a time, as Barley re-worked mentally all he had and had not done in the matter. Finally, he concluded, "He wouldn't have moved into town, no matter what. Couldn't stand people. But I wish I could have done something, somehow …

"You did smell wood smoke up there. When I went in the cabin and looked out the one window I could barely see faint traces of it down the path that leads to the still. Your 'shiner, when possible, always likes to keep an eye on any comings and goings. Notice how the front door overlooked the path up to the cabin? Well, his one window was placed to overlook the path from the cabin down to the still beside that little run at the bottom of the ravine.

"After you've built up the fire and distilled a run of hooch, it takes a day or two to let things cool down so you can tap the product into your mason jars or whatever. The sumbitch who shot Sam was waiting nearby for that very thing, so he could make off with a whole fresh batch in addition to what was already bottled when he murdered Sam. He'd have moved all the stuff some ways away, cached it, and then come back to carry off small loads one at a time, as he disposed of it."

"So the killer was sitting there all this time, watching us?" Tom's stomach gave a queasy lurch.

"Yep. Bet on it. Just in case, that's why I wanted to have you bring us up in the Gravely. With the racket it makes, I could be sure of giving the killer plenty of notice we were coming, so he could find a good spot to watch us. 'Course, he *did* tend to watch what there was to look at: two men beside a fire at the back side of the cabin. In the darkness at the cabin's front side, I didn't figure it would be hard for Dick to slip out of the cart and make the three steps or so through the open door. He's inside now, waiting. He's got that Savage double-barrel so he can use the .30-.30 or the 12 gauge, depending on what the range turns out to be. If there's more than one of them he's also got his revolver.

"All the killer knows is that two men arrived, spent the night, loaded up the body, and then the two men left. That much he could plainly see with his own eyes. He knows the place is deserted now, so he'll resume what we interrupted—stealing the latest run of Sam's hooch."

They rode further in the jouncing cart beside the corpse, not speaking. Finally, Tom's frozen silence extracted at least a partial apology from the Chief.

"Look, it was important to act normal. Predators—people like this killer, whoever he is—sometimes really do have a sixth sense or something. They actually can pick up 'vibes,' or a 'feeling' when something's not exactly right. They themselves can't explain it rationally, but there are countless cases of predators somehow just sensing a trap or setup, and waiting patiently for as long as it takes to neutralize it before they move in—or just turning around and silently vanishing over the horizon if things don't feel right. Your behavior, body language, *everything,* had to arouse not even the vaguest intuition of anything not quite right—and that, in the eyes of some predator who was watching you more attentively than anyone's probably ever studied you in your life. I couldn't tell you."

"Jesus," Tom said with a shudder. "I guess," he finally muttered, half-accepting Barley's half-apology.

When they reached Mountainview, Barley had Tom drive into the police station garage again and close the door. He removed a clean white cloth from a shelf and placed it in the Gravely cart alongside the body. Then he took the crutch and bag of Sam's personal items from the cart and placed both in an enclosed locker, which he padlocked.

It was the first occasion Tom had had to look closely at the crutch. It astonished him. First, there was the selection of two absolutely perfect clear ash pieces for the long uprights. Both had grown with the exactly right slight

126

curvature required, matching each other to perfection. God knew how much searching it had taken to find that perfectly matched pair of ash pieces. The two cross-pieces, one to go under the armpit and one to be gripped by the hand, were made of close-grained oak that looked as hard and durable as marble. But the carving was, really, the most astonishing thing. For nearly its entire length, each upright had been carved with an intricate pattern of vines and leaves and berries. The woodcarving must have consumed more days of painfully careful precision work than Tom could even imagine someone doing.

"You didn't see that crutch," the Chief told Tom in no uncertain tone. "You've never seen it. You know absolutely nothing about it. Understand?"

Tom had given up trying to understand anything. He just nodded.

The corpse was so rank Barley decided to wash it outdoors, so they left the garage and drove to the churchyard. They let the sexton know a grave was needed promptly, and he rounded up three helpers to get it dug right away. Tom and the Chief borrowed a pair of heavy rose-pruning shears from the sexton to cut off the clothing, got buckets of water, and pulled the Gravely out to the edge of the churchyard, out of smelling-range of the crew laboring at the gravesite.

They cut off the clothes, washed the body as well as feasible, and sewed it into the clean white shroud. It was getting toward noon by this time, and the Chief seemed to be listening for something. Finally it came: the sharp report of a rifle echoed off the mountainside in the distance. Barley immediately glanced at his watch.

"Shush," he told Tom, and kept his eye on his watch. They paused in their work on the corpse.

Soon another gunshot boomed off the mountainside—this one the heavy blast of a 12–gauge shotgun.

"Yep," Barley said with satisfaction, "Three minutes exactly after his first shot. Dick got him, all right. That was our signal. Let's head back up to the cabin."

Borrowing a pick and shovel from one of the gravediggers, and leaving the shrouded body beside the partly dug grave, Tom and Barley headed back up to the cabin on the Gravely.

They arrived to find Dick Peters sitting on the cabin's doorstep. He gestured down the path overlooked by the single window, toward the still.

"Sure enough," he said. "He waited a long time after you left, still watching. Careful sonofabitch. There was only him. Finally came out of the rhododendron thicket over there. Must have been up in that big oak all the while. He went down the path toward the still …"

"And that's when you called loudly 'HALT! POLICE!' and he reached for his gun and you shot him." The ring of cold steel in Barley's tone of voice left absolutely no doubt about the matter.

"Uh…um…right, Chief. Yeah, uh, that's what happened."

"Okay. We'll spell each other digging a grave. Needn't be regulation size or anything." Barley handed the pick to Tom, who was standing there open-mouthed at what he'd just heard. "Down there's as good a place as any," he gestured down the path toward where the body lay in a crumpled heap.

They walked down the path about ten yards to the body. Barley turned the head this way and that with his foot, as if moving road-kill to the side of a highway, but gave no sign he recognized the corpse. He looked at Dick and then at Tom, both of whom shrugged that they didn't know him either.

"Some roamer probably, just passing through. Maybe saw Sam or his cabin, or smelled the smoke from his still; maybe he was casing Mountainview, looking for easy pickings on the outskirts of town; could be anything." Barley shrugged indifferently.

While Tom and Dick set to work on the grave, the Chief went into the cabin and got one of Sam's empty pint Mason jars, with a flat and ring. He took a sheet of Mountainview police department letterhead paper from his notebook and dated it, then wrote in careful ballpoint:

This is the unknown person suspected of murdering Sam Stone three days ago. He was killed today by Mountainview Police Officer Dick Peters while resisting arrest. Signed: Jack Barley, Chief, Mountainview Police Dept.; Dick Peters, Officer, Mountainview Police Dept.; Tom Jeffson, Witness.

When the three of them had signed it, Barley placed the note in the Mason jar and screwed the lid on as tightly as possible. He then relieved Dick on the shovel, till they had a grave a couple of feet wide and about three feet deep.

"Good enough for this shit," Barley said, straightening up and handing the shovel back to Bill to hold. Without further ado, Barley rolled the corpse into the shallow pit with his foot, placed the sealed Mason jar in the pit, and said "Cover him up. I'm going to roll a couple of those rocks over here if I can."

By the time Tom and Bill had shoveled the loose dirt on top of the corpse, Barley had succeeded in moving two large rocks to the site. The three men managed to end-over-end them up on top of the fresh grave. That completed, Barley started up the path toward the Gravely, obviously considering his work here to be done.

"Uh, Chief?" Peters called after him uncertainly. "Um…should we sort of put up a cross? Or mark the grave, or something?"

"Suit yourself. I don't need to take a dump right now or I'd shit on it. Otherwise, I have no plans to mark it." He continued toward the Gravely.

With a brief glance at each other, Tom and Bill Peters followed silently.

After making sure the cabin window was closed, and the door closed and latched, the three men rode back down the mountain path toward town, each lost in his own thoughts.

Upon reaching Mountainview, Barley directed them first to the police station, where he talked briefly with the shift officer on duty, issuing him instructions. Then he turned to the two men with him.

"The funeral's in one hour. I'd appreciate it if you would come. Get something to eat first, if you want."

And he turned away from them so abruptly—almost bolting for his house next door—that both men were left wondering at his sudden loss of composure.

Tom, feeling starved and wanting to check in with Sophie, walked the few blocks to his house. She was out, probably at Maybelle's, so he left her a note, wolfed down a sandwich, and headed back toward the churchyard.

There, he found Parson Miller had arrived at the just-completed grave. The gravediggers were placing their tools tactfully out of sight behind a nearby headstone. Moments later, Chief Barley, his Senior Officer Dick Peters, carrying a shotgun, and an honor guard of six other police officers carrying matching rifles all made their way to the graveside.

With some brief words from the Parson, and the reading of the 23rd Psalm, Sam Stone's shrouded body was gently lowered into the grave. Barley nodded to Peters, who turned to the honor guard and began that awful series of commands the nation had witnessed so many tens of thousands of times—at Arlington and countless other cemeteries across the land—year after endless year—for more than a decade of the nation's longest war:

"Preeeesent ARMS!"

At the moment of the volley—dry-fired by the six honor guards to save ammunition—Peters discharged his 12–gauge shotgun in salute. The blast echoed back and forth off the nearby towering mountainside, whose forests and ravines had provided Sam Stone a home all those years with the peace and solitude the poor, damaged man had needed.

As the service was completed, the Parson thanked, and the honor guard dismissed, Tom turned to go when Barley caught him gently by the sleeve.

"Got a few minutes?"

"Sure, Chief."

"Let's sit over there a bit while they fill in the grave." He led Tom to a nearby stone wall surrounding the churchyard.

"What I'm going to say goes no further. Understood?"

"Yes."

There was a long silence between the two men as Tom waited patiently while Barley collected his thoughts.

Chapter 17

Poor, Poor Bastard

"Somebody needs to know," Barley began, "about Sam. It's not right that he just...just vanish. Somebody needs to know. Attention must be paid. He deserved that much, at least.

"Sam just showed up here in Mountainview one day, around 1952, '53, something like that. He must have been about six or seven: technically, old enough he was supposed to be in school. I got all this years later from Jake Sneed, when he retired and turned over the police chief job to me. He kind of filled me in—informally, you know—about who'd done what to whom in town over the past years. Made my new job a lot easier, having that background.

"Anyway, Sam had these two old bachelor uncles—Silas and somebody— who owned about 100 acres of that mountainside where the cabin is. They'd lived out there since day one: harmless old coots who did some trapping and jacklighted a deer now and then, and cut some firewood to sell in town—and maybe helped themselves once in a while to a little excess produce going to waste in somebody's garden, or quietly took care of a chicken that got lost from its backyard flock. They were a harmless old pair, and nobody minded.

"Best anyone could figure, Sam's parents must have died, or left him, or whatever—anyway, he'd been sent to live with the two old uncles. You got to remember: this was in the early Fifties; in West Virginia, in a tiny little country town. We didn't have all the Social Services paperwork, and Department of Child Welfare caseworkers, and all that stuff like we have today. The old uncles took him in. He showed up in town once in a while. Bought a penny candy at Gump's Five and Dime. Looked well-fed enough, always had on old but adequate clothes; had shoes and a jacket in winter...Well, that's about all people looked for back then. You know, things were not like today."

Was Barley simply anxious that his (or Mountainview's?) acts be clearly understood? Or was he seeking some sort of forgiveness? For whom: himself? Mountainview? Humanity at large? Tom nodded encouragement, wondering.

"Technically, he was supposed to be in school. And he was, fairly often. He'd walk into town for grade school here if the weather wasn't too bad. When he was old enough for Junior High he'd walk into town and catch the school bus to Grayson with the other kids. Kept to himself, apparently, but hell, he wasn't the only kid from some remote holler who didn't have much to do with town kids. That happened a good bit. People from outlying farms—usually lacking an all-weather dirt road to their home—often didn't have a whole lot of contact with people from town.

"From what old Jake told me when he retired, it must have been about 1962 or thereabouts when unsettling rumors began to quietly spread. I guess Sam would have been a sophomore in high school by then, or maybe a junior. There was nothing specific, Jake told me, and nobody would go on record saying anything detailed; but it just seemed some parents felt Sam might have an unwholesome interest in their boys. Complaints their sons brought home that he spent an awful lot of time in the locker room, changing—that sort of thing.

"Well, hell. In Mountainview, West Virginia, 1962 might as well have been 1900, for all any of us knew back then about gay rights, and lifestyles, and that whole load of crap. I mean, Jesus—what the hell did any of us out here know about that? We're not exactly New York City. The world was different back then.

"But anyway, there just seemed to be some vague rumors about Sam, but nothing was done—well, Jesus, what *could* we have done?—and he graduated in 1964. Vietnam was just heating up then, and when Sam went into the Army right out of high school the town breathed a sigh of relief and figured everything had worked out all right—for him and us both.

"He served two hitches, and afterwards apparently spent a lot of years in and out of VA hospitals and dead-end jobs. It was ten years before he showed up again in Mountainview. By then the two old uncles had both died so he owned their property. When he returned after all that time—well, he owned property here, didn't he, however worthless those scrub-timber, cutover mountainside acres might have been in financial terms. And people had generally put aside whatever feelings they'd had from his high school days. So there was no problem with him coming back to his uncles' old place.

The Grayson VFW Post back then made it a point to give each returning vet a welcome home—maybe the only one he got that didn't include spit and accusations of baby-killing."

Barley paused, recalling those awful days, and what they had been like.

"Eventually, a fellow in the Grayson VFW tracked down someone out in

Texas or someplace who'd served in Sam's company during Sam's second tour in 'Nam. The VFW member in Grayson told me what I'm about to tell you, in strict confidence, because he felt Sam had had a raw deal. In a whole lot of ways, I expect, though he didn't go into all of them.

"What happened was, the Grayson VFW Post sort of *insisted* they be allowed to give Sam a 'Welcome Home' dinner when he got back. Well, Christ: he had no family, he was shy, didn't know anybody here really…he'd served his country and he *deserved* to be thanked for it. So, maybe, they might have insisted a little bit too much that he be honored at the Post, despite the lack of enthusiasm he showed. They meant well, for Chrissake.

"So, comes the evening of the dinner: in walks Sam with a proud host on either side of him, the members all rise to their feet, applauding—and Sam takes a handful of medals out of his pocket, throws them on the floor, and walks out.

"He left Mountainview the next morning, staying away fifteen years this time. From what was learned later, his previous life of VA hospitals and dead-end jobs sank another notch to a life of dead-end jobs and skid row bumming.

"The reason this guy in the Grayson VFW looked into it, and quietly clued me in later about what he'd learned, is the nature of the medals. Sam was a genuine hero—as real and as decorated as they come. When the Grayson VFW members scooped the medals up off the floor and looked at them, and each other, in horrified astonishment, they realized Sam was no way an ordinary soldier.

"My pal in the Grayson Post quietly contacted buddies of his all over the country, working from one referral to another, till he tracked down this guy in Texas or wherever who'd served with Sam during Sam's second tour. What he learned was this: Sam got one of his Purple Hearts from shrapnel during his first tour. When he went back the second time, he got another from a close mortar round that left him partially deaf in one ear and injured an arm. He spent some time in hospital in Hawaii, then returned to 'Nam as a 'replacement' to be put into whatever outfit needed fresh meat.

"He wound up with an infantry unit northwest of Saigon, in VC-owned heavy jungle. That's where he won his Silver Star. The Army has only two higher awards for valor: the Distinguished Service Cross and the Medal of Honor, which is usually posthumous.

"Apparently, a good portion of Sam's company got into a very carefully prepared kill zone, thick with improvised booby traps, captured claymore mines, punji stakes—the whole works. The VC had prearranged lines of fire into the zone from their undetectable spider-holes. They were simply picking off the grunts one at a time, and the grunts had no line of retreat available without brushing a trip wire somewhere.

"The grunts could stay hunkered down until the Cong got around to shooting them one by one, or they could attempt to fall back and be blown up by the mines or impaled on the punjis. They frantically radioed for air support, artillery support, *anything*—and were told basically 'Sorry, pal, it's a busy day today. We'll add you to our list …'

"In the course of three hellish hours, Sam saved a lot of lives. For lack of anyone else willing and able to do it, he took over the painfully slow process of extracting the men, one by one, from the trap. This one he'd signal to stay in place; that one he'd direct to fall back along a route he knew was clear; the ones on the edge of breaking down, he'd encourage till they kept their heads; all the while he was checking other possible routes for withdrawal, looking for the single, near-invisible thread across a trail that meant explosive death, or the one disturbed leaf that might mark the edge of a pit full of punji stakes.

"Sam cheated the VC that day: what should have been the unit's total annihilation was held to 'only' about sixty percent killed or injured."

Barley paused, and the two men gazed across the peaceful grass of the churchyard at the workers just placing their last shovelfuls of earth on the new grave mound. The workers picked up their lunch boxes, checked they had all their tools, and after a final tidying up began to depart, leaving the earth to receive its latest son in peace.

"His greatest heroism, though, was not something they hand out medals for.

"When he was getting to be short-time, down to about two months left in his tour, the unit got a hotshot new Second Lieutenant. On a sweep, they entered a village where all the adults had fled, except a half-dozen or so ancient peasants who were so far gone they probably couldn't have walked two hundred yards anyway.

"They were about to call the village clear and move out, when one of the last search teams discovered the pit. The brand new lieutenant went bananas. First, he was embarrassed that his men had come within a hair of not finding the pit, then he was terrified by what was going to come pouring out of it, guns blazing, when they opened it up.

"'Take cover! Prepare to fire! Watch it! Look out for 'em!' he screamed to nobody in particular, smacking an ancient granny-woman with his rifle butt to let people know he was nobody to pull this kind of 'hiding' shit with. They carefully secured a wire to the pit's trap door, took up positions with M-14's on full 'rock-and-roll,' and slowly pulled the cover off the pit.

"What stared up at them, paralyzed in mute terror, were a dozen or so children: infants to pre-teens.

"KILL 'EM!' screamed the lieutenant, now completely unhinged by the totally unexpected. 'Give 'em a Willie Pete!'

"W.P., or white phosphorus, was an incendiary grenade designed for roasting alive people in bunkers.

"Sam walked up behind the screaming Lieutenant, drew the man's .45 from its holster, and jammed the muzzle hard between the dumbfounded officer's ass cheeks.

"'Leave the kids alone. Move your men out of this village. Right now. Or I'll blow a hole from your ass out through the top of your head.'

"For one, eternal-seeming moment, the entire cast of characters froze, silent, death hanging over all of them, licking its chops, waiting.

"'Ah, hell with it. Move out,' the Lieutenant finally croaked when he could speak once more.

"The grunts looked at each other silently as they shouldered their packs and formed into file. What the fuck?! Whatever crazy shit had just gone down, every grunt knew the least hassle for him in any investigation was to have been somewhere else at the time, doing something else, seeing and hearing nothing. Keep your head down and get home alive: that was all this shitty little war had ever amounted to, and every man in the unit knew it. As for the direct assault they'd just seen on their officer: fuck him. It would be a chilly day in hell before any of their hearts would bleed for some mo' fo' officer. Nobody saw nothin', nobody knew nothin': the eternal creed of all men imprisoned—conscripts and convicts—came automatically to their minds. Shouldering their packs, they walked silently on down the trail.

"'Soldier, you just signed your death warrant.' The lieutenant—his .45 restored to its holster—turned and looked at Sam. 'You're going to die for this.'

"Sam turned and followed the file of men.

"The lieutenant was right, of course. He wasn't about to have a court martial pry into all the various issues involved in the incident. He didn't need to, and he knew it.

"In that time and place, there was a terrible attrition rate for the men up front walking point. They were, to be blunt, the bait a unit put out ahead of it to draw fire or to 'discover' the trip wires across the trail that would blast the legs off a soldier. With luck, a grunt could survive his turn pulling point every now and then—but nobody was going to last long if he was assigned point time after time, until he was butchered. The other grunts in the unit weren't going to bitch if Sam got their turns at point. And the noncoms and officers weren't going to make an issue of it either: they all knew discipline in the field had to take unusual paths at times. They'd look the other way. So Sam was a walking dead man from the moment he pulled that officer's .45 on him—and he knew it.

"But fate has its whimsical ways. Just a week after the incident, the lieutenant got a three-day pass to Saigon, where he enjoyed going to beat up the whores. The lieutenant's taste in such matters was well known throughout the company, and that common knowledge forms the basis for this assumption about what evidently occurred.

"He was in Saigon, beating up a teenage whore, when her pimp became annoyed by this needless wear-and-tear on his merchandise. So the pimp quietly walked up behind the busily engaged lieutenant and thrust a sharpened steel rod in one of his ears and out the other.

"By the time the body was discovered, of course, the whore and pimp were long gone. Nobody in the entire neighborhood had seen or heard anything, nor did anybody know anything about anything—if that much. The bored MP's 'investigating' the matter met with bored shrugs from the half-dozen or so locals they perfunctorily questioned, filled out the routine paperwork, and that pretty much closed the case on that. The affair was marked down as yet another typically barbaric VC atrocity; the lieutenant's next of kin received the standard boilerplate letter from a grateful nation's government about his heroic death serving Freedom's Cause; and the matter was all wrapped up.

"Fate's whim had been for Sam to sign his own death warrant saving those kids in the village—and then for the warrant to be torn up by a teenage child and her pimp in Saigon. Sam served out the rest of his tour and shipped home."

Barley and Tom sat on the graveyard stone wall, looking at the fresh mound under which Sam Stone lay. It was such a beautiful day: a day on which people should be alive, enjoying the earth, not rotting in a hole six feet beneath it.

"So Sam came home—or at least what was left of him did. In 'Nam, he'd seen too much of what the strong do to the weak. He'd seen it in too much detail; smelled it; walked through the cratered remains of too many peasant villages where the charred and blasted surrounding trees were freshly strewn with body parts of what had been peasant farmers, who asked nothing more than to be left alone to be misruled by their own people, instead of being misruled by the round-eye giants from 10,000 miles away.

"When Sam got back to Mountainview that first time, what he wanted most was never to see another human for as long as he lived. Not one other species

136

behaved toward its own kind with a human level of savagery. But even isolation was not something we understood how to give him, back then.

"When he came back to Mountainview the second time, it was simply because he'd hit bottom and had no place lower to go. He'd held onto the acreage the two uncles had left him, and it was apparently a last refuge to hole up in—the sort of hiding place a mortally wounded animal will seek out to lie down in and die.

"He had a small disability check from the military—not much, but his expenses weren't much, either. He refurbished the half-ruined cabin a bit, to make habitation possible, and immediately set about meeting his other need: oblivion. The only way Sam could make it through the day sometimes was with enough booze to dull the edge of the world's unbearable reality.

"Grayson County's dry, of course. Sam could chip in for gas-money and get rides from people going into nearby towns, where he could stock up at an ABC package store, but that was not too practical for long. He needed too many bottles to make the trips inconspicuous. On the other hand, getting his own car, leaving it in Mountainview, and driving himself, was out of the question: by this time, Sam couldn't have gotten or kept a driver's license, even here.

"So Sam quietly expanded his shopping list, and began adding assorted items a suspicious person might consider components of a still. When he couldn't quietly get necessary things in nearby towns, he paid the Scouse brothers to accept and hold for him various strange parcels delivered by UPS and FedEx.

"Sure enough, within a few months Sam was ready to start running a little batch now and then. In the meantime—partly from necessity and partly from a newfound curiosity about plants, fermentation, and its products—Sam began turning out batches of wine. He sent away for books with all kinds of old-time wine recipes: dandelion, elderberry, buffaloberry, wild cherry, peach, apple—you name it.

"There's an astounding range of plants that grow wild on these mountainsides, and Sam could turn an awful lot of them into wines of one sort or another. Some were rather tasty, I'm told, and some were downright vile—but, hell, they all provided the anesthetic Sam needed, and what was wrong with that? Some folks in town knew, and others suspected, but I'm proud to say the people in Mountainview had common decency enough not to call the government about it. The government had already done about all it needed to in destroying Sam.

"And so this ruined, mostly dead remnant of a human lived year after year in his isolated shack, getting a few necessities now and then with his disability check, and brewing for himself the liquid oblivion he had to have. He brewed a lot of it. Over the years, he couldn't help but get fairly good at it.

"Eventually, some of the local folks began quietly asking Sam if he might favor them with a little nip of something, in return for money or food or whatever he might happen to need. Just a drop of something medicinal, you understand: a quart of sovereign remedy to combat the chill, say, or fight snakebite—or even to have on hand for potential snakebite. Folks tasted a small drop or two of Sam's product and liked what they tasted. By God, it was pretty damn good, they said. And that led to another strange turn in this poor man's life.

"For the first time in a long while, Sam was doing something people liked and praised him for, something he liked doing—something that even, well, began to draw him into the company of other human beings. You see, people began asking Sam to deliver them a drop or two on a regular basis. He got to know them, in a way, and he experienced the feeling of having people—a fair number of them throughout Mountainview—actually *depend* on him. They came to look forward to his deliveries. He realized they were sitting up and waiting for him on nights of a full moon partly just to pass a few words with him, and tell him they liked the last batch, and share some leftover fried chicken, and say how hot the weather had been, or how cold it was.

"Something whole teams of white-coated shrinks in VA hospitals all across the country couldn't come close to doing, the people of Mountainview were accomplishing right well with Sam: he was becoming whole again.

"Funny thing was …"

Barley had to stop and sit quietly a few moments. When he was able, he went on.

"Funny thing was: Sam's own drinking sort of tapered off. You see, he got so interested in making all kinds of different wines, and he had the responsibility of scheduling production with his still, and making sure his deliveries were made, and maintaining the quality folks had come to expect and praise him for…well, he just couldn't manage all that and drink every day, too. So he cut back his drinking to about nothing. And he recommended others consider the same, if he began delivering a bit too much to some.

"Oh, he knew all kinds of things about folks in this little town. He knew all kinds of things. Alvin Baker, Tim Baker's father, was one of Sam's customers. Sam must have heard an awful lot of pain from Alvin, when that boy's leg had to come off.

"I'll see Tim gets that crutch Sam made for him after a few days have passed—in some roundabout way, so no one will suspect. You are not to tell a soul where it came from—or any of this."

The chief got to his feet, stiffly after sitting on the stone wall, and he and Tom walked the few feet to the mounded heap of raw earth. Barley took a pint of water-clear moonshine out of his coat pocket, passed it to Tom for a sip, took a sip himself, and poured a few drops on the raw earth mound.

"Poor, poor bastard," he said softly.

Then, with a clap on the shoulder, instead of trying to put anything more into words he left Tom and headed back to the police station and his home.

Chapter 18

Construction Work: Restaurant Renovation and Central Five-year Plans

If Sophie wasn't at Maybelle's then Maybelle was at Sophie's. By the time Sophie had been in Mountainview six weeks or so, the two were thick as thieves, day after day. Even Tom, in his innocence, realized with dark foreboding that whenever women are this closely involved in something together it does not bode well for the relaxation, peace, or comfort of any men in the vicinity.

"Johnson slaughtered a small pig last week," Sophie casually remarked to Tom one morning at breakfast, her opening gambit clearly a feint, aimed at distracting his attention.

"Hmm," he countered.

"About 200 lbs live weight, or thereabouts," she chattered on.

"He's going to wait another month, for colder weather, before killing a larger one, but he decided to kill this one now to get in some practice processing it before doing the larger one. He's still got most of the old equipment that was stored away in the barn—big iron kettle, bristle scrapers, meat saw, hand cranked meat grinder, sausage stuffing machine, etc—but it hasn't been used since his parents' time, so he wanted to get it all out and make sure people remember what to do with it.

"Hmm," observed Tom, noncommittally.

"Maybelle and I made a deal with him to cook for the crew he had over for the butchering and processing, in return for a slab of the meat," she added, offhand.

"Oh, so that's what you've been up to," Tom replied, cunningly pretending to have not a suspicion in the world.

"Yep. Got that pork slab sugared, salted, and now being slowly smoked—even as we speak," Sophie continued, calling his innocence and raising him.

She put butter and honey on a slice of her delicious bread.

"Should turn out to be pretty decent bacon in a few weeks," she opined, offhand.

"Bacon." Tom was determined his tone would contain no trace of begging.

"Well, from the looks of it so far it should be a pretty tasty first attempt. Of course, we plan to make larger quantities once we've got our cure adjusted the way we like it."

With an innocent purity so earnest it would have impressed an angel, she twisted the knife ever so slightly. "Tell me, Tom; do you like bacon a bit more sugar-cured...or a bit more salty...or with a more smoky flavor?"

He had had no bacon for over four months, since the time of The Collapse. Afraid he'd moan if he tried to speak, Tom just eagerly nodded his head. Bacon.

"Uh...Need any help with it—or anything?"

"Oh, Tom, that's so nice, thank you." She accepted his surrender with the serene poise of the Empress Victoria receiving word that India had just been added to her dominions.

"Actually, Maybelle said she just *knew* you and Owen would be willing to help us. The Gumps have agreed to rehab their storefront! Isn't it *great?*"

Tidying up the last minor detail, she casually threw out, "Of course, they're too old to actually do the work themselves. So naturally we explained that you and Owen could take care of that part easily enough. It's just putting in cooking and dishwashing facilities, setting up tables, decorating the walls, fixing up a stage...that sort of thing."

She casually waved a hand to convey to him the minor nature of these details.

"Gumps? Kitchen? Stage?" He understood the trout's first faint trace of alarm at the prick of the hook taking hold in its jaw.

"Oh yes. Only a small stage, of course. But that can come later. First things first. Owen's going to be there today around noon to get started, Maybelle says. Do you think you could look in on him for a few minutes, just to make sure things are going all right?"

In silence, Tom glumly nodded. First bacon; now this. It wasn't *right.*

When Tom arrived at the former Gump's Five and Dime, he found Owen somberly sitting in the dust of the storefront window, like a discarded mannequin or a sculpture portraying Dejection.

"Thanks a whole heap, Tom. I oughta be exercising Invincible right about now. If it wasn't for you." He regarded Tom bitterly.

Heart sinking, Tom gazed around the dust-covered, thirty-by-seventy-five-foot-foot room, taking in the piles of trash in the corners, the holes in the sheetrock walls, the complete and utter absence of anything remotely approaching cooking, dishwashing, dining, or—God help him—*stagecraft* facilities.

"*Me?*" he replied to Owen's accusation.

"Maybelle said Sophie told her you'd *just love* to fix up this garbage dump. And, sure enough, here you are. So of course Maybelle said the least I could do is give you a hand with it."

He kicked at an empty beer bottle with enough force to have sent it through the flimsy sheetrock wall if his kick had connected.

"Invincible, you know, is on a *schedule,*" he pointed out. "You don't just work a horse like that any ol' time whatever. But what the hell does Maybelle know? Has she ever worked a horse like Invincible?"

The answer to this was so clear, and the justice of Owen's position so obvious, that Tom could only sigh and punch him halfheartedly on the shoulder.

"Well." He sighed again. "Let's start getting all this crap moved out of here. That ought to be enough to claim we're on the case, anyway. I'll go get the Gravely with the cart. If you move this trash out to the door we can load it in the cart and make however many trips it takes to haul it off."

By late afternoon, when Maybelle and Sophie arrived together to call them to supper, the women had genuine cause for their delighted exclamations. With all the trash gone, and the holes in the walls patched, it was possible to imagine the place being fixed up a bit.

Tom allowed as how he could use his electric cutting torch to cut one of his spare 55-gallon drums in half lengthwise, thereby making two sinks when the halves were set up on bases of the right height. A hole cut in the bottom of each sink would be stopped with a plug while in use. Removing the plug would allow drainage into a piece of six-inch PVC sewer pipe which could run through the back wall and out into a small, improvised septic tank and drainfield. Tom could dig that in a few hours with the Gravely. For occasional use, with less than 100 gallons or so of waste, the primitive system should provide adequate graywater disposal.

"If you're going to have customers here, you'll probably need an outhouse, too," Tom pointed out. "I expect the back corner of the property would be as good a place as any for a basic pit privy. Might as well dig that at the same time.

"And if you put two 55-gallon water drums up on a stand there," Tom pointed to a back corner of the room, next to where the sinks were to go, "you can use gravity flow to get cooking and wash water from them, and fill your sinks, and so forth. There's no well here, so you'll have to pay Bill Etter to fill your 55-gallon drums. We'll run a filler pipe through the back wall, and put in a small window, too, so he can just pull his cart up out back and use his hand pump to fill the drums. By looking through the window, he can see when the float indicator on the drums indicates they're full.

"Have you got any leads on a wood-fired cook-stove? A real one would be a lot better than anything we could jury rig out of scrap iron."

"Yes!" Sophie cried, excited beyond measure to add her latest good news to the progress already being made toward her dream. "Since you're doing so much to fix up their store—making all these improvements—Mr. and Mrs. Gump have offered us an excellent kitchen range. It's the real thing: it has six burners, a huge oven, and a hot-water tank built right into the stoveback, where the stovepipe comes out.

"Their son and his wife were storing in their barn, but when we explained how much we needed it, Mr. and Mrs. Gump agreed to get it back and loan it to us. Isn't that terrific? All it needs is to have a broken leg welded back on, or maybe it could just be propped up on some bricks."

"Well, that's a stroke of luck," Tom agreed. *Like it's a stroke of luck for a freight locomotive to overpower a stray ant on the track,* he privately added. "I guess they won't mind if we cut a hole in the back wall here to run the stovepipe through. I hate like hell to ever cut a hole in a roof if it can be avoided. In this case, running the stovepipe out through the wall then up will mean a lot less risk of water leaks when it rains or snows. The only other thing we'll need is to make storage bins for stove-wood and kindling here next to the back door. With your food ingredients, water, and firewood delivered in back, and an interior wall to partition off the kitchen, that will keep the front of the place nice for your customers.

"For starters, when we put up the interior wall partitioning off the kitchen I guess we'll cut some vent holes in the top of the wall and some at floor level. When they're open, the hot air from the kitchen should pass through the ceiling holes into the restaurant area, and the cold air from the restaurant floor level should flow into the kitchen, where it will be warmed, and rise, and make another cycle. If that system's not effective enough when the weather gets really cold we'll have to think about a small stove in the restaurant, or some other heating method. But let's try simple first."

Despite themselves, Tom and Owen had become enthused by the project. They were intrigued by the challenge of solving problems using ingenuity and "make-do" methods, instead of simply spending money to buy a solution to every problem, as people used to do. If converting a bare room into a restaurant was possible, using nothing much more complicated than ingenuity, perhaps there was hope for overcoming far larger difficulties in their post-Collapse world using the same approach.

The next day, unseasonably warm for late autumn in the West Virginia valleys, Chief Barley huffed and puffed his footsore way to the scene of the restaurant-under-construction. Tom was out back, using the Gravely to till up the dirt along the distribution lines for the septic system he was putting in, so he could plow the lose dirt out of the way in preparation for laying coarse gravel in the bottom of each trench. The Chief drew his finger across his throat to signal Tom to cut off the machine so they could talk.

"Jaysus Key Riste," he grumped, settling himself on a pile of dirt directly in the path of Tom's work, to make it plain he was out-of-sorts. "Never know where anybody is anymore. Wander all over the damn town lookin' for people.

"That damn woman," he jerked a thumb at Sophie, visible through the open back door, happily painting a far corner of the room, "Doc says she's the best medical person we got. So she wants to be in the restaurant bidness. Naturally. You're supposed to be working on a steam engine for when the gasoline runs out—which is pretty goddamn soon, if you care to know—and you're in the sewer-line bidness or something. That one," he aimed a glare at Owen, who had just come out the front door for some more lumber to use in the kitchen partition wall, "is supposed to be in the Police Equine Unit, training a horse, for Chrissake. So he's in the damn carpenter bidness, looks like. Jee-sus! How 'bout I get in the damn hootchy-kootchy dancin' bidness, like those Chippendales or Chipmunks or somethin' used to be in the newspapers? Reckon this new place needs an entertainer, to go with all its gormay kwizeene?"

"Chief, you have no idea how close things came to that." Tom grinned, remembering Sophie's initial plan for a "respectable strip joint." "If I were to tell you some of the original plans ..."

"Oh Lord; don't," Barley sighed. "I don't want to know."

He sat there with his friend, enjoying the unaccustomed freedom to be honest about his ill temper—a deeply tired, overworked man—who had never wanted to be more than police chief of a three-man force in a tiny rural village, who now found himself effectively Head of State for a miniature nation. 'Why me?' he had wondered to himself night after night, lying awake as a dozen of the day's most pressing items ran over and over though his head—all of them important for Mountainview's survival, none of them things he had the experience or ability—let alone the other necessary resources—to undertake.

"What I do want to know," he sighed, "is whether you can interrupt your steam engine and septic system projects to help move a whisky still and set up a salt-making works. It's a big project, but I think we need to get it done before winter sets in. Counting what's left in the tank at Jared's Conoco and at the police station, we want to be sure we've got enough gas left to finish those construction projects. Then we're down to whatever remaining few gallons people have in drums or five-gallon cans at their homes. Might as well try to get the construction finished before the last of our gas and last decent weather of the year both run out."

"Sure, Chief. Tomorrow morning first thing? I'm to the point here that Owen can take over most of what needs doing till I get back."

"Well, I'll need Owen too, and he'll be tied up for a couple of weeks most likely. You'll be able to put in a few days at a time, maybe, coming home some nights. Trained or untrained, Owen's going to have to use that horse to move some heavy timbers."

The Chief sighed. "Probably need that damn woman, too, off and on. Maybelle says she's about the smartest person around here next to Doc when it comes to figuring out scientific, chemical-type stuff. Doc agreed: he's still hoping she'll come back as his helper, once she gets this restaurant thing out of her system. Here's what it looks like we're going to have to do..."

And Barley outlined for Tom the dual nature of the whisky-still and salt-works project he judged a vital Mountainview priority.

"I've rotated deputies on four-day tours, living in Sam's cabin to guard the still, ever since he was killed. Obviously we have to do something more long-term for security in that area: the still's a priceless, irreplaceable source of alcohol for medical and morale-boosting use, and for producing barter goods in the future.

"At the same time, Doc pointed out to me that we're going to need salt—lots of salt. It's not just to sprinkle on your food, you know. We'll need it for preserving all sorts of things, from meats to sauerkraut to pickles to cheeses. We'll need it for tanning leather. All our animals, from draft horses and cattle right down to the rabbits and chickens, need salt in their diet. And putting out a salt supply will be about the easiest way to bait an area for pot-hunting deer, turkey, rabbit, wild pig, and so forth. Funny, how something as common as salt is a very big deal for us, now that we can't just call and have a few hundred pounds delivered. Doc rates it about on a par with food as a vital need, in the medium to long run.

"So I've put two-man teams on each of the four-day guard assignments up at Sam's cabin. One man would secure the still while the other scouted the area for any signs of a natural salt lick. Sure enough, Pete Thompson followed a deer trail about a mile and a half down that same little run the still's on, till he spotted a tree-stand Sam had built to hunt from. About forty yards from the tree-stand there's a little clearing with a depression in it, covered with animal tracks. It's a seep containing a natural salt deposit.

"There's not a whole lot of salt—I mean it's not piled up in dried salt crystals or anything—but the water in the seep does taste a little bit salty, and sticks lying on the ground there have been licked or chewed on. Doc figures there should be enough salt for our needs, once it's concentrated.

"What he suggests we do is move the still to that area. Then make some big, shallow metal pans that will each hold fifty gallons or so of water from the salt seep. When we re-assemble the still, set it up so the water pans get as much heat as possible from firing the still. We can get double use out of the same firewood, doing that. It would be quickest to actually boil the salt pans to concentrate the salt out, but that would take an awful lot of precious firewood. Just heating the pans will do the same thing over time.

"So," the Chief concluded, "we'll want you to pull a cartload of tools and supplies for a work-gang up to the existing still. While they disassemble it and carry the pieces down to the salt lick, you'll need to haul whatever metal you'll need to make some big, shallow evaporator pans. Then bring the generator to run your arc welder so you can construct the pans on-site. Then help us with any welding we might need to re-assemble the still so the evaporator pans can share its heat.

"Owen's going to have to use his precious horse to drag some heavy timbers to the site, to mount the still and evaporator pans on, and also to construct some rough sheds to shelter the firewood, and some roofs to keep rain or snow out of the salt evaporator pans. If you can use the Gravely circular saw attachment to square the timbers into beams, and to make planks for building the firewood sheds and roofs for the pans, that would sure beat trying to do it with chainsaws. Same thing with laying in several cords of cut firewood for the still.

"During all this, I'll have some men see if they can bore a well a few yards down into the seep. Doc said he's read that the subsurface water in these places is often saltier than that on the surface. Once everything's in place, we can pump water out of the seep to fill the evaporator pans and we'll see if it all works. With any luck, we'll eventually produce both salt and moonshine from one, securely guardable plant."

He sighed sourly. "Hell of a note, for a so-called *police* department."

The two men sat silent for a time, weighed down by the almost indescribable magnitude of the tasks the Chief had so briefly outlined—the sheer amount of backbreaking drudgery the project would involve. Finally, in part to relieve the gloom by a change of subject, Barley poked a thumb at Sophie, still happily painting the restaurant walls.

"Do you know, that woman has some kind of fixation on socialism," he confided, as if passing on the news that she was inclined toward nudism or vegetarianism, or a belief in flying saucers. "I mean it. She's always bending my ear about 'social ownership' and 'central planning' and God-knows-what-all. But you mark my words: what it comes down to is socialism. Can you beat that? And yet, she *seems* like she has perfectly good sense ..."

The Chief shook his head, baffled—though not surprised—by the strange ways of humankind.

"Hell of a looker, I'll say that for her. And everyone says she's smart as can be. Well, I guess there's no figuring ..."

He shrugged, with a tolerance due in equal measure to his basic decency and to having seen some of everything in his years running a small town police department.

"Anyway, Doc and others I've talked to say she's our best bet to help get the still up and running when we re-assemble it. They say she can probably read up on the subject in whatever books we can find, and just look at the existing setup and figure how it works, and what we'll need in terms of grain and sugar and water for the mash, and proportions, and run times and temperatures, and so forth. Wish to hell poor old Sam had written it all down— or we'd had sense enough to get it from him somehow. But Doc says that woman's smart, and she can figure it all out if anyone can. I sure hope so. You think she'll be interested in doing it?"

"Chief, she will be dancing on air from sheer joy." Tom sighed. "You think *you* get to hear from her about the wonders of socialism. *Jesus!* Try living with her. When the police department took central ownership of all *three* Mountainview draft animals, you'd have thought she'd seen Karl Marx himself rise from the grave. Now that we're going to have a socialist government monopoly producing booze and salt, she'll think she's in Heaven. And I'll get to hear *all* about how progressive and wonderful it is, believe me. Every waking hour of every day."

"Well, better you than me," Barley grinned. "Come by the station tomorrow morning and we'll have men and a load of supplies for your cart. Bright and early, Comrade Worker: we have a Central Five-Year Plan to accomplish."

"Power to the People," Tom sighed, limply raising a fist.

Chapter 19
More Construction: Distillery, Salt Evaporator, and Guardhouse

The next morning, Tom gave Sophie a lift to the police station in the Gravely cart. *I can see why the Chief was so footsore yesterday*, he thought, *if he rounded up this mob from all over town.* There were over a dozen workers, mostly laid-off agricultural labor now that Halloween had passed and fieldwork was slowing down. In addition, Tom was surprised to see young Tim Baker and his father, Alvin. An exquisitely handcrafted crutch had been discovered a few weeks previously, leaning against the Bakers' front door. And although no one knew how it had gotten there, it proved a godsend for young Tim. He was young and strong and adaptable. He'd been up and about with the crutch early on, and seemed to be adjusting as rapidly to his new life as anyone could have hoped. Alvin, too, seemed to be pulling out of the despair that had hit him so hard with his son's misfortune.

"I'm going with the group!" Tim reported excitedly to Tom and Sophie. "Dad and me are going to cook for the work gang. Gives us a chance to get out of the house and get in on some of the action."

"Well, that's great, Tim. But, uh, you know the ride up there in this unsprung cart would be awfully rough…"

"Yeah, it would be. We thought of that. I'm ridin' up on Invincible! Owen said I could. He's saddle-broke now, and he'll be a whole lot smoother than the Gravely cart."

As if in response to hearing his name, around the corner plodded the mighty Invincible, Owen beside him holding the lead rope. The huge Belgian was dragging a crude wooden sledge which, Tom discovered, held a dozen square bales of hay and two fifty-pound bags of cracked corn, under a tarp lashed down with a spiderweb of rope to keep the load on the sledge. The horse had a saddle blanket secured on his back with a leather strap which held it in position and also provided a loop for a rider to use as a hand-hold.

Tim, game as any kid could be, gave his crutch to Tom to be brought up in the cart, and offered the huge, gentle horse a piece of carrot he'd brought. Then his father and Owen helped boost him up onto the animal's broad back, where the boy half sat and half lay, holding on to the strap. With a quiet word from Owen to his horse, they set off along the trail toward the still. It was immediately apparent that the plodding of the ponderous Belgian, dragging the loaded sledge as if it weighed nothing, was gentle and rhythmic enough to present no problem for Tim on the giant's back.

"See you at the cabin!" Tim called to the assembled crowd.

The work gang loaded the Gravely cart with the heaviest items collected at the police station: food and cooking utensils, chainsaws and other tools, bedrolls, and a mountain of related paraphernalia, tying it all on as best they could. Carrying the rest of their gear, they set off after Invincible, making a sort of impromptu parade of it in the clear autumn sunlight, Sophia and Alvin Baker talking quietly as they walked beside each other.

Tom started up the Gravely and had soon overtaken the walkers and the horse, arriving far enough ahead of them to unload the wagon and have those items stored in the cabin by the time they got there.

"Let me know what you'll want us to haul back to town," Tom told Sophie. "We'll take all the moonshine and wine, of course. There should be room in the cart for anything else you think we should take. Use all the time you need to look at the still, make your notes and drawings, and so forth: we don't have to head back to town till around four-ish."

Sophie gazed quietly around the interior of the tiny cabin, almost as if she were sensing its previous occupant's aura.

"They say he was a Vietnam vet, gone sort of crazy," she offered in a sad, quiet tone, perhaps recalling her own anguish in Berkley during that terrible time, committed to seemingly endless, futile protest about how the nation— year after year after year—callously threw away its young men.

"Yes. He was."

Tom left her to look through the haunted little shack for any scraps of information she could unearth. He went along the path to the still, to get some ideas about how it might be re-assembled to incorporate the salt evaporation pans. The work gang split up, some preparing to disassemble the still while others with chain saws headed down the deer track toward the salt lick, marking suitable trees to be felled for use at the new location. Owen and Invincible went with this group. Tim and his father began setting up their cooking operation using the cabin's tiny potbelly cast iron stove, plus a campfire just outside the door. Tim seemed spry as a cricket, hopping about energetically with his crutch, and Alvin was fairly glowing with happiness, seeing his son so active and productive.

By the time shadows began lengthening, Tom had loaded the cart with all the wine and hootch in stock, plus an old leather satchel of what Sophia said were notes and papers Sam had left that might prove useful. With a final check among the men for any requests about items to be brought up on the next trip, Tom and Sophie headed back to town in the Gravely cart. There, they assured an anxious Chief Barley at the police station that things were going well. Tom arranged with him to go together to the Scouse Brothers the next morning to buy materials, then Tom and Sophie headed for home.

The tone next morning was set right from the start, as Tom drove Chief Barley to the Scouse brothers in the Gravely cart. When their god awful pigsty came into view, Barley gripped Tom's arm like a vise, and muttered through clenched teeth, "Don't let me kill them."

The ensuing negotiations amounted to two solid hours of root canal work, during which the Chief's blood pressure never once left the Red Zone.

Jimson (or Jackson) Scouse opened the proceedings by expressing his and his brother's determination to do everything possible—indeed, even more—to assist the worthy Chief and their dearest friend Tom in every conceivable way—not for recompense of any sort whatever, but merely for the deep inner satisfaction of Doing Good.

Breathing deeply to keep from gagging at this load of bull, Tom very calmly mentioned the sort of materials he needed to construct some shallow metal evaporation pans.

Jackson (or Jimson) could hardly express his desolation that those *exact materials* were, by appalling mischance, ones he and his brother had set aside that very day for projects of the utmost importance they were working on themselves. The materials, both brothers agreed, were of such rarity and unimaginable value nowadays they would scarcely even know what to ask for them. *If* they were even for sale.

Well, try to imagine a price, just for example, Tom urged the brothers, as he listened to the audible grinding of the Chief's teeth.

The brothers leaned close together, each keeping one eye on Tom and the Chief as they muttered back and forth from the corners of their mouths. This went on for quite some time.

When they straightened back up and announced their suggested price, Tom saw the Chief's hand convulsively reach for a rock lying on the ground nearby.

Rising hastily to his feet and pulling the Chief with him, Tom announced they would consider the offer. But the real purpose of their visit, he explained, was to examine the progress being made on the wooden fence under construction to keep the Scouse Brothers' zoning violations out of sight.

At this, both brothers assured the group that progress on the fence was being made rapidly and in workmanlike fashion. In fact, the fence was lately requiring so much of the brothers' time—being their first priority, after all— that they might not be able to use all the various materials Tom had mentioned needing. It would hardly be sensible to hold those materials if there were no time to spare from fence building to use them. Perhaps, in light of that, they could think further about a price.

The men sat back down. The Scouse brothers again put their heads together and muttered back and forth for what seemed like an hour. They straightened up and announced their newly revised price. Chief Barley again seemed on the edge of committing an unprofessional act. Tom changed the subject, mentioning that booze was a nice treat, on occasion, and salt was a downright necessity—and both would be available from only one source. *IF* they were available, he added pointedly.

The brothers discussed the implications of this new fact at length, heads close together, their mutterings inaudible to the other two men.

After several more thrusts and parries back and forth, extending past the morning and into the early afternoon, a deal was finally reached.

Tom would bring his Gravely generator to their establishment and run it for them a total of three days, so they could use their electric cutting torch and welder to make two horse carts from the rear ends of junk pickups. Chief Barley would then buy the two horse carts, after certification from Tom as to the quality of their construction, for 100 gallons of police department gasoline. A paper was quickly written out with these details, dated, and signed by all parties.

In a completely unrelated matter, the Scouse brothers—as they had generously indicated from the very outset—would gladly *give* Tom and the Chief the materials Tom had mentioned. For these materials, the brothers would absolutely accept no payment except the good wishes of their dearest friends, Tom and the Chief. On this point, the brothers must insist; honor demanded it be so.

But Tom and the Chief, as it happened, entirely by chance, had with them six gallons of the purest and most exquisite moonshine, in gallon jugs, right there in the Gravely cart. Perhaps the Scouse brothers could accept such a gift, merely to seal the bargain between friends and as an indication of the pleasure Tom and the Chief felt in doing business with such public-spirited citizens.

Considered in this light, both brothers agreed such a course would be entirely proper, so the items were exchanged as gifts.

So Tom and the Chief handed over the hootch, loaded the sheets of galvanized steel and pieces of angle iron Tom needed, and bid the Scouse Brothers adieu without the Chief ever once actually doing violence.

"I'm going to kill them," the Chief muttered as they drove away. "I swear to God—one of these days I'm going to kill them."

The next morning, guided by a deputy who knew the location of the salt lick, Tom hauled his building materials up there, offloaded them, made another trip to haul up the generator and welding equipment and some food and camping gear, all of which he stashed under a tarp, then made a third trip to haul up the Gravely's circular saw attachment and additional supplies requested by the work crew at the site.

Two welcome features of this location were its closer proximity to town—about three miles instead of four—and especially its lower elevation compared to the still's original site. There were fewer sharp ravines to traverse, so progress was quicker: getting to the new site by Gravely took barely forty minutes, compared to the hour previously required. The new location's greater accessibility would also make it easier to maintain security, and more convenient to haul grain and sugar to the still, and hootch and salt away from it.

At the new site, Tom found a place where a smooth, level rock slab about two feet high made a convenient "table top" to slide timbers across and into the Gravely's 30-inch diameter circular saw blade. That size blade could make a cut 14 inches deep, so Tom was prepared to square off timbers to as large as 14-by-14 inch dimension, in any length they could physically handle. While he was setting up a tarp for his camping shelter next to those of the other workers, he heard Owen and Invincible approaching.

The chainsaw teams had selected nice, straight, 18-inch diameter southern pines to serve as foundation timbers for the still and evaporator pans. The sap-sticky wood had plenty of resin in it to resist decay for years. Having felled the selected trees and bucked off the branches and tops, the sawyers had watched in awe as Owen attached the log chains from Invincible's collar, spoke a quiet word to the Belgian, and strode off down the hillside, skidding a thirty-foot length of tree trunk weighing over a ton through the woods as if it were nothing.

With a bit of careful positioning—Owen's and Invincible's mutual delight apparent in the careful, precision ballet they executed together—the team placed the butt end of the trunk on the flat rock "table top" next to Tom's saw, and disconnected the logging chains from the tree trunk. Then a crew attached one end of a lever-operated "come-along" winch to the trunk, and ran the other end of the winch's wire cable to a stout tree some forty feet away. Operating the "come-along" would slowly pull the tree trunk across the "table top" and through the saw blade.

Tom fired up the Gravely, clutched in the saw, and signaled the crew to slowly ease the tree trunk into the blade.

After making the first cut down the tree trunk's entire length, the men used another come-along to pull the tree back to its original position on the rock table-top, then they rotated the tree trunk ninety degrees, placing the just-sawn flat side against the saw's "fence," or guide, and made a second cut. Then twice more the tree trunk was put through the same procedure, each time rotated ninety degrees, cutting off the rounded slab-wood, until all four sides were straight and the now-square timber measured about 14-by-14 inches by about thirty feet long.

By the time the first timber was sawn, Owen and Invincible were back with another tree trunk. Placing it as they had the first one, they then went around to the squared off timber, hooked onto it, and dragged it into position for the still's new foundation.

In the coming days, more similar-sized trees were squared into foundation timbers. The still was to be rebuilt on two parallel lines of these timbers, instead of having a foundation on all four sides. Leaving the open space at each end would make it possible to position the salt evaporator pans close to the still's firebox, and would make stoking the fire and removing the ash easier. To give the desired height, each of the parallel 14-inch foundation timbers had another laid on top of it and pinned securely to it with heavy spikes, making about 28 inches total foundation height. This would allow sufficient firebox room below the still and keep the firebox up out of any light snowfalls.

By the time the still's new foundation was completed, workers were arriving with pieces of the still from its former site. Owen and Invincible continued delivering sap-laden pines to Tom at the saw, for use as foundations for the evaporator pans. When those were completed, they delivered oaks to be cut into 4" X 4" inch corner-posts, 2" X 4" frames, and 1" X 14" planks for construction lumber.

Once the crew had a sizeable stock of cut lumber to work with, Tom removed the saw from the Gravely and attached the generator. Carefully assembling and clamping his flat sheets of steel plate together, he arc welded them to make a pair of 4-foot-by-8-foot pans about six inches deep. To the bottom of each pan, he welded a protruding flat tongue of scrap steel that would extend about three feet into the fire itself, absorbing heat and conducting it to each steel tank and its salt brine contents.

The men were lucky: as one week's hard work gave way to the next, the autumn weather held fair, cool and clear each day but without significant rain. The crimson, gold, and russet leaves piled up deep on the forest floor, making clear how little time was left before outdoor work would become much harder, and making clear how little time they had before improvised tarp lean-to's would no longer provide adequate shelter for the men.

About sundown each day, muscles aching and brain spinning from the ceaseless physical exertion and mental calculating he was doing, Tom gobbled down a hot meal and crawled into his sleeping bag more dead than alive. He was delighted to see that Tim Baker had had no trouble reaching their new site from the still's former location. The boy had simply hung onto the strap on Invincible's broad, flat back as the giant Belgian sure-footedly picked its way down the mountainside trail to the new camp. Tim was constantly busy helping his father with the cooking, making up for any dubious culinary skill with an infectious enthusiasm that kept the work gang too amused to pay much attention to the finer points of cuisine.

"*Well, it's hot and there's plenty of it!*" he would crow delightedly each mealtime, ladling great gobs of dubious goo into the men's mess tins till they couldn't help but grin at his high spirits. More and more often lately, they discovered, the stuff even tasted rather good—despite its regrettable appearance of pureed roadkill that caused more than one man to gingerly take very small bites, while steadfastly looking away from whatever it was.

On a couple of occasions, Tom saw the boy suddenly wince in pain, even though nothing had struck his stump or given any other outward sign of causing any hurt. As Tom was staggering, dead-tired, toward his sleeping bag one evening, he noticed Tim silently rocking back and forth on the log the boy was sitting on in the darkness. Tom paused and gently laid his hand on the boy's shoulder.

"Did Doc or Sophie tell you about phantom pain?" he asked softly.

Tim silently nodded, not willing to trust his voice at the moment.

"It doesn't mean anything has gone wrong; it's just something that happens when any limb is amputated. The nervous system is mixed up, and sending those signals out of confusion. Even though it hurts for real, it doesn't indicate any 'real' physical problem to be alarmed about. But if there's anything I can do to help, will you let me know?"

Tim nodded, glancing briefly up with a smile at the man, who poked him gently on the shoulder and continued on to his lean-to, there being nothing to say.

The crews completed an open sided post-and-beam shelter roof over the rebuilt still to shed most of the snow and rain, and did the same above the now-installed evaporation pans. During any snowfalls of about three feet or more, the men on duty at the site would be responsible for shoveling snow away from the still and salt pans.

A ten foot high wooden platform with a series of steps was built in the middle of the salt seep, so a man could stand at various heights from two to ten feet above the seep and wield a sledge hammer. Then a ten-foot length of one-inch iron pipe was steadied against the platform, and painstaking pounded down into the soft mud of the seep until it was almost completely driven down out of sight.

Using a come-along attached to the top of the wooden platform, the pipe was then pulled back up out of the hole it had made, while the men held their collective breath. Quickly but gently, they threaded a ten foot length of three-quarter-inch plastic pipe, with a dozen holes drilled through it in its lower couple of feet, down into the bore-hole the one-inch iron pipe had made. Their luck held: the bore-hole did not cave in, and the smaller plastic pipe could be gently pushed all the way down its ten foot length.

A cap had been placed on the plastic pipe's bottom end, but not secured there. After the pipe was seated fully ten feet down in the hole, it was then pulled back up a few inches, pulling off the end-cap and leaving the pipe's end open to allow the salt water in, adding to what could enter through the holes drilled in the pipe's lower end.

When an old hand-operated well pump was installed and water was pumped up out of the plastic pipe, it was indeed noticeably saltier than that on the surface of the seep. Starting with the more concentrated brine made the job of the evaporator pans easier, and greatly improved the salt-works' efficiency.

With the distillery and salt-works completed, the men set to work building a cabin for the deputies who would pull one-week tours tending and guarding the works when they began operation.

The cabin, designed to sleep two men routinely on beds, plus another three or so on the floor if necessary for limited periods, was in fact an ordinary looking shell concealing a bunker. At the sixteen-by-sixteen-foot cabin site, the

Gravely was used to assist in digging a cellar six feet deep. When the cabin was built over it, the cellar would be accessible via a ladder through a trap door in the cabin floor – the trap door to be concealed by a small rug.

The cabin floor was raised about a foot above ground on 14-by-14-inch foundation timbers like those used for the still and evaporation pans—but these timbers did not quite meet at the corners. Each of the four corners had barely enough of a gap to serve as a loophole for a firearm. In addition, close inspection would reveal that at the center of each sixteen-foot cabin side the foundation timber had been notched away sufficiently to provide another firing point. It would have taken quite a close inspection to notice it, though, because some weeds happened to get planted in exactly the right locations to hide these loopholes.

The cabin cellar contained wooden shelves to store food, water, and other supplies up off the floor, and had a small, foot-deep sump hole in the low corner to collect any water that found its way in.

The cabin's four rather small windows all had heavy wooden shutters that could be locked from inside, with viewing slits in each one. The heavy oak door had an iron bar standing upright just inside the cabin entrance, ready to place across the door from jam to jam, and prevent entry by anything less than a truly hellacious battering ram. The cabin roof was deliberately pitched steeply enough that any items thrown up onto it—definitely including items that were on fire—would tend to roll off.

Instead of the single, inch-thick oak plank walls used elsewhere at the site, the cabin sides were two walls of such planks, with a one-inch dead air space between them for insulation. A tiny, sheet-metal stove with a flat top for cooking and heating was installed on a base of bricks in one corner.

All in all, though it would shelter only a few men at the site, the cabin/bunker's design would serve as a significant force-multiplier, giving a handful of men the effectiveness of several times their number in any conflict.

By the time all the work was completed, fall was threatening to become winter. The detachment chosen for the first week's detail at the site was glad to move into the cabin, where they would live while spending their days cutting and hauling more firewood, and pumping the evaporator pans full of the first batch of brine water. The rest of the men were happy to pack up and get back to their warm homes in town. Tom was so anxious to get back to his workshop and his most important project, the steam-powered Gravely, he was even willing to face cheerfully the endless "honey-do" lists Sophie was bound to come up with for her crackpot restaurant scheme.

Chapter 20
To Every Thing There Is a Season

Tom was surprised by what seemed new in Mountainview after a mere three weeks away at the construction site. Perhaps it was the approach of Christmas, or the greater physical proximity to other people, who were spending more time indoors as the weather grew colder, or perhaps it was the "people-oriented" ramifications of Sophie's restaurant project he'd been unwillingly dragged into.

Whatever the reason, Tom began to notice a most curious thing about the people of Mountainview: three distinct generational groupings had become identifiable, and people's reaction to the post-Collapse life they all now faced depended heavily on their generation. The correlation did not hold in every case, of course, but in most cases it was sufficiently clear Tom was surprised he'd not seen it earlier. Mountainview's Christmas-gift project, begun while Tom was away, illustrated as well as anything what was happening to the generations in the little hamlet.

Old people, who had experienced the Great Depression firsthand as children, were adapting surprisingly well to life since The Collapse. It was not a matter of their having some deep inner well of "Pioneer Lore" or any arcane knowledge of old-time methods for doing things: some had been the privileged children of small-town merchants or lawyers, and had never once personally extracted milk from a cow, made soap, or mended a shoe.

But they had, early in their lives, acquired a comprehension of the term "making do." That was not a foreign, or incomprehensible, or personally demeaning concept to them. The old people had grown up in a pre-consumerist world, where it was considered perfectly respectable to live by the maxim "Use it up/ Wear it out/ Make it do/ Or do without." For them, living that way was merely common sense—not a bewildering, humiliating or frightening blow to their self-esteem.

The children and teenagers, at the other end of the age spectrum, also adapted amazingly well to post-Collapse life. Partly, of course, that was because young people are by nature still supple and able to adapt readily to almost anything. Also, because at first it was exciting: a chance to play hooky, living out *The Adventures of Tom Sawyer* every day.

But in time (though the youngest might have had trouble putting it clearly into words) they began to enjoy something else about their lives in the new world: they had suddenly become *valuable*—to their family and their community—in ways young people had not been for decades. Water *needed* to be carried and kindling split, stoves *needed* to be lighted and stoked, eggs *needed* to be gathered and cows milked, gardens *needed* to be planted and weeded and watered and harvested ...

A huge array of tasks very quickly developed for young people of various ages. And the tasks very clearly and obviously had to be done for life to go on. For immediate and convincing proof about the value and importance of a child assigned to bring water from the creek, try running out of water.

Children and teenagers, who had previously had no valuable role in their family or their community (and who knew it: they were young, not stupid) now had something more important to do with their lives than get tattoos and piercings, lounge around in the latest silly "whigger-gangsta" clothes, exercise their thumbs into exhaustion on the latest electric games, and hang out at the local mall telling each other how pissed off they were at Life. Suddenly they had things to do, things that were indisputably important, things that made *them* indisputably important.

They flowered! They were filled with pride and maturity and self-respect. From being grudgingly tolerated pains in the ass for their family and their community—and knowing it—they had suddenly become valuable and valued partners—and they knew that too. How could any human not thrive, undergoing such a transformation?

The Difficulty—both grandparents and grandchildren agreed—was the sadsack generation in between. That cohort, the Baby Boomer yuppies and yuppie-wannabees, had almost immediately become a real problem. For many of them, unlike their parents and their children, The Collapse had destroyed their most deeply held values and their avenues to self-worth.

The Collapse, to take one example, eliminated for all three age groups a huge variety of electronic toys: computers and espresso-makers and 72" Orgasmatron-sized TV's and so forth. But the old people had not felt entirely comfortable with those things (or their price tags) all along; and the young people were too busy having actual lives, for a change, to notice their absence after the first few weeks. It was the Boomers and Boomerettes for whom the now-absent toys had become The Central Fact of their lives and the key to their sense of self worth.

"You are what you own" had become the fundamental rule of their existence. And although they would have denied it to the death when stated that nakedly, they nevertheless believed it with every fiber of their being. If your toys all "go away" one day, and you suddenly *own* next to nothing, then you suddenly *are worth...*

With The Collapse, Boomers and Boomerettes could not anticipate their upcoming Caribbean cruise aboard the *Carnivale Princess*—and it hit them hard. Neither their parents nor their kids had been planning to go: it was no big deal for them. With The Collapse, any Boomers and Boomerettes who had been Important People at The Office suddenly had no office—and were therefore no longer Important People. Neither their parents nor their kids were involved in corporate rat-racing: it was no big deal for them. With The Collapse, Mountainview's more affluent Boomers and Boomerettes could no longer drop by the Starbucks in nearby Grayson and take a carryout decaf mocha grande latte Cinnamon-Lite Diet Supreme DeLuxe to the tennis club down the street there. And Mountainview's less affluent Boomers and Boomerettes could no longer spend their days searching for the very best bargains on the Home Shopping Network. Neither their parents nor their kids did those things anyway: it was no big deal for them.

After several weeks of utter despair when the implications of The Collapse hit home for the Boomers, leaving them trailing clouds of misery through their respective homes, their lives suddenly reduced to hollow nothingness, the Boomers were rather coldly advised by their equally impatient parents and children to "get over it."

"Oh Mother!" tearfully confided Muffie Anstett one day, "With no tennis club, how am I going to stay in shape? In six months I'll look like a potato dumpling—and *then* won't Harold be pleased! Oh *Mother!*" the svelte, forty-ish matron wailed in adolescent anguish.

"Well, dear, speaking of potatoes, perhaps you could dig three or four rows of them to stock the root cellar. And then get the new cutting of hay put up into the loft in the Andersons' barn. And then set up that big cauldron with the tripod we're going to use tomorrow for apple butter. There will be hours of stirring to be done, and I'm sure that will provide exercise galore for everyone there."

"Oh *Mother!*" came the anguished reply, "You don't *understand!*"

When Mildred related this conversation to her pals in the Grannies' Circle the next day, while they spent six hours trading turns with a huge wooden paddle stirring thirty-five gallons of boiling apple butter, the Circle's response was as grimly impatient as Mildred's own reaction had been.

But the incident did establish an instant tradition. From that time on, Mountainview's older population shared a code phrase summing up their collective view of the Boomers. Any time they wished to make their point, the oldsters in a group could be depended upon to glance at each other meaningfully and wail in unison: "Oh *Mother*! You don't *understand*!"

The more impatient the old and young became with the age group in the middle, the closer they grew to each other. Tom first noticed this in connection with the Christmas-gift project, which involved much secretive scurrying-about among the grandparents and their older grandchildren, and frequent clandestine evening meetings in the Mountainview Elementary School's art room.

The grandparents, Tom learned, had become concerned that, with Christmas approaching and no toys commercially available, the little kids would suffer disappointment. When the grandparents gingerly raised this matter with their own Boomer-generation children, the only response was a morose torrent of despair. The Boomers knew all too well how completely impossible it would be to give the little kids a decent Christmas: there was no more Pokemon, no Nintendo, no video games of *any* sort. And (crushing final point) where would you get batteries? There was *nothing* any more! There was *no hope* of a decent Christmas for the kids – no hope at all. "Oh, *Mother*!" they would heartbrokenly wail, "You don't *understand*!"

Jaws firmly set, the grandparents brushed off their distraught children and sought out their older grandchildren. They explained the problem. Would the older kids help make some toys for the young ones? The grandparents had several books illustrating home-made toys, and memories from bygone years, to provide ideas …

The project took off like an overturned kerosene lamp in a barn full of dry hay. Night after night, the older kids would sneak out of their houses and meet their grandparents at the elementary school. Types and numbers of toys were decided on. Supplies were obtained from all over Mountainview—not always through strictly legitimate channels. Various adults were asked about any tools or help they could provide. Sophie, of course, offered that Tom would love to help, committed him to cutting out three wooden jigsaw puzzles, and then informed him how simple it would be.

Tom sighed, quietly vowing he would get even some day. He explained that, actually, the coping saw in his shop could cut a stack of quarter-inch plywood ten layers thick, thereby simultaneously making ten copies of jigsaw pieces, or whatever parts were being made.

"Yes, exactly," Sophie countered, quick as ever. "I said you could easily do three different jigsaw puzzles, making ten copies of each. That will be wonderful, Tom! You're really super! And with the restaurant rehab about finished, you'll have more than enough time."

But Sophie, to give her her due, drove herself as hard as she did Tom or any other hapless conscript in her constantly expanding band of "volunteers."

Obtaining a Mountainview phone book, she had systematically grilled Maybelle about each name listed in it, thereby compiling a chart of every person with knowledge—or access to knowledge—concerning any subject Sophie was interested in. And Sophie was interested in just about every subject there was.

"Do you know what the temperature is?" she demanded, opening the prosecution's case one frosty morning at breakfast, an hour past sunrise.

"Uh, thirty-four degrees," Tom replied, glancing at the thermometer mounted outside the window.

"Well? What do you think that's going to do to marginally hardy plants?" Her tone left no doubt as to whom she held accountable in this matter.

"Kill 'em, I guess. Happens every winter. You just hearing about it?"

"Don't take that tone with me, Mr. Jeffson. You know perfectly well—or should—how vital it is we keep certain plants alive, using whatever greenhouses we need to, with whatever heat they require. We may be losing plant material right now we will *never* be able to replace."

He didn't exactly shrug, but his silence was not acceptable either.

She spelled it out for him, in the simple way men seemed to require. "Do you like tea?"

"Yeah, sure." He looked at his steaming cup, considering a re-fill.

"Where does it come from?"

"Tea plants: they pull off the leaves and dry them."

"And what are 'tea plants'?"

After enough silence to make her point, she drove the nail home.

"Camellias. Not, of course, the flower *Camellia Japonica,*" ("of course not," interjected Tom, under his breath) "but instead a very close relative, *Camellia sinensis.* Camellias—I would point out—are marginally hardy plants. Or were you planning on dropping by the local Safeway for some more tea when yours runs out? And that's not even considering opium."

162

"Well, no, I guess not," Tom admitted. "I hate it when they're out of tea *and* opium."

"That would be rare: they had entire shelves full of diluted opiate-derivatives—in the patent-medicine aisles, among other places. Wouldn't it be nice if we had a few truckloads... But there's no time for wishful thinking: I need you to take me to Judge Parker's first thing this morning."

Losing whatever conversational thread they were following, as he always did with the damned woman, Tom explained, "He's one street over, on Second; next to last house at the east end—a big brick place like a judge would live in."

"Well I *know* that, of course. So get your coat. It's early, I realize, but we have no time to waste. I need you for an introduction. Maybelle says Arlene's been sweet on you forever."

The damned busybody had her snout into every tiny crevice of Mountainview life. Arlene was Judge Parker's long-in-the-tooth, career-woman daughter, almost Tom's age. Whether she was afflicted by feminism, which Tom loathed, or merely lesbianism, which he didn't much care about one way or the other, Tom neither knew nor wished to know. Either way, women who wore man-tailored pinstripe pants-suits to Important Corporate Positions were not his type. Arlene had probably not been interested in Tom, either, but had merely seen in whatever "Corporate Success" book she was speed-reading at the moment that a husband was considered a desirable accessory for the top-level Corporate Woman Executive. Hence her businesslike attempt some time ago at merger negotiations. Tom had fled like a spooked deer, and Arlene resumed her fast-track climb toward partner at Long and Gibson, the toniest corporate law shop in Grayson.

"Arlene's not 'sweet on me' for Chrissake, and never has been, and is not to be dragged into whatever your latest scheme is. So the answer is no. Good luck with the Judge, or Arlene, or whoever you plan on seeing."

"It's Mabel, of course, that we're seeing. My God, you're slow! Don't you even *know* about 'Mabel's Herbs & Spices'? Arlene just *happens* to be the main reason her mother's 'hobby' pulled in more money than the Judge's retirement pension last year. Give her ninety days and I bet Arlene could even make this Gravely Dealership show a profit. Though I wouldn't bet very much on it. But that's neither here nor there. Arlene thinks you're OK, and she has her mother's ear, and her mother has a greenhouse and an herb-and-spice garden. And there's also, of course, the distillery and salt-works you've just built that needs to be run. Do I have to draw you a diagram? And comb your hair: I want you to exude that youngest-full-partner-in-the-firm look when you tell Arlene what a great person I am."

It was time, Tom realized, for Sophie to become aware that he could put his foot down.

"No." He said it with a quiet, manly dignity that rather impressed him.

She glided over to his chair and stood close behind him. Very close. Close enough that her full breasts pressed gently against his back. She brushed his cheek with her slightly parted lips. With one long finger she slowly traced the line of his cheek, down to his lips.

"Poooore wittle Tommeykins," she softly breathed, "so scared of mean ol' Arlene.... Don't worry, precious lamb, your Sophie will protect you."

Despite himself, Tom couldn't help leaning back in his chair the least little bit, sinking slightly into Sophie's twin pillows behind his back. He felt her nipples grow erect. Jesus, was she kidding, or serious, or what? You never knew with the damned woman! You never knew what was what with her...

"After we've finished with business, won't it be nice to get back home again? We'll put some more wood in the stove, and have a glass of wine in the library, and talk about this and that...I've never told you how I was initiated sexually, have I?"

"Jesus, Sophie!" Tom sprang up. "Now look! Now you just listen here! I have no intention of being..."

But as he wagged his finger forcefully in front of her, she gently took his hand in both of hers and placed his finger between her lips, moving it into her mouth and stroking it with her tongue in a way that left nothing unsaid.

He gulped, adjusted his pants for propriety's sake, ran his pocket comb through his hair, held open the coat he'd given her, wrapped his arms around her in a hug when she had the coat on, and grabbed his own coat on the fly as he hurried her down the stairs on their way to the judge's.

"Now just try to keep up, silly," she instructed him, as she used the ornate knocker on the door of the elegant old brick mansion, eyeing the curved brick walks sweeping round to the back where the greenhouse, croquet lawn, and ornamental fountain were.

"Good morning, Mrs. Parker. I know it's early, but Sophie so wanted to meet you and Arlene before you got wrapped up in the day's business. Sophie, this is Mrs. Mabel Parker—Mrs. Parker, this is Sophie Fein."

"Oh for Heaven Sakes, Tom, come in. I'm Mabel, Sophie; I've been so wanting to meet you, ever since I've heard about you—but people never come by here anymore; I never get to see anybody. Tom, you're back in my will for this kindness."

"Henrietta," she instructed the maid, who had just arrived in the foyer, "tell the Judge that Tom and Sophie are here! And breakfast's in thirty minutes. You *must* join us," she simultaneously demanded and implored, looking at Tom and Sophie.

With just the tiniest slight pause—oddly, it reminded Tom of seeing young Tim experience a twinge of phantom pain—and then a determinedly cheerful smile quickly in place, Mabel continued to Henrietta, "See if Arlene's free. I'm sure she'll join us…if she can…."

"Wonderful!" Sophie didn't miss a beat. "If it's not too awful to impose a 'business breakfast' on you, that's what we really came for—to discuss some business possibilities with Arlene and you."

"*Business*! Good Heavens – I'm afraid I'd be out of my depth there: Arlene's got the head for business in this family. Henrietta, be sure to mention to her we need her for *business* matters."

"Yessum!" The colored maid suddenly beamed, pleased by the good tidings she was to bear to Arlene.

"Now. Sit here by me, won't you, Sophie, and you over there, Tom. Surely you're not going to try to sell me one of your huge lawnmower-things for my little herb garden? I couldn't possibly…."

"Oh no; of course not," interjected Sophie. "But one item does involve your herb business. I'm sure you must realize how very valuable some of your plant material now is. You may have things that are *extremely* important for all of Mountainview—things that couldn't be replaced for generations if they were to die."

Mabel sighed, nodding. "Well, you know, I've thought that—since The Collapse, and so forth, I mean. Even more valuable in some ways…now that nobody has any money to buy them. It's all very strange. Of course, I'm not a businesswoman… I suppose economic conditions nowadays are very different…I have tried to get Arlene's ideas about it all—she's actually the one who built the so-called 'Mabel's Herbs & Spices' business: I just enjoy piddling around and growing things—but…." The elegant, gray haired lady used all her very considerable inner powers to maintain control. "Well, to be frank, The Collapse has hit Arlene rather hard. She's, ah, been hit rather hard by it all, you see." Mabel had to stop.

Spontaneously, Sophie reached across the Hepplewhite end table—six months ago, probably worth a quarter of what his house had been, Tom guessed—and gently patted the elegant old lady's hand. Now, Tom saw, the two women were merely two women—a younger comforting an older—and the formerly near-priceless antique was nothing but a small, old table.

Sophie's gesture was so clearly sincere, and Mabel had been so long without anyone to unburden herself to, she couldn't hold back.

"She expected she'd be made partner at her law firm within the year. It was her life."

"She needs a business to run," Sophie said gently. "That's the other reason we're here. Tom's just come back from helping to build a distillery and salt-works, owned by the town of Mountainview. Chief Barley told Tom he needs someone to run the combined operation, and Tom pointed out there's no better business executive in town than Arlene."

Tom's jaw dropped at this blatant, barefaced lie—but his astonishment at least kept him silent.

"Tom, good to see you!" exclaimed the Judge, entering the morning room with his hand extended. "Good Lord, who's the looker? Is she my early Christmas present?"

With much rolling of eyes, Mabel turned to Sophie. "He's gone simple in his later years. Don't worry, he's harmless."

"*Simple! Harmless!* You little carnal plaything, you—I'll show you simple and harmless!"

And the Judge delivered a swat to the seat of his wife's elegantly tailored tweed skirt that sent her bouncing, with a shriek, through the Breakfast Room doorway, nearly colliding with Henrietta coming the other way bearing a loaded tea-tray.

"*Lord, they at it again…*" she muttered under her breath—from years of practice nimbly sidestepping the Judge's giggling wife, swiveling the tea-tray up out of harm's way and averting disaster.

"If people can manage to *behave* theyseves," she announced, "breakfast is served." She saved the best for last: "And Miss Arlene commin' right now!"

Tom made the introductions, glad to present Sophie to the old gentleman he'd long admired, and curious to see her interact with Arlene—the two women so opposite in terms of their sexual vibes. The judge insisted Sophie sit next to him, and Tom sat between Arlene and Mabel.

As Henrietta brought out the breakfast, the food itself was a fascinating study in aristocracy, Tom mused: it was painfully plain and awful—an assortment of gruels made from the few basic storage-food ingredients people now had available to them in Mountainview. These privileged residents of the town's finest white-columned brick mansion, eating food served from elegant silver platters onto the most exquisite paper-thin china, were eating the same grim stuff everyone else did. The mansion and its elegance were *then*, the available food was *now*—and these aristocrats paid the stark contrast no attention whatever. They were pleased to offer the hospitality of their home and hearth to friends. Making a display of fashionable brand-names of objects was as foreign to them as would have been pointing out the prices paid—or emphasizing how far below their accustomed fare this morning's breakfast was by making a big to-do about the regrettable nature of the food now available. No such ideas crossed their minds. Whatever they had they gladly shared—and thought nothing more of it. Because the Judge and his family had been born to privilege, their *guests,* not their own home or food, were the focus of their attention.

As they ate their peasants' gruel off the museum-piece table settings, Tom and Sophie saw to it the other three people were caught up on all the latest Mountainview goings-on. During a brief lull, Mabel smiled and pointed at Sophie.

"At least he didn't try to 'help' you tuck your napkin under your chin. The first time we ever ate together—at an undergrad 'tea-dance' at the University of Virginia, in 1935 (they had such things, back then) he gave me so much 'help' I had to use a salad fork on his hand. It never pays to let them get away with anything—only makes training them that much harder later on."

The old woman smiled and sighed, thinking of former times—and (Tom suspected) thinking of how her pain just a few moments ago over her daughter's distress had been lifted when her husband appeared.

"Nuisances though they are," she gazed at the Judge, "I suppose they're still worth keeping around."

"*Some of the time,*" Sophie replied firmly, folding her napkin and placing it beside her plate. "Other times, things have to get done. Tom, dear, don't you and the Judge need to oil the guns or something? I bet he could tell you stories of that little blonde item he thinks Mabel doesn't know about. We girls have some business arrangements to make...."

While mannish Arlene looked on, grimly righteous in her solidarity with the sisterhood, and her mother barely contained a giggle, Tom and the surprised Judge excused themselves, heading down the hall toward the Judge's library.

"I'm just here with her," Tom apologized with a baffled shrug when they were in the library. "Damn if I know what's going on. I never seem to, anymore."

"Smart move, young man: let them think they're in charge."

The Judge's grin slowly turned serious and he was silent a moment. "That way," he continued slowly, "the transition's easier when the world turns upside down one day—and they actually *are*."

His mind drifted back to a long-ago time when young ladies and gentlemen attended "tea-dances" at the best universities, and the more daring of the young bucks sometimes attempted the very napkin ploy he'd tried.

"About a hundred years ago, seems like, I graduated UVA Law with a *Magna*, and in hardly any time I'd made partner at my firm, and shortly after that I was elected judge for the sixth circuit. We've always lived sensibly, Mabel and I. Arlene was our only child, and she was sought out by recruiters handing out scholarship money at every school she ever went to, so we didn't have a lot of expenses in that department. By retirement, we had a very comfortable investment portfolio—as conservative and secure as any investments could be.

"And we had Arlene's successes, one after another, to share with her and to pleasure us during our old age. She's ferociously bright, you know: far more than I. I'm a country lawyer who became a country judge—and did okay by it, and knew when to quit. Arlene would have *made* law, on the national scene, if she'd stayed in that field—or would have become one of the executives they use in their case studies at Harvard Business School if she'd gone over into business."

The old judge ran a bony finger slowly down the spine of one of his treasured old books.

"And now? My legal training and entire career have about as much relevance as if I'd devoted my life to alchemy. An impeccably safe retirement pension from the government, and our own portfolio of the bluest-possible blue chips, have a total value of zero. My child's bright future has collapsed, and with it she has too. She spends day after day sitting in the leather seats of that fancy Lexus she'd just bought—crying.

"And my wife's herb garden—an *herb garden*, for Jesus Christ's sake!—is what we have for living on now and for securing our future."

He smiled, wanly. "You never know, Tom."

"Yes, sir."

They settled into the huge, overstuffed leather armchairs the Judge had insisted on for his private domain, and he poured them each a tiny bit of his irreplaceable whisky—J.W. Black Label, not moonshine.

"Mabel and I—hell, we've had a good long life. We've loved each other deeply, done all right by the world's standards, I guess. Neither of us has anything left undone. We're both ready to go when it's time. Till then, she enjoys piddling with her plants, and I get to spend time reading."

He gestured at the warm, oak-paneled room's floor-to-ceiling bookshelves.

"Fact is, that's all I ever really wanted to do. The law was just a way to make a living. I was never driven by career advancement, the way Arlene is. But *books*, and the leisure to read them …! Ah…!

"I'm old and selfish, Tom. Sure, Mabel and I both hurt for the pain Arlene's in—for the fact that her life's not going to be remotely like anything she wanted, or worked so hard for, or is so capable of. For Arlene, life is hard, and it will be for the rest of her days. But for just Mabel and me, I've got to admit I have no real problems with the world collapsing. I'm about halfway through Toynbee's *Study of History*. You haven't read it, of course: it's twelve volumes, for Chrissake—who's going to read a twelve–volume history these days, except someone with nothing better to do.

"Besides," the old Judge smiled mischievously, "it's a thoroughly old-fashioned history, completely discredited in today's more advanced academic circles. You see, Toynbee thought civilizations rise and fall in a cyclical pattern, the wheel always turning, one civilization after another riding it up and up, to the top—and then over—and then down and down… until the cycle begins again.

"But people in our era became enchanted by the notion of *Progress*. Surely, with all our intelligence and courage and hard work we were going to make things ever better in our nation and our world, moving onwards and upwards. Toynbee would have smiled and simply asked 'Make progress toward *what: the high point on the wheel? From which we head downward?*'"

He took a sip from his cut-crystal whisky tumbler, ordering his thoughts.

"Ever pay any attention to the politicians making speeches about U.S. military might? The worst of the old Cold War fools – Kennedy and Johnson and Nixon, that bunch – used to shovel their flag-waving crap on television by the hour, trying to scare the Russians. And of course the Russians would respond in kind. ICBM-this and ICBM-that, and 'we've got bigger ones than you do,' and similar impressive-sounding bullshit about each side's technical prowess."

He signed, thinking back.

"But even more inexcusable than such silliness during the Cold War is this: we kept *on* with it after we'd *won*! Once the Soviets were defeated, we just expanded our enemies list to include the entire Islamic world—a fifth of Mankind—plus some primitive, dirt-poor Asian dictatorships, plus any former European allies who didn't click their heels and join our parade promptly enough. Creating so many enemies posed no risk, you see: we were invincible. We had the ultimate military technology: stealth bombers, nuclear subs, ICBM's."

The old Judge slowly shook his head.

"Want to know an example of *really* big-time military technology? A technological breakthrough many, many times more powerful than the stealth bomber or nuclear sub or ICMB? One that changed the fates of empires and altered the history of entire continents? The stirrup."

He laughed shortly.

"Toynbee tells all about it. Our deep thinkers could have looked it up. At least they could have if they hadn't been too busy Making Progress and Being Powerful to bother with a twelve-volume history of every previous society's experience at Making Progress and Being Powerful.

"Toynbee could have pointed out to the patriotic American yahoos—or their moronic leaders if they hadn't been too dumb to read anything much deeper than *Timmy The Turtle*—that America's pathetic little flicker as an 'invincible world power' had lasted about seventy-five years. That's compared with *thousands* of years for the Egyptian, Babylonian, Chinese, and other empires that really *were* important.

"Toynbee could even have shown the members of the FED, had they been interested, what happens when a country prints more paper currency than it has actual value in the vaults to back it with. There's almost no idea in economic history that's been tried more often with more uniform results. Every attempt in Man's history to create wealth out of nothing – by issuing unbacked pieces of paper—has failed. Every one—given time—without a single exception in the history of the world! The idea of using unbacked paper currency, called 'fiat,' goes back to a time almost before there even was such a thing as paper.

"The Chinese (a superpower far too militarily advanced to ever be defeated) used mulberry bark, stamped with impressive-looking official inscriptions. Some of the earliest European travelers, though they feared being ridiculed for passing on such a far-fetched tale, returned home with reports that in China people would hand over gold for these pieces of mulberry bark.

"The travelers explained that when they had first witnessed this transaction—not willing to believe their own eyes—they stammered to their hosts 'but…but…why would anyone exchange a piece of *gold* for a piece of mulberry bark with ink on it?' 'Because,' explained the Chinese patiently—keeping it simple for the primitive, round-eye barbarians from the backward West—'if they don't, we chop off their heads.'

"And so the European primitives acquired two new ideas on the same day from their more advanced cousins in China: the concept of 'fiat,' or unbacked, inherently worthless currency, and the concept of 'legal tender,' whereby the rulers forced their subjects to accept it. Not a bad day's work—except for its impact on the subsequent economic history of all Mankind…"

The old man chuckled gleefully, settled comfortably in his huge leather chair, and slowly savored a pull at his whisky.

"I fancy old Aristotle—quite the speechmaker—knew how important timing is for a well-delivered punch line. Back in 340 BC he said, in effect, concerning fiat money: There is nothing inherently wrong with it—*provided* we have perfection in Authority, and God-like intelligence in kings."

Tom gazed out the library's leaded window at the little hamlet of Mountainview, where several hundred of his neighbors would succeed in finding some way to survive—or else die.

"I don't have your God-like, dispassionately amused view, Judge. I can't help thinking of all the human suffering—past, present, and future—produced by our failure to learn from human history. So *much* entirely avoidable suffering! It's not right that humans should have been placed in a world we were too stupid to cope with."

The old judge shrugged.

"No, probably not. That's why, if I had to sign up for some religion, I guess I'd have to be a Jew. The Old Testament writers never made any pretence about God being kind, or reasonable, or even minimally decent. He was simply Power—raw, unbridled Power—not constrained in any way by even the most basic notions of fairness, compassion, decency, or reasonableness that we'd expect of a normal human two-year-old. Just sheer, absolute Power …"

The old Judged smiled faintly. "Which corrupts, so we are told… "

He savored a quiet delight. "As much as I loathe the Jews in certain political and cultural respects, it's amusing, isn't it, to think that theologically I probably am one. Oy—such a sense of humor has Yahweh.

"But as far as your frustration and outrage are concerned, Tom—both of them pointless but fully justified, let me hasten to add—this old man hasn't any sage wisdom to offer. Historically, I guess, the Jews have reacted to their God's loathsomeness by trying to build the Heavenly City themselves, without Him, here on earth. Commie-socialist-leftwing-liberal-utopian do-goodery of every sort is almost a defining characteristic of Jews. I suspect they're attempting to achieve with their own efforts here in our world some of the compassion and justice their bloodthirsty God so conspicuously lacks in His.

Well, Hell: if it works for you…Whatever gets you through the night. If we survive, we're going to have long, cold ones for many generations to come.

"But I suspect you have more sense. Building Zion, or utopia, or whatever you want to call it, is a project driven by emotion: the feeling we've *got* to do *something.* Since you're motivated, I suspect, more by rational than emotional needs, just doing *something* isn't going to be good enough: you'll need to do the *correct* thing. But if there *is no* 'correct, rationally justifiable' action to take in our present fix, I'm afraid you're out of luck. And what—except your desire for one—makes you think there has to be some rational action to take in today's situation? Where was that guaranteed?

"Perhaps, rationally, there is nothing you *can* do except read about our ancestors," the Judge pointed to the sixth volume in Toynbee's series, open on his desk, "and observe our contemporaries," he pointed out the library window, "and see what happens.

"Maybe the 'God-like, dispassionate amusement,' as you disapprovingly term it, is merely a last resort: a fallback position for lack of any intellectually honest alternative."

Chapter 21

Aaanndd the Winnnerrrrr, by Technical Knockout, Is: Mountainview!

Wrapped up in their discussion, the two old friends lost all track of the time. A couple of hours must have passed, Tom realized with a start, when Henrietta finally appeared at the library door to announce the conclusion of the ladies' chit-chat. As the men made their way back to re-join them, she confided "Thank you, Mister Tom, for whatever you figured out to get Miss Arlene up and about. We been worried sick about her."

"Well I don't know that I did anything. How've you and Abner been keeping?"

Henrietta and her husband, Abner, who served as chauffeur, groundskeeper, and all-round handyman, had lived the past forty years in the former guesthouse behind the Judge's main house. They had expected to remain there for life, even before The Collapse eliminated any other alternative, and were in practice as much a part of the Judge and Mabel's family as Arlene was.

"Oh we been doin' as well as can be, thank you, sir. We was both really hit hard that we lost our families, looks like. I got folks in N'awleans and Abner's people are in Atlanta. Don't seem like they made it, most likely—do you reckon, Mr. Tom?"

"I don't think I'd hold out hope for it, Henrietta." He patted her on the shoulder. "The chances look awful slim."

"Yessir. That's what me an' Abner figure. We just put our trust in the Lord to see us through. He got a plan for us all, don't you think, sir?"

"Maybe so. It's good to see you and Abner doing all right; maybe Arlene will pick up a bit now too."

"Oh yessir."

Henrietta's eyes grew round and she fairly burst with overheard secrets demanding to be shared with her longtime friend.

"Miss Arlene, she been picked up, all right—and set down, too! More'n once! Lordy me, I ain't seen *that* before, 'cause you know how Miss Arlene is. That Miss Sophie you brung—she some pistol, let me tell you sir. She ain't *nobody* to mess with! Dey sittin' round that table, and dey goin' back and forth and back and forth like I don' know whatall, and I ain't never see anybody do some hard dealin' with Miss Arlene the way that Sophie lady done. I'm sure enough glad I ain't got a dog in *that* fight, lemmie tell ya, 'cause when them ladies get down to 'compensation' and 'fringe package' and 'net-versus-gross,' dere is some serious eye-starin' and figgerin' on paper and 'counter-proposals' happenin.' Hoo-*wee*! Lord save us!"

"I know what you mean, Henrietta," Tom sighed—as always, on the same wavelength with his old friend. "Lord save us."

The ladies, who had moved from the breakfast room into the parlor when Tom and the Judge rejoined them, were making polite chitchat while sipping delicately at tiny little cups of mint tea.

As he entered the room, Tom's imagination suddenly flashed a bizarre image of the trio: Mrs. Mabel Parker, gracefully poised on her chair in the most impeccable finishing-school posture, primly correct in white gloves and Mamie Eisenhower hat, with a fat, rubberbanded wad of hundred dollar bills negligently tossed on the end table beside her, like all-night poker winnings. Then Sophie Fein, a mite pale and weary-looking but still upright, with a few tens and twenties visible in the patch-pockets of her lovely Orvis fullskirt-and-sweater set. Lastly, Arlene, her Anne Klein "Dress for Success" lawyerette-suit ripped in several places (and contrasting strangely with her army boots, in any case) slumped on the floor in one corner, a dazed, post-fight "Rocky" look on her battered face, clutching a single crumpled dollar bill in her bleeding fist.

Trying to shake off his fantastical vision, Tom glanced over at the Judge—and he could have sworn the Judge had seen exactly the same picture! Then Tom realized, with a start, the experienced old man didn't seem the least bit surprised.

With their farewells said, Tom and Sophie headed back toward the Gravely Dealership. They walked in silence, Sophie apparently not yet choosing to make any comments, Tom certainly not fool enough to do so.

Finally, when they were back home, in the kitchen together fixing lunch, Tom offhandedly asked "Whatja think of Arlene?"

"Pussycat." Sophie dismissed Arlene with a casual wave of the hand.

A little bit later, emboldened by his success, Tom tested the ice a bit further from shore. "So…whatja think of Mabel?"

Sophie turned twin laser beams fully on Tom, with a force that could have drilled steel. She spoke slowly and quietly, making sure Tom fully got the message.

"Don't—even—ask."

All she can do is kill me, figured Tom. *What have I got to lose?*

"Tough as that, huh? She's the sweetest looking old lady you could ever hope to meet. The Judge says, with his pension and all their investments gone, the whole crew of them—he and Mabel and Arlene and Henrietta and Abner—are all living off what 'Mabel's Herbs & Spices' brings in. Amazing, isn't it?"

"No. Not with her in charge. That …"

Then Sophie began to sputter and twitch, and Tom had to calm her down with a steaming bowl of rabbit stew and a slice of her by-now truly delicious bread. Finally, with an effort, she collected herself enough to fill him in on the morning's business agreements.

"Well, there was a certain amount of back-and-forth, but we got things decided," she began.

"Easy part first: Arlene, with a partner, will run the still and saltworks, she and her partner together receiving as total compensation their housing plus three percent of the booze and salt produced. You can sell that to Chief Barley. He won't want to lose the services of two deputies stationed out there all the time; they won't be keen about week-long tours away from their homes and families anyway; and Arlene will run the operation better than any of them could for less than it would otherwise cost. She really is bright, and a real go-getter—and she is also willing to be slightly underpaid for the moment because she has another little issue going on.

"Arlene—perhaps you'll be relieved to know—actually *is* sweet on someone: a musclebound little cupcake here in town who was a UPS driver. UPS was a thoroughly Progressive company—in other words, it discriminated in favor of women in its hiring policies. I guess Arlene's beloved—one Billie by name—must have borrowed a dress for her job interview. I saw her photo. Yikes!

"So Arlene and Billie will have their own private love-nest in the cabin you built out at the still and saltworks. It's far enough from town for everything to be cool, and with Arlene's brains plus Billie's muscle the operation will do well. So far, so good. They start as soon as you get Chief Barley's OK.

"The *real* issue we hashed over is how to keep alive—and eventually propagate and cultivate on a large scale—certain vital plants, without which we would truly slide back into barbarism.

"The four basic groups—and believe me, Mabel has been way ahead of the rest of us on this—are foods, spices, medicinals, and 'others'—mainly fibers for making ropes, textiles, and so forth.

"First, foods. Within a week of the terrorist nukes starting the economic Collapse last summer, our dear Mabel—that sweet, kindly, little gray-haired old lady, who hasn't the faintest idea in her head about business—understood full well the significance of obtaining open-pollinated seed.

"Most food grown today—wheat, corn, tomatoes, cucumbers, whatever—comes from hybrid seed that will not reproduce itself. Each new planting therefore requires a new batch of seed. Burpee and the other seed-sellers loved that arrangement, of course—and so did a lot of growers because the hybridized plants did in many cases have features to recommend them: greater yield, or better drought or disease resistance, and so forth.

"But some old-timers (and a handful of new-age organic-and-natural-foods types) stuck with the old fashioned varieties, called 'open-pollinated,' in which seed saved from one year's crop is used to plant the next year's. Thanks to Mabel's quickness—immediately phoning in orders to all the little sources she knew about, which sold open-pollinated seed—for just a few hundred dollars she laid in quite a supply before the nation's commerce and transportation collapsed. In addition, she sent Henrietta and Abner to the stores in Grayson, and quietly went all over Mountainview visiting any locals who might have some open-pollinated seed, buying part of their supply.

"Thanks to Mabel, it looks like Mountainview will be able to grow most temperate-climate food crops for as long as there are people here to till the soil.

"Next, spices and seasonings. Typically for a man, you still don't fully appreciate their importance. They are literally a matter of life and death. People today simply can't, or won't, live on a medieval diet. A daily bowl of unseasoned gruel may contain sufficient food value to sustain life—calories and nutrients and such—but over time, modern people will just quit eating it. Unseasoned glop, if there's no improvement in sight from such a diet, will literally kill people by destroying their morale and sending them into apathetic decline, where they just give up and die.

"But, alas, so many of our spices and seasonings are tropical plants. There's a reason the spice trade, by sailing ship or camel caravan, was the earliest and most profitable long distance commerce: for temperate-climate medieval Europeans, living on bland, unseasoned glop, tropical spices were often literally worth their weight in gold.

"Black pepper, nutmeg, cinnamon, coffee...these and similar items we'll never see again once our supplies run out. They're tropical plants, and we couldn't grow them even if we had the seeds. Say goodbye for the rest of your life and for generations to come.

"But at the very start of The Collapse, shrewd Mabel, making her list and checking it twice, added to her existing herb garden various spices and seasonings we will be able to grow here. Lacking black pepper, we'll still have several kinds of hot red and green peppers. Lacking nutmeg and cinnamon, we'll still have something rather close: allspice, *Pimenta dioica,* which is in the myrtle family. Lacking coffee, we'll still have chicory, for those who can stand it; and for the rest of us, tea, *Camellia sinensis,* which Mabel's growing right now in her greenhouse alongside her common flowering Camellias. Lacking sugar cane, we'll still be able to grow sugar beets and grain sorghum, or 'sorgo,' which we can press the juice out of, then boil to concentrate it for sweetener.

"Till that gets done," Sophie added parenthetically, "when our sugar runs out we'll have honey, which is a project Maybelle's been working on. She's organizing kids to follow bee-lines into the surrounding woods to locate the nearest wild colonies. She's given Mr. Baker, Tim's father, some 4-H Club beekeeping books showing how to construct proper hives to house the wild colonies, so eventually we hope to partially domesticate them, or at least move some wild colonies to closer-in, more convenient locations.

"Anyway, from what we discussed this morning, it seems Mabel has the resources to keep alive at least a few examples of all the marginally hardy spices and seasonings she obtained, plus the ones she normally grew in the course of her hobby business. While you and the Judge were away in the library, philosophizing your heads off no doubt, Mabel showed us something a tad more practical. She's turned a south-facing room in their home, the former music room, into a bizarrely elegant auxiliary greenhouse. It now contains tubs of dirt on the beautiful parquet floor, with plants of every sort packed in tight as can be. It's quite a sight.

"But even more astonishing is the now-unheated interior room next to it, a small ladies' sitting room that's an absolute knockout. It's got the works: textured silk wallpaper, crystal chandelier with ceiling medallion and crown moldings—the whole bit—and is furnished with the sort of antique chests and tallboys the Vanderbilts would have used at Biltmore. Open the door and you expect to see Prince Albert or Kaiser Wilhelm or somebody sitting there."

Sophie grinned maliciously.

"I wish my Aunt Esther could see it, right now, as I just did. She'd feel right at home—until Mabel showed her what she just showed Arlene and me, which would have locked old Esther's bowels for a month.

"I'm standing there in this painfully elegant room—a chamber-of-horrors out of my childhood, come back to haunt me—when old Mabel proudly pulls open drawer after drawer of those priceless antique chests and displays: *plant material!*"

Sophie chortled, enjoying the memory of Arlene's stunned reaction and her own subversive pleasure.

"Seeds! Scads of 'em—the label on each little envelope carefully done in fountain pen in Mabel's own spidery handwriting. Roots! Corms! Rhizomes! Bulbs! Scion cuttings! Dormant shoots of this and that! You name it. If it was something a 17th, 18th or 19th century European peasant would want to grow, there it was: carefully stored in those priceless antique chests and tallboys like it was the crown jewels.

"Uptight Arlene—Ms supposedly tough-as-nails-cutting-edge-Upscale-Yuppie-Career-Woman—nearly shit. All she could say was a sort of strangled '*Mother*!'—which damn near sent me into a giggling fit.

"'Oh—this?' Mabel answered her, casually shrugging off a hundred thousand dollars worth of furniture, 'Heavens—that was all *then,* dear. These plants represent our *future.* We must keep up with the times, you know.'"

"So you think it's surprising the entire household—Judge, Mabel, Arlene, Henrietta, and Abner—can live off the proceeds from just 'Mabel's Herbs & Spices'? Ha! Let me tell you something, pal: I give Mabel about five years before that sweet little gray-haired granny *owns* this town! Mabel Parker does not have *one, single public-minded cell* in her body. She is a moneymaking, capitalist swine—right to her very core. This morning, she and I had a few little exchanges on that matter, believe me."

Tom certainly did believe her.

"It's an *outrage,* the way she thought she should be able to dictate financial terms for sharing her plant material with the community! By God, it's people like her that *really* make me long for the Revolution ..."

Sophie struggled for composure, grudgingly admitting (to herself, certainly not to Tom) the excitement she'd had in her morning's combat with a sweet little old lady who'd all but wiped the floor with her.

"Revolution, eh?" Tom grinned. "What do you think today's world turned upside down has just gone through? You lefties have such quaint, old-fashioned 19th century notions of revolution! I'll give you 'revolution:' how about considering the social and economic changes ideas like Ayn Rand's would produce if, say, a Collapse lead to their actually being implemented? If, for example, we suddenly had a world in which the tiny handful of people smart enough, farsighted enough, and productive enough to save irreplaceable plant material for their community could then reap the personal reward commensurate with the good they'd done for the community?

"Or would you rather cling to your tattered, old pre-Collapse morality—in which the 'unfairness' of some people getting rich by providing vital resources for all is replaced by a 'fairness' in which everyone shares equally an absence of those vital resources?"

But Sophie had already done valiant battle that morning at Judge Parker's home on behalf of Progress and Righteousness, bearing away the scars to prove it. She decided to postpone Tom's offer of a repeat match.

"Well, anyway, to get back to the subject, come spring Mabel will have the starter-stock we in Mountainview will need to grow the basic seasonings: garlic, chives, mint, basil, thyme, sage, oregano, tarragon, rosemary, horseradish, and so forth. And before next winter we'll get large, heated greenhouses put up to do production-growing of the more tender plants we've propagated from Mabel's specimens.

"During The Collapse, she even grabbed all the different citrus fruits she could come by, and dried their seeds for storage in case any might breed true and produce usable fruit when we build greenhouses big enough and warm enough to try growing citrus. That's probably going to be some years off—and we agreed the likelihood of any of the seeds producing usable fruit is rather slim—but it goes to show how far ahead that cunning old lady thinks in pursuit of a profit."

Sophie continued her summary.

"The third plant category is the medicinals. Surely, Chief Barley has enough common sense to see to it the town doesn't go all hysterical about *drugs* and *dope* and so forth. Have a word with him, Tom, to make sure he does what's needed in that area: privately tells the fundamentalist mullahs at the local churches to 'can it' if they start looking to make problems, or whatever.

"We've had a stroke of luck with one of the commonest age-old medicinal plants, good old *Cannabis*—alias hemp, ditchweed, ganja, marijuana, grass, or pot. It grows wild everywhere, of course, and if we had to I suppose we could selectively breed it to increase the amount of THC, the active ingredient, in our mild local variety. But that's where Arlene's Billie gave us a break.

"UPS drivers, believe me, know it all. They pick up things the post office doesn't handle, for delivery to and from places U.S. mail-carriers wouldn't dream of going. Billie's UPS route included a little hippie 'family'—too small even to call itself a commune—at the far end of a dirt road on the other side of the county. They supported themselves making wooden folk-toys and handmade samplers and needlework crafts and suchlike, which Billie picked up every other Wednesday for shipment to Yuppies in the cities. More to the point, Billie's *deliveries* to this unworldly bunch sometimes included small packages from interesting places like Mexico and Hawaii.

"After the nukes went off and the nation began to panic, Billie found no one at home during one of her regularly scheduled Wednesday pickups. Instead, there was a note from the hippies saying they'd had a vision telling them to travel to the summit of 4800-foot Spruce Knob, West Virginia's highest peak. There, they would find 'positive energy vortices' which they could tap into to overcome the nation's spiritual crisis.

"Bye-bye hippies: no sign of them ever since. But upon discovering their empty shack and the note, Billie—no fool she—searched the place. Sure enough: tucked into cunning little hidey-holes here and there were some carefully screened-out seeds and stems from the Acapulco Gold and Maui Zowie they'd received occasionally from Mexico and Hawaii. That stuff is to common pot like 190-proof grain alcohol is to 3.2 beer.

"So Billie brought back the seeds and gave them to Arlene; who, thank God, had sense enough to give them to Mabel; who is now, in her quietly elegant and refined way, growing some of the most mind-blowing weed anyone could imagine. Good for our side! Between the Judge's daughter brewing moonshine, and the Judge's wife raising fantastic-voyage pot, we'll have at least two of Mankind's oldest and truest friends to comfort us in the many physical and emotional sufferings the flesh is heir to.

"Mabel's also, naturally, compiled a list of traditional folk-medicine plants, many of which grow wild here. She's assembled pages of descriptions and botanical drawings: chamomile and comfrey, ginseng and Saint-John's-Wort, and more than a dozen others. We'll recruit people to scour the local area, search for any plants on Mabel's list, and bring cuttings back to her for verification. After being verified, the plants can be carefully dug up and moved to 'Mabel's Herbs & Spices' for propagation.

"But when it comes to medicinals, I'm losing hope we can acquire the vital Big Two. That's a bitter blow, because Mabel agrees with me they'd both grow here if we had them. I refer to coca and the opium poppy: the South American shrub, *Erythroxylon coca*, with miraculous leaves, and the

Eurasian flower, *Papaver somniferum,* like the common red flower we see everywhere, but with miraculous sap. There are no other painkillers even remotely as effective, or as useable in the crude state of refining we're capable of. Ether, chloroform, nitrous oxide and so forth are way beyond our abilities in chemistry—now and for years to come.

"Even the most potent marijuana is merely a calmative, not a painkiller—and alcohol in sufficient amounts to reduce pain is too strong a depressant to be safe. I dread to imagine going back to the days of pre-anesthetic surgery or dentistry—or how it's going to be for the inevitable cancer cases... *Jesus!*"

Sophie paused, grimly taking stock.

"Well, chalk one up for the Conservatives: their precious strong-arm government and its forces of Law and Order have finally won a huge victory in their war on drugs—even if the government itself is no more. I'm sure any staunchly right-wing moralists in Mountainview who find themselves facing surgery or a steadily growing tumor will be pleased."

She tried to put aside her bitterness and sense of foreboding, moving on to the next item.

"The last of our four plant categories includes those grown for fibers to use in textiles and ropes, plus other miscellaneous plants. Within a year or two, our existing supply of clothing will be increasingly less patch-able. But reverting to wearing animal skins would mean sliding back to an even more primitive level than people occupied before they had anesthetics.

"We do have the wool from our flock of sheep. But 100% wool clothes are not ideal, especially in summer heat, as the early settlers here soon learned. Cotton won't grow this far north, even if we had the seed. However, there is an old-time product called 'linsey-woolsy,' a fairly comfortable and durable homespun fabric combining linen and wool, offering the best features of both.

"Being able to grow the flax plant, *Linum,* represents one more debt we will forever owe Mabel. Once we begin cultivating the seeds she acquired, we should be producing enough linen from our flax in time to replace our clothing with linsey-woolsy as the existing items wear out.

"Hemp—plain ditchweed, not the primo smokin' stuff," Sophie grinned, "will give us fiber adequate for making crude rope and burlap bags. Altogether, using our wool, hemp, linen, and leather—alone or in various combinations—we'll get by in the textiles and ropes departments. Though let me tell you: a year from now you're going to be praying to the God of Synthetics and Plastics, begging Him to reappear on earth.

"Anyway, summing up our four categories of plants, I'd have to say in the foods category we're doing fine; in the spices and seasonings we're OK; in the medicinals our situation is bad, though not quite as bad as it might be; and in the fourth group, fibers for rope and textiles, plus other miscellaneous plants, we're doing all right.

"And if Mabel thinks we're not going to re-visit, sometime in the future, her little capitalist Plant Empire and its monopoly financial arrangements…"

She paused, dreams of Social Justice dancing like sugar-plums. "Come the Revolution…."

Then she held out her glass to him as they sat together on the sofa in the den.

"Meanwhile, get me another drop of wine," she said, smiling, "and as I promised, let's discuss more exciting things than plants. Have you ever thought much about geishas?"

Chapter 22
Crime and Punishment

The next morning after breakfast Sophie sent Tom to ratify with Chief Barley the various agreements she'd hammered out. As Tom's body trudged down the street toward the police station, through a 35 degree temperature made vicious by a biting, gusty wind, his mind was far, far away, lost in replaying and analyzing each detail of the previous evening's conversation.

Sophie, as he now realized he'd known almost from the start, was a sexy, bright, and fascinating woman; one he wanted. Well, perhaps—just for the sake of argument—let's say possibly even *needed*. And as if that weren't problem enough, he fumed, she seemed to indicate she felt a similar attraction to him.

For Tom, who by and large preferred Gravelys to people—Graveleys being far more reasonable, understandable, and predictable, not to mention useful—the whole damned business was a complicated mess. His positive feelings of elation and his negative feelings of worry were both overpowered by his rational sense of outrage at having to admit the illogical absurdity of holding the previous two contradictory feelings simultaneously.

"It's *ridiculous!*" he muttered to himself, causing needless offense to Mrs. Crinwald as he brushed past her unawares on the sidewalk, leaving her with the impression he was referring to her hat—one she had always felt rather flattered her.

The few other people out and about on this cold, blustery morning also noticed Tom—particularly his use of a sternly wagging forefinger as he lectured himself while striding along the sidewalk—but they all knew him well enough not to expect him to notice their presence, or remember their names if he did see them. An advantage of small towns—one that had drawn Tom back to Mountainview, truth be told—is their easygoing acceptance of people like Tom who are considered "harmless."

Reaching the police station, Tom halted with a sudden jolt and stood for a moment on the sidewalk, trying to recall what he'd come for. Remembering, he went inside and presented his message to Chief Barley.

The Chief, ever the realist, jumped at the chance to hand over occupancy of the cabin and operation of the still and saltworks to Arlene and her "good friend."

"What the hell do I care what the pair of them do in their spare time? As long's they produce plenty of 'shine and salt, I'm happy, and as long's they do the rest of it out of sight, other folks in town won't care. Sounds like a good deal to me."

Then he sighed, thinking of the next agenda item.

"As for the Judge's wife growing pot…." The Chief carefully weighed the politics of the matter. "It's obviously the right thing to do. Thank God she has whatever that strongest variety is: I expect we'll need it."

Then he sighed again. "Well—we can't keep pot-growing a secret. I guess I'll have to go see Brother Stainfuss and try to get some kind of understanding worked out. Jeeze, Tom—that's going to be a bitch. You know the righteous brother…"

Tom did indeed.

There were three churches in the little hamlet of Mountainview: First Methodist, Woodside Baptist, and Foursquare Baptist.

First Methodist was headed by The Reverend Robert ("call me Bob") Billings. He was young, fresh out of seminary, and clearly enjoying ("to the max" as he would put it) his pastoral and teaching roles. Most of his congregation was secretly very excited to be let in (confidentially) on what Call-Me-Bob implied was the cutting edge of the very latest theological thinking. And so, with considerable tact and skill, he led his flock gently toward an awareness of ideas that actually were the latest in Protestant thinking—or at least had been, about 75 years ago; which for Mountainview was quite radical enough, thank you very much.

Woodside Baptist, and its Parson, John Miller, were a solid, stabilizing influence in the community. They could be counted upon to gently drag their heels when confronted by any wild new ideas, painstakingly mull over the continued usefulness (or not) of long-held old ideas, and eventually come up with pretty sensible decisions avoiding either extreme. Woodside—set on a beautiful little rise at the edge of town—was the Establishment's church in Mountainview.

Foursquare Baptist, on the other hand, was most definitely not. Its fervent little band of True Believers was lead by Brother Emanuel Stainfuss. Tom and

Chief Barley both sighed inwardly, thinking of the problems ahead.

"Hell of it is, Chief, they're undeniably good people. They live clean lives, work hard, mostly pay their bills…"

Tom grappled with the conflict inside himself. "And they have a *right* to their views, Dammit! If freedom still holds any value for any of us, they have a *right* to believe whatever goofy nonsense turns them on!"

"Fine, Tom; I'm impressed by that ringing defense of Freedom. I doubt you'll have any trouble with Brother Stainfuss. Let me know how it went when you get back."

"Now Chief. Wait a minute here. I didn't say anything about *me* going: that's definitely in your area. Surely you can reason with him, or make a deal with him, or something. Look: Call-Me-Bob and Parson Miller are both sensible. Maybe *they* could talk things over with Stainfuss—sort of preacher-to-preacher, like—taking into account freedom of conscience, and so on and so forth."

"*Ha*," said Barley. He did not sound amused. "You know perfectly well they'll both just grin and wish me the best of luck—just like you're doing. I'll tell you what Freedom is: a royal pain in my ass."

He killed off his tea, set the cup down with a thump, got up, and put on his official hat and jacket.

"I sure as hell never would have taken this job if they'd told me Chief-of-Police work included convincing a religious nut what a swell idea it was for the Judge's daughter to make moonshine while the Judge's wife grows pot. *Jesus*!"

And he stomped out the door, not a happy man.

Two days later, when Tom was finishing up his renovation work at Sophie's restaurant, the Chief entered. As quick on the uptake as ever, almost immediately Sophie produced a cup of genuine coffee—actual, real, precious, irreplaceable coffee. The astonished and delighted Chief gratefully cupped his hands around the mug, warming them, deeply savoring the coffee's aroma, luxuriating in such unexpected wealth. He gazed at Sophie with the look of an eighth-grade boy toward the girl he'd just written his first poem for. He flicked a brief, appraising glance toward Tom.

"You lucky bastard."

Then he sighed and got down to business.

"Hard to tell," he mused. "He went right through the roof, of course. I had to listen to more Bible verses than I've heard in the past ten years. He carried on about Satan's Power, and my own prospects after death. He hauled out big color pictures of Dope Fiends—some of them dying in flophouses and others down on their knees praying for redemption. He beseeched me to keep the Devil's Weed out of Mountainview 'for the children's sake.' I listened to him for about ten years, or so it seemed, and we finally—near as I can tell—arrived at sort of a compromise.

"First, he's going to document this whole affair, with sworn statements, and turn the entire matter over to The Authorities the minute there's some government somewhere to turn it over to. Second, he's going to lead his followers to 'prayer vigil' the Judge's house, day and night, until Arlene and Mabel—and maybe the Judge, too, for all I know—repent and seek forgiveness. And third, he's going to pray for us all, especially me."

They sat silent for a bit, thinking.

"Let's hope he confines himself to that—and none of his followers hears a Call to go off the deep end," the Chief said in anguish. "Let's just hope. Jesus, Tom, the risk of fire…the things that could happen…Even just a bitter, divisive social battle, without any physical violence…Jesus. But I just don't know any other choice we have: rejecting alcohol and pot, in our circumstances, simply is not sane."

"That's true," said Tom. "We don't have any other choice." He deeply felt the other man's anguish, and his own inability to lessen it. They sat silent. "Let's just hope Stainfuss and his flock don't decide *they* don't have any other choice …"

The two men sat glumly, at an impasse.

Sophie, though, did not appear quite so hopeless.

"It might be a good thing if they really do make an all-out effort at prayer vigiling the Judge's house," she thoughtfully mused. "I can't help but think how my Aunt Esther would deal with that …"

And on this cryptic note they parted, the Chief returning to his office, Tom to his shop to resume his interrupted work on the steam powered Gravely, and Sophie to the restaurant kitchen to finish preparing for the Grand Opening—each one of the three holding his or her breath.

The temperatures dived into full-scale winter, keeping the next several days and nights below freezing. Brother Stainfuss, true to his word, led his followers in shifts, day and night, witnessing through prayer and song on the sidewalk in front of the Judge's house.

Sophie, who by this time knew Maybelle very well, was not too surprised when Maybelle and Owen began showing a noticeable lack of fervor about their church's vigiling crusade. They participated several times, on various day and night shifts, but indicated less and less enthusiasm after each occasion. To Sophie's intense relief, Owen and Maybelle showed no hard feelings toward herself and Tom. If anything, Maybelle seemed increasingly tense yet drawn increasingly close to Sophie during the endless kitchen chitchat as they prepared for their Grand Opening. Sophie remained as interested in Maybelle, and as receptive to her ideas as she'd always been, but otherwise made no moves toward bringing up the searing controversy that threatened to split the people of Mountainview.

After a week, Maybelle suddenly blurted out "I don't think little *kids* should be kept out in the cold! Isn't none of their business, what things the grownups are doing. I wouldn't do *my* kids that way—when the Lord sends me some!"

"I know you wouldn't, Maybelle." Sophie put her arm around the woman's shoulder. "That is one thing I am absolutely certain about."

And it all came out, in a tearful rush, Maybelle and Sophie sitting down in their restaurant's kitchen with cups of tea as Maybelle unburdened herself.

At the start of the first prayer vigiling shift, when Mabel Parker had glanced out her window one morning and seen Brother Stainfuss and his band assembling to pray and sing on her sidewalk, Mabel had immediately sent Henrietta out with steaming hot thermoses of tea and cider. They were left untouched on the curb, but at noon she'd sent out sandwiches. Those also, of course, were left untouched.

"Never know what she might'ev put in 'em," Brother Stainfuss said.

When it became clear the group was determined to remain throughout the night, Abner placed a small lamp on the sidewalk to spare the group the expense of using their own valuable kerosene or candles. Brother Stainfuss blew out the lamp, continuing to lead the praying and singing in the dark. And so things went. Day after day the standoff continued. Matters seemed to have reached an impasse.

But as abundantly as Brother Stainfuss had been blessed with zeal and determination, his skills at tactical maneuver and practical psychology were less impressive.

For one thing, his crusade's luckless timing meant that almost every day and night were colder than the previous day and night. After a few days, that couldn't help but gnaw at the morale of his followers.

For another thing, he displayed more fervor than common sense in encouraging his followers to bring their children with them on their vigiling shifts. Parents, however zealous their convictions, are still loving parents—and it was growing bitterly cold.

For another thing, his rhetorical skills were not up to the task of demonizing a little gray-haired old lady who, day after day, presented him no argument or challenge whatsoever, but merely kept sending out hot drinks and sandwiches.

For Maybelle and Owen, the final straw was the evening it turned coldest. Making the awful temperature even worse, a bitter wind picked up as the daylight began to wane. Conditions were clearly approaching the point where the vigilers could become seriously at risk.

In the fading light, Abner appeared, making three trips from around behind the house, lugging piles of boards, a hammer, and nails. In a few minutes, he had nailed together a rough windbreak for the curbside vigilers, several of whom held children in their shivering arms.

In a burst of stupidity that Tom later claimed could only have been sent by God, Brother Stainfuss deliberately moved his remaining followers away from the shelter and exhorted them even louder to pray and sing.

That did it, for Maybelle and Owen—and, as things turned out, for most of Brother Stainfuss' other believers too. The vigiling was maintained through that bitter night, but for the next morning shift there were too few volunteers to continue without it becoming clear that Brother Stainfuss had lost the bulk of his flock.

Seeing no other option, Brother Stainfuss strictly forbad anyone from joining him, and prepared to convert the crusade to a one-man demonstration: himself against the very Powers of Darkness, *mano a mano*.

Alone, Stainfuss returned to Armageddon, to battle for the Lord.

In mid-morning, the old Judge came out to the curb, accompanied by Abner carrying two straight-backed chairs. Placing the chairs on the sidewalk, Abner withdrew. The Judge took one, and gestured to the other.

"Please have a seat, sir. You're still young and vigorous but I'm past that stage of life, I'm afraid. Nowadays, I need to sit—and it's much easier to hear what you have to say if you'll sit here beside me."

Not knowing quite how to react to this unexpected move, Brother Stainfuss prayed and sang all the louder, marching back and forth across the sidewalk. The old Judge seemed in no great hurry. He quietly observed the birds in the trees and the clouds overhead. Matters continued in this fashion for about an hour and a half. By then it was noon.

Henrietta came out, bearing the usual sandwiches and two thermoses of steaming-hot tea. Placing a thermos and some sandwiches on the vacant chair, she handed the others to the Judge and withdrew.

"I'd like to hear your position, you know—stated clearly and directly," the

Judge remarked, nibbling at his food. "You might be surprised by the admiration I have for you. And what I seek from you."

This truly caught Brother Stainfuss off guard. Was the Judge a possible convert? Was this the opportunity he'd prayed for so long, to bear witness to someone as deeply lost in sin as this Judge? Stainfuss agonized—but he had to take the chance.

Removing the sandwiches and tea from the chair-seat, and placing them on the sidewalk, he forcefully announced, "I'll not eat your food!"

"Smart move. It's awful." The Judge grimaced, placing his own sandwich on the sidewalk beneath his chair.

"All this time I've been telling Mabel to let Henrietta make them. Henrietta's a fine cook; my Mabel couldn't butter bread. But Mabel wanted to make them. She was worried about you and your people, you know, out here all this time, and she wanted to do what she could."

The Judge took a deep breath, steeling himself to continue. "I've been worried by all this, too. As I said, I doubt if you know how much I admire you. We think different things about this marijuana-growing plan, you and I. But the biggest difference between us is that you're brave enough to stand by your views. I haven't been.

"You see, throughout most of my career as a lawyer and then a judge I disagreed with the idea of punishing people for voluntary involvement with drugs, especially ones like pot. I thought it was deeply hypocritical for a Judge to send some kid to jail for puffing a joint, then go home to his daily feel-good prescription pills and a stiff martini. I thought it was wrong, as a matter of policy, to encourage contempt for all law by failing to enforce stupid laws that were obviously unenforceable and were generally winked at by the privileged classes anyway. I thought it was utterly self-destructive to take cops away from actual crime-fighting—not to mention risking having them corrupted by the huge sums of drug money floating around—in a hopeless effort to protect people from their own folly.

"Well, anyway—agree or disagree with them, those were my views. But I was too cowardly to live by them. Unlike you, I was willing to go along to get along.

"Oh, I tried to 'go easy' on drug prosecutions when I was a young State's Attorney; and I sentenced any drug convictions at the lowest end of the acceptable range throughout my time as a judge. And I bit my tongue, and played the game, and made money, and finally retired with numerous honors – and I'm ashamed. I'm deeply ashamed. I could never muster the courage you have, and stand up for my beliefs. Can you offer me any…any….?"

Brother Stainfuss sat dumfounded; mute. With all his heart, he begged God to tell him what to do. How should he turn this undreamed-of situation into a successful witnessing for the Lord's Truth? What should he say? Or do?

God did not help his servant.

The two men sat, silent—their silence on earth matched by God's silence above. Time passed.

Finally the old Judge got stiffly to his feet, a mute Brother Stainfuss doing likewise, still frantically trying to think of what he should do. The Judge reached out and they shook hands.

"Live with it, I guess, eh?" said the old Judge, and turned and shuffled toward his front door.

Chapter 23
Visitors—and Steam Power

"Got time for a break?"

In the cold mid-afternoon, Sophie had come downstairs to the shop, bringing bread just out of the oven, with butter and honey. She was increasingly worried about Tom, who had become noticeably tense and preoccupied as the time drew near for testing the steam-powered Gravely.

"You're a lifesaver!"

He pulled up another chair next to his rocker beside the workbench, got a second mug to match his own, sprinkled tea leaves in the teapot on the bench, and poured in some water from the kettle he kept simmering on the shop's woodstove. They sat together, enjoying their snack.

Partly to divert Tom from his nearly obsessive fixation on the steam Gravely, Sophie asked "Why do you think we've had no contact from any other people since The Collapse? It's been…what…some four months now? There were the three of us at my arrival, then seven or so Amish, and the man who killed Sam Stone up at his still. Wouldn't you think there'd have been more people reaching Mountainview than that?"

"There have been. This is not to be taken any further, but Chief Barley's told me on a few occasions his patrols have found signs of some person or persons—in all cases keeping well into the forests a half mile or so from town. He doesn't want alarm pointlessly stirred up, and he's told me that on each occasion the signs indicated just one or two people involved, never a sizeable enough group to pose a threat to us.

"A couple of months ago, a party out to the east, scouting for desirable lumber-trees, came across a cat-hole somebody had dug to crap in. Animals had subsequently dug it up—which is why they happened to notice it—but it had clearly been used by a human, and none of our people had been out there.

"Two or three weeks later, a Citizen's Patrol one night at the west edge of town reported faint wood smoke coming from further west. Barley waited a couple of days before sending out scouts, not looking to stir up trouble if it could be avoided, and sure enough, whoever had been there had moved on. The scouts did find signs of either one or two people, they couldn't be sure, and it seemed clear he or they were just passing through.

"A couple of weeks ago, when they'd just settled in at their new cabin, Arlene reported she and Billie may have had possible indication of some person or persons moving through that area. The women were both in the cabin, cooking supper, and had the door open for a few minutes to air the place out, when something spooked a deer so badly it ran right past the cabin's open door, not three feet from it. They buttoned up immediately, and kept a silent, careful watch from the viewports throughout the night and well into the following day.

"They didn't see or hear anything further. Possibly, the deer might have been spooked by a bear or mountain lion, or even a coyote—but that's not very typical. Most often, deer just give those animals a careful, wide berth and go quietly about their own business: usually, only humans really panic them to the point they'd run right past the open door of an occupied cabin.

"Anyway, if there was a person moving through the area, he must have moved on, since the two women didn't encounter any further sign, despite searching the area thoroughly. Each is careful not to leave the cabin without her .44 Ruger Blackhawk. Barley issued a pistol to each of them, and oversaw their familiarization with it, till he was satisfied they're both proficient. They make it a practice, when feasible, for one of them to stay in or near the cabin while the other's away from it, to provide covering rifle fire from a secure location if that should be necessary.

"As far as one or both of them being picked off from ambush—sure, it's always possible. Far as that goes, any of us working in the fields all around the edge of town could be picked off by someone in the woods with a rifle. But what would anyone doing that stand to gain? He wouldn't be able to steal anything before we were onto him. He'd know ahead of time there are lots of us, and working as a pack we'd probably be able to track him down and kill him. So except for some irrational nutcase—which is a risk we've always faced— there's not too much to worry about from any outsiders unless they're numerous enough and well-armed enough to be tempted to mount a serious attack on us. Groups that big would find it hard to move quietly enough to get into position without our Citizen's Patrol deputies all around the edge of town discovering them and alerting us.

"What I think we've seen is a handful of lone survivors passing through the area. They've survived this long by hiding from superior forces, not taking them on, and the last thing they want is a confrontation. Once they see we're a fully populated town—with a perimeter defense system we've taken care to make very obvious—they quietly go on their way. God knows I would: in today's situation, if you're a stranger, suddenly popping up without warning among an armed group of townspeople would not be a prudent move. Witness the 'Amish' and their arrival."

"Well, they came through Grayson on Rt. 12," Sophie pointed out. "But what about Grayson? Isn't it strange there've been no further contacts from that direction—just the knife-man and Carl and me, then the Amish? Carl and I must have walked right through Grayson—Chief Barley told me Rt. 12 is Grayson's Main Street—and I've tried so hard to remember what I must have seen there, walking through it. But, you know, that whole experience has become a sort of blur in my mind."

She concentrated, finding it hard to comprehend that her terrible, bloody arrival at Mountainview had been scarcely three months ago—in what now seemed a different age in a different world.

"The best I can come up with," she continued, "is that we must have walked through Grayson at night. I do vaguely—very vaguely—recall passing through various deserted, or at any rate silent, towns on various nights we were walking. Perhaps one of those blurred memories is from one or two nights before our arrival here, and Grayson's the town involved. By that time, we'd been walking for a couple of weeks or so, I guess; to tell the truth we were just in a sort of exhausted trance by then, walking blindly in hopes something might turn up, not really thinking clearly anymore. All I remember of whatever towns we walked through at night is that they seemed quiet and dark and deserted; and we just kept putting one foot in front of another; and then we were back out in the country again."

Tom sipped his tea, glad for this chance to sort out his thoughts with her on a subject that had long puzzled him.

"Damned if I can explain it," he said. "I assume Grayson's population must have nearly all died amazingly rapidly—or surely we'd have heard something from someone by now. I've wondered about it. When I asked Chief Barley about sending an expedition there he indicated he leans toward my own view: it's an undertaking for when we have the time, energy, and resources to spare – in other words, later.

"We'd have to go in sufficient strength—twenty-five men or so—to avoid merely serving ourselves up as a tempting target for any people with hostile intent. That requires transportation at least twenty-five miles each way for

193

men, arms, food, water, and camping supplies for a few days, plus related gear. And, of course, we'd need sufficient transport to bring back anything of value we found to salvage—or barter for, if there are still people in Grayson

"Now that we have Invincible, who can easily pull Johnson's largest hay-wagon, plus the water-cart mule pulling that cart with the tank removed, I guess we've got the necessary logistics capability for a trip to Grayson whenever Barley decides to stage one.

"To a considerable extent, it's a matter of not raising a question until you can cope with whatever answer you get. If Grayson has a strong, thriving, but militant population, are we prepared to defend ourselves from them if need be? Or if we find only a pitiful group of sick or starving wretches, are we equipped to take on a load of charity cases? Or if we find not a single living soul, are we prepared for the effect that might have on our own morale? There are good reasons for letting the sleeping dog called Grayson go right on sleeping, at least for a while.

"Our ham operators still maintain a basic listening watch on the frequencies people would use for short to medium-range transmissions—from twenty to 500 miles, say—and they've picked up nothing anywhere near us for months.

"From a security standpoint, we're certainly safer from attack now that winter's arrived. Lacking fairly modern transportation, travel in wintertime is simply too difficult to be practical. There's a reason armies in the old days entered 'winter quarters' when fall came, and stayed there till spring when warfare could resume. My guess is Barley will put off any trip to Grayson until very late winter—just before our men, animals, and other resources will be needed for the start of farm work in spring."

"Well then," Sophie asked, "what about a trip in the other direction: south on Rt. 12 to the Amish settlement? You wouldn't have the security considerations, heading in that direction. Also, it's only eleven miles or so—half the distance to Grayson. Christmas is coming, Tom: a time when people reflect back over the past year and ahead to the coming one. I think public morale would get a real boost from knowing we're not, after all, the last people on earth. There are others, good people, we can stand together with to face the future."

"Well put," Tom agreed. "You've summed up clearly some vague ideas I've had floating around in my own head for a while. When's your restaurant going to be ready to open?"

"A week from now, with luck."

"Would you and Maybelle be willing to delay it another week, till the day after Christmas, if we could persuade the 'Amish' to visit us and join in a Grand Opening then? December Twenty-fifth, I know, is a solemn religious time for them: they devote it to celebrating Christ's birth, not the wonders of Visa and Mastercard. But on the Twenty-sixth their custom is to visit friends and relatives and enjoy holiday merriment. That would be the day to have them visit. Since we in Mountainview number about 400, while they're maybe three dozen all told, it's obviously our place to serve as hosts. How do you think Maybelle would react to the new restaurant's involvement in such a visit?

"It sounds wonderful, Tom! Funny thing, I believe Maybelle would be delighted. I think Owen's been talking with her about what he encountered during his visit with the Amish to get Invincible, and she, in turn, has been pumping me for information about the Amish and their customs and beliefs. I wouldn't be a bit surprised if she and Owen both are seeking a home. They seem disillusioned by Brother Stainfuss and his Foursquare Baptists, but they don't feel comfortable as part of Woodside Baptist's Establishment crowd. Needless to say, the hip, totally with-it vibes of Call-Me-Bob at First Methodist don't do much for them. I've suspected for some time now that they're both searching for something closer to what the Plain People—the Hutterites, Mennonites, Amish—might have to offer. A Christmas visit from those neighbors, especially to help formally open the restaurant, might thrill Maybelle and Owen beyond measure. Let me talk to her. You check with Barley to see if we can work out a visit for the Twenty-sixth and the following days."

And so it came to pass. Two days later at dawn, Owen set off on Trigger, the old gelding Jensen had sold the police department, clip-clopping slowly down Rt. 12 toward the Amish settlement. Unlike the mule and Invincible, Trigger was not considered worth training in harness, and was retained for saddle use only. A Gravely with a cart or riding sulky would have been far faster, but the town's only remaining gasoline amounted to a few precious gallons devoted to the winter's firewood cutting.

Tom—obsessing over the final details on the steam Gravely—was hardly aware of anything outside his shop.

On December 23, Owen returned to Mountainview with the news that the Amish were delighted by the invitation and planned to arrive the afternoon of the 26th to spend that day and the next. From the grilling they'd given him about items needed in Mountainview, Owen reported, they seemed determined to bring an abundance of goods with them.

Mountainview Elementary School was turned into a temporary dormitory to house the town's guests. Sophia and Maybelle worked nonstop finishing their restaurant's decorations, laying in huge quantities of food and drink, and finalizing their menus. The townsfolk, suddenly starving for the stimulus of new people to interact with, prepared their own gifts and trade goods for the visitors.

Speculation raged throughout town concerning their guests' strange beliefs and customs—a dialog almost totally unconstrained by even the slightest trace of actual knowledge. Some of the wilder speculation that reached Sophie's ears took her back across the years to her summer on a hippie commune, overhearing locals in the nearest town confidentially inform each other, in scandalized amazement, about "what those hippie-people are *really* like."

Tom finished his work on the steam-powered Gravely. The Reliable steam engine was big, heavy, bulky, and clumsy when mounted on the two-wheel tractor—but it worked. He filled the boiler with water, carefully laid a fire in the firebox, lit it off, and began slowly building up sufficient heat to make steam. As the kindling burned down to coals, he placed heavier chunks of stove-wood in the firebox, building up more heat while he watched the indicator needle on the steam pressure gauge flicker, tremble, and begin to slowly rise as pressure built in the boiler. Once steam was up, he privately tested the modified Gravely in his back yard, tilling up a patch for use next spring as a garden. Then he brought the machine back into the shop, removed the tiller-tines, connected the generator, and used that to provide electric power to the well pump to top off the 55-gallon water tank upstairs.

"Want to go for a ride?" he asked Sophie that afternoon when she got home from the restaurant.

"Oh Tom, is it working?" At that moment she was far more thrilled for his sake than for what the machine might do for all of Mountainview.

"So far. Hop in the cart. I'll hook the generator on behind, and we'll try it out at the restaurant."

After further stoking the firebox, they *chuff-chuff-chuffed* their way along the village's frozen, deserted streets through the evening's lengthening shadows to the restaurant. There, Tom parked the tractor and connected the generator they'd towed with them, then ran a power cord from the generator to the electric service box on the restaurant's wall. Opening the steam valve a bit to increase engine revolutions, he instructed Sophie to turn on the electric lights they'd left in place during their rehab of the storefront.

In the restaurant, she flipped switch after switch.

"They work!" she cried. "They work! It's beautiful!"

Using dusty light bulb spares that had been stashed in a cupboard long ago, from a different, pre-Collapse world, Tom and Sophie replaced any bulbs which had been broken or burned out, then stood in the electric glare admiring a brighter nighttime sight than either had seen in months.

"Well, we knew the restaurant's wires and light bulbs worked. We knew the steam engine ran. And we knew when the generator was spun it would generate current. Still, I confess, it's reassuring to see it all happen together," Tom admitted dryly, concealing the relief in his voice.

Sophie hugged Tom, who began disconnecting the generator from the restaurant's power lines and prepared to tow it back to his shop. He devoted the ride back home to explaining why their little outing by no means meant unconditional success for the project.

"Durability is a key factor we won't know about for months yet," he pointed out. "To be of any practical use, the machine has to run dependably for months or years, not just once for a demonstration. Also, it has to work successfully with a wide range of accessories, not just the generator. It has to operate as a stationary engine, powering things like a generator or saw or wood splitter or water pump—and it has to operate as a tractor, going up and down rows in a field cultivating or plowing or using the sickle bar mower to harvest crops. It has to transport a rider on the sulky at a horse's canter, pull a wagonload of stone at a horse's fast walk, and skid tree trunks at a slow, careful pace like Invincible does. When it can do all those jobs, and more, for months on end – then will be time to say we've succeeded. Meanwhile, it will light up the restaurant for a few hours at the Grand Opening, using nothing more high-tech than some stove-wood to generate the current."

When they'd parked the equipment in the shop, locked up securely, and gone upstairs to fix supper Sophie ordered Tom to remain in the den while she prepared the meal. Within a few minutes he was at the kitchen door, sniffing like a starving wolf on the scent of prey.

"Sophie! What is that?"

"What is what?"

"You're cooking *bacon*!"

"Well of course, silly. I always do that when a wonderful man persists and persists and persists, until he's made a machine that will improve the lives of hundreds of people around him. Good thing it's been cold enough outside to keep nicely: I've had it for weeks awaiting this day."

Chapter 24

Christmas; High-tech; Societies Built on Sand and Relationships Built to Last

It began as an awkward, hesitant, tentative Christmas that year. People weren't sure quite how they felt: devastated by the year's catastrophe, adrift after losing so many family members and the entire culture in which they'd lived, grateful and filled with wonderment that they themselves were still alive, anxious about what lay in store for them in the coming year. People were having to learn a whole new set of responses to a season they had previously navigated each year mostly by unthinking habit.

With this year's unprecedented circumstances rendering useless their "automatic pilot," some of Mountainview's most faithful churchgoers—lifelong pillars of their churches—were astonished to discover themselves becoming, of all amazing things, actual believers in Christianity!

Who wore what to which service, and who controlled whom on the Building Committee—even who said what about which hymns the choir director ("And you know what *she's* like") chose for the service—all these formerly life-or-death matters unexpectedly fell away into irrelevance for at least some of these lifelong churchgoers. And they were suddenly dumfounded, struck by the enormity of what was reported to have happened so long ago, so far away—and what it perhaps meant for them personally, right here and now.

The changes seemed random, unpredictable. Other, equally solid lifelong pillars of their churches and stalwarts of the community quietly drifted away from any further involvement in either. After all, they had conspicuously upheld their side of an unwritten agreement for twenty or thirty or forty years, often at a very genuine personal cost in commitment, time, money, and effort—and now *this*. Let God (or the civics textbooks) find some other sucker to dupe.

The Christmas-gift Project probably did more than anything else to help get the people of Mountainview through that year's December 25—a day so unlike any other Christmas Day in anyone's experience.

During the past month, the town's grandparents and their older grandchildren had made toys and gifts for every one of the younger grandchildren. Many of the Baby Boom generation in between—equally remote from their parents and their children—wrung their hands in helpless agony. These well-meaning but culturally lobotomized parents were increasingly distraught as Christmas approached. *They had no Nintendo games for their children*! And they *certainly* had no faith in the simple items of the grandparents' devising. With mounting dread, they awaited the bitter, tearful disappointment that loomed closer with every passing day.

Corn-husk dolls, wooden alphabet blocks, stick horses, wooden swords and rifles, cardboard or plywood jigsaw puzzles, sock puppets, stilts, slingshots, yo-yo's, reed whistles and bullroarers—there were dozens of items the grandparents had remembered and set about helping their grandchildren make. But the parents knew it wouldn't work; it wouldn't work at all. None of these things had been advertised on television. The parents couldn't even know *what* this year's totally hot, "gotta-have-it" toys were. Not that they could have bought them anyway. It was hopeless…hopeless …

And yet when Christmas Day dawned, cold and clear and bright, the young children *loved* their gifts! And the older children could hardly contain their own pride at having made them, excitedly telling again and again their tales of secret evenings at Mountainview Elementary School, working with their grandparents.

And the grandparents watched the little kids' delight and the older kids' self-importance and shrugged. Why wouldn't an older child enjoy choosing and making a gift, all in the deepest conspiratorial secrecy? And why wouldn't a younger one be delighted to receive it? And why, in God's name, were their own Boomer and Boomerette offspring such…such…?

And they sighed. As they would optimistically tell each other at Grannies' Circle meetings in the days to come, "Maybe they just need some time to adjust."

Christmas that year was an entirely new experience for everyone. Tom and Sophie, both hesitantly groping toward some new response to the new conditions of this strange holiday, celebrated quietly at home at noon on the 25th.

Pork, like any other domesticated meat, was terribly expensive; but Sophie had prepared a savory Christmas meat pie using just enough pork mixed in with the pie's venison and vegetables and herbs and seasonings to make it indescribably succulent.

The aroma wafting from the oven, as the wine-rich gravy bubbled up onto the pie's golden top crust, drew Tom into the kitchen where he stood with his arm around Sophie's waist, beholding the wonders of her latest triumph. The pumpkin pies were cooling on the kitchen counter as they began their Christmas dinner. Tom had made some eggnog laced with a shot of moonshine, and as they sat down to begin the meal they raised their glasses to each other.

"Thank you," he said, "for all the lives you've saved, now and in the future—mine especially."

She smiled at him. "You're the one who's been saving lives—cursing away in your shop month after month, building a thoroughly old fashioned machine to give us some hope we can cling to the modern world. If we do remain alive, your contribution will make our lives worth living—mine especially."

After their Christmas dinner, when they brought their eggnog into the den, Tom gave her an old fashioned wind-up wristwatch.

"It's beautiful! I love it, Tom! You must have seen how crazy I get lately, always having to guess at the time. Trust you to think of something that combines beauty and usefulness."

"It was my mother's. It's got a jeweled movement that should run for many years yet. It certainly won't run for all the generations it's going to take us to regain the technology of battery–powered watches—but it'll start you on that road, and take you some years along it.

"When we get *there* again," Tom gestured toward the dead LED watch Sophie still wore, unable to discard that last fossil from an extinct high-tech world, "perhaps we'll have built a more durable society, on a more dependable foundation. Sand, including silicon chips, has its uses—but providing a firm foundation for a society or its economy is not one of them.

"Those little diamonds on the watch face and the band are today no more useful than sequins. But someday, in generations to come, precision machining will be possible once again: they'll have genuine value for use in machine cutting tools."

Sophie kissed him in a long, slow way.

"Tom; dearest Tom; my very own Gravely mechanic. Believe it or not, diamonds have value even aside from precision machine tools. Thank you for them.

"As for what happens in the future: people will go where they go and do what they do," Sophie said softly, giving him another kiss, "and they'll reap the consequences whatever those may be." She handed Tom his present from her. "Somehow, that's becoming less and less urgent for me. What I care most about is keeping special people warm and happy on the journey."

Maybelle had taught her sufficient knitting skills for Sophie to produce a beautiful, luxurious, all-wool scarf. She placed it around Tom's neck, smoothing the ends across his chest.

"It's perfect, Sophie." Tom hugged her. "Thank you. I don't know what I'd do without you, any more."

"Well you're in luck, Buster, because you won't have to find out. I'm going to let you volunteer to come along with me to the restaurant. Maybelle's going to be there, and after he's taken care of the draft animals so will Owen. We're making up food parcels for the Citizens' Patrol deputies to distribute to people who need them. Then there's work to finish before the Grand Opening tomorrow."

She smiled sweetly. "You'll probably want to bring the Gravely and generator, because you may end up volunteering to work past nightfall."

The next day, December 26, fully twenty-nine people of the thirty-four total in the 'Amish' community arrived at Mountainview in late afternoon. Only those too old for the trip, plus a few people to care for them and do essential chores, had had to remain behind. They'd left their community in mid-morning, bundled into two large hay wagons on soft, warm hay, with tarps available to erect as windscreens or snow covers if needed.

The two huge wagons, each effortlessly pulled by an enormous Belgian gelding, turned off Rt. 12 at Mountainview and rolled down Main Street toward Mountainview Elementary School, where the visitors were to stay.

The impromptu parade instantly collected a crowd of children, several doing wheelies on their bikes, two of them walking on homemade stilts, one on a pogo stick, and assorted others on foot, some pulling younger siblings in their Radio Flyer wagons. One child played a bugle, with limited musical skill but extreme gusto—causing several adults to be grateful no one else had thought of that possibility.

All along the parade route, Mountainview adults came out of their houses to stand in their front yards, waving and calling greetings to the visitors. At the head of the procession, leading the way like De Gaul liberating Paris, rode Owen Paks on the old gelding, Trigger. As if to place the capstone on this procession of the surreal, Tom hastily left the restaurant on the steam Gravely, towing the generator, overtook the parade at speed, and went chug-chugging furiously ahead of it, trailing a cloud of ash and smoke from his antique contraption, as he headed for Mountainview Elementary.

By the time the guests arrived there, Tom had the generator running and connected to the carefully limited loads he'd decided to power during the visitors' stay. There were barely adequate lights to illuminate the four classrooms which had been turned into dormitories for men, women, boys, and girls. There was sufficient electric power to run the building's oil heating furnace. Two bathrooms were illuminated. And—surely the crowning touch—both of them actually functioned: with the well-pump receiving power, water came out of the taps, and the flush toilets flushed. Carefully juggling the loads imposed on his generator, Tom was able to direct power to one load or another in sequence, rather than simultaneously, and thereby maintain barely adequate current for the entire range of carefully limited demands.

It was improvised, it was jury-rigged, and at times it was touch-and-go—but it *worked*. A group sizeable enough to have imposed a genuine strain on the resources of many private dwellings—in terms of heated space, water, toilet facilities, etc.—could be housed at the school in greater comfort and convenience, while costing Mountainview very little in the way of scarce resources. To his immense relief and pride, Tom's careful planning and calculating were being validated right before his eyes.

Where his meticulous computations went awry, of course, was in the perfectly natural (to him) assumption that human beings could exhibit some minimal trace of common sense. But even as the visitors were getting settled in at Mountainview Elementary, word spread through the village like wildfire about the wondrous things to be found there.

Mountainview's children of all ages—including some well into their late 60s—swarmed into the school to behold the marvels: electric lights that came on when a carefully taped-over switch was thrown; water that gushed from a faucet when someone ripped the tape off the tap, opened the tap to full volume, and stood back in gratified delight; toilets in previously blocked-off restrooms that flushed and flushed and flushed—each time arousing the ever-increasing crowd of village onlookers to greater cheers and applause. The baffled visitors, just moments earlier the center of so much attention, now found themselves suddenly forgotten, as their hosts excitedly swarmed the school, seeking more light switches, more water taps and more flush toilets to try.

The puzzled "Amish" (who had by now given up trying to explain that they were actually Mennonites and Hutterites, not Amish) didn't need or expect to be the beneficiaries of Mountainview's very latest, cutting-edge, steam-powered High Technology—and they were very soon its beneficiaries no more. The surging electric demand quickly outstripped the available generating capacity, the automatic overload-protector shut the generator down, and

Mountainview Elementary suddenly became once again the same lifeless hulk of a building it had recently been: no lights, no heat, no water, and no usefulness to humans.

"Hell, I never thought it would work," Mountainview's disappointed yokels confided to each other as they trudged, disheartened, out of the darkened school and back to their homes. Leaving the school, they cast an occasional cold glance in Tom's direction, but at least (they were pleased to admit) they were too courteous to confront him directly about his failure.

When the last villager had left the school, and the guests quartered there were unpacking and lighting the candles they had expected to use all along, Tom went through the building with fresh rolls of duct tape from the supply closet, re-taping all the switches, water faucets, and restrooms that were not to be used. He was explicit in his mutterings as to precisely what he thought of the yokels: their ancestry, their defining qualities, their prospects in the future life, and precisely what they could all do to themselves and each other in the present one. Then he re-set the generator's tripped overload shutoff switch and resumed supplying current. And once again the school building came to life.

The "Amish" silently glanced at each other, blew out their candles, and shrugged. Whatever.

It was only three blocks down Main from Mountainview Elementary to the restaurant, and their horses had been unharnessed and stabled in the school garage, so in the late afternoon's cold winter twilight the town's guests, led by Chief Barley, promenaded on foot to the restaurant's Grand Opening.

Tom arrived with the generator ahead of the crowd, and the restaurant seemed to explode into a magical scene of brilliant light and festive sound. After using candles for several months, the electric lights seemed indescribably brilliant; and after going without any but the simplest homemade music, the Christmas tapes and CD's on the stereo system sounded like something from heaven itself.

"I *knew* it would work!" cried the villagers to each other, as they pressed forward toward the magical restaurant to join in the excitement.

The Amish were seated at a long trestle-table on the slightly raised stage platform at one end of the room. In the center, by popular demand, their patriarchs Caleb Yoder and Amon Yoost were flanked by Chief Barley in his capacity as de facto leader of Mountainview, and by Owen Paks, who had become Mountainview's ambassador to the guests.

The rest of the room was packed tightly with all those from town who wished to attend. The cost was thirty cents silver—a formidable sum of money—but all who could do so handed it over at the front door eagerly and entered the festive room. Others milled about in the street outside, enjoying the music and peering in at the brightly lit scene, excitedly commenting on everything displayed—who'd come and who hadn't, who was wearing what, who was talking with whom—showing the same unselfconscious, childlike fascination their forebears would have exhibited gawking in wonder at a Grand Ball held by Louis XIV or Henry VIII.

It soon became clear there would have to be two seatings for townspeople, to make room for all who wished to attend. Sophie explained to the Amish as she seated them that they would be expected to eat twice, in fairness to the townspeople coming to the second seating. The guests—by now hardly attempting to make much sense of the English and their peculiar ways—smiled and nodded in puzzled agreement.

When all was ready, each of the three Mountainview ministers offered a brief prayer. Call-Me-Bob implored all present to strive unceasingly toward social justice; Parson Miller mildly suggested it was always good to remember the Reason for the Season; and Brother Stainfuss delivered a dark warning against the all-too-tempting snares the Evil One had laid for the weak and fallible.

Then the visitors' designated representative rose to offer a concluding prayer. To everyone's surprise, this turned out to be five-year-old Aaron Hite, who in his clear, high voice, without the slightest trace of "ceremony," simply asked God to bless and keep all those in both companies, and, if it be His will, see them safe through the days ahead.

The banquet began.

And continued.

And continued.

In days to come, there were some earnest disputes between townspeople who'd been at different seatings. Chief Barley's after-dinner address, some claimed, had been somehow *better*—more pithy, perhaps, or slightly more nuanced—at the first seating. Others stoutly maintained that what they'd heard during its repetition at the second seating was superior—as was only reasonable, practice making perfect. Some held that the special vocal rendition of *White Christmas* offered by basso profundo Bill Etter was better at the first seating, because it included nearly all the words. Others pointed out that he'd had to dash to the creek with the mule cart to fetch an additional load of water for the restaurant between seatings, and to do that he'd naturally strengthened himself with several additional well-fortified eggnogs, and the resulting state of...*relaxation*...during his second rendition of the ballad gave it an added piquancy not attained in the first, which more than made up any shortcomings from his forgetting almost all the words the second time around.

To the surprise of nearly everyone, the dinner crowd contained an unexpected pair of referees in a perfect position to rule on the issues: the Scouse brothers had attended both seatings of the banquet. They had gone so far as to shave, and apparently even bathe, for the occasion—and since they weren't wearing their overalls no one recognized them when they lined up after the first seating and paid another thirty cents each to be readmitted a second time.

When the matter of the Chief's after-dinner remarks was brought to them for judgment, Jimson held that the first-seating version was indeed slightly more pithy—but Jackson maintained the second-seating version was marginally more nuanced. A tie was declared. On the issue of Bill Etter's Special Vocal Rendition, Jackson held that the first-seating version was slightly superior because Bill was able to stand without assistance through most of it. And yet Jimson countered persuasively that the second-seating rendition had a more, sort of, "informal" quality from being delivered while seated on the floor—and the song's words weren't all that important anyway. So on this matter, too, the dispute was adjudicated a draw, and members of both seatings agreed the evening had been a roaring success.

It was after midnight before the Amish made their festive way back to their quarters in Mountainview Elementary—a late night indeed for people accustomed to five a.m. milking. The children had long since curled up on pallets Sophie and Maybelle had prepared for them in a corner of the warm kitchen floor. They were roused to sufficient consciousness to hang on while being piggy-backed to the school by adults—or just carried in arms if too small and sleepy for that tactic.

Specially marked bowls of punch and eggnog had contained liberal amounts of Arlene and Billie's most recent batch of White Lightning—which was, everyone agreed, "breathtaking." Though the Amish had intended to sample these beverages only for politeness' sake—and even then in the most moderate amounts—there may have developed some confusion as to which bowls contained the "plain" and which the "fortified." In any event, even after walking three full blocks through the freezing night air back to the elementary school, more than a few of the Amish were still singing with amazing gusto.

Leaving the restaurant to close by lantern-light, Tom sped the Gravely and generator to Mountainview Elementary and set them up for use there. He found the Deputy promised by Chief Barley waiting, as arranged, next to the pile of firewood beside the school. Tom showed him how to read the steam pressure gauge and feed more wood into the firebox occasionally through the night as required to maintain operating pressure. Satisfied the steam engine and generator were functioning properly and the man would have no problems, Tom left instructions to send for him if ever in doubt, then walked back home, where he arrived just after Sophie.

"Sophie, that was splendid!"

"Do you really think people liked it?"

"I think it was truly a once-in-a-lifetime event – on an occasion when we all needed it more than anything else in the world. You and Maybelle have absolutely outdone yourselves."

Sophie glowed with pleasure.

"It made all the difference, your providing electricity for lights and for music from the stereo – not to mention those floor fans we set up to move the air around a bit. My God the place was packed! Doing it with Maybelle really made it possible. She's priceless."

"What happened to her? Last I saw of her was midway through the affair—she didn't get sick or anything?"

"Of course not. She's just being Maybelle-The-Priceless. An hour after the first seating began she informed me she'd made arrangements with a half-dozen or so of the Mennonite women to meet her there early tomorrow for cleanup—so I could stay as late as I wanted tonight and not show up till noon-ish tomorrow. She went home early for some rest, and I get to come in late tomorrow to a cleaned-up restaurant. That's Maybelle, to a "T.""

"When *does* the next event start?"

"Well, officially mid-morning—but that was planned before anyone knew what a blowout this evening would turn out to be. I suspect noon-ish is a more likely time for people to start re-appearing. We'll have a lunch—hopefully a bit more restrained than this evening's bacchanal—and there will be trading and gift-exchanging and a chance for the guests to visit with Mountainview people, either in their homes or at the restaurant. And then the next morning the Amish will set off on their return trip. I'll miss having them here. I didn't know how hungry I was for the sight of new faces and the sound of new conversation."

For all her thrill at the evening's success, he could see Sophie was obviously nearing the point of utter exhaustion. She weaved a bit as she removed the shoes she'd borrowed from a friend of Maybelle's for the party.

Seeing her sway, Tom held her in a tight embrace and delivered a lingering kiss. He was thrilled beyond words to feel her respond as he did so.

"You're fantastic. Everything about you…what you do…who you are… You're the woman I've been waiting for all this time, my precious Sophie. Can I persuade you…?" He gestured toward his own bedroom.

She giggled. "Goodness gracious, Mr. Jeffson! From the looks of things in the Boiler Room, you seem to have a full head of steam up. Well, if so, I'd better come with you to help monitor the gauges and so forth, don't you think?"

As she went ahead of him into his room, in stocking feet, with his eyes fixed on the gentle sway of her— left and right and left and right and left and right— he knew at that moment his life had reached its peak. For whatever incomprehensible reason, this fabulous, incredible woman actually wanted *him*!

Because they were both at the point of exhaustion, it was all so peaceful it was nearly dreamlike. He gently undressed her, placed her in his bed, caressed her, and took her. She floated in a gentle bliss, crying out sharply at the moment of orgasmic surrender, then immediately falling asleep in his arms. Before many minutes had passed, he too slipped into peaceful, sated, sleep— still holding her, enveloped in her warmth.

Chapter 25
Love, and Other Exchanges

The next morning they prepared to part briefly, Sophie going to the restaurant while Tom went to the elementary school to move the Gravely and generator to the restaurant. As they dressed, neither could stop smiling, or even fully gather sufficient wits to concentrate on any business at hand.

"Oh God, Tom—they're all going to take one look at me and laugh. I've *never* been so utterly obvious!"

"Mmmmm," Tom counseled her—but without interrupting his nuzzling of her inner wrist, which nuzzling casually wandered up the length of her arm to her shoulder, which then led to…

"*Stop it!* I can't get myself together when you do that! Tom, now let's be sensible! We both have things to do…"

"Mmmmm," he replied, causing her in desperation to grab a glass of water from the kitchen counter and dump it over his head.

"Agggkkk!"

"Now *behave*, Steamboy! Go rev your motor and bring it to the restaurant."

She hugged him fiercely.

"Quickly, Tom; get to the restaurant quickly. I don't want to be away from you even for minutes."

She re-buttoned the blouse she'd just cross-buttoned, mind and fingers both distraught, scarcely able to function. "But don't talk to me, or touch me or anything when you get there; you'll drive me crazy. No: give me one kiss and a hug when you get there. But not a really big kiss. Unless we can be alone for a minute. Oh no, that would be worse! Look, just be totally casual. Or maybe …"

"Ummm," he agreed, nodding with manly composure as he pecked her on the cheek and stumbled down the stairs on his way to Mountainview Elementary, one arm in his coat, the other flailing ineffectually behind him at a sleeve turned inside-out.

"I declare; I think he's worse than usual," muttered Mrs Crinwald when Tom strode past her on the sidewalk, oblivious as ever, spastically flapping one arm behind him at his half-on jacket in the bitter cold.

When Sophie arrived at the restaurant, Maybelle and her Mennonite volunteers had the restaurant spotlessly cleaned up from the previous evening, as promised, and had laid out a buffet lunch for the guests and townspeople who were beginning to filter in.

Theoretically, the lunch was to have cost twenty cents silver. But in practice, the young Mountainview man who'd volunteered to collect payment became so engrossed in his discussion with Joshua Yoder, Caleb Yoder's son, on methods of curing hams that he insisted on taking the young giant to his home nearby to show him some examples. Not one to shirk his duties, though, before leaving he scribbled TWENTY CENTS on a piece of scrap paper, and stuck it in the register's open cash-drawer at the restaurant's entrance.

The tactic proved very fortunate. Most people thronging into the restaurant had the necessary coins and deposited them, but some customers—either lacking coins or not being believers in a cash economy—left barter goods next to the register. The growing pile of odds-and-ends, some of them very odd indeed, came to include three dressed fresh rabbits wrapped in a clean cloth, eleven fair-sized perch, a lump of lard, several jars of assorted jams and preserves, a paper grocery bag full of dried mushrooms, dozens of eggs, the wretchedly inevitable jars of canned tomatoes, and various other foodstuffs.

When the buffet lunch drew more customers than even the wildest estimates Sophie and Maybelle had previously made, and food began running low, they snatched up the edible barter-goods left at the register and incorporated those into additional things to serve the crowd. Some of the improvised dishes, frantically thrown together with whatever ingredients were available, produced expressions from Sophie and even Maybelle that ranged from the dubious to the downright queasy.

"Ach! Fret not!" cheerfully reassured the bustling Mennonite women, who by now had largely taken over the kitchen, speedily turning out one peculiar concoction after another.

"Tis good food, all of it, the Lord has sent. Besides," one sturdy, lace-capped matron assured Sophie, handing her a dish of fried perch in gooseberry jelly on a bed of scrambled eggs to take out to the dining room, "they'll eat it all up sure. You'll see. They're mostly menfolk," she explained.

"Ach—and would not the menfolk any dish eat, when brought to them with such a smile as yours?" teased another of the Mennonite cooks, nudging her companion with her elbow and setting off giggles throughout the kitchen.

Sophie, reduced in an instant from Progressive Intellectual Firebrand to squealing fifteen-year-old at a Beatles concert, fled through the kitchen door into the dining room with the food, nearly braining Tom, who'd cautiously poked his head through the kitchen door in hopes of catching a glimpse of her.

The door's resonant, hollow THUD as it impacted Tom's head set off a burst of delighted laughter among the Mennonite women, with much rolling of eyes and many furtive glances of appraisal cast in his direction.

"Not so bad, maybe, that one. A big engineer, they say. He's the one who the electric lights makes, and the indoor water at the schoolhouse, you know."

"Ah? So? Still—there's time for him to find something useful to do. He's an English: maybe it's with him a hobby. It's harmless. This one," with a thumb toward Sophie, "maybe she soon helps him find the right furrow to put the plow in, no?"

As the kitchen erupted in shrieks of laughter, Sophie summoned her last remaining shred of composure to cover her retreat, announcing, "Well *somebody* had better check the cash receipts or this restaurant's going to be bankrupt before it's even gotten started!"

And with that she strode in calm and regal dignity to the register up front, where in the thoughtful pose of a Captain of Industry she looked down at a drawer full of dimes, and wondered who had bartered seven Superman comics for his lunch, and whether a small assortment of reading material might be a desirable addition to the restaurant during normal times.

"What's going on in your kitchen?" inquired a puzzled Dick Peters, just coming in from his police shift. "I could hear some kind of squealing or shrieking or something from clear out in the alley."

"I do *not* have the *slightest* idea," Sophie flash-froze the poor man, holding out her hand for his two dimes, and forcefully slamming them into the drawer. "Nor did we *intend* to serve fish with jelly on scrambled eggs. I had planned a *Greek* theme. *GREEK*!" she emphasized, her inner turmoil making her a bit shrill, but trying her best to make him understand. "*The origins of Western Culture!*"

"Yes ma'am, I see," soothed Officer Peters as he edged carefully away, praying she didn't have a knife or gun under the counter.

The many exchanges of gifts between townspeople and their guests developed into a sort of "pay-what-you-like" medieval trade fair in the restaurant, once the dishes had been cleared from the tables to make room for the items both groups had brought. There was such a generous array from the

Amish that one of their Belgians had to be harnessed to pull a wagon from the elementary school to the restaurant.

There were foods of every sort: hams and smoked fowls and rabbits and corned beefs and jerked lamb and kid, along with sauerkraut and honey and preserves and canned vegetables. There were Amish horseshoes and assorted items of tack for Mountainview's Belgian and mule and gelding. There was Mountainview salt for the Amish community's animals and their other needs. Clothes and toys and books were exchanged. Quilts were swapped for music-boxes and windup alarm clocks; beeswax candles for fish hooks and china teapots; a handmade banjo and mountain dulcimer for a pair of harmonicas, a child's xylophone, and two duck-calls. A veritable Ali Baba's Cave full of treasures was spread out on the restaurant tables before the wide eyes of the hosts and their guests, and members of each group sought excitedly from the other the particular items their own community lacked.

"Good to see it's working out so well," Chief Barley quietly confided to Tom as they watched the activity. "The Amish, although they're totally honest, are generally known for driving one hell of a hard bargain. Best way to deal with them is to overwhelm them with generosity on your side: leaves 'em no choice but to reciprocate in equal measure because of their religious values."

On the sidewalk outside the restaurant, where they had gone to bring in additional items from their wagon, Caleb Yoder quietly counseled his sons Jacob and Joshua.

"God has blessed us with a wonderful exchange to meet both groups' needs. Heed the ways of the English: they are not ordinarily given to great honesty in their dealings. But if thee offer them measures pressed down and heaped up and running over, they respond with like abundance—for their Pride doth require it."

As the afternoon progressed, Tom chatted with several visitors about the various machine-shop services he could offer: welding, drilling, and other metalworking to fabricate new items or repair existing ones. The Amish had a primitive charcoal forge for basic metalwork, but they quickly saw with delight that Tom could perform far more sophisticated tasks for them in his shop.

For his part, Tom explained there were several items Mountainview hoped to obtain. Foremost were various types of presses: one for pressing cooking oils from oil-seeds, and another for pressing juice from sugar beets or 'sorgo' grain sorghum, and a third for pressing apples and similar fruits into cider, and grapes into grape juice.

After much consultation back and forth, the Amish explained they had only one of the small, very high-pressure presses used to extract oil from oil-seeds. It was made from an old hydraulic auto jack and some thick-walled steel pipe. If Tom wished to borrow it to make two copies they would be delighted to purchase one of the copies from him.

They did have a substantial mill for extracting juice from the sugar beets and grain sorghum they grew, and it was a fairly simple item they could easily duplicate for Mountainview, but they advised against it for the time being. Enormous amounts of beet-pulp or sorgo-pulp were left after extracting even small quantities of the sugar-juice. The pulp made excellent fodder, and they had sufficient animals in their own community to consume it. But until Mountainview's flocks and herds greatly increased it seemed unlikely there would be sufficient demand there to prevent the fodder going to waste.

Perhaps it would be more efficient, they suggested, for them to increase their own sugar beet production and trade the extracted sugar-juice to Mountainview. A few hundred pounds of the juice was easily transported to Mountainview—in contrast to the many, many tons of raw sugar beets required, and the mountains of crushed beet-pulp fodder from the early stages of sugar-production.

Tom agreed with their reasoning and decided to advise Mountainview to obtain sugar juice from the Amish for the first few years, until Mountainview's own animal population increased several times over. Considering Mountainview's production of salt—an urgent necessity for the Amish community's livestock and other needs—trading sugar juice for salt was obviously the sensible course.

Regarding the simple press for squeezing juice from apples, grapes, and other fruit, the Amish were delighted to offer the services of Abraham Hite, who had built several such wooden presses and could oversee the job. He, in turn, suggested Jacob and Joshua, the two huge young sons of Caleb Yoder, as useful artisans to assist him in completing the job quickly. The project was good indoor work for winter, Hite explained, and if desired he and the Yoder sons could remain in Mountainview when the rest of their party returned home and get started immediately, so as to finish up before their presence was needed for early spring tasks in their own community.

This sounded fine to Tom, who could borrow any specifically woodworking tools his machine shop did not have, so he offered Hite the bedroom Sophie had been using, and asked him to compile a list of metalworking and other jobs the Amish wanted done in exchange for his and the Yoder boys' services.

A quick check with Owen Paks confirmed he and Maybelle would be happy to board Jacob and Joshua Yoder. Tom was delighted at the speed with which the cider-press project was set in motion.

Perhaps the most important of all the many exchanges between the Amish and Mountainview was conducted by Mabel Parker, that genteel little old lady and capitalistic plant-grower who was on her way to becoming Mountainview's John D. Rockefeller.

When Mountainview's guests had arrived the previous afternoon, they had scarcely reached their lodgings at the elementary school before Arlene, Henrietta, and Abner were quietly nosing about among them, meeting and greeting, sizing the visitors up, and reporting back to Mabel at Corporate Headquarters.

In a trice, Mabel's three agents then reappeared at Mountainview Elementary bringing some of the visitors her warmest personal invitation to dinner, along with the gift of some samples of scion-cuttings to use in grafting superior varieties of tree fruits, and some starts of various highly coveted spice and medicinal herb plants, with the innocent question "did any of them know if these plants were of any value?"

During their visit with her, once Mabel displayed such of her inventory as she wished to divulge, there was no doubt in any of the Amish guests' minds that there was very serious business indeed to be done here. Some of the guests—including Klara Yoder, who oversaw her community's medicinal herbs, and Ephram Yoost, her brother-in-law, who was their leading orchardist, and Rachel Yoost, who worked with textiles—ended up spending almost their entire visit at the Parkers' home, too absorbed in working out plant exchanges even to attend the evening's dinner or the next day's buffet lunch.

As in the larger barter fair at the restaurant, both sides benefitted from the plant-trading agreements reached across Mabel's dining table. But the stakes and the long range benefits were incomparably greater at the plant sessions. Mabel obtained agreements for the Amish to deliver almost a dozen varieties of medicinals she badly wanted, along with written indications for their use, dosages, and so forth. She discovered several types of melons, black beans, apples, and turnips the Amish could provide her to help fill out Mountainview's inventory. The Amish were ecstatic to learn of Mabel's supply of flax seed: the linen it would produce would be vital for their future clothing needs. Likewise, they were overjoyed that she had some tea plants: in time, they would help somewhat to soften the near-mortal blow of losing their beloved coffee, without which they sometimes wondered if life itself would be possible.

Each party understood its own interest in the fullest possible exchange of plant material: if disease, weather, pests, or other calamity should wipe out a particular plant in one community, it would be possible to re-introduce it from survivors in the other community, so benefitting both groups.

Mabel mentioned that Mountainview could supply certain wines and any quantities needed of "medicinal alcohol," for which the Amish offered malt and several beers made according to their European ancestors' ancient recipes.

After extended, carefully disguised probing all around the subject, Mabel decided not to introduce the subject of high-potency marijuana—or her desperate desire to obtain opium poppy seeds. Time enough—with these religious people—to raise issues of that sensitivity later, she decided.

Back at the restaurant, as the afternoon waned, the last trades were being concluded. The visitors carefully stashed their acquired treasures in their big hay wagon, while the hosts took their own to their homes nearby, or placed them in the corners of the room like piles of gifts on Christmas Morning. Then, from their wagon, several Amish brought in box-loads of a peculiar song-book entitled *The Sacred Harp,* while others began arranging the room's chairs into a large hollow square.

Old McClintock, who'd been having fewer clear days and more fuzzy ones the past decade or so, and was recently more and more often insisting he'd helped found Mountainview in 1781, immediately cleared up.

"*Shape note singing!*" he exclaimed joyfully, shuffling about excitedly and getting in everyone's way as he tried to help arrange the square of chairs.

"So! You the shaped notes are already knowing! Soon everyone knows, for you help us teach, yes?" encouraged Abraham Hite in a warm and gentle acceptance of Old McClintock that instantly won the heart of everyone in the room.

"The shaped notes is very old. Like us," Abraham said, putting an arm around Old McClintock. "But we still are working good, you bet! All choose now which side of the square you sit on: here treble, here alto, here tenor and here bass." He indicated for each group one side of the hollow square.

"But you not sitting over there," he mock-cautioned Old McClintock. "Too many innocent young girls in treble section. Not safe. Anyway, I need you here in center for helping me."

As the crowd sorted itself into the four sections, according to their respective parts, the townspeople had a chance to look at the hymnals the Amish had brought. The music had its notes written on the usual horizontal lines, called staves, as in the modern notation, but the notes themselves were different. There were only four notes—called Fa, Sol, La, and Mi. Unlike modern notation, each of these notes was represented by its own shape: a triangle, oval, square, or diamond respectively.

"Not always were people so educated, back in the Old Days," explained Abraham with a smile, standing with Old McClintock in the center of the hollow square. "Used we then the different shapes to make music simple for everyone to read, 300 years ago. But one thing they were very smart back then: they knew singing the right note is only second importance. Singing LOUD is first importance! Wonderful system for anyone like me: music ability so-so, but strong and healthy lungs. You see. Let's on page 306 begin, with 'Oxford.'

"First we set a tone ..." and he hummed a note, slightly raising or lowering the "Fa" on which the rest of the notes would be based, until the four sections nodded approval that the resulting scale would be comfortable for their own parts.

And then he led off, marking time with a vigorous up-and-down beat of his arm to keep the sections together as the room exploded into joyous, full-throated harmony, catching up the astonished townsfolk in a flood-wave of sound and sweeping them along in it, scarcely able to resist.

Shepherds rejoice! Lift up your eyes, and send your fears away:
News from the region of the skies – a Savior's born today!
No gold nor purple swaddling bands, nor royal shining things
A manger for His cradle stands, and holds the King of kings.

When all the verses of the first song were finished, leaving the room still reverberating, even the least musical of the townsfolk understood: this was music for ordinary people, not musicians. The "harp" of the songbook's title referred to the untrained human voice, and the guiding spirit of the music was to "make a joyful noise."

Amazingly, the simple lyrics and the four-part harmony of the rousing old hymns were transmuted by a mysterious alchemy into something beautiful and inspiring far beyond the sum of its individual parts. People who "couldn't sing a note" were caught up in some kind of spell, producing music they couldn't possibly produce—and yet ...

Abraham glowed as he saw their hosts' puzzlement turn to increasing enjoyment.

"One of our Elders, Caleb Yoder, has for our next number asked. He says it recalls his mind to his first meeting with a Mountainview person, who talks with him at night on the road beside a campfire. Page 66: 'Jordan.'"

And with that he led off—the volume surging even greater this time as Mountainview people joined in with increasing spirit. Tom, himself never a singer, had little doubt as to whom the song was directed.

There is a land of pure delight, where saints immortal reign,
Infinite day excludes the night, and pleasures banish pain.
Sweet fields beyond the swelling flood stand dressed in living green.
So to the Jews old Canaan stood, while Jordan rolled between.

Oh could we make our doubts remove, those gloomy doubts that rise,
And see the Canaan that we love, with un-beclouded eyes;
Could we but climb where Moses stood, and view the landscape o'er,
Not Jordan's stream nor death's cold flood should fright us from the shore.

As evening drew on, with the darkness falling and the winter's cold night settling over the dark immensity of the endless fields and forests all around them, that tiny handful of people in the brightness of a single room seemed both pathetically insignificant and yet charged with an all-important, radiant light of hope. Unreasonable hope, perhaps—unjustifiable in strictly rational terms—but hope. There perhaps *could* exist some future for their kind; or at least the possibility of one.

How deep our roots go down through time! Tom thought, gazing down at *The Sacred Harp* he was sharing when the group came to its next-from-last song of the evening.

"By the calendar, it's now the early 21st century. Socially and technologically, we're living somewhere in the mid-1800s. The song we're singing was written by Isaac Watts in 1719. It's been taught to us in shaped-note form by a group whose origins and beliefs date back to the early 1500s. And as for the song itself—why it could have been sung by Paleolithic hunter-gatherers at this time of year, huddled close around the fire at the mouth of their cave:

His hoary frost, His fleecy snow, descend and clothe the ground;
The liquid streams forbear to flow, in icy fetters bound.
He sends his Word and melts the snow, the fields no longer mourn;
He calls the warmer winds to blow, and bids the spring return.

"Uh, is there any...ah...*news* you'd care to share with me?" Sophie whispered to Tom as the singing came to an end and it became clear Abraham was planning to come home with them from the restaurant when the evening ended.

"Oh, Jeez! I plain forgot! How about if we share a bedroom, while Abraham's in the one you've been using? Also, I meant to ask you—will you marry me? It's because Abraham's staying here to help us build a press."

Things couldn't get any worse, so he gave her his goofiest, slavering leer.

"It's going to be used to draw forth sweet nectar from the juicy, softly rounded, ripe and luscious fruits we gently place in it: grapes and apples and pears and all manner of sinfully delicious treasures—from which the sweet, dripping nectar will be slowly, gently coaxed for our sensual gratification..."

"Tom! *Stop it!* I swear you're going ga-ga... And you're making *me* goofy! Yes, of course I'll marry you. Now quit it! Stall him here for ten minutes and I'll have my things moved into your bedroom. *Not now!*" she commanded urgently, as his fingers crept slowly up her ribcage.

She was so flustered she unthinkingly dashed back toward the kitchen, where work had largely come to a halt as the entire staff crowded the open door, not wanting to miss a thing.

Tires squealing in a sharp u-turn, Sophie then headed toward the cash register, where she began elaborately counting dimes.

"A widow, they say," mused old Widow Yoder approvingly, nodding to herself. "Not like the silly young ones today. And a big engineer, eh? So? If he can make for her the water indoors in wintertime, is that so bad? Maybe is nothing wrong with such a thing. I think she's not a fool."

And that conclusion, from a widow of twenty-seven years, noted for her upright adherence to each and every one of the Old Ways, truly put the seal on Tom and Sophie's union more than anything else ever could.

Chapter 26
Loyalties: Living, Learning, and Loving

The following morning, 26 of the Amish visitors and the trade goods they'd acquired, nestled snugly in their two big hay wagons, left Mountainview Elementary School, proceeded down the town's Main Street amid the farewell waves of the townspeople, and then onto Rt. 12 South for the eleven mile trip home.

The departure evoked a mixture of feelings. Abraham Hite, struggling to raise a large family on a comparatively small acreage, had remained in Mountainview because he needed the income from a winter's work on the cider press. His helpers, Jacob and Joshua Yoder, the twenty-one year old twins, remained in Mountainview because every day in such a huge, bustling metropolis was another day of wonders and splendors beyond anything their young lives had yet encountered. And in Mountainview, ironically, the pangs Owen and Maybelle felt as they waved farewell to the departing visitors made them almost wish they were in the wagons with the Amish, going...strange to say..."home."

The Amish community's life—its people and ways and values—had exerted a pull on Owen ever since his first stay there in late summer to get Invincible. His more recent visit to invite the Amish to Mountainview for Christmas had only increased his interest in their community. The more he told Maybelle about what he'd seen and experienced, the more keenly she felt a longing of her own for such an environment in which to bear and raise the children she so greatly wanted. Since their commitment to Brother Stainfuss and his Foursquare Baptist flock had begun to cool, both Owen and Maybelle were each seeking, in their own way, the security of a nest, a shelter to provide themselves and their longed-for children as much stability and safety as their world's desperate insecurities would permit.

Maybelle, who had never known anyone remotely close to Sophie's degree of worldly sophistication, continued to discretely question Sophie about what she thought of the Amish and their lives and beliefs. Owen, for his part, directed cautious, experimental comments to Tom concerning what he'd seen of the Amish, eagerly hanging on the older man's reaction.

"They break my heart," Tom flatly told Sophie one evening when their house-guest, Abraham Hite, had withdrawn to his room and Tom and Sophie in their own room were preparing for bed. "Owen and Maybelle are the most decent people I've ever known. I wish events had not let them, and their future children, down so badly. Is moving to the Mennonite community really the best option they have?"

"People have done worse—far worse," replied Sophie. "I've been trying to stay as neutral as possible when Maybelle brings the subject up. She knows I'm not a religious believer, of course, any more than you are. But I'm sure she understands I love her and want the best for her, and will support her and Owen in whatever decision they reach. What else can either of us do?"

"Fight ignorance, for one thing." Tom's jaw set in a tight, rigid line.

"Look around," he continued, "at the unimaginable death and suffering people have heaped on our world through their stupidity. Don't blame greed: greed played a minor part in The Collapse. The childish, oh-so-cunning scheme to 'print ourselves rich' by creating unlimited amounts of worthless paper 'money' out of thin air, to drive real estate values and stock prices endlessly higher, and fund ever-expanding 'free' government programs—that fantasy was always so breathtakingly simple-minded, so dependant on magical thinking, that it's unworthy of being dignified by the term greed. Without mind-boggling doses of stupidity such a scheme would never have been concocted by ignorant leaders, nor accepted by their ignorant followers. In light of recent history, I repeat: is there anything in the world more important than fighting ignorance?

"Offering Owen and Maybelle an unqualified warm and well-meaning supportiveness in the name of 'kindness' sidesteps that little issue, doesn't it? The religious community Owen and Maybelle are drawn to has fine people, no question. As you point out, countless people have lived lives infinitely worse. But, Jesus, Sophie: religious communities do not fully educate their young! Granted, at least our so-called 'Amish' neighbors are not really Amish, where the kids finish eighth grade and are sent to the fields to hoe 'taters. The Hutterites, and especially Mennonites, do go on to obtain college degrees, although typically at their own, carefully oriented colleges. But, come on, Sophie: they impose a religious indoctrination from birth that confines their minds within certain, clearly specified boundaries of acceptable thought—and is *intended to*! Don't you have enough still-glowing embers of good old 1970's feminist rage to be furious about the Chinese binding the feet of their girls? Well? Then what of a culture that binds not merely the feet but the *mind* of a child, confining it for life within certain 'theologically acceptable' limits by indoctrination?"

Sophie was as put out by his blindness as by the point he was making, and (a deeply committed believer in her own right) felt as threatened as any other believer confronted by the militant skeptic. She returned him measure for measure.

"Why should all people devote their lives to endless questioning of abstractions, just because that's been your choice? Without people to fell trees and haul the timber home, and cut it up for firewood and boiler fuel—or people to cook for the timber-cutting crews who felled those trees—how long would you be around to wring your hands and play Hamlet? You and people like Judge Parker, endlessly poring through libraries full of deep and weighty tomes in search of Wisdom—and finding only still further reasons to doubt the doubts you've already had about doubting the doubtful worth of doubtfulness. For God's sake, Tom: be as well-intentioned as you can, then *act*!"

"For God's sake, Sophie: learn some humility and skepticism from the tragedies and pratfalls of history. Before acting, *think*!"

"Implementing a well-intentioned public policy is better than having none at all: you can clean up the mistakes as you go."

"Thinking through a public policy is better than implementing one which proves disastrous: you can make do somehow till you've thought things through."

"You'd *never* get anything done!"

"Well, By God you and your kind certainly got *plenty* done! 'Seek you his monument? Look around you.' We're now living in the *nineteenth century,* for Chrissake!"

"Well, we're *living*! Yes, all right, in the nineteenth century. We did the best we could at the time. We made mistakes, and we're paying for them, and we'll go on: to try and perhaps to fail, again and again and again. Until we succeed in forming a world that's humane and decent for all, not just for a favored few at the top."

"Trying and failing, again and again, you blithely say. As if it were merely a matter of monkeys harmlessly typing away until by random chance they banged out the works of Shakespeare! But those are human lives with which you're so willing to 'try and fail, again and again.' Those eggs you're so willing to break, to make your utopian omelet, are human beings. Those piles of human carrion heaped up in the streets of this country's now-dead cities—silent testaments to the stupidity and hubris of ill-thought-through economic and social policies: they scream to me there is nothing—*nothing*—more important than combating the ignorance which made such horrors possible. I repeat: there is nothing in the world more important than promoting careful, searching, skeptical, unfettered inquiry—in brief, combating ignorance."

"Fanatic!"

"Fanatic!"

Stung by the injustice of her charge, Tom carefully delivered one of the gravest accusations he could imagine, by way of a coup de grace: "You're inconsistent."

The damned woman merely shrugged.

He expanded on his point, making it irrefutable. "You deny the primacy of unfettered rational inquiry, and yet you've been working to foster exactly that all along. You haven't fooled me one bit: I've figured out what you've been planning for your so-called 'restaurant.' Once the Christmas commotion dies down, you're going to use it to draw people in so you can dose them with 'Greek Civilization: The Basis of Western Culture.' And then God knows what-all, given that starting point. You've been planning to set up a *university*, right here in Mountainview, on Main Street, right out in broad daylight."

"And if I have? Lord knows, you and Judge Parker are as widely read as most of the professors I dozed through. And from the titles I've scanned on your shelves, the two of you have libraries that together will form the basis of an adequate—if typically bourgeois, elitist, and reactionary—college collection. It's a start."

She smiled sweetly, twisting the knife ever so slightly.

"Not an ideal start, perhaps. Not one that has been thought through in every last detail, with every conceivable flaw or weakness raised and carefully considered and analyzed to the point of absolute metaphysical certainty. But, nevertheless, a well-intentioned start—from which we can proceed to clean up any mistakes and make any possible improvements along the way, once we get going.

"I was not planning to accept applications from prospective faculty just yet, but I believe I will make exceptions for you, Judge Parker, Chief Barley, and Doc Billings in the faculties of the Humanities, Law, Political Science, and Natural Sciences, respectively. That will elevate you four to the status of Founding Members—and perhaps entitle you to the use of specific colors on your academic robes, though I've not made up my mind on that point yet."

Tom made things as comprehensible as he could for her.

"First: I wouldn't teach there in a million years. Second: I wouldn't set foot in it for a million dollars—real ones. And third: I don't plan to even *breathe* when walking past it on the sidewalk, for fear of what I'd catch!"

"I plan to call it," she went on sweetly, "The New School for Progressive Social Policy Research."

"That figures. Let's hope you can get enough copies of the *Little Red Book* so each of your three students can have his own copy to wave—as part of the academic coursework, while chanting quotations from the Great Helmsman in unison."

"Ah, that will be the least of it," she mocked right back at him. "Group calisthenics, self-criticism sessions, identification of any 'Capitalist Roaders' and the reporting of 'Unreliable Elements'…Why, there's just no telling, Mr. Jeffson, what horrors we might end up embracing for lack of any counterbalancing input. We might go far beyond mere blood-soaked Maoist Revolution and, in our frenzy, commit the truly unimaginable for Mountainview: *social improprieties*! For, mark my word, we mean to revolutionize the life and thinking of this town—and a revolution is not a dinner party."

"*We* who?"

Not for the first time, Sophie's rhetorical exuberance had gotten her into a corner. Unwilling to admit that her royal or editorial "we" amounted to a single person, she sputtered and stammered, bursting out with the first name that popped into her head.

"*Plenty* of us. Hockley Beener and I, among plenty of others, for a start."

Suppressing a horselaugh, Tom contented himself with giving her the sardonic fisheye. Hockley Beener was just the sort of flakazoid loser who really would be drawn to Maoism—after brief stopoffs at the Rosicrucian, vegan, Wiccan, naturist, Lyndon Larouche, and Scientology booths in the Nuthouse Carnival of the Weird.

"Uh, Sophie? Hockley's about fifteen years old. And I think he talks to Martians. If any will talk to him, which I doubt. That's *it*? That's the entire revolutionary cadre planning to terrorize Mountainview and shake us to our core?"

"Hockley's brighter than you think. And anyway, there are other people too. And anyway…." She burst into sobs.

As Tom held her close, gently rocking her, he understood for the first time just how important the restaurant-university was to his beloved.

"Ah, Jeez, Sophie. Come on. It'll work out all right. You'll see. Hey, if I was going to take over the world there's nobody I'd rather have at my side than Hockley Beener. No, really; he's ok, just a little…But maybe you might want to start out with 'A Thousand Points of Light' or 'Compassionate Conservatism' or something, then work them up to full-scale revolution from there."

His snickering, chortling enjoyment of the situation didn't help any, and Sophie's sobs intensified until he couldn't help but be affected.

"Aw, hey, look, come on. All right, if I promise to think about teaching a course sometime can we get married next week?"

Her sobbing slackened. "Married? Just so you can enslave me in a domestic prison as a sex object, keeping me as chattel, barefoot and pregnant, subjected to the Male Gaze and deprived of a Voice to protest sexist hegemony? Is that what you're proposing?"

"Well, yeah. Unless you're not cool with some part of it. I could see negotiating a bit over the length of your chain…"

"You are a despicable sexist pig, Mr. Jeffson. What sort of marriage: where and by who?"

"*Whom*, please, my dear. We in the professoriate do feel it necessary to insist on minimal standards in spoken as well as written converse, not to mention AAWKK…!"

Pleased to have found his tender spot, just below the lowest rib, she jabbed him again for confirmation, this time on the other side.

"AAWKK…! Don't *do* that! I can't stand to be poked there. Now listen; let us be mature and rational. Ground rule Number One for our forthcoming Holy Union: no poking people in…AAWKK!"

"Civil ceremony? By Chief Barley? In the restaurant?" she inquired.

"Oh Jesus, my beloved," Tom murmured gratefully, nuzzling her, "Anything you want. Colonel Mustard, in the pantry, with the candlestick, for all I care. Just marry me and be with me forever. I love you so much I can't ever be without you again."

"And you will support Owen and Maybelle if they decide to join the Amish?"

"Why not? Damn if I know what they should do. On the one hand …"

Showing scant respect for the value of free and unfettered inquiry, she limited his response to a single hand.

"And you will teach?"

"Comrade Directress, I swear undying loyalty to you and Comrade Hockley Beener as together we vanquish the lickspittle lackeys of the imperialist running dogs and march valiantly onward to build a Glorious Future for the proletarian workers of the world."

Chapter 27
Stupid vs Smart:
The System vs the Oddball

Tom knew Hockley Beener only by sight. But that was enough to convince him about what he needed to do next. Judge Parker, Chief Barley, and Doc Billings were the other three "volunteers" Sophie planned to conscript for duty in her restaurant-university. Knowing those three, Tom decided it was only decent to contact poor Hockley first himself. Maybe he could somehow get the kid to…well…*shape up* or something, before the other three men dealt with him in less kindly fashion.

The house itself gave fair warning. Mr. Beener had been on his "beat-the-capitalist-system-through-economy-and-efficiency" kick he seldom strayed far from. Mrs. Beener had been in an "organic-natural-earth-substances" mode at the time. And their only son had, as usual, been deep into a combination of *Scientific American, Hustler,* and *Mother Earth News.* Accordingly, the Beeners had obtained a 55-gallon drum of recycled waste creosote from the power line company and, using rollers, coated their entire house with it: roof, siding, trim, doors, and all.

"People wouldn't believe how cheap this is for total protection," Mr. Beener had gloated at the time, as his admiring wife and son looked on.

During hot summer days, the Beeners' downwind neighbors had considerably less complimentary things to say.

Hip to the system, Tom picked up a pebble to tap gently on the front door, avoiding smearing his hand with creosote.

"Hi, Miz Beener. Is Hockley in?"

"In what?"

"At home, Miz Beener. If Hockley's at home could I speak with him a minute?"

She checked the sun's position in the sky.

"Well…yessss," she considered, dubiously. "It's time he got up anyway, I suppose. Come on in."

It was late afternoon. Mrs. Beener explained Hockley was currently in a "night phase" and seldom ventured out during daylight. "It's amazing, he says, what a different perspective one gets, living nocturnally. He's only been doing it a few months, but he reports it's made all the difference in his aura. I can't undertake that journey right now, because I'm having auric issues I need to work through. My current program of high-colonic cleansing seems to be doing the trick, though, and I expect to become nocturnal myself once my alignment's favorable."

"Ah."

Reaching Hockley's bedroom, Mrs. Beener stopped a good three feet from the closed door and explained.

"You'll want to step up quite high, going through the doorway. About two feet high should do it. Hockley's set up a photo-voltaic 'electric eye' in the doorframe that if interrupted triggers a lightning bolt from his Van De Graff static generator. It's all quite harmless, of course, but many people find an unexpected 250,000-volt electric spark quite disconcerting—even though the amperage is so low it's nothing to be concerned about.

"Hockley! Wake up, child! It's Tom Jeffson, the steam engine man."

No response. Lengthy pause. Still no response.

"Hmmm." She considered carefully. "I don't know about knocking on the door…He was fiddling with something the other night that makes me think that might not be wise…Ah, I know."

She retrieved a torn rubber galosh from the dining room china cabinet, and a broom from the kitchen, where it was being used to prop the oven door closed.

"Insulation!" she told Tom with a triumphant grin, as she held one end of the broom in the rubber galosh, stood well back, and used the other end of the broomstick to bang on Hockley's bedroom door.

All hell broke loose, with lightning bolts passing floor-to-ceiling directly in front of the door, where the unwise would have been standing.

"HA!" Mrs. Beener gloated. "He's quite bright, you know. We had him tested as a child at Duke—they flew us down there after some preliminary screening because they were quite interested in having a look at him. He scored 200-some-odd on the Wechsler. But he's all technically oriented: doesn't know a *thing* about human interaction. For example, I picked up clues to his plan just by watching him assemble his apparatus the other night. *And thereby we defeat his technological prowess!*"

Yikes, Tom thought. *Speaking of 'human interaction,' Mrs. Beener, have you ever considered...?* But he just took a deep breath and smiled.

"The capacitors have discharged by now. There'll be no problem," she assured Tom, and thrust the door open. "He has to rely on solar cells for electricity nowadays, and that really cramps his style. Takes forever to fully recharge his apparatus. Hey! Hockley!"

The pimply fifteen-year-old was awake, working at his desk, earphones on, with a headbanger-industrial-ska CD so mind-bendingly loud the hellish thumping and screeching was audible at considerable volume outside the headphones. He looked up from his work, surprised, peering at his two visitors through coke-bottle lenses that made his eyes resemble those of a grouper Tom had once seen in the Baltimore Aquarium.

With a sigh, Hockley turned off the "music" and removed his headphones.

"How did you get in here?" The question was clearly prompted by curiosity, not hostility.

"*Rubber!*" exhulted Mrs. Beener. "I will leave you two now: it's time for my Vedic chanting." And out she swept on the crest of her triumph.

The kid sighed and nodded morosely, conceding his mother's victory.

"I had to promise: no lasers," he glumly confided. "They tie my hands, and then think they've achieved a triumph."

"Ah. Uh. Well—what I came about is...I understand you're going to be involved with Sophie in her restaurant, um, sort of 'school' project ..."

"Oh yeah. She originally wanted me for general EE—but I'm, like, down for IT and maybe some AI too. I mean, who else is she gonna get? What I'd *like* to teach is a historical analysis of obsolete languages – COBOL, FORTRAN, that sort of thing—but she says there's not enough interest *at present.*

"They always say *at present,*" he muttered, "like I'm not gonna realize ..."

"Uh ..."

"Electrical Engineering. Information Technology. Artificial Intelligence. I've still got my textbooks from the Cal Tech Advanced Placement courses I'd been taking. I was gonna move out there next year to finish any courses I couldn't do ahead of time by AP. That way, I'd have been able to wrap up my Bachelors in two years and get on to grad school, where they do the good stuff. But then, with The Collapse...." He shrugged.

Suddenly, Tom was hit by a realization: Hockley Beener was a human. Yes, he was an oddity, a freak, a surpassingly weird little geek who dwelled behind those coke-bottle lenses in a family as weird as he was, but—notwithstanding all that—a *human.*

"Most people are a pain in the ass!" Tom himself didn't fully comprehend why he said it; it just popped out.

Hockley looked up from his desk, where he'd been working on what may have been a circuit diagram for a doomsday bomb. He regarded Tom with new interest, as if just noticing his presence in the room.

"Yeah."

"I was always physically big for my age," Tom mused, looking at scrawny little Hockley. "That's important to boys. And—I say this proudly, and screw anybody who has a problem with it—I acquired very young the ability to use words as weapons when it suited me. I could combine quick-wittedness, sarcasm, and aggressive ridicule into a verbal slicing-and-dicing machine other kids wanted no part of. They left me alone. I wasn't nearly as bright as you are—though I had ideas and interests other people didn't share—but there was no bullying: people didn't mess with me."

He sighed. There was silence for a time between them, each of them wondering what this sudden outburst of candor was all about.

"It doesn't get any better, you know: the Good Guys don't necessarily win in the end. Throughout your life, you will never be more than a tiny fraction of what you could have been, Hockley, because you will never get the education necessary for someone with your gifts. We see far horizons only by standing on the shoulders of giants—and you will never have that opportunity. Cal Tech and all other such places of human excellence have been wiped out. In the endless war between stupidity and higher human culture, stupidity has won. Maybe only a temporary battle—or maybe the entire war—but in either case has certainly won for the duration of your own personal lifetime, and for generations to come.

"You get accustomed to being on the losing side, eventually," Tom confided. "But you never do completely accept it. At least I haven't. It rankles."

Tom couldn't believe he was revealing himself so nakedly to this …this…he finally understood it: this teenaged version of himself.

"Fuckemall," he concluded, his voice betraying a note of anguish. "Stupid Goddamn people. There was nothing anyone could do, all those years, but sit and watch, day by day, as their childlike, carefree stupidity slowly brought the inevitable Collapse down upon us all. Bottom line: stupidity's more powerful than brains. Don't kid yourself."

"Fuckemall," Hockley replied soberly, raising an imaginary toast.

"Well. Anyway. Good luck with your teaching. There's not three people in Mountainview who give a rat's ass about anything you have to teach them— or who could understand it if they wanted to. So stick to explaining the difference between an open circuit and a closed circuit. Imparting that concept will take however long Sophie plans for the courses to run. What's all this stuff?" Tom gestured at bits of equipment that seemed intended to go together, piled in a corner of the bedroom.

"A television receiver I'm making."

"Hockley, I don't think they broadcast TV any more."

"Yeah; I know. So I'm also making a camera and transmitter. That's that stuff over there. It's tricky when you first have to create almost every component you need, before you can assemble those components into the finished article. It's good mental exercise, though, devising workarounds when you lack the proper tools and materials. It's an entertaining relaxation from my real interest: computing."

"I reckon. Can you see if the electric output of my Gravely generator is 'clean' enough to use for powering a computer? What have you been using so far, solar cells to charge lead-acid car batteries?"

"Yes and yes. If I could just charge my batteries with the generator now and then it would be great. Cloudy days: no computer—man, that sucks."

And then Hockley surprised himself with unexpected candor, fully as much as Tom had done moments earlier.

"I need computer power these days because the stash of porn on my floppies has gotten old and stale. I downloaded all I could, of course, before The Collapse brought down the entire web. But it, like, gets old, man, you know?"

"Yeah," said Tom, remembering worn and tattered girlie magazines from his own time, a hundred years ago.

"However, since I have plenty of images on file, why not write programs that will, in turn, re-program the sounds and motions of those existing images to create new activities, new settings, new combinations of images—whole new amalgamations of the existing material in the databank to produce, in effect, new porn? At least, that's the basic idea. Actually doing it's a good bit more complicated."

He began having second thoughts.

"But don't, like, shout about it, you know? My dad's down on porn because Capital shouldn't have that much power to exploit the proletarian wage-slaves who act in it. And my mom gets bent out of shape because she claims the actresses risk serious misalignment of their chakras, or primal forces, by having sex commercially without orgasmic culmination. Well, on the one hand, Mom or Dad, or both, might be right. But on the other hand …"

Tom understood reasoning involving the use of several hands.

"Hell, I'm not going to tell. Show me some, if you ever get it to work, ok? But don't yak about it to Sophie. You never know when she's going to go all 1970's and turn feminist on you, or some damn thing."

After weighing the next issue carefully, Tom gingerly broached a subject he and Sophie and a few others had come to dread ever since she'd helped amputate Tim's leg.

"Do you have reference material on floppies you can run in the computer? I know *Encyclopedia Britannica* was distributed that way, and some other reference works."

"Yeah. I got *Britannica*. Also some AI technical reference works and some other stuff. Need something looked up?"

"Yes. But I need it to be kept quiet. I mean it. It's an issue that could truly damage community morale."

Taking a deep breath, he plunged in.

"You see, once Doc Billings' supplies run out, which they've mostly done by now, we're without any effective anesthetics. The closest we can come is pot and alcohol, neither of which is really a pain-killer. Without anesthetics, dentistry and surgery revert back to the 'sturdy wooden table with strong leather straps' techniques. You get my drift? Would you have *any* reference materials where you might dig up *anything* of possible use for anesthesia? Any mention of plants or other substances we haven't already thought of? Maybe simple chemical processes we're capable of duplicating? Anything?"

"Why not use opium poppies?" Hockley said with a casual shrug.

"Well, yes—something we could grow would be ideal. But we'd have to have some of the plants, or seeds, or scion-stock or whatever. That's our problem. Maybe you could find some mention of an opium substitute that we could obtain locally …"

Hockley got up from his desk, rummaged in a footlocker which contained— among other items Tom chose not to notice – two bongs, *The Anarchist's Cookbook,* and an inflatable sex doll—and eventually produced a cigar box containing a floppy disc, a pill bottle, and a half-dozen small bottles of commercial spices.

"Here ya go, man. I can't guarantee all the seeds, either for viability or potency, but I bet at least some will do the job."

"You've lost me. Seeds for what? And what's the floppy disc?"

"Poppies.org—I copied it off to diskette while the internet was still up. I was just surfing around, like always, and came across it and I'm like 'Whoa, Man—cool!' Tells you anything you wanna know about opium poppies: how to use 'em, how to grow 'em, where to get 'em. Easiest thing in the world.

"Like—you can read this on the diskette—simplest way to use 'em is crush the entire bud, seeds and all, into a fine powder. For each bud-sized batch of powder, pour two cups of boiling water on it, steep the tea for ten to fifteen minutes, add some sour fruit juice or other acid to help leach out the maximum amount of opiates from the poppies, and drink the stuff. Tastes so bitter it's hard to drink. An overdose will kill you, the website warns, so you know it's gotta be good.

"Growing 'em's even easier. They're a hardy wildflower, originally from the area that's now Greece and Turkey, and they grow without any care at all throughout most of the forty-eight states' climate range. Just drop the seeds in the dirt and come back in a few months to harvest the buds."

Tom's mind boggled. This was a *hugely difficult* problem he and Sophie and Mabel and a few other carefully chosen adults had been desperately agonizing over for months. And this goofball kid just shrugs and hands him the answer?

"But the *seeds*! Are these *opium* poppy seeds? Because, you know, there are lots of different kinds of poppies. What we need is the *opium* poppy."

Hockley grinned.

"Gotta love the internet, man. The info was available all along: with the internet, it could no longer be kept secret, that's all.

"Yes, those are opium poppy seeds. Technically, you could always buy them in the U.S.—and technically there was no law against possessing the seeds or even the mature plants: only the plants' opiate sap and products made from it were illegal. But in practice, the Federal drug-goons simply ignored the law's technicalities and used to raid any 'druggie-looking' individuals who bought or sold opium poppy seeds: beat 'em up, trash their homes, perp-walk 'em in shackles for the local TV news—that sort of thing. It played well with The Folks when politicians were up for re-election—and the drug-goons were plenty smart enough to understand that in a choice between helping win re-election versus enforcing the law, as they'd sworn an oath to do, that was not a hard choice at all.

"So that's where divulging secret info came into play. Ever eaten a poppy-seed roll or bagel? The seeds used on those are—yep—the opium variety. Cooking the roll or bagel kills the seeds, though, so what you do is buy the seeds in bulk, uncooked. Just stay away from the shady criminal underground and score your seeds from respectable Capitalist Corporations: McCormick, Watkins, Sauers—all the spice companies—sell jars of poppy seeds along with all their other spices. Drop some on the ground and come back a few months later to harvest the crop. Who knew, eh?

"As word started to get out, the spice companies began trying to sterilize the seeds so they wouldn't germinate. But according to 'poppies.org' they had only partial success. Anyway, even if that had worked, you'd just go down the street from the grocery store to a crafts-and-hobbies supply shop. Those places carry dried flower arrangements, dried wreathes, and similar dried floral stuff—a very frequent component of which is dried opium poppies, including seeds which are perfectly viable.

"I got several jars of spice, then just for fun bought some dried flower arrangements and harvested the seeds. Those are the ones in the pill bottle."

The strange little kid exuded a quiet satisfaction.

"Never bothered growing any—that wasn't the point. I just wanted to beat The System for the hell of it."

He concluded with a calm, defiant pride, handing the cigar box to a dumbfounded Tom, "Fuckemall, man."

Chapter 28

Justice: Social and Personal

When Tom handed over the precious seeds to Sophie, she thought long and hard before she made her way to Judge Parker's imposing brick mansion.

To Mabel's surprise, Sophie asked the Judge for some time with him "on a legal matter." The two of them went into his library, where Sophie showed him the seeds and recounted Tom's meeting with Hockley.

"These right here are the only source of pain-killers we have—or will ever have for generations, most likely," Judge Parker said in wonder, eyeing the ordinary-looking spice bottles on his desk. "These are indescribably valuable."

Sophie smiled a cold, wintry smile.

"You mentioned some legal business. Does it concern these?" he gestured to the spice bottles.

"Indeed it does, Judge. As you've pointed out, those seeds are valuable. *Very* valuable. I want some legal arrangements made concerning the financial benefits which will accrue from those seeds.

"First, I want ownership of the seeds—and all plants, plant-materials, and products derived from them, in perpetuity—to be legally vested in a foundation, with myself as president, Tom as secretary, and Arlene as treasurer. I suggest we call it The Mustard Seed Foundation."

The Judge cast his eye along one of his bookshelves toward his Concordance, but before he could get out of his seat, Sophie continued.

"I had to look it up, too, Judge—pair of heathens that we are. Matthew 13: 31-32: 'Another parable He put forth unto them, saying the kingdom of heaven is like to a grain of mustard seed, which a man took and sowed in his field: Which indeed is the least of all seeds: but when it is grown it is the greatest among herbs, and becometh a tree, so that the birds of the air come and lodge in the branches thereof.'

"Second," she continued, "I want all income received by The Mustard Seed Foundation, for the use of its valuable seeds and plant products, to be disbursed according to this ratio: 1% to 'Mabel's Herbs & Spices' for growing, propagating, harvesting, and processing the plants in question."

The Judge's eyes grew wide.

"*One* percent?"

She sailed on as serenely as a player holding four aces with two more up her sleeve.

"89% to Doc Billings in his capacity as President of a corporation to be established called 'Mountainview Medical Care,' which will provide such care for free, or as nearly so as possible, under the direction of Doc as President, Chief Barley as Secretary, and Arlene, once more, as Treasurer."

"But ..."

"And the remaining 10% to Master Hockley Beener, paid to his parents on his behalf until he becomes of legal age."

He had scarcely had a chance to take a breath when she added her final requirements.

"By accepting a full one percent paid to 'Mabel's Herbs & Spices,' instead of the half-percent I had considered, you agree that your legal work in setting all this up will be done *pro bono*, you agree to teach, *pro bono*, in a soon-to-be-established academic institution, you agree to make your library available for use by students of said institution, and you agree to contribute forty-three dollars silver (one dollar for each year of your legal career—I looked it up) to establish a 'Parker-Beener Scolarship Fund' in said institution for the assistance of needy students."

And with that, she sat back in her comfortable armchair.

There was a silence, as the judge tried to collect himself.

Finally, he said "Well now, Sophie, I have no problems with the general outline of what you propose. You seem to have a very sound plan, and I commend you for it. But we may need to think further about the precise ratios for distributing the profits from these poppy seeds. You see, *one* percent for doing all the work—growing them, propagating them, harvesting them, extracting and processing the sap from them, et cetera—well, that's just not a proposal I could seriously present to Mabel. I'm afraid she wouldn't consider it. Perhaps something more like, oh, say...*ten* percent would be a figure we could take to her."

"We? I'm not taking anything to anybody. You've jotted the numbers down correctly on your legal pad, I see. I'm sure you can use your influence."

As the Judge sat in dumfounded silence, Sophie continued sweetly "Thank Heavens my Tom is willing to use *his* influence with the current owner of those seeds, one Hockley Beener. Hockley thinks the world of Tom, and would do anything Tom suggests. So I feel pretty sure Hockley won't demand ten and three-quarters percent of the profits, leaving only one quarter of a percent for Mabel's Herbs & Spices."

"This is extortion! This…you're…Do you realize, young lady, what you are trying to do here is …"

When the Judge's sputtering had diminished somewhat, Sophie said thoughtfully "Well, I won't be a party to strong-arm tactics of any sort—what you describe as 'extortion.' That sort of thing is just so…so…well, *Capitalistic.* After all, we don't *need* to reach any agreement about the seeds: Hockley and Tom and I can easily grow anything we might need for ourselves in a window-box or two. And, fortunately," she directed a long, ice-cold gaze at the old Judge, "*We're* young and in good health …"

There was a long silence.

"You'd DO it, too, wouldn't you!"

"Life's a bitch," she casually observed.

The Judge writhed in his elegant leather armchair. He twisted this way and squirmed that way and wiggled in yet another direction, his sharp-honed legal mind rapidly running through every conceivable tactic. But he found no alternative.

At last, Sophie gently spoke to him.

"Look, Judge, you did very well indeed in the old world." She indicated the beautifully appointed library with a wave of her hand. "And Mabel already has so many high-profit plants she will do, relatively speaking, even better in the new one. So think of this as merely a graduated income tax: your opportunity to give back something to the worlds, past and present, your family's done so well from."

"Did Brother Stainfuss send you here?"

It was Sophie's turn to be perplexed.

"Stainfuss? No; what's he got to do with it?"

"Oh nothing. I was just thinking back…"

He pondered the grim future awaiting him. "Mabel's going to kill me, you know. She's going to kill me. *One percent*? She's going to *kill* me!"

"Try to stall her till the first crop's harvested—in case you need some of it," Sophie deadpanned.

And they both broke out laughing.

"By *God* you'd have made some lawyer!" the old judge acknowledged, full of admiration for a fellow professional cutthroat.

She smiled. "For a man holding almost no cards, you did everything you possibly could. That's usually the situation we Progressives were in: I wish you'd been an advocate for our side, instead of a judge."

The old man smiled rather sadly, thinking back over his long career.

"Looks like I may yet end up working both sides of the street—on the drugs issue and who knows what else. If you see Brother Stainfuss, tell him I got my answer—however roundabout its delivery may have been."

And with that, and a polite word or two with Mabel about the weather, a slightly puzzled Sophie went on her way, pleased with her morning's work.

At noon three days later, on December 31, the affected parties gathered around Judge Parker's gleaming mahogany dining table to sign the assorted paperwork: setting up The Mustard Seed Foundation and the Mountainview Medical Care Corporation, installing the officers of each entity, formalizing the Beener family's agreement to Hockley's 10% profit share, and the agreement of Mabel's Herbs & Spices for its 1% share, and formalizing Judge Parker's undertakings regarding Sophie's forthcoming restaurant-university.

That evening, their house-guest, Abraham Hite—perhaps fearing a riotous New Year's Eve bacchanal—bid them an early goodnight and withdrew to his bedroom. Tom and Sophie cuddled on the couch in the den with a glass of wine, quietly taking stock of the passing year and marking the arrival of the new one.

"Next week, you know, it will be six months," he said, still struggling to grasp the incomprehensible. "It was on July Fourth those four little home-made nukes caused a mere couple-hundred thousand or so casualties in four cities—a mere pinprick for a nation of 300 million! But enough of a pinprick to pop the nation's economic bubble.

"How fragile our seemingly wealthy world, our house of cards built on financial make-believe, had become! Economic folly on an unprecedented scale, government corruption and incompetence so pervasive and so obvious they produced only a widespread shrug of amused contempt toward the Rulers, incessant foreign adventuring to profit the well-connected and divert the attention of the ignorant, flag-waving masses... Well, hell: with so many straws on the camel's back, how could just one more do any real harm?"

He grinned. "As they said in the Soviet Union, around 1989 ..."

"But, you know," he paused, reflecting, "since today's Great Opium Conference at Judge Parker's I actually see possibilities we might survive – and even a few reasons why a sane person might want to.

"According to people I've talked to who are raising them, our crops and animals appear sufficient to provide us an adequate, palatable diet. It looks like we'll produce enough fiber, leather, and so forth to provide clothing and shoes—and enough medicinal plants and substances to maintain at least a tolerable degree of health care, now with the vital addition of opium.

"We have almost unlimited renewable wood for fuel and building material. And with the steam Gravely looking like it's going to work long-term we have the ability to cut and haul the wood—and do countless other jobs in farmyard, field, and workshop. With the existing steam Gravely to run the generator, we have electric power for our shop equipment, so we can repair broken tools and make new ones, including building more steam engines from the parts of our now-useless gasoline and diesel engines.

"Our social structure seems cohesive, and at our small scale our government can be kept accountable, honest, and efficient. That's a huge advantage we have over the former system, where a professional caste of bureaucratic priest-kings ruled behind closed doors, living in their own private world, thousands of miles removed from their subjects: the 'little people' in flyover-country they regarded with contempt.

"Our newly revamped Mountainview Elementary/Secondary School is re-opening next month, I hear. And thanks to you, we're going to provide higher education, too. So we needn't lose our grip on civilization and slide back into a dark age of feral savagery as many other societies have done throughout history.

"We have substantial arms and ammunition, a well-constructed defensive perimeter, and sufficient trained men to make an attack on Mountainview unappealing to any group except a sizeable military force; and we're far enough off any beaten path to make that highly unlikely—assuming such military forces still exist.

"We have wonderful, helpful, non-threatening neighbors to the south of us—the Amish—and nobody from Grayson on the north has caused any trouble, whatever the situation is there. To the east and west we're protected by steep, forested mountains.

"I expect the rest of our lives, yours and mine, will be spent in…oh…say around 1850 or thereabouts. And that's not so bad. Hell, it's *way* ahead of where most of Africa and other parts of the third world were in 2006. In some ways—socially, culturally, governmentally, even economically—you could make a pretty strong case it's ahead of where the *United States* was in 2006!

"Best of all, I have the most wonderful, intoxicating woman in the world. She's agreed to marry me next week and spend her life with me. And I'm looking forward to that. More than I can tell you. You make life worth living for me."

She clinked her wineglass to his. Her vision was a bit blurred by the moisture in her eyes; and yet she was certain she'd never seen the future so clearly in her life.

Chapter 29
An End – and the Faint Beginnings of New Hope

The day it occurred, Tom knew it would. After all, he'd been concentrating obsessively on the subject, six or seven days a week, since the earliest days of The Collapse, six months ago. He was so quiet and preoccupied when he got up that morning, anticipating it, he didn't notice at first that Sophie was equally grim.

During their near-silent breakfast, awareness dawned on Tom that Sophie and their house-guest, Abraham Hite, were both awaiting the event as fearfully as he was. *Of course*, he realized with a start, *I mentioned it yesterday. Of course they're waiting too.*

"If you can, would you folks want to give me a hand in the shop today? I, ah…there's some cleanup and nuts-and-bolts sorting and that sort of stuff to do. I never get around to doing it. If you've got time…"

And so, after breakfast, the three of them went down to the Gravely shop together, and quietly puttered about, sweeping up, sorting parts, and generally imposing some order on the chaos.

Since near dawn (work started early in Mountainview these days) the noisy rasp of a chainsaw had been carried on the freezing January air to every corner of the village from the racket's origin at Dean Jacobs' log pile on the east edge of town.

At ten forty-seven a.m. (Tom jotted the time in his pocket notebook, in case someone several hundred years in the future might care) the chainsaw racket suddenly stopped.

After the three had waited a few moments it became clear the silence had not been caused by something else – a need to repair or replace a broken saw, or reposition a log, or halt work for some other reason. Unmistakably, in the continuing silence, what they were waiting for had happened.

"Well, I guess that's that," Tom remarked.

When the four little terrorist nukes had detonated on July Fourth, triggering The Collapse, it had taken barely three weeks before people in Mountainview stopped using cars, trucks, full-sized tractors, and similar gas-guzzling machines. Their irreplaceable gasoline was carefully siphoned into 55-gallon drums and gas cans of every sort, to be carefully portioned out, gallon by gallon, to only the most efficient machines available. Other gasoline, obtained a few expensive gallons at a time from Jared's Conoco Handimart or the police department tank, was likewise stored or transferred to Gravely tractors and chainsaws, gallon by precious gallon. The Graveleys, sipping tiny amounts of gas compared to larger machines they replaced, had made it possible to finish up the year's agricultural work under mostly mechanical power.

By late October, with the harvest and threshing completed and agricultural work going dormant for winter, most of the Gravelys had joined Mountainview's cars and trucks, carefully tucked away in permanent storage. The last irreplaceable gallons of gasoline were devoted exclusively to the town's chainsaws to help meet the desperate demand for firewood.

There was no secret about the diminishing amount of gas the woodcutting crews had left. The quiet *chuff, chuff, chuff* of the steam powered Gravely had been going six days a week at the firewood pile, alongside ever-fewer racketing chainsaws, as the last three five-gallon cans of gas diminished to two, and then one, which was then half-full, and then…empty.

When the last chainsaw in use—a Stihl MS260—ran dry at ten forty-seven a.m. on January 11, the town of Mountainview officially returned to the Steam Age.

People throughout the town had been listening: everybody knew somebody on the woodcutting crew, or knew somebody who knew somebody. The bush telegraph had made everyone aware of what was going to happen.

Interestingly, without any planning or forethought whatever, most other people in town did exactly the same thing Tom, Sophie, and Abraham Hite did that morning when the sudden silence hit them. They opened the door and looked out. All over town, the other residents were doing the same thing – yearning for contact with other human beings in the new era they'd just entered, yet surprised to see everyone else in town was doing exactly what they were: opening their doors or windows in the freezing January air and looking out, just to see…other people. Just to not be alone. They waved to each other. Some smiled. Some flashed a V-for-Victory, or a thumbs-up. They stood there for a long moment—scared, embarrassed, self-conscious, frightened, defiant …

And then, with a final wave to neighbors up and down the street, they closed the door or window and went back to their own daily work and their own daily thoughts.

The previous afternoon, Bob Jenkins, delivering a garden cart load of stovewood to the kitchen quarters of Judge Parker's residence, had told Henrietta the maid what a pal of his on the chainsaw crew had told him was going to happen the next day. Henrietta had told her husband, Abner, who'd passed the information on to the Judge that evening while bringing in some wood for the fire in the Judge's study.

The Judge had scoffed when Abner said "Pretty big day tomorrow, don't you think, Suh? Kind of a milestone? More important than a birthin' or a buryin'—looks to me like—cause them things happen every year. But folks say won't be no more gasoline for who knows how long. Why, babies born this year—their great grandchirren's grandchirren might never have no gasoline...never drive a car...mow the grass with a power mower...ordinary things like that. Lordy, Judge...just don't make sense."

The old servant shook his head in perplexity. Such commonplace activities, disappearing for such an unimaginable span of time ...!

"Aw, tomorrow's not the real Milestone, Abner. It doesn't mark some decisive event, some decision taken, a fork in Mankind's road that really counts," Judge Parker had said. "It's merely the day when the last chainsaw uses up the last teaspoon of gasoline."

But later, alone in his study, the Judge had thought to himself: Dates...Milestones... On which *day*, exactly, did the Roman Empire "fall?" Before noon or after? At which hour and minute? Silly. Forget tomorrow as a Milestone for our own age: there are far more significant dates to choose.

Why not August 15, 1971, when Nixon broke the dollar's last restraining link to gold, thereby disabling the 'off' switch of the FED's printing presses, ensuring that they (like the mad, runaway brooms in *The Sorcerer's Apprentice*) took on a crazed, unstoppable life of their own. Now *that* was a historical milestone: it made tomorrow's event inevitable, given time.

Or why not pick November, 1910, and the founding, in deepest secrecy, of the FED itself: *The Creature From Jekyll Island*, as that book title so eerily termed it. For once the Federal Reserve System had been put in place, the days were numbered for anything placing limits on paper dollar creation.

Tomorrow's random date, he mused, will scarcely merit a footnote compared to those truly momentous Milestones which made our coming chainsaw-halt inevitable.

And yet, despite himself, the old Judge listened in his study all the next morning. And when the predicted silence hit him it hit with totally unexpected force. He sat in his big leather chair, Volume IX of Toynbee's *Study of History* lying unseen before him, ambushed by a wave of emotion that took him by surprise. And then he got up and walked over to a bookshelf on the opposite wall, reaching up far over his head for the book he believed he sought.

"Yes …" he muttered, consulting the index, talking softly, as old men will mutter to themselves.

He shuffled back to his desk with the book. "After all this time… Well, the least we can do is make sure we get the name and date correct for what is perhaps the *real* milestone that made today's event inevitable.

"Edward, Viscount Gray of Falloden, British Foreign Secretary, August 3, 1914: the eve of the War to End All War. The War to Make the World Safe for Democracy. The War that ripped the guts out of Western Civilization—not just culturally but, more relevant to today's event, economically.

"For it was that war's mutual economic suicide that made it politically impossible to continue the gold standard which had worked impeccably for centuries. All the governments of the 'Civilized' World—driven to desperation by their war costs, and by the popular pressures on them for ever-expanding government services, by the democratic forces the War had unleashed—eventually abandoned fully gold-backed money and took up the wanton printing of paper scrip, backed by less and less and less—and eventually by nothing.

"Gray's 1914 epitaph for Western Civilization was early—farsighted men tend to be—and it was surely broader than even he knew when he uttered it. But the sudden silence that began a few minutes ago bears out his judgment."

The old man read softly to himself, lips moving, a mottled forefinger tracing the line on the page: *"The lamps are going out all over Europe; we shall not see them lit again in our lifetime."*

He sat silently—an old man in no hurry—long past the point in life when this or that pressing concern seemed so urgent.

"Gray. Foreign Secretary. 1914.

"I'll have to work that into the course that damn woman wants me to teach in her restaurant. Completely pointless, of course. The ignorant little shits have no time or interest for the yammerings of some Dead White European Male they never heard of, from back in 1914. After all, they have to deal somehow with the fact that to avoid freezing or starving now in Mountainview they must cut, split, and deliver…oh…at least a *ton* of firewood *daily* I suppose? With almost no mechanical assistance."

240

And he signed, and marked the passage from Edward Gray with a small slip of scrap paper, and gazed absently out the study's window at the now-silent town for a long time before turning back to Toynbee in his patient search for the answer to a single question: *Why?*

Weeks before the last gas chainsaw died, Tom had realized he needed an assistant to operate the steam powered Gravely. Owen would have been the most knowledgeable candidate but he was more than fully occupied with Invincible, dragging felled trees from the surrounding forests to the four wood-piles around the edge of Mountainview, where they lay waiting to be cut and split for firewood.

Casting his mind over who might be available for the engine-operator job—someone capable but not already fully committed in Mountainview's now-typical sixty-to-seventy-hour workweek—Tom glumly concluded that anyone capable was not available, and no one available would be capable. As usual, he took his lament to Sophie. And as usual, she resolved his problem, casually tossing him the solution without even breaking her stride as she pressed on with problems of her own.

"Have Tim do it. Look: Barley's giving me a stall job on the course we've agreed he'll teach. I think he's just afraid of standing at the head of a class—simple public-speaking stage fright. You know him: what's the best way to put the whip to him?"

"*Tim?*" Tom thought it over. The engine-operator's job required moving cut pieces of firewood to the steam engine, monitoring the engine's water and steam gauges, adding water and stoking the firebox as necessary to maintain the water levels and steam pressures within prescribed limits, ensuring there was adequate oil in the engine's oil reservoir, and occasionally using an oilcan to lubricate specified external points on the engine and the attached saw. Tim's missing leg would not make the job impossible for him: it would be the perfect opportunity for him to join the men in the firewood crew, doing work he was fully capable of "right in the middle of things" where he always wanted to be.

"You're a genius!"

"Genius, ha. That's the term for somebody who can make Barley commit—in writing, signed in blood—to February Twenty-eighth: opening day for classes. I really am getting frantic, Tom. Eight students are signed up for 'Democracy: Athens' Gift to Mountainview'. What am I going to do when the Twenty-eighth rolls around?"

"You say you and Barley 'agreed' he'd teach the course? Could you be a bit more specific about the agreement itself?"

Very quietly, through clenched teeth, she clarified. "We agreed it would be less painful for him to teach a course than to have his lungs pulled out through his nostrils, inch at a time, using a rusty fish hook and needle nosed pliers. At least, when I put it to him in that light, he didn't argue the contrary position—so for all practical purposes that's effectively an agreement."

"Yeah. I kind of thought so."

Tom sighed, considering the options. "Look, I'll pull *your* lungs out if you tell him where this came from—but here's a suggestion. Offer him the option of teaching a more contemporary, more 'relevant' course if he'd prefer. Explain there's been a lot of interest shown about issues concerning the extent of Government's rightful powers to enforce zoning-type local ordinances: requirements to screen eyesores on private property from the public view, privacy fences around junkyards or garbage dumps, that sort of thing. See if he'd rather cover that topic than 'Athens' gift to Mountainview,' and offer to change the course if he'd like.

"But," Tom fixed upon her the Evil Eye, full strength, "if he *ever* finds out where this came from, you're dead. And I'll have Brother Stainfuss officiate at the funeral. And I'll tell the righteous brother your last wish was to bequeath him the university, to be renamed 'Foursquare Bible College."

His "Southern" was impeccable: "fo'squa Babble Colludge."

He could see her grow visibly pale.

"I swear to God, Tom: I'll never let on," she said very softly, her demeanor indicating a gratifying amount of horror. "I won't even ask any questions about anything, OK? Because I don't even want to know anything about anything, OK? It was just a random idea that popped into my head, right? But, look, Tom…when I die…"

She gulped. "Brother Stainfuss…'Foursquare Bible College'…"

He let her stew a moment, to make certain his point was taken. In measured tones, giving the matter its full weight, he stated "Well. Let us hope things don't reach that pass."

And so, to Tim's unspeakable delight, he had become engine-operator for the steam Gravely at the town's firewood-cutting sites. Six days a week, in the pre-dawn gray darkness, he arrived at Tom's shop, fired the Gravely's boiler, coupled the machine to a cart, and drove off to the site on that day's Gravely schedule. He then coupled the Gravely to the wood saw, assembled a day's worth of boiler fuel close to hand, checked lubrication points, and was ready for continuous operation till early afternoon.

The other workers at each site, typically fifteen to twenty men carrying axes, wedges, and splitting mauls, a couple of two-man saws, even assorted pruning saws and similar garden tools, arrived just after dawn.

Their spirits were always lifted on the day the steam Gravely appeared at their site to help them. The steam power at least tripled their output of firewood on that day, compared to what they could achieve manually. Hour after hour, the men muscled logs into the Gravely's spinning saw blade, then used mauls and wedges to split the rounds the tree trunks were sawed into, then hauled loads of the split wood off in garden carts for delivery to homeowners, or to storage in garages for additional drying if necessary.

Since The Collapse last summer, the wood-scouts had concentrated on locating and hauling to town all the standing-dead trees and any unrotted downed timber for a mile or so around Mountainview. People had been lucky: for this first, terrible winter such sources were providing a barely sufficient amount of usably dry firewood. Subsequent supplies, harvested from trees that had been girdled and left to dry standing, would furnish ample amounts of seasoned wood for future years—if the huge amounts of labor required proved sustainable over the long run.

Any people in Mountainview who had their own land generally cut their own firewood, but the rest of the townspeople bought theirs—mostly from the four biggest firewood-dealers. Each of these dealers was in fact an extended family, whose members owned fairly large acreages of what had been low-value mountainside timber. Each family had sent its own tree-felling crews with chainsaws to fell selected firewood trees, buck off the limbs, and use ropes to drag manageable-sized pieces of the limbs back to town, where they were cut up and sold. Then each family paid the police department 1.5 ounces of pure silver (about $2.10 in face value of 90% silver coin) per ten-hour day for the services of Owen and Invincible to skid the tree trunks and large limbs to their family's woodpile on the edge of town. There, the chainsaw crews and splitting crews turned the logs into usable fireplace and stove-wood.

Each of the four wood-dealers paid Tom one ounce of pure silver (about $1.40 face value in 90% silver coin) plus the necessary boiler-fuel for a day's services of his steam Gravely, which he rotated among the four different wood-lots, spending a day at each in turn. Tom paid his machine-operator, Tim Baker, a daily wage of just over 1/5th ounce of silver: 30 cents in 90% silver coin. For the men working at the wood-lots – moving tree trunks, sawing and splitting them, pushing full garden carts of the split wood all over town for delivery—the typical day's pay was also 30 cents in silver coin, plus a pair of heavy leather gloves and a warm jacket, if needed, and a steaming-hot bowl of pinto bean or split-pea soup and a hunk of buttered cornbread with jam or preserves.

Mountainview residents who bought their heating and cooking fuel, delivered, for about $2.00 face value in 90% silver coin per cord complained, naturally, about the extortionate prices they had to pay, and threatened to quit doing so. In fact everyone involved at every stage in the process—the police department which rented Owen and Invincible's services, Tom who furnished the steam Gravely and engine-operator, and the hired hands who provided their labor—swore the compensation paid them was totally inadequate, and threatened to quit. And all four major firewood dealers howled that after paying all their costs they were losing money on every stick of wood they sold, and they too threatened to quit.

It was, in short, a superbly efficient free-market system for distributing the energy resources that kept Mountainview alive.

Each afternoon, when the winter light began to wane at four o'clock, firewood cutting at the wood-lots halted for the day. Tim uncoupled the saw and drove the Gravely and cart back to the shop, where his own workday ended and Tom's began.

Coupling the engine to the shop's generator, Tom made power to run his electric lights and shop machinery as he worked doggedly through the night into the early morning hours. With agonizing slowness, piece by piece, he was machining from scratch the parts he would need to eventually create a second steam engine from an assortment of gasoline engine bits and pieces he had selected. He was desperate to complete the second steam engine, to permanently power his shop's generator, so the steam Gravely could be freed up for use throughout Mountainview and the surrounding fields when farming and related outdoor work resumed in spring.

In the early, pre-dawn hours each morning, Tom would end his workday, carefully check the steam Graveley's lubrication and do any other needed servicing, bank the fire in the engine's firebox, and trudge upstairs to bed, leaving the machine ready for Tim to collect before dawn for the new day's firewood cutting.

As they used the last few gallons of gasoline in their chainsaws (God, how quickly *those* had been able to cut wood!) the people of Mountainview understood the coming month or two was going to be make-or-break. Either they would somehow manage to produce a sufficient amount of fuel by hand and with the steam Gravely to heat their homes and cook their food...or they wouldn't. With daily highs in the teens, dropping to nighttime lows below zero, no one had any doubt what the consequences of failure would be.

They were helped immensely in that first crucial winter by any home heating oil they'd already had in their furnace tanks, and propane in their propane tanks, and stored firewood in their woodpiles when The Collapse hit. They had made the best possible use of their gasoline, fueling the dozens of chainsaws they'd been operating since The Collapse. And they wore layers of sweaters and coats in their cold houses, most of the rooms closed off, as families congregated by the kitchen stove until it was time for bed—to sleep in freezing bedrooms beneath a mountain of blankets.

The town's three churches quietly kept an eye out for any of their members who might need a bit of fuel to help get them through the winter, and the Citizens' Patrol deputies likewise discretely monitored the town for any potential problem cases. There were a few people, mostly aged, who woke up some mornings to discover a pile of firewood had somehow materialized in their front or back yard overnight. And there were some other people (younger, usually with kids) who were approached privately by their pastor or Chief Barley with the news that a job had just opened up for the next few weeks at the church, or the police station, or one of the firewood dealers—which by chance happened to involve exactly whatever skills it was thought the person in question might possess.

No one in Mountainview had ever lived through such a cold, frightening time of seemingly endless hardship.

But no one froze that winter, or ate his food raw.

And as an even more bitter February replaced the freezing cold of January, people in Mountainview became filled with a deep, growing pride in themselves. Slowly, gradually, it was becoming clear they were going to make it, at least as far as heating and cooking fuel were concerned: their production was holding even with consumption.

The firewood cutting crews, starting their brutally hard work shifts six days a week, in the winter's zero or subzero dawn, could eventually cut back to five days a week. Morale soared, and all over town people who had been virtually holding their breath gave a huge sigh of relief. Allowing two days off work reduced the amount of exhaustion and therefore the risk of terrible injury for the men moving heavy tree trunks and working with axes, saws, and splitting mauls in the numbing cold.

They were very lucky, too. In the past few weeks, Bill Stott had lost half the ring-finger on his left hand, pinched off between a steel pry-bar and a suddenly shifting log ("about as neat as I could have done it" Doc Billings commented, shaking his head as he applied a dressing). And two other men had lain in bed for several anxious, terrible days, lacking X-ray facilities, until it became clear their ankles were only badly sprained, not fractured. There had been some mild cases, and several worse scares, involving frostbitten fingers, ears, and noses. And many of the men had put a decade's worth of abuse on their knees and backs during the past few months—something they would pay for in rapid ageing during their coming years.

But no one in Mountainview froze that winter, or ate his food raw.

"I think we're going to make it, as far as firewood's concerned," Tom reported to Sophie as he stumbled up to bed one morning about two a.m. during the first week of February. "You just can't overestimate the benefits in morale, and the reduced likelihood of injury, now that we can give the firewood crews two days off each week. I think we're going to make it."

And he fell asleep as he was talking.

She didn't wake him to finish removing his pants. Instead, she simply made sure his shoes were off, then covered him warmly with the feather comforter and promised herself she would deal with him however she had to the next day. There was no question he had to reduce his own hours in the shop to a sustainable level. It was simply a matter of deciding which, of a wide array of possible threats available to her, would prove most effective. She lay beside him, considering.

Chief Barley had seemed gratifyingly appalled when she raised the possibility of changing his university course to something about property zoning and privacy fences around junkyards—or whatever peculiar nonsense it was Tom had suggested. Perhaps there just might be enough leverage left in that threat, whatever it was, to conscript Barley into leaning on Tom to cut back Tom's hours—a reverse-bank-shot she rather fancied.

What was it about men, she lay there wondering, that made them incapable of doing what any woman could see was obviously the right thing—until a woman taught them that resistance was futile?

Chapter 30
Genius – In its Wildly Varied Forms

"Oh hell yeah: brilliant. I'll give you that, in spades. Damned genius, for all I know. I'm just saying she's touched, Tom. Happens with geniuses—what I hear. They just, you know, sort of lose *contact,* so to speak…"

Tom sighed his agreement. Chief Barley wasn't telling him anything he hadn't figured out for himself months ago. The two friends sat in the far corner of Tom's shop, talking quietly enough they hoped Sophie upstairs wouldn't hear them—not *hiding,* exactly, but…well…her "Honey-Do" lists were as extensive as her range of volunteer "Honeys" was lengthy, and neither man needed additional assignments at the moment. They sat, commiserating in buffaloed silence, studying the coals glowing in the potbelly stove.

"Well. I think the key to it is this wretched 'university' bee in her bonnet. Look: you've gotta come up with some line of bullshit about 'Athenian democracy: a gift to Mountainview' to get her off your case. I think I know just the person can help in that regard. Let me see what Hockley can come up with on his computer. He's got *Encyclopedia Britannica* you know, among other things, and I bet he could print you off a six-inch-thick pile of crapola and all you'd have to do is skim through it, highlight some of it, and stand there in her damn 'university' reading it like you made it all up yourself. Eh? How's anyone gonna know—Hockley won't tell."

"Jesus. That kid's even crazier than Sophie! He flat-out scares me. Lemme tell ya, Tom: we got some genyouwine cases runnin' loose in *this* town!"

The Chief thought a bit.

"But—since you mention it – there just might be something to the idea. The *other* crusade she's on is that I should make you do less work on your steam engine. Can you believe it? Like I'm gonna tell you how to spend your time? She's gonna blame *me* because *you're* working on a steam engine? I gotta tell you this, Tom: you married a woman who's not altogether stable.

"But anyway…if you make a big enough deal about spending time with Hockley, working with him and me on her 'university' stuff—blah, blah, blah—

247

then maybe she'll get off my case about you working on the steam engine all the time. I mean…if that's what it takes …"

Tom could see the sense in this.

"Mmmm. You may have a point. In fact…I may know just the thing to get her so worked up over her 'university' fixation she'll leave us both the hell alone for a while. Al Platt still got that monster seventy-two inch TV of his? That he was able to watch for about three weeks before television ended?"

"Far's I know. What's that got to do with anything?"

"Look at it this way: at Sophie's 'university' the speakers are going to need some way of illustrating various points they make. Can't very well say 'look at the picture on page fifty-six of your textbook' because we don't have multiple copies of most textbooks. But if we can find even one copy of a picture—in a book or any other place, anywhere in Mountainview—Hockley can scan that picture into his computer, then run it from the computer to a huge TV screen in the front of the class, and shazzam: there's a big picture of the Acropolis or Parthenon or whatever, for the whole class to see."

"Yeah? They can do that nowdays?"

"Hell yes. Hockley knows how, and he's got all the computer stuff he'll need. We just need the donation of a really big TV screen to put at the front of the classroom. Like that set Al's not going to watch a Superbowl on for the next several hundred years. Which is just taking up space in his house. Which we'd be doing him a favor if we offered him a hand moving it.

"Then, anybody teaching a course just tells Hockley what sort of pictures or graphs or whatever he'd like for illustrations, and no matter where something might be, if there's a single copy available anywhere in town, Hockley puts it in the computer. And there you go: displayed for the whole class to see. Or in the case of music, for the whole class to hear."

Barley thought a moment in silence. Then he saw the weak point in the plan.

"*Hockley* scouts these things up? From all over town? I never seen him leave his house. Which, frankly, is fine with me—I mean…talk about *weird* …"

Tom considered a moment. And then the inspiration dawned. He displayed the slow smile of contentment, the gently patronizing amusement inevitable when the superior mind of a Holmes confronts the spectacle of an earnestly plodding Dr. Watson trying to keep up.

"Just leave it to me."

He stretched, luxuriating in the sheer abstract perfection of his crystallizing plan: it's starkly elegant simplicity combined with its awesomely stunning effectiveness.

"You see, Chief—let me put it this way: to deal with women you've got to be able to *understand* them. It just takes a certain…well…let me say experience plays a part in it…but there's also a basic, innate *ability* I doubt can ever be acquired if you're not born with it. I'm going to solve all your problems with Sophie, *and* solve Al's problem about what to do with that useless monster TV of his, *and* solve Sophie's problems about what to do with all the excess energy she's got, *and* solve my own problem of being left in peace so I can get a steam engine built—*and*, in the meantime, out of the sheer goodness of my heart, solve a certain young man's problems that I can sympathize with because, hell, who hasn't had problems of that kind?

"Finesse, Chief, that's really all it takes: just a matter of experience…knowing women and how best to work them around till they're delighted to do whatever you want them to do. Leave it to me."

"You? *You* know about women? *YOU?* "

This last was said in a tone which, to Tom's ear, suggested the Chief might feel somewhat less than total confidence in Tom's fitness for his self-assigned mission.

Rising from his seat, Tom clapped the other man forgivingly on the shoulder, manly decency requiring no less, and said gently "Couple days, Chief—shouldn't take much longer than that."

Walking back to the Station in a fuddled daze, Barley kept shaking his head and muttering to himself. That damned crazy woman…and the kid Hockley, who, if possible, was even crazier than she was…and now Tom Jeffson, of all people on this planet, suddenly thinks he's an expert on *women*?

"I gotta get outta here!" the Chief muttered in desperation.

Tom, bathed in the warm glow of genius humming on all cylinders, strode confidently through the little town in a slightly different direction, toward the Fludd residence. And even as he walked, he savored the way genius can solve one problem after another, effortlessly, even down to the smallest operational details.

"The Next Generation"—that's the term he would use, thereby demonstrating the finesse, the inborn savoir faire, with which the sophisticate moves effortlessly through life, leaving a trail of worldly charm in his wake from salon to…to…well, not *exactly* boudoir, in this case, but, still, the point was …

The point *was* that to ask for "Myna Fludd" would endear him to her painfully straight parents, but at the cost of permanently alienating the young woman herself. And yet to ask for "Starshine" would endear him to the young woman in question at the cost of permanently alienating her parents.

"The Next Generation!" He chuckled, turning onto Hickory. How easy finesse came, to those with a basic gift for it.

And how necessary an ability in the present case, he soberly reminded himself. For Herbert and Martha Fludd, land surveyor and housewife respectively, were of the absolutely straightest, most devotedly square, bourgeois, middleclass sensibilities Tom had ever encountered. While their fifteen-year-old daughter— The Next Generation, in Tom's brilliantly neutral phrase—was determined to be "Starshine": fullblown hippie earthchild from the Summer of Love, born 3000 miles from the Haight-Ashbury, and forty-some years too late—but not the least bit deterred by that.

Starshine, one of those rare genetic "sports," or throwbacks to the genetic makeup of some far-distant branch of the family tree, had taken after her Aunt Maxie, now aged sixty-one, who was physically as close to the Fludds (two streets over, on Walnut) as she was ideologically remote. For Aunt Maxie— a frightening example of Bad Seed and a humiliating cross to be borne through life by Herbert and Martha Fludd—was an unreformed, unregenerate, unrepentant, actually was-*there*-when-it-was-all-going-down HIPPIE.

In 21st century Mountainview, West Virginia, Tom reflected, Aunt Maxie – still groovin' to the Sixties' beat of The Haight—admittedly did stand out a bit. And her influence on her worshipful young disciple, Starshine, promised to extend Herb and Martha Fludd's shame and agony about their only child's misguided course even unto the parents' grave and beyond.

Moments after his knock, the Fludd's door popped swiftly open to reveal both females, slightly breathless. Apparently his knock had set off a genteel footrace, each contestant expecting some visitor of her own— certainly neither of them imagining Tom.

"Hi, Mrs Fludd." (Warm, confident smile for the lady of the house. Warm smile plus nod for the daughter.) "I wonder if I could ask you—and The Next Generation (second, smaller nod, same warm smile)—if you could help my wife a little bit promoting education."

"Oh, Tom! It's good to see you! Come in, come in. Education? Why that certainly seems like a Good Thing. Here, have a seat. Would you like some milk – I've just taken a pan of cookies out of the oven…"

Tom pantomimed a life-threatening need for milk and cookies. Martha, fussily adjusting her apron over her print dress and patting her hair, bustled into the kitchen. The blue-jeaned Next Generation rolled its fifteen-year-old eyes, sighed wearily from the very depth of its soul, and sank, utterly without hope, into a living room chair, one Doc-Martens-booted-foot slung casually over the chair's arm.

Good. Can't resist hanging around to see what's up…curious about what ole' Tom has in mind. Ha! *Women* ...

"Here we are! Oh, be sure to take one of these, too. Would you care for one, *Myna*?"

"KWAAAK!" uttered The Next Generation, rolling its eyes yet another notch.

But then, to ensure the effect was not lost: "A mynah is a *bird*, mother. Do you have any *idea* what that grease and sugar are doing to you?"

Turning to Tom, to maintain the confidentiality of the diagnosis: "It affects her brain." Shrug of pity, mixed with helplessness.

Yikes, thought Tom, sitting between them. *Anyone with less savoir faire than I, in a situation this fraught…*

"Well! Brains! The very thing that makes us human! You probably know my wife, Sophie, plans to use the new restaurant as a location for classes. All sorts of subjects…whatever people might be interested in learning about…expanding our minds …

"But there's going to be a need for illustrations—pictures, graphs, that sort of thing—to accompany some of the courses. And also a need to present things like music or movies in some of the other courses. We need someone to collect such material from wherever it might be scattered all over Mountainview. As we track down what's available, we can provide each item—picture, music, movie, whatever—to Hockley Beener, for him to put on computer. Then the original item's returned to its owner and the copy stored in Hockley's computer can be used to help with teaching classes.

"I told Sophie you'd be the perfect people to help us. I'll bet that you, Mrs Fludd, would have plenty of music you'd be willing to loan us for copying. And who better than Mountainview's own Next Generation to find other items scattered throughout the town and take them briefly to Hockley for copying? These materials, you know, are now irreplaceable."

He reached for yet another of Martha's cookies, smiling appreciatively toward her. Turning, he dangled a perfectly crafted piece of bait toward The Next Generation: "It's a matter of transmitting the cultural *Values* each of us holds most deeply."

Neither Martha Fludd (disciple of Martha Stewart) nor The Next Generation (disciple of Aunt Maxie) ever had a chance. The deal was done forthwith.

Martha excitedly headed upstairs to make sure all eighteen boxes of her *Longines Symphonett* cassettes and all twenty-two boxes of her *101 Strings Perform the Big Bands' Biggest Hits* were ready to lend to Hockley. Starshine excitedly headed for Aunt Maxie's house, to enlist her guru in this grand opportunity to actually Make a Difference in Mountainview's Level of Awareness. And Tom contentedly strolled toward his next meeting, reflecting on how easy things are, really, for those who have the gift…the inborn…*ability*… to let women find their deepest fulfillment in pleasing the rare sort of man who effortlessly understands them.

For the first time in his life, Tom wished he owned a smoking jacket: something in a tastefully light burgundy—corduroy, of course – but with just a touch of velvet facing on the lapels and collar. He strode purposefully along the sidewalk.

Al Platt's house was on the way across town to the Beeners.' Al, typically small-minded, held out for a free meal at the restaurant in exchange for his giant TV, but that deal was also soon concluded. From there it was only two more blocks to the Beeners' house.

Tom explained to Hockley about Chief Barley's need for "research assistance" involving printing out anything Hockley might have concerning Athenian Democracy and its imaginary relevance for modern government. To encourage Hockley's more enthusiastic cooperation, Tom explained that what would be involved was outright plagiarism of the rankest, rawest, most inexcusable sort. That did the trick.

Then Tom explained the plan to load every cultural artifact available in Mountainivew into the computer, partly for use as needed in the university, but mainly for the safekeeping of such irreplaceable material.

"Basically, I want you to create on your computer here Mountainview's own version of the Library of Congress, or antiquity's great Library of Alexandria: a repository of every obtainable intellectual, cultural, and artistic achievement of Mankind—to be kept safely in trust by the present generation, and passed on as the inheritance of those to come.

Hockley was, as expected, bored by such a trivial task. Tom was undeterred.

"Now of course the problem's going to be tracking down every suitable item we have, anywhere in Mountainview. There's…what…eighty-five or so homes here…plus stuff in attics, basements, barns, garages…We're talking about all significant photographs and paintings, in books or elsewhere; all music on records (78, 45, and 33 rpm) and on reel-to-reel recordings, or even wire recordings for all I know, and on 8-tracks and cassette tapes and on CDs; movies on eight mm or sixteen mm film, video tape and DVD...You can see how tracking down and borrowing all this material is going to be a big job. So I've got you some help. Best person I know for finding stuff here in town, no matter where it might be stashed away: Starshine."

Hockley's eyes widened, his pulse picked up, his breathing quickened and became shallow. This was so easy. Tom cruised effortlessly on, closing the deal.

"Yep. If you'll take on the job, you two will have to work out how you're going to proceed. You decide how you're going to categorize and index the material, arrange your priorities as to types of items you want for copying, let her know what schedule you can maintain so she can return materials without undue delay—all those sorts of issues. She's about the best there is when it comes to finding things in every out-of-the-way nook and cranny of Mountainview. Think you two can handle this?"

"Starshine..." was all Hockley could manage, breathing heavily, gulping and nodding as he gazed worshipfully at Tom.

Answering Sophie's inquiry at supper that evening, Tom was elaborately casual.

"Nah," he commented offhandedly, "I've been taking a break from the shop for a while. Doing some other stuff. Chief pointed out I've been spending an awful lot of time lately working on the steam engine, and I think he's got a point. I'm helping him put together his course for the university: doing some research, that kind of thing. It's going quite well. Hockley's a great help. I got to admit your choice there was perfect for the university."

Sophie gave him a huge smile of gratitude and encouragement. She wondered what, exactly, Tom was up to. Did he actually think, for one moment, he was going to put something over?

Then, to her surprise, there was still more.

"Oh, speaking of the university: Hockley and I were working out a way to use a huge TV screen in the front of the room to present anything lecturers might need for their courses: pictures, graphs, music, movies, whatever. Hockley's going to put all that sort of thing into his computer, then you can display it on the TV in the university as required."

After which (as if all this sensible cooperation did not strain her credulity) Sophie was surprised to learn there was still more.

"By the way—ran into that Fludd girl: 'Starshine' the hippie. Did you know Hockley's absolutely goofy about her? Don't tell him I told you, of course: it's a sworn secret between us guys. He's too scared to speak to her, goes without saying. Anyway, she's big on natural health, physical fitness, organic wellness—all that crap—and wouldn't you know: she jogs out to the creekside and back almost every day, right past the Beeners' house.

"Well, poor ol' Hock: he's just sitting there in his bedroom with his computers all day long, pining away from sheer lust and frustration. So, Mrs Jeffson, your university's going to benefit from one of Man's most primal needs: I fixed it up for Starshine to locate and borrow every cultural/artistic item we have in Mountainview, and take each one to Hockley for scanning before she returns them. Hockley'll gladly work on the project twenty-five hours a day, if it means a chance for contact with Starshine."

Sophie bathed her husband in warm appreciation, effusive congratulations for his helpfulness, confessions of feminine awe at the brilliance of his manly competence—while wondering quietly now what, exactly, does he think *he's* up to?

Tom leaned back from the supper table, contentedly accepting the accolades his genius was due. Women, he mused, with a wry, worldly smile: you gotta love the simple hearted little creatures.

In fact, Starshine really was just as much of a genius at locating things as Hockley was in transferring them to computer files. With Aunt Maxie's guidance, Starshine had for years been combing every part of Mountainview and its surroundings for "back to the good earth" treasures to furnish the private little reality in which the two hippies dwelt.

Whether it was locating long-forgotten wool-carding brushes or old-time spinning and weaving equipment, packed away in a barn or attic by earlier generations, or turning up footlockers full of grubby, mildewed old books ("antiquarian volumes" as Starshine and Maxie thought of them) or talking dubious housewives into allowing her free access to their basements to search for vats or tinctures or notes having to do with early settlers' natural, plant-based dyes—Starshine was a whiz at turning up deeply buried junk from long-gone previous generations. She took to the task Tom had offered her with an aptitude that was breathtaking.

Perhaps it was the slowly gathering rays of hope in Mountainview that February—the relief that their basic fuel needs could be met, and the town's cultural resources could be preserved for the long run—that made the sudden violence in late February all the more terrible. After the initial shock, no person in Mountainview could escape the continuing feelings of dread—for how many more such horrors might lie ahead, to explode into sudden death equally without warning?

Chapter 31
Death—In Hot Blood and Cold

The steam Gravely was scheduled for Dean Jacobs' wood pile that bitter late-February day. Broken thick clouds hung low, seeming almost pregnant, in the dim gray sky.

Tim had arrived at the site on the southeast edge of town just before sunrise, as usual. Leaving the Gravely parked, flames glowing cheerfully in the firebox, boiler gently hissing as it vented steam, he began gathering up a day's fuel-wood ready to hand, tossing especially dry, convenient-sized chunks of hardwood into the cart still attached to the machine. He waited to be told which of several huge logs were next to be cut up before moving the Gravely into position, detaching the cart, and attaching the saw-blade. The wood-lot contained a dozen or so tree trunks, some nearly three feet in diameter, strewn about haphazardly. The first dozen or so men began arriving, slapping their gloved hands and stamping their feet, breath steaming in the bitter cold.

A rifle shot rang out through the frozen air, sounding as if it were not more than six feet away.

"What the hell?!" It was not deer hunting, at this hour. Men stared about in alarm, looking in all directions.

"Look! There!"

Marv Fisher pointed southeastward, directly into the blinding glare of the rising sun, at a small group of figures about seventy-five yards away. They had just emerged from the tree-line at the far edge of a field and were running across the snow-covered field toward the wood lot. They were all armed, but they carried their weapons at their sides as they rushed forward in the attack. The shot, the woodcutters now realized, had come as a warning from the Citizens Patrol lookout post, also on the edge of town but one block to the side of the wood-lot.

The warning shot did not slow the band's assault across the frozen field. The town's lookout fired a second shot, this time aimed for effect. The astonished woodcutters saw one of the attackers spin around and fall, but then get back up and continue his rush, apparently hit but not seriously wounded. That man called out something, and two of the attackers paused, knelt, and fired at the group of woodcutters, apparently the only targets they presently had. The men who had fired then rushed forward while two other men in front paused, knelt, and fired repeatedly toward the wood crew and also toward where they supposed the Citizens Patrol lookout to be.

Sustained rifle fire then began in the distance, and the wood-cutters now saw at least two more figures hidden in the treeline at the far edge of the field, providing covering fire for their attacking comrades. Bullets thocked into the tree trunks as the woodcutters dived behind them.

"Get out of here! Head back to the shop!" Marv screamed at Tim, and threw some large pieces of wood in the back of the Gravely cart.

Tim hopped into the front of the cart, opened the throttle wide, and began lumbering across the frozen dirt back toward the center of town, steam whistle held down in a continuous shriek that would have awakened the dead.

The woodcutters lay on the snow and frozen dirt behind tree trunks in the jumble of the wood-lot. The attackers— six men coming, all armed—were now within forty yards. The woodcutters, dispersed across the wood-lot, were pinned down by the gunfire behind logs big enough to hide them. They gripped their axes and other tools and waited.

The Citizens Patrol lookout hit another of the attackers, this time putting him down. The remaining five, alternately rushing forward and covering each other in the most basic but brutally effective infantry squad tactic, advanced to within 30 feet of the wood-lot. At that point it was impossible for the Citizens Patrol lookout to continue firing from his position a block away: there were now Mountainview houses behind the attackers in his line of fire.

"Stay hidden. I'll holler at the right moment. Then kill the bastards," Marv whispered to his fellow workers, peering around the end of his log, watching the advance of the attackers. The dozen workmen, unarmed but for their axes and other tools, swallowed hard and nodded, hoping they could at least injure some of the armed men before being shot.

And then the attackers made their first really stupid move. They all made their final rush into the wood-lot in unison, instead of leaving some behind to provide covering fire and keep the workmen pinned down.

"NOW!"

At the moment the attackers reached the wood-lot, workmen leapt up from behind the jumble of logs, swinging frantically with axes, mauls, sticks—

anything they had—hitting back at the five gunmen from all directions.

Rich Albertson, with his double-bitted ax, lopped a leg clean off one of the attackers coming over a log just as the attacker gut-shot him. The two men fell together, screaming and beating at each other with ax handle and rifle butt as the crimson arterial blood spurted from them both for yards across the snow.

Another of the attackers, standing calmly atop a huge log, methodically gunned down three of the wood-cutters before the Citizens Patrol lookout running toward the scene could get off a shot, catching the man in the back and blowing half the man's chest out his front.

The Citizens Patrolman, just as he reached the wood-lot and shot another of the attackers in the thigh, suddenly lurched, stumbled, and went down like a sack of meal, hit in the pelvis by one of the attackers providing supporting fire from the tree line seventy-five yards away.

The attacker shot in the thigh had hardly hit the ground and raised his hands in surrender before a woodcutter crushed his skull with a splitting maul. The Citizens Patrolman, his entire midsection a mass of gore, feebly tried to claw his way toward cover behind a log, leaving a smear of blood, fecal matter, and stench, until he mercifully shocked into unconsciousness on the frozen ground.

Another attacker, appearing as a bizarre picture of calm in the frenzied, screaming chaos, used a short, lever-action carbine, methodically killing four workmen one after another, until Bill Keeter, in desperation, popped up over a tree trunk behind him and threw a hatchet, tomahawk-style, at his back. The hatchet hit the man handle-first, bouncing harmlessly away. But as the man spun around, startled, he stepped on a round bit of wood that rolled under his foot, and fell awkwardly. Before he could get his carbine into position, he was swarmed by three workmen who beat him to a pulp with short lengths of firewood, frantically going on beating long after the corpse was lifeless.

Within minutes, a half-dozen Citizens Patrolmen, sprinting toward the scene, converged on the wood-lot from several directions. The last attacker dropped his rifle and fell to his knees with hands raised, pleading for his life. A careful, deliberate shot rang out and he pitched forward into the bloody snow.

"Looked to me like he was going for a pistol in his pocket," observed one of the Citizens Patrolmen quietly, and the rest of the townspeople nodded in grim agreement.

The gut-shot Rich Albertson and his attacker with one leg hacked off had both bled out, lying locked together on the frozen ground in what seemed a final dying effort by each man to use his teeth on his enemy.

"Don't let them…in the treeline…get away," gurgled Marv Fisher, leaning back against a log, bleeding heavily from a gunshot to the throat as he shakily pointed the location to the arriving Citizens Patrolmen. "Make sure…one in the field…is dead too. Don't get fuckin' ambushed. Be careful."

And his blood gurgled and bubbled and he sobbed softly, sitting propped against the log, quietly weeping from fear and regret—till after a few minutes he relaxed his grip on life and slipped gently away.

At the first sounds of gunfire, Chief Barley had issued the pre-arranged signal on the air horn at the Station: three longs, pause, and three more longs. As every Citizens Patrol deputy knew, and could double-check on the three-by-five card of code signals he carried at all times, Barley's signal meant that all Citizens Patrol lookouts on duty were to remain at their posts on high alert, any townsman who could assist them was to report to his nearest lookout post to offer his services, and all deputies not currently on duty were to report immediately to the police station.

Within minutes, two women and twenty-three men of the Citizens Patrol had assembled at the Station.

"Runners have come in from all the lookout posts," Barley told them. "There are no reports of any other attacks anywhere around town. I figure the bunch that hit Dean's wood-lot are probably all that's out there. At least two of them, maybe more, who stayed in the tree-line opposite the wood-lot, are still at large."

He turned to his Number One, Dick Peters.

"Pick fifteen men who can move fast. Take three days' food, canteens, sleeping bags, two CB radios and two Sterno stoves. Move out right now, and deal with whoever got away—at least two hostiles, maybe more. Be careful. Call for backup if you need any. If the damn radios don't work, as usual in the hills, use gunshots to signal us." He flashed his own three-by-five pocket card listing the signal codes and their meanings.

"Those not selected by Dick spread yourselves among the lookout posts as reinforcements there. Work out a shift-rotation at your post to keep it manned at all times—remember, people have to sleep to remain effective—and make sure each person at a post knows where to locate every other member of his post if needed. We'll try to get a hot lunch out to every post, but take cold food out with you when you report, just in case. Let's go."

Peters quickly selected his fifteen men. They were fully clothed and supplied, arms and equipment checked, and trotting east out of town in a broad skirmish line long before the bodies had been brought in from Dean's wood-lot.

At the Gravely shop, Tim swiped viciously at the all-too-visible tears running down his cheeks, batting in a hot fury at what he considered shameful evidence of his body's betrayal. He was so angry with himself he could hardly tell Tom, when he reached the shop, what was happening.

"I didn't run away, you know! Mr. Fisher *said* to get out. He yelled, and I just didn't think. And I just did it before I thought what I was doing. I was *not* running away!"

"Hey! Tim! Look: you did exactly the right thing. It is absolutely vital to protect this machine. One stray round in the wrong spot could blow it to smithereens. Marv knew that—that's why he yelled. There was nothing else in that wood-lot—not even a dozen men—anywhere near as valuable as this machine. Thank goodness you had sense to get it to safety, and to use the steam whistle on the way. That's given the whole town the earliest possible warning."

Glancing about, Tom could see the boy did not have his crutch.

"Look, I'm going to go by the police station. I'll try to get back shortly and tell you what I learn. Meanwhile, I'm going to let Sophie know where I'm going. I want you to stay here to guard her, the shop and its equipment, and *especially* this machine."

He ran up the steps, filled Sophie in and advised her to stay in the building till things were sorted out, and informed her that Tim would be downstairs, armed and on guard. Then Tom grabbed the Mossberg 500 twelve-gauge, with its sling-bandoleer holding twelve shells, six of them 00-buckshot and six slugs, plus a T/C Contender carbine with five .45-Colt cartridges for it in an elastic cartridge-holder on the carbine's stock.

He ran back downstairs to the shop.

He looked closely at Tim, making what he fully knew might prove to be a life-or-death decision.

"Listen to me, Tim." He took a deep breath. "*NOT* shooting is as important as shooting—and almost always a lot harder when you're under stress. Can I trust you to be *absolutely certain* you must shoot this, before you do so—and not accidentally kill somebody who merely comes running in here intending no harm? You *must* wait before pulling the trigger, until you are absolutely positive it's necessary and you have no other alternative. Do you understand me?"

"Yes."

"You swing this lever over to the side, like this, and the barrel breaks open. Put in a cartridge, snap the barrel up to closed position, verify the safety, here, is 'off', aim, and pull the trigger. Keep your finger *outside* the trigger-guard unless you have definitely decided you must kill someone. Keep the muzzle pointed down, like this, unless you have definitely decided you must kill someone. Do not even consider waving the gun around to scare anyone, or aiming for an arm or leg to wound him: if you are *certain* you must shoot, aim for the middle of his torso to kill him. Do you understand? Can I trust you to keep your cool?"

"Yes."

Handing him the carbine, Tom cautiously opened the shop door and looked both ways, somewhat reassured that the firing had stopped by now. Then he stepped out, closed the door after him, and ran for the police station, shotgun in hand.

When Chief Barley saw Tom he beckoned him.

"An attack by about eight or more men, all armed. They hit at Dean's wood-lot. No other attacks around town anywhere we know of. At least two hostiles got away—we're sending out a party to try to catch them."

He looked up at the gray, low-hanging cloud cover.

"Easy enough to track them now, with snow on the ground. Let's hope to God any more snow holds off long enough for us to get them."

As usual, Barley was thinking a step or two ahead of the moment's hectic action.

"What I wanted to check with you: If we can do so at reasonable cost, I'd like to try to warn the Amish. They're sitting ducks, with that 'nonviolent' crap they believe in. If they're killed, and/or have their possessions stolen or destroyed, that would be a real blow to us here. We need the Amish and the cooperation they can provide. We sure as hell *don't* need their buildings, animals, food, and equipment falling into the hands of armed hostiles. Can you make the eleven miles or so down Rt. 12 using the steam Gravely? That would certainly outrun any hostiles on foot."

Tom thought a moment.

"Yes, I can, Chief. I'll go if you want me to. But I don't think I should use the Gravely. Our long-term future may hang on that steam engine: I don't think it's worth risking damage to it for anything. *Anything.*"

Barley sighed, considering, trying desperately to weigh probabilities he couldn't possibly know enough about to judge accurately.

"Hm...May have a point." He gazed out at the commotion, the police station alive with deputies drawing supplies, checking instructions, and heading off on the run to their duty posts.

"Look, Chief, how about going on horseback, on that old gelding Trigger?

That would still be faster, for eleven miles, than men afoot."

"Hmm. Yeah. But who? Owen knows horses, but he won't carry a gun. There's Abraham Hite and the two Yoder boys staying here, finishing up that cider press—but of course they won't carry a gun. We can spare that old horse, and frankly we could spare Owen and the three Amish too, if we had to: but what's the point of sending someone who couldn't do any more to help than throw rocks at the attackers. If the Amish believe in throwing rocks."

"They don't, I'm pretty sure—at least not with intent to injure. How about if I ride Trigger? Worst come to worst, Owen knows enough to make progress on another steam engine. The one we have will be safe. I'll go armed, and I'll do what I can to kill anyone attacking the Amish—high moral principles be damned. But I'll try to kill them lovingly—in some way that won't permanently alienate the two communities.

"Tell Sophie bye for me: I'll get back as soon as I can. Tim's armed with a single-shot .45, guarding her and the shop and the steam Gravely inside the shop. I think he's steady, but holler and knock before anyone enters."

So Tom headed off at a run to Johnson's place, where Trigger was now stabled, and with the farmer's help got the gelding saddled and bridled. When they were done, Johnson said "Just a sec," and disappeared into his house.

"Here," he said, reappearing moments later, with a wool muffler, a filled canteen and a small canvass bag. He tied the canteen and bag onto the pommel of the saddle as Tom wrapped the muffler around his neck and secured the ends under his parka. "Water, some more 12-gauge shells, piece of roast pork, and some bread and cheese. Good luck to you."

"Thanks. I appreciate it. See you soon."

Tom, no horseman by any stretch of the imagination, slung his shotgun over his shoulder, lacking a saddle-scabbard, then swung up into the saddle and got the lazy old gelding headed down Fourth Street toward Rt. 12 at the other edge of town. He wasn't sure what pace the animal could maintain for an eleven mile trip—or for that matter what he himself could maintain, unaccustomed as he was to riding.

He gingerly experimented with the disgruntled beast, trying different gaits in hopes of chancing on one that might seem clearly superior. Trigger, already thoroughly put out by having to leave his cozy stall in such weather, and transport a novice rider, was soon in an even more vile temper because of the changing gaits.

Going down the middle of Fourth Street, then turning onto Rt. 12 and heading south down the middle of the highway, the horse was disappointed to find no convenient trees to swipe his rider's leg against, or low-hanging limbs to duck under to brush him off his back. But Trigger, grown steadily older and more ill-tempered with the passing years, had also grown more canny. He had acquired plenty of other little moves and techniques. He cantered moodily along Rt. 12, mulling over his many grievances, biding his time.

After cantering for nearly an hour, Tom figured he must surely be well in front of any men on foot, assuming they were even heading in the same direction. It was vital to conserve Trigger for the entire round trip. And the heavy 12-gauge slung on his back, rhythmically slamming up and down as the horse cantered, was killing him. Tom decided to halt briefly and secure the gun to the saddle in whatever way he could devise, ready access be damned.

Choosing a spot where the roadside ditch was easily accessible, he reined in and sat for a moment in the middle of the road, looking around and listening. Seeing and hearing nothing, he dismounted and tied the reins to a roadside bush. He found a sizeable rock and slammed it down hard on the ice in the bar ditch, breaking open a pool of water for Trigger to drink. As the horse did so, Tom examined the leather thongs affixed to the cantle, or rear part of the saddle.

There's no way to tie the gun crosswise to the saddle behind me, he mused, *that would never work. Obviously can't tie it lengthwise along the horse's side: I couldn't have it under my leg or over my leg either. Can't just tie it vertically and let it dangle and bounce around. Can't hold it in my hands conveniently while holding the reins. Damn! Why didn't I have sense enough to leave this wretched artillery piece at home with Tim and carry that light little Contender carbine?*

While Trigger drank and rested, Tom wiggled his aching shoulder, cursing and fuming as he re-learned the same lesson every fighting man has had to re-learn, one generation after the other, since the day of the stone-headed club: a weapon too heavy to carry easily is a liability, not an asset.

After a few minutes of badly needed rest, fruitless experimentation, and frustrated cursing, Tom wearily slung the shotgun over his other shoulder ("Might as well equalize the damage," he muttered, furious at himself) and re-mounted Trigger, continuing down Rt. 12 toward the Amish, this time at a walk. The gentle walk made the gun infinitely less punishing to his shoulder.

Tom resigned himself to the coming hours of boredom as the horse sullenly clip-clopped along the county road. He forced himself every few minutes to scan 360 degrees around the empty winter landscape to verify what he already knew: there was nothing there but desolate, snow-covered fields and woods— scarcely a trace of evidence that Man even existed any more.

Early in the second hour of his three hour trip, Tom felt the first snowflake on his face. He knew, from Barley's concern, what terrible news this was. If the Mountainview party had not yet found the remaining attackers—and he'd heard no gunshots to indicate as much—this snowfall would make their task infinitely harder and more dangerous. With tracks obscured, not only was escape much easier but also ambush.

As Tom rode on through the steadily increasing snowfall, his gut knotted in anxiety. The Mountainview patrol—more precisely its food, clothing, boots, arms, ammunition, and other equipment—was fast changing from being the hunter into being enormously desirable prey.

Eventually, knowing he was now too far away, he gave up listening for any possible gunshots from the patrol and concentrated on trying to decide what he'd do when he reached the Amish. He knew their settlement consisted of four or five large farmhouses, plus numerous barns and other outbuildings, grouped in a rough horseshoe around Rt. 12 where the road ended. They owned and worked several hundred acres of land fanning out from their central cluster of buildings.

"If anyone attacks them, I *will* do my best to kill him," Tom mused, "if not for their sakes then for ours. Mountainview simply cannot permit armed attackers to hole up in the Amish community, just eleven miles away, with all that community's resources at their disposal. And yet…I can't just ride into their community armed: that offense could have longterm consequences almost as disastrous."

The horse plodded steadily along the county road, Tom desperately turning and twisting the dilemma every which way in his mind, trying to find some solution.

Around ten-thirty, some three hours after he'd set out, Tom saw in the distance the houses and outbuildings of the Amish community. He halted about a quarter-mile before the highway ended, sitting silently on the horse for a time, watching and listening, seeing and hearing nothing amiss. With a heavy, bitter sigh, and a heartfelt exclamation of "Shit!" to express his feelings of fear and frustration, he dismounted.

Removing the horse's bit and stuffing it in his jacket pocket, he used the reins to tether the animal by its halter to a sturdy roadside tree growing next to the bar ditch. He broke the ice in the ditch to make water available, and dragged some dead bushes and loose brush to form a line upwind of the horse's location, to make what shelter he could for it. He kicked some loose snow off the long, dead, dry grass at the edge of the ditch where Trigger was staked to

263

give the animal a clue about grazing.

Then he dug out some chunks of the frozen dirt from where he'd pulled up one of the dead bushes. He removed the food from the bag Johnson had given him, putting it in his jacket pocket, leaving the shells in the bag. He removed all the shells from the bandoleer sling and from the shotgun itself, placing them in the bag too, then buried the bag in the hole, scuffing enough dirt over it to conceal it.

A few yards down the road, he found the next spot he was hunting for. With a deep sigh—his heart breaking at such abuse of a fine tool—he took the unloaded shotgun and gently placed it in the dirt under the edge of a long, flat rock he'd moved slightly aside. Then he piled enough brush, smaller stones, and snow on the area to conceal the gun.

When he was content that he'd done what he could, he walked toward the Amish settlement. It would be very hard for any thief to ride Trigger, lacking the bit he'd taken with him. The animal had water, grass, and as much shelter as he could provide, staked in the roadside ditch. The gun and its ammunition, hidden separately, would both have to be found for anyone to use them against him. And—most important—they were hidden on the County road's right-of-way, not on Amish land. It was all he could do, he reflected; but was it wise or deadly stupid?

As he came within shouting distance of the homes he gave a loud "HELLO! I'M TOM JEFFSON! FROM MOUNTAINVIEW! ANYBODY HOME?"

Scared to death, his legs trembling as he walked, Tom visualized all too clearly what an easy target he made for anyone in those buildings with a rifle.

If I can just get somebody to reply, he thought, maybe I can tell from their reply whether things are normal here or whether there are Amish dead or being held hostage—with their attackers still around. With any warning, and a lot of luck, maybe I'll have time to dive for the bar ditch and crawl along it back to where I buried the gun and shells. Oh Jesus. His legs trembled as he walked, making him jerky and uncoordinated. He dreaded he might piss himself.

Chapter 32
One Form of Counterattack

He called twice more, steadily walking closer, before anyone inside the tightly closed buildings heard him.

Finally a door in the nearest barn suddenly swung open, making Tom flinch, and a clearly astonished man looked out. Nonplussed, the man called to Tom, "Ho! Welcome, friend!"

Then he recovered his wits sufficiently to turn and call to someone in the barn. "Amon! Comes here an English! On the road!"

A man Tom recognized from their Christmas visit as Amon Yoost strode out of the barn heading for Tom, delight mixed with surprise on his face. Tom could see no indication that the man was under duress of any sort. Anyway, if there were attackers hidden in the settlement it was too late now.

"Welcome, friend! Thou art Tom, I believe?" His eyes traveled up the road to Trigger, staked at the roadside.

"Thy mount is gone lame?"

"No, Amon. I left it there because I did not know if you had been attacked by armed thieves and your settlement occupied. Are you all well here?"

"Oh, aye. We've no trouble here," the Mennonite replied in some puzzlement. "We wish no one ill: there is no reason for us to be attacked."

If I hear that again I'll knock the teeth out of whoever says it, Tom thought, giddy with sudden relief. Amon looked at him with concern.

"Caleb can fetch thy mount to the barn and tend it. Come now inside to have some warm drink and rest thee."

As if dumbstruck, Tom silently fished Trigger's bit from his pocket and handed it to Caleb. Walking beside Amon to the kitchen door of the nearest house, Tom almost slumped against him in sudden relief and letdown.

"There has been an attack against Mountainview. Several of our men were killed, about eight or ten I think, before we killed most of the attackers. At least two other attackers, with rifles, escaped. We wanted to warn you in case they came this way."

"Thank you, friend. We are grateful. We will gather at once to pray for all those involved."

They reached the nearest farmhouse and went inside, into the peaceful warmth of richly varnished honey-oak flooring and paneling, maple and hickory rockers and kitchen chairs, with bright quilts on the couches and needlework samplers on the wall.

"*Pray*," Tom said in anguish.

It was exactly what he'd feared. He made no effort to conceal the despair in his voice.

Amon and his wife and daughters seated Tom with them at the kitchen table, and produced mugs of steaming tea and a kind of shortbread on which they drizzled molasses.

In a moment, Amon, who had heard full well the unspoken part of Tom's comment, clasped his friend's shoulder and said softly, "It is hard for each of us to credit the other with having much sense. You believe the Good people can arm themselves with mighty weapons, to rain fire and death upon the Bad people. And when enough Bad people have been killed then the Good will triumph and all will be well in the world."

He sighed, and Tom felt he had never heard such grief in a simple sigh.

"Ach. Would not the Good have triumphed long ago, were things that simple?"

The farmer, trying so hard to communicate with Tom, explained. "We of the Plain People do not have entirely the right of this matter either, I sometimes fear. Perhaps it is a problem without a solution. But we pray—in part that a solution may be shown to us. At least, praying, we offer harm to no person. That makes us feel easier in our minds."

He turned to the women. "Go and summon all to gather here. There has been great killing in Mountainview, and we must meet to seek strength before sending aid."

Utterly taken aback, Tom exclaimed "No—you don't understand! *We're* trying to help *you*! We're ok. We beat off the attack. But some of the attackers may be heading your way. So I'm here to help *you*!"

"Well, then," Amon gently offered, "If we each help the other, will that not be best? Will thou lend thy strength to our meeting here? It would mean much to us."

"Yes. Of course."

Tom made one last effort. "But—if you dispersed your people, instead of grouping them all together...If you were widely dispersed...It might be safer…In case of trouble, some might escape…hide …"

"Thank you for your concern, friend," the farmer said gently. "I do understand your reasoning, and I do feel grateful for your concern."

He smiled. "But we have our own little customs for times of trouble, and—like cockroaches and fleas—we haven't all been killed off yet. So who can say, really, which way works best?"

As the settlers gathered in Amon Yoost's home, receiving the news Amon murmured to each upon arrival, Tom could not stop his mind racing frantically in all directions. Where was each of their buildings located; what were the highest vantage points; which would give the best fields of fire; what were the likely approach routes; where could people be stationed, with pitchforks or sticks or whatever they had; were the killers at this moment quietly closing in, softly whispered words and hand signals finalizing their attack?

The settlers—male and female, young and old, healthy and feeble—quietly heard the news as they arrived and took seats on the chairs and sofas and floor pillows until the parlor, hallway, kitchen, and stairs were filled with people, all seeming lost in quiet reflection while Tom's mind darted frantically, against his will, in a dozen directions at once. *That window*! A single shooter, standing outside the house aiming through the window, could kill every person in here! Could they not SEE what was possible?

They seemed not to. When the last person had arrived, received the news, and settled quietly into an attitude of contemplation, Amon, who had finally located the book he'd been hunting through his shelves for, took it up: one of the few Bibles the community had in English. He stood, opened it, and spoke softly to the group.

"Our English brothers and sisters have suffered injury and death. For them, and for those poor wretches so lost in the darkness of sin as to do such terrible things, I read from this English translation. You will recognize Our Savior's words, though this language is not our accustomed one.

"You have heard it said: thou shalt love thy neighbor and hate thine enemy. But I say unto you: love your enemies; bless them that curse you; do good to them that hate you; and pray for them that despitefully use you and persecute you. For if ye love them that love you, what reward have ye? Do not even the publicans the same?"

Then they sat silent for a few moments, heads bowed.

When they looked up, Tom nearly gasped at the sudden, steely resolve that had filled the group. These people, it suddenly hit him, are not the least bit soft and impractical and unworldly. There's not a trace of sugary sentimentality here: just a gritty, iron-willed *determination to prevail*—in the most practical, down-to-earth manner. A sufficiently evil person could indeed kill these people, Tom understood with a shock; but short of that, he'd be an awful fool to mess with them.

"So," said Amon, "Now is dinner, yes? Then we send help. Klara makes the medicines to take. Put we all some little something to eat in the baskets: there are widows now to feed at funeral dinners and beyond—and children without a parent who need a treat for coming days. Have you maybe a small toy or a doll? Caleb, see to the hay wagon. Maybe Daisy, I think, likes to pull it to say hello again to the people who gave her grain when she first arrived here. Be quick now."

As he spoke, the women were darting about the kitchen so fast as to almost blur before Tom's eyes, doing their incomprehensible food-magic. In scarcely more than the blink of an eye, the routine lunch prepared for seven in the Yoost home had transformed—with items hastily brought over from the neighboring houses, and instant additions from the Yoosts' own larder—into a buffet-style feast for the entire community of thirty-four. The smiling women, in their white lace caps, working together with the highspeed precision of a gun crew in a battleship's 16-inch turret, gave not the least indication there was anything unusual in their awesome performance.

Truly, thought Tom, as a hot, multi-course lunch was served, precisely at noon, to thirty-four 'Amish' and himself: these are not a people to be trifled with.

By 12:45, Daisy was in the shafts of the big, rubber-tired hay wagon; Klara Yoder, the community's medicinal herb woman, was in the wagon with her basket of medical supplies; Caleb, who was to drive, was on the wagon seat; and a huge assortment of foods and other care-gifts was in the wagon—to be delivered to those who had sent Tom to help the Amish.

Still taken aback by the speed at which everything had turned upside down, Tom mounted the recently fed, combed, saddled and bridled Trigger to ride alongside the wagon back to Mountainview.

They waved farewell to the rest of the assembled Amish and set out. Tom, burning with embarrassment, muttered an explanation to Caleb that he needed to briefly pause at the tree where he'd initially left Trigger in order to dig up the gun and ammunition he'd buried there. "On the roadside right-of-way," he emphasized, "not on the community's land."

"Buried in the *dirt*?" the startled Caleb asked. "Is maybe not so good for it, buried in the dirt, I think…"

268

From inborn politeness—the natural aristocrat's unwillingness to cause embarrassment to a guest—and aware that the strange ways of the English often made no sense anyway—Caleb prepared to drop the matter, turning with great attention to a buckle on Daisy's harness when they reached the tree and halted.

Tom dismounted, retrieved his shotgun from the snow and dirt, dug up the sack with the bandoleer-sling and extra shells, attached the sling to the gun and slung it over his shoulder, put his left foot in the stirrup, and swung back up onto Trigger. He had not had time to get his right boot into that stirrup—which may have saved his life—when Trigger's pea-sized brain suddenly realized a long-awaited opportunity.

The horse lunged toward the little tree, intending to swipe Tom's right leg against it. Tom, realizing at once he couldn't pull Trigger onto a new course, swept his right leg back over the horse's rump just in time to prevent the leg being crushed against the tree. He was lucky to kick his left foot out of the stirrup as he slid in a clown's exit over the horse's rump, landing hard on his back in the frozen dirt on top of the shotgun.

Stars and a burst of white light accompanied a searing pain in his left side. Too stunned to think, let alone speak, Tom lay there in a heap.

Caleb was off the wagon-box in a flash, kneeling beside him, knowing not to move him until he'd assessed his condition.

"Rib," Tom sobbed, each breath a searing agony. "Broke. Rib."

By this time, Klara was out of the wagon and beside him. She soothed him with a gentle touch and softly murmured words of reassurance, even as she rapidly ran down a thoroughly professional checklist of diagnostic signs and symptoms.

"I am receiving *extremely* competent medical care," Tom's wandering mind registered in amazement, as he mentally swam about a bit before returning to full awareness. "This woman's every action *exudes* professionalism—from her diagnostic evaluation to her bedside manner. Her technical skill is simply fascinating. I will just hover here beside myself and watch, I think. Anyway, the embarrassment of returning to Tom's body is more than I could stand."

"Yes. One broken rib, I think. You do not worry: it is painful, yes, but not medically so bad. I will bind it to limit further movement and in a few weeks will be ok with no further treatment. Often happens this thing among us, working the farm and especially the animals. I give you now some little thing to drink so you feel better, and you can stand up for me to bind with some good cloth I have, yes?"

She stood and waved gaily at the mass of suddenly concerned people who were standing, uncertain, back at the barn where they had just seen the party off.

"No problem! All ok! We go fine now!"

Tom, his eyes streaming tears and his nose running snot, struggled in agony up off the dirt and onto his feet—spared at least the added humiliation of becoming a spectacle at the center of a crowd.

His mind (his "real" self) still floated a few feet overhead, gazing with revulsion at this fiasco, too mortified to re-join the physical body of some humiliated, clownish oaf that called itself Tom. He, It, finally stood—trying very hard not to sob.

"Thank you," he rasped between gritted teeth.

She understood—well enough to pretend not to.

"Ach; busybodies! Always their own cures they want to sell. What worked for Uncle Jacob...what was such a blessing for Widow Hite...Like I never spent no time learning something myself."

She had him hold on to the wagon's tailgate while she deftly wrapped a wide cloth firmly around his chest and upper left arm, securing it with safety pins.

"Now, Caleb, we help him up into the wagon, where he stands. Soon he is home again, yes?"

And in a moment Tom was standing with Klara in the front of the wagon holding on, Caleb had tethered Trigger to the wagon's tailgate, placed the gun and ammunition in the wagon and returned to his seat, and the wagon set out once more for Mountainview. They rolled gently along the snow-covered county road.

"You are a very kind person."

He watched her mind sort at computer-speed through her range of options for a response.

Klara was an oddity in her community because she was still unmarried at twenty-seven. She had had more experience than she wished in dealing with the sudden, irrational infatuation of a male patient for a female medical caregiver. Long ago, she had accepted it as a common secondary symptom of stress, generally no more serious or long-lasting than a patient's brief bout with constipation or depression—and to be dealt with just as briskly, in common-sense fashion. But it was inevitably a matter requiring considerable tact and skill on her part.

Tom watched as she weighed—with an experienced clinician's

shrewdness—the pros and cons of blowing a smokescreen of aw-shucks countrified claptrap, versus smoothly withdrawing into a clinically professional coolness, versus a gently patronizing putdown by way of some 'how-are-we-feeling-now' governess/nursie talk …

His awe was intensified by the option she selected: simple honesty.

"I wish to be professional—even without the professional medicines and equipments and training it would be nice to have."

She smiled gently and explained. "Is good, in medical care, to be seen as a kind person. Many studies show patients do much better in such a person's care. So. What we have, we use, eh? Simple matter of efficiency, in our business. But if you have an X-ray machine, that would be nice too …"

Her smile broadened a bit, lightening the mood. "Perhaps now, with no more X-ray machines, I will become a big doctor and make millions of dollars from my great efficiency."

They were silent for a bit.

"And also—perhaps …"

She studied him unhurriedly, considering carefully whether she wanted to proceed…"Perhaps no situation is ever so bad we can reduce the amount of suffering by forsaking kindness and adding more suffering to it. Maybe not even the suffering from killing is that bad," she added, to make her point unmistakable.

Tom stood, gently swaying in the wagon, as some of the most obvious certainties he'd acquired in fifty-nine years of life swirled crazily upside down. He groped for something, anything, solid and reliable—but found nothing.

"I came to try to help *you*, you know. And now *this.*"

She thought a bit, trying to phrase her point clearly.

"You *do* help us. At a time of great sorrow of your own, you come to warn us. You ride here alone when terrible men are about. You do a very kind thing to not give offense—putting your fine, expensive gun into the dirt and snow. You walk into our home without this thing you imagine will make you safe, not knowing what you will find. You accept our own ways of dealing with these terrible killings, willing to temporarily put your own lifelong ways aside. You show respect for us as humans, not just curiosity about how we are strange. For anyone, that is a help—maybe for us especially. Amon Yoost said well, I think, at dinner just now: is best when each of us can help the other."

They were silent a bit.

And then she added "Because our ways, too, do not have all that is necessary, I think. With scientific medicines and equipments—and especially training—so much more suffering could we help to ease …"

Changing the subject (or was she, Tom wondered) Klara said with a tiny hint of malicious pleasure, "So: You are the engineer who makes the school building into a luxury hotel for us when we visit at Christmas time. Until the people turn the lights and the water on too much and break your machine for a little bit. Ach! Such *language* I heard you say to yourself! And you a big engineer yet!"

After enjoying a moment or two of his confused sputtering—a muddled mix of technical explanation, heated self-justification for his behavior, and, perhaps, in theory, apology if, hypothetically, there were valid grounds for anyone to have taken offense at certain language, who shouldn't have been eavesdropping anyway in the first place—she grinned and waved him to a halt.

"Oh well. I grow up on a farm, all my life. And I work with people making babies, and old people, and sick people. Not many of these words you say I have not seen the real things. Ha! But, of course, you are still very bad to say such language."

"Very." (Teeth gritted. Wanting simply to get off this particular subject.)

"In our community, you would be in big trouble for speaking so. But (judiciously weighing his case) in our community you would not be making electric lights and indoor water from burning wood in a machine. So maybe you would not feel the need for saying such words. And that is maybe not a small thing. When someone is too high above the heads of others, he maybe demands things from them they are not able to do. And then says very bad language about them when they fail to satisfy him."

She paused a moment, phrasing her point. "The atomic machines for making electricity must have been much more big and complicated than the machine you use. I do not like to think what such big engineers who can build those things might say about us who are not so smart…Maybe I prefer not to have the electricity, than to think they say such language about me …"

They were silent in the wagon for a time.

"But, still…some things…the scientific medicine and the training…I think perhaps they are better in some ways …"

After a bit she asked him "Has your gun been harmed, from putting it in the dirt and snow?"

"Maybe not. I'll clean and oil it as soon as we get home. I'm sorry if having it in the wagon here is troublesome. It's not loaded."

"There is no problem, but thank you for considering our beliefs."

"Do you have a sharp knife in your basket of medical things?"

"Yes; a scalpel, of course." Her puzzlement was obvious.

"I suppose you have kitchen knives in your homes, too, and knives in your barns and other places for use on the farm?"

"Yes ...?"

"You know, surely, that in the past thousands of years many, many more people have been killed by knives than by guns. Still, it would be hard for you to do some of your medical work without something sharp—or to run a kitchen or a farm."

He struggled to find non-confrontational words for what he wanted to express.

"In the hands of evil, arrogant men, guns can be used for evil. The steam engine I've attached to a generator can produce enough current to electrocute a person, killing him. You seek medical training? The U.S. Government, for many years, has trained people how to use very advanced medical knowledge and equipment for torturing political enemies in countries all over the world— how to keep them alive while inflicting indescribable pain. The nuclear powerplants you mentioned...their capacity to produce death and destruction is unimaginable.

"But merely avoiding guns, or steam-powered generators, or medical technology, or nuclear powerplants, is no more sensible than trying to live without knives. You have achieved peace by sacrificing progress. I think we achieved progress by sacrificing peace. Perhaps each of us—desperately— needs the other."

The huge Belgian mare plodded along the road, pulling the wagon through a sparkling white wonderland. The morning's snow, falling steadily for four hours, had added a foot or so to what was on the ground, then ended, giving way to bright, cold sunshine and a brilliant blue sky. They rolled quietly, the rhythmic clop, clop, clop of Daisy's huge hooves blending with the continuous, soft squeaking the wagon tires made in the loose snow, punctuated now and then by a snort of steam from Daisy's muzzle and a gay shake of her head. It was a world peaceful and lovely in all directions, as far as the eye could see.

Klara piled up a nest of loose straw in a corner of the wagon to make a soft seat, where she sat lost in thought, looking out over the snow-sparkling countryside. Tom, who had to remain standing to minimize the pain of his rib, swayed gently with the wagon's motion, holding lightly to the front edge of the wagon-bed with one hand. All three people silently wished they could continue voyaging through such beauty for a long, long time. They knew perfectly well that gruesome things awaited them in Mountainview.

Chapter 33
Another Form of Counterattack

Just before five in the afternoon, the wagon rolled to a gentle halt in front of the Gravely dealership. Before anyone got off, Tom shouted "Hey Tim! It's Tom and some other people here! Open up, will you?"

The shop door cautiously swung open, Tim bracing himself in the doorframe, carbine in hand.

"Hi, Tim. Make sure your weapon's unloaded and leave it on the shop bench. Then get the shotgun out of the wagon here and put it with the carbine. Then help Klara and Caleb here take a message to Chief Barley at the Station."

Tim dealt with the guns while Klara and Caleb helped Tom out of the wagon, then returned to the group. Tom saw the boy had found a sturdy piece of hardwood dowel which he'd padded on one end to form a makeshift crutch.

"Abraham Hite is already rooming here, so if you'll share his room tonight, Caleb—and Klara, if you'll room with Sophie—we'll be all set for lodging. I'm going to sleep down here in the shop awhile, instead of going up and down all the steps. Tim, you ride in the wagon now to direct Caleb and Klara to Chief Barley at the police station. Barley will advise you about casualties, Klara, and whatever else he needs done first, and where to unload the things you've brought for us. Then, Tim, show Caleb to Johnson's place. Johnson will stable and feed the two horses, and shelter the wagon in his barn. Can you find some way home from Johnson's, Tim—or spend the night there? You don't need to report for work tomorrow: I expect work's going to be halted for a few days."

By the time Sophie had gotten downstairs, the wagon was already rolling toward the police station. In a few minutes, while filling her in on her latest two houseguests and his own situation, Tom helped her locate the folding army cot in the backyard shed, bring it into the shop, and set it up.

He then went to work on his shotgun, stripping, cleaning, oiling, and re-assembling it, relieved to find no indication it had suffered harm. Then he did the same for the Contender carbine Tim had had.

As he was finishing up, Sophie brought down their supper: steaming bowls

274

of split-pea soup, a potato-venison casserole, and fresh oat-wheat bread with butter. Placing the food on the shop workbench, she had just pulled her own chair up next to his rocker to join him when Chief Barley arrived.

"Do *not* say a single thing till I get back," she warned the men, jumping up and heading to the kitchen.

Returning, she added a plate, bowl, teacup and utensils for the Chief where he'd drawn up a chair of his own.

"Right." She sat down and tore off a sizeable hunk of warm bread. "Proceed. You *both* have some explaining to do."

"You're fantastic," sighed Barley, with a lovesick gaze at her. "First chance I've had to eat since dawn today, except for a handful of jerky around noon."

He luxuriated in the steam rising off the hot soup, inhaling its peace and fragrance as he began to unwind a bit for the first time in almost twelve frenetic hours.

"We've been very fortunate, considering. The attack came at a time and place I should have given more thought to: directly out of the rising sun at dawn, from that too-close tree-line on the southeast edge of town. We were very lucky the workmen had arrived at the wood-lot literally minutes before we were hit. We lost nine woodcutters and one Citizens' Patrolman killed. We couldn't save any of them. I doubt even a trauma unit would have had much chance, given the situation: high-powered rifles used at short range...freezing temperatures...The five attackers who reached the wood-lot, plus one in the field, are all dead too. I'll get to the others in the tree-line in a minute.

"If the workmen had not been there, or if the attackers had been smart enough to keep them pinned down and just go around them, they could very well have occupied two or three houses adjacent to the wood-lot. There's probably...I don't know...say five or six people living in each of those houses. Once inside—with hostages, food and drink, shelter, and the threat of killing their hostages and firing the buildings—they'd have been in a hell of a strong negotiating position. I suppose we'd have tried to meet their demands— probably thus encouraging additional demands—until sooner or later we'd eventually have run up against some demand we couldn't comply with. Then what: tell them to kill fifteen or twenty hostages and fire the buildings and die themselves in the process?"

The Chief, who had kept a tight hold on himself throughout the long, long day, desperately needed a chance to release the pressure that had built almost beyond endurance.

"Any decision like that…..*Jesus*. We'd have had real, *real* problems in this town—long after the attackers were dead …

"I should have considered that particular place and time more carefully— southeast edge of town at sunrise—and strengthened our defenses there."

He sighed, slumped in his chair, devouring the hot food as if seeking in physical nourishment some moral rejuvenation.

"Thanks for contacting the Amish, Tom. I guess. Gonna be Hell to pay, I expect, when that Amish woman treating the prisoner gets an earful of his sad tale." The Chief sighed.

"Dick Peters got his fifteen men moving toward the treeline immediately. They put a couple shots into the body on the field first, for good luck, but he was dead. When they reached the treeline and found the rucksacks and sleeping bags the attackers had stashed there, they realized how lucky we'd been for the second time this day. A little ways from the equipment cache a person was lying, well hidden in the snow with pine branches over him, rifle trained toward where our men had just walked across seventy-five yards of open field without a speck of cover—but unconscious. God knows how many he could have killed if he'd waited till they were halfway to him and then opened fire.

"Anyway, he was unconscious, mostly from cold-induced shock and the pain of a broken ankle. Dick left two guys to bring him to and interrogate him, while the rest of them followed tracks of at least two others heading south through the woods. Don't know what's become of that: the snowfall set in heavy within the hour. We've heard no shots. I guess Dick's bunch is still trying to track them. Hope to hell they don't get themselves ambushed…

"Meanwhile, the guys with the prisoner brought him to and began asking questions. He wasn't going to talk. It was pretty bad. Folks could hear the screams clear in town from where the guys were working on him in the tree-line, seventy-five yards away. One of the guys said they concentrated on the broken ankle…Took a while …"

The Chief was so distraught he was physically shaking.

"Nothin' else to do, of course."

He collected himself.

"Guy finally talked. Said there were two others who'd been in the treeline with him, assigned to provide covering fire. They were all originally from up near Johnstown, Pennsylvania, and drifted together as a group in the weeks following The Collapse. They all had wives or girlfriends with them at first, but the women had died off by wintertime. They've been occupying a series of farmsteads and small towns since a few weeks after The Collapse, living at each place till the food's gone then moving south till they found another place to hole up. Most places were abandoned, he said. Some had people still living in them, and those they killed. They planned to keep on heading south in this fashion till they reached a warm enough area—South Carolina or beyond—where winters would not be a problem and they could 'live off the land.'

"Had to be outsiders, of course, I see that now: locals would have known about the Amish just eleven miles away and hit them, instead of an obviously populated town like Mountainview where they could expect resistance.

"They decided to hit us because it was hard to keep moving with the guy who'd broken his ankle a few days earlier in a fall, so they wanted to hole up for a while, also because they didn't realize workmen would be at the wood-lot at dawn, and because they were tired and hungry and wanted to feed and rest awhile. From the looks of the bodies, I'd say they may have been hungry but they were sure as hell not starving: those were fit, able men. They were well armed, with scoped .30-06's and some AR-15's, mostly. If the guy we caught hadn't lost consciousness, our men would have been slaughtered coming across that field: he had an AR-15 and all the ammo in the world.

"They didn't enter Grayson on their way down here. All the prisoner knew was they'd seen some town bigger than Mountainview when they were north of us, but decided to go around it. They'd just snared several rabbits, he said, and didn't need food at the time.

"After our guys questioned him they brought him into town—alive, if you can believe it."

Barley sighed.

"Which, of course, shows a fine respect for the Constitutionally protected rights of the accused. And genuine humanitarian concern, no doubt. And a surprising degree of restraint, too—considering one of the guys lost a brother and the other one lost a brother-in-law, killed at the wood-lot. Also shows I got to explain very clearly to Dick Peters—who is a hell of a good man, but we're all new at this—that you leave *one* guy to deal with matters of this sort, not two. Makes it easier, all around.

"So now your Amish lady is helping Doc do whatever they're gonna do for this animal's broken ankle—and hearing every last detail, no doubt, of the trying time he had in the custody of my men before deciding to share his knowledge. And after he's been given enough time to stir up all the trouble he possibly can, then I guess we'll have to stage some sort of bullshit 'trial' before we execute him."

Barley spoke in a low voice to his dinner plate. "If that bastard's two

277

remaining buddies kill or injure any more of my men…"

The Chief's anxiety, intensified by his powerlessness to affect matters, was nearly overwhelming. He almost pleaded with Tom and Sophie for reassurance.

"*Surely* Dick will have sense enough not to press them, once he's lost their track in the new snow…Maybe I shoudda gone. But, shit, as old and fat as I am …"

Sophie spoke up, with that steel in her voice Tom had come to know.

"Chief, there's absolutely *nobody* who could have done as well as you have—before the attack and throughout this long, terrible day. Thank you for being here for us all. Long-term, I don't know whether Mountainview could make it without you."

"That's kind of you to say, ma'am. Thank you for the delicious food, too. I needed it. I've got to get back to the Station. The Amish lady's with Doc and the prisoner there, and the wagon-driver is too. I'll have a patrolman walk the two Amish here as soon as they're ready. Thanks again for the supper and kind words, ma'am. Tom…*Jeeze*…try not to fall off any more horses, huh?"

When Barley had left, Sophie said thoughtfully, "Well, Tom…what *should* be done about that prisoner?"

He considered the matter until he admitted defeat. He spoke almost helplessly.

"This morning I'd have said 'hang him'—with or without some hokey trial, but right away, before any more medical attention and supplies are wasted on him. It would have been so simple and obvious. We're not a stable, secure, affluent society that can afford luxuries like the moral preening, posturing, and hand-wringing of an ACLU. But now, to tell you the truth, I just don't know what to do. Things that were so obviously sensible before… now…just seem …"

Sophie gave him a long, surprised look.

"I'd be happy to kill the bastard with my own two hands—just for what he's doing to the Chief, if for no other reason. And I'm a Life Member of the ACLU."

She grinned, but with that same undertone of cold steel Tom had come to recognize in her.

"True—might be grounds for expulsion. But I'd terminate the membership myself, if there was anywhere to send the notice to."

"My. Haven't *you* changed," Tom said, with a sad, thoughtful smile. Then, trying to lighten the mood, he added "I'd love to see my new Sophie in action at a Stanford Faculty Club tea."

She did not retreat an inch.

"That was then. This is now. It used to be theoretical; it's now very, very personal. Ten families here have lost a husband, father, brother...The morale throughout my community has been badly shaken. And Chief Barley—a decent, caring, hardworking man, doing his best to keep things going for all of us—has been placed in agonizing, no-win moral dilemmas no one should ever have to face."

Instead of reacting with the harsh "better-late-than-never" bitterness that would have marked his reply until recently, Tom's response to her now reflected recent changes of his own, fully as wrenching to him as Sophie's were to her.

"I don't know," he said, bewildered. "I honestly don't know any more. Those Amish, with their pacifist, turn-the-other-cheek stuff...They couldn't be *right*—I mean, well, let's be reasonable: they're not right. Obviously. But I'm not really certain they're wrong. I just don't know."

Sophie had more hot food ready to serve upstairs in the kitchen when Caleb and Klara arrived an hour later. Watching out for them, Tom took care to dodge out into the backyard, on pretext of an outhouse visit, when they approached the shop, leaving Sophie to deal with the two guests who'd just come from the prisoner.

"Good luck, he muttered, heading out the door.

"Luck," Sophie replied evenly, with a certain set to her jaw, "will have very little to do with it."

But when he steeled himself the next morning to face the Amish, especially Klara, Tom was astonished to find no trace of tension between her and his new—exceedingly post-ACLU—Sophie.

To his flabbergasted relief, the women had hit it off famously, and were only too eager to tell him the arrangement they'd arrived at overnight.

"Doc needs a medical partner. The Amish community needs improved medical care. Klara needs training, supplies, and equipment. What could be more obvious? She does an internship with Doc, returns to her community to provide routine care, and when either community has a serious medical case Doc and Klara join forces in whichever community is involved. By the way, tell Hockley we'll need a radio in each community capable of transmitting and receiving reliably across that distance. He can work out whatever antennas might be required, and batteries and solar chargers—that sort of thing."

"A radio of such a kind would not be considered a telephone, I feel sure," explained Klara, with perhaps a hint of mischievous daring spicing her moral trepidation in a way that made Tom's eyes pop open, "and so such a radio could maybe help us here in this world without the risk of harming our moral fitness for the next."

"By the way," Sophie interjected, "be grateful the Amish haven't been as uptight about their opiates as we've been with ours. The liquid Klara gave you when you broke your rib was laudanum: opium dissolved in alcohol. It made your trip back home a lot more comfortable.

"The medical representative of the Amish community and the President of Mountainview's Mustard Seed Foundation—her and me—have just concluded a meeting in which it was agreed to stop keeping Mountainview's opium and 'herbal relaxant' seeds a secret. We plan to divvy them up between the communities. I'll see Mabel about it later today.

"The financial arrangement for funding medical care—which I had to beat out of old Judge Parker—won't be required for these old-fashioned Amish: they're a hundred years or so ahead of us in that respect. For them, medical care is just something any civilized humans naturally provide their own kind— to the extent they're able—not a business opportunity for squeezing private profit out of human suffering."

Concerned that her devoutly conservative people and their ways were being cast by Sophie's leftwing perspective in something less than an accurate light, Klara spoke up.

"Actually, you know, we are not so quick to give things away free. We work for what we have, and we expect all to do the same. Is good for people—honest work—and very bad to have things free, we think. Medical care—most times you do not need, ya? Only once in a while. Some need little, other people need much. Is best, we think, for all to pay some little thing each week—then all to receive care they have paid for if they need it. Not so good, we think, for some people to pay nothing. Because then, if they need, we must either give them care for free or else charge them huge amount they cannot pay. Not so good, either way, eh? Our system Sophie tells me is very 'Progressive'—but is really just old-time way we have for being fair: everybody pays and everybody gets. Is no free handouts with us."

Sophie was a bit taken aback by this sudden shift from the Leftist Lady Bountiful's free-handout orthodoxy she habitually thought in terms of to a hardnosed system run on a strictly enforced "pay your own way" basis. It sounded frighteningly close to something rightwing Republican cost-accountants wearing green eyeshades might approve of.

280

But she was thoughtful enough to find Klara's comments intriguing: her Amish notions (describing a healthcare system that had been functioning quite well for many centuries) undeniably held a certain pragmatic appeal, even if some aspects were, perhaps, in theory, a bit morally scandalous. Perhaps even like... like... well, maybe a bit like Klara's initial moral qualms about establishing a radio-telephone link between our two communities, Sophie realized with a start.

Listening to this interchange, and knowing his Sophie well enough to virtually read her mind, Tom thought: sweetly gentle, pastoral utopian sentimentalists? *Ha!* The Amish are about as tough-mindedly realistic as any group could be, right down the last penny owed, plus interest. They are—most definitely—not a people to be messed with. He smiled. Any more than my Sophie is, come to that.

As much as he'd tried to steer clear of mentioning the prisoner Klara had worked on with Doc, Tom could finally stifle his curiosity no longer.

"Could you and Doc help that prisoner yesterday? What did you think of the situation?"

"Ach—we help his pain from broken ankle." She shrugged. "Some medicine he drinks and broken ankle is not feeling so bad."

Then she sighed, and Tom and Sophie could sense the depth of the woman's sorrow.

"I work only with broken bones and simple things like that. Other things broken is much too difficult for me—for anyone here on earth, I think. This man has done terrible things—maybe *most* terrible thing there is: attacking people; killing. His broken ankle is nothing—truly nothing—compared to his broken...well...we say 'soul.' I feel so sorry for him. He will be judged, like me and you and all of us—this I believe. And so I pray for him—yesterday, and today, and in the days ahead. For his judgment will be a hard one I think. That is what he has to fear truly, not just a little nothing like broken ankle. So I pray for him and I will ask all our people to pray also. That poor man, so broken inside to do such terrible things, needs every prayer."

Tom's compulsion to understand her made him ask, even at the risk of creating a rift: "I expect Mountainview will try him and execute him as an accessory to multiple murder. What would you, your community, do with him?"

She'd obviously thought long about it herself.

"I am not sure. Never have we had such a thing that I know of. Usually, for someone who acts very bad, we make a judgment of all our people not to talk to this person. Our silence to him lasts until we believe he repents and will not do such harm in future. In case of even worse bad acts, I think we would make a judgment to put him out from us completely, and make him go. But I do not know of any from our people who have done such terrible things as this man: killing others. So I do not know what to answer you."

She added, as the group sat in somber silence, "But what our people do with him, or your people do with him—this is not the important thing, I think. Whatever…it is finished in short time: a few hours if he is hanged, a few years if he is spared. What is that—compared to all time eternal that lies ahead till the very end of the world? That is the serious judgment he must face, and that is why I hope all will pray for him. The poor, poor man …"

Overwhelmed by the dept of Klara's simple sincerity, the former ACLU-Sophie could not fall back on her knee-jerk sociological mantras. Nor could the current, post-ACLU-Sophie exhibit any of the newfound, hard-edged moral clarity of a neo-conservative: a liberal who's been mugged. Even Tom, for once, could not carefully set forth in a clear and neutral fashion numerous hands-worth of alternative ways to consider the matter, all deserving of endless, agonized consideration before concluding that the issue required further study.

As Sophie arranged with Klara for her to return soon to Mountainview to begin her internship with Doc, The Jeffsons' other houseguest, Abraham Hite, announced that the cider press he'd been working on was near enough to completion for his two young helpers, Jacob and Joshua Yoder, to finish it. He would take the opportunity to return to his community in the wagon with Klara and Caleb. With breakfast over, Caleb set out on foot for Johnson's to fetch Daisy and the haywagon.

Abraham Hite collected his belongings and told Tom and Sophie how much he appreciated their hospitality ." . . and all the many new things I see here in so big a town. I think you like the press when it's finished, ja? But if any problems you have it with, you tell me and I make it good, ok? And thanks for the work you do for us on those welding jobs. Is very good we help each other, I think."

Tom and Sophie thanked the Amish again for the care-gifts they had brought, which had been stored at the police station pending distribution.

Caleb clucked his tongue at Daisy and the big hay wagon with Abraham Hite and Klara Yoder in back rolled away from the Gravely dealership.

As Tom and Sophie waved goodbye to these strange people from some bygone century, Tom said to her "we could not possibly have been any luckier regarding our neighbors. I think…I'm not clear about this…but I think maybe in some way our human future might depend on successfully blending elements of the two worldviews, theirs and ours, each group providing what the other lacks. At least when it comes to building any future *worth* living for—not just some endless, meaningless cycle of civilizations' rise to power and fall from power, over and over, forever and ever, around and around the same futile circle that Judge Parker claims is all history has to offer us."

After the hay wagon was lost to sight around a corner, they split up. Tom picked his painful way through the early morning's freezing streets, slowly and carefully, toward the police station, intending to learn what he could from Barley about any recent developments, and then see Hockley Beener to arrange a radio link between the communities.

Sophie went—in an uncharacteristically preoccupied amble, not her usual brisk march—to the Judge's house to advise him and Mabel about Klara's forthcoming partnership with Doc, and about the two communities' soon-to-be-pooled medical resources, including the sharing of Mountainview's opium and pot.

Chapter 34
Trial...and Tribulation

"Still no sign from Dick and his guys tracking the two who escaped," Barley told Tom at the Station. "I don't know. They took three days' food. I guess they must figure they have some chance of catching them. But anyway, here and now, how about if you use your steam Gravely to help dig graves. It's a bitch in the frozen ground, considering how many we need. Once you get that underway, come back here to confer with your client."

"Client?"

But Barley just smiled a thin, chilly smile and sent Tom on his way.

Before seeing Hockley about the radio link, Tom went by Tim Baker's to give him his instructions and return his crutch, which had been recovered from the wood-lot killing field and brought to the police station.

"Go fire up the Gravely, attach the cart, and put the roto-tiller tines and a full load of firewood in the cart. Drive up to Woodside Baptist, to the graveyard there. Chief Barley's going to send a deputy over to actually run the Gravely, but you'll be there to make sure it's properly fired, operates within acceptable steam pressures, has proper lubrication, and so forth.

"What I've suggested they do is use the tiller tines to break up the dirt where they're digging, so they can shovel it out of the graves more quickly and easily. Chief says they plan to dig one large grave for all the attackers and lay them in side-by-side, so they'll probably figure, say, foot-and-a-half width times six bodies—plus a bit more maybe," (to include space for the prisoner, in a few hours, Tom thought but did not tell the boy) "say—something like a trench about six feet wide by twelve feet long. Then there's ten individual graves for our own people. It's going to be a huge amount of work: thank God we have the Gravely to help.

"Also, Tim, thanks again for your own help yesterday: you got the machine to safety and you set my own mind at rest, knowing you were there, guarding it and the shop and Sophie. No man could have done better."

He used the word "man" deliberately, and it had the effect he intended. Almost before Tom's eyes, Tim seemed to gain four inches, fifty pounds, and a sober new maturity.

"Well," Tom sighed to himself as he left the shop, "From the looks of the kid, it seems I've just made a disciple. Now if I only had a faith ..."

At the next house he visited, Tom spoke briefly with Hockley. The young man, still giddy with gratitude over the deal Tom had cooked up for him to work with his lust-object Starshine, would enthusiastically have agreed to set up a radio link from Atlantis to the moon. After a few minutes outlining what needed to be done, Tom headed back to the police station.

"*Client?*" he demanded when he encountered Barley once more.

"Yep. I've met with Judge Parker and he agrees we'd better go through some motions with the prisoner. We considered attempting a genuine 'trial'— or as close as we could get. But the fact is, neither of us wanted to chance it with twelve jurors. Simply too damn much risk we might get one out of twelve who'd hang the jury: Bob pissed at Bill because his yard next door's always a mess; Mildred miffed at Molly because of what Susie said Alice told her at the church picnic; earnest young Harold in his first year at community college, who's just encountered sociology, and believes society's the root cause... And so forth. Hung jury, re-trial, jurors disqualified (on what grounds? by who with universally accepted legitimacy? in accordance with what process?) and endless, endless community division. A lot of families here have lost a man: for them it's not theoretical. Long-term, the social bitterness and divisiveness of a screwed-up trial could be more destructive than the murder of the ten victims.

"So Judge suggested, and I've agreed, that we consider ourselves under a sort of martial law. Accordingly, conventional legal process is suspended. The trial will be before a court martial, consisting of the Judge, whom I've just deputized, with a prosecutor, who'll be me, and a defender, who'll be you. Raise your right hand."

"Hey! Now wait one effen minute! In the *first* place I've never taken a single course in the law, and in the *second* place ..."

"I'm no lawyer either. Judge will advise both counsels on matters of law and procedure. Right hand up."

And so, upon his swearing in, Tom acquired his first capital case.

"Here's a pencil and some paper. Come to court sober and stay awake throughout the entire trial: that'll put you way ahead of plenty of Public Defenders assigned to capital cases in the former system," Barley advised with a grin. "Now, come and confer with your client. I want this wrapped up by the time the grave's dug."

"*Jesus,* Barley…!" was all Tom could exclaim.

The prisoner was lying on his cot in the police station's one jail cell. He did not look up. Barley swung open the door, admitted Tom, said "give me a holler when you're done," closed and locked the cell door, and departed.

"My name is Tom Jeffson. I've been appointed to defend you in your trial. I'd like to, uh, well, for a start, let me get your name and date of birth."

"Screw you."

"Um, well: can you give me any information I can offer the court on your behalf?"

Silence.

"Did you actually fire your rifle during the attack? Were you in such pain at the time you didn't fully know what your comrades were doing? Did you feel you had to pretend to go along with them, for fear they'd turn on you if you didn't? Anything you can offer? Are you remorseful now about what happened?"

Silence, followed by more silence. The two men might as well have been in different worlds—as indeed we soon will be, thought Tom.

"I want to do whatever I can to help you. Whether or not you want me to for your sake I *need* to for my own sake. If you no longer care about yourself, will you help *me* do the best I can—so I can live with it?"

Further silence.

Finally, a bang on the door and loud call from Barley: "'Bout done in there? We're all ready soon as you are."

The court martial had been convened in the police station's garage. A desk had been positioned for Judge Parker to sit behind, card tables and folding chairs had been set up for the prosecution and defense, and three rows of folding chairs had been arranged along the garage's far wall for any spectators who wished to attend the open trial. About fifteen people, mostly relatives of the victims, had chosen to do so.

When convened by Judge Parker, the court heard a brief statement from Chief Barley summarizing the attack at the wood-lot and subsequent capture of the prisoner. When asked by the Judge if he wished to dispute this account, Tom did not contest it.

When the prisoner was asked by the Judge if he had anything to say about the matter—or would at least provide his name and state whether he pled guilty or not guilty—the prisoner remained silent.

The Judge explained that Western legal tradition had long held accomplices to criminal acts generally liable for the acts of their cohorts, whether they themselves actually engaged in all the specific acts or not; that in this case the acts of unprovoked multiple murder were extremely serious; and that in the event of being found guilty the prisoner was subject to the death penalty or to very long imprisonment.

"Slavery, you mean," the prisoner spoke out.

"Well, in a sense. It would be the only alternative, if found guilty, to a death sentence."

"Kill me."

The Judge was unable to elicit any further comments from the prisoner. He asked Chief Barley and Tom if they had anything to add regarding guilt or innocence, and neither did.

The Judge pronounced the court martial's verdict of guilty.

"Do I understand correctly that the prosecution seeks the death penalty?"

"Yes, Judge."

"What statement do you have to make on the defendant's behalf?" the Judge asked, turning to Tom.

"We need labor, Judge. There must be all sorts of work the prisoner could do in his cell, with the amount and type of food he receives being dependant on fulfilling his work quota. We also need to make a firm statement about our own humanity, Judge. This prisoner is surely the least guilty of all the attackers, and most worthy of mercy. We should take the opportunity to grant that mercy—for our own sake, if not for his. And we need hope, Judge. This man, if left alive, might change. He might repent of his acts, and serve his penance for them, and in time become a different man—a more worthwhile man—than he is today. I do not strain your credulity by claiming such a thing surely *will* happen. But I suggest that if he is left alive what also remains alive is the hope that it *might*—and hope is something we all badly need; all of us." He sat down.

The Judge reflected for a few moments and spoke to the prisoner.

"You have an effective and persuasive spokesman arguing for sparing your life. I am persuaded that, on balance, his arguments slightly outweigh those for executing you. But if you are determined not to be imprisoned, I will place your own wishes above the case for imprisonment that your counsel has argued. Do you wish to be executed instead of imprisoned?"

"Yes."

"It is the decision of this court that you be executed before the end of the present day. Because this is a court martial, it is within the court's power to specify that the execution be humanely carried out in such manner as the Chief of Police shall dictate. I am sorry for you, prisoner. I hope all who are so inclined will pray for you. This court is now adjourned."

Chief Barley helped as the prisoner, using a crutch, was escorted out of the garage's back door into the police station's back yard. He was placed against a large oak, a rope passed under his armpits and around the tree to secure him in position, and a blindfold placed on him. Chief Barley drew his own Colt .45 pistol, held the muzzle three feet from the prisoner's chest, and fired.

As several deputies took the limp body down, Barley went back into the Station, where the 'courtroom' chairs and card-tables in the garage were being folded up and removed, and the Judge's desk was being hauled back into one of the police station's offices. He was glad to see that Tom had not yet left.

"Come into my office, would you Tom? You did well, you know. You have absolutely nothing to reproach yourself for." The two old friends settled in their chairs in Barley's room. "Grave's just being finished, I hear, so I'm headed there next for the service."

Barley sighed. "The seven attackers are together in this first batch. Then, tomorrow, the hard burials begin: all ten of our own people. While they're transporting this latest body, there's a related matter I want your input on.

"The attackers had gold coins in their pockets: fourteen one-ounce gold American Eagles, all told. Money they'd stolen, I assume. Imagine how many supplies they could easily have *bought* from us for a tiny fraction of that gold! Obviously, their minds just didn't work that way—which leads me to suspect they were most likely criminally inclined even before The Collapse. Though who knows whether they were already professional criminals or just latent wannabee's. Lots of tattoos on them—but that ancient mark of the criminal subculture became so common among middleclass suburbanites toward the end it's not much of an indicator any more."

The Chief gave a gentle, sad little sigh. "Hell of a note ...

"Anyway, their weapons—some of which are excellent—and their ammunition I have ruled to be police department property. As for the coins, I'd like to distribute one coin to each victim's widow, or in Bill Jeffries' case to his mother since he wasn't married. The remaining four coins I want to declare to be police department property, to be deposited on Mountainview's behalf with old Miz Strewk, for her to lend out at interest. Poor Arthur, of course, had all those silver dimes and some $20 gold pieces he left Miz Strewk when he died...."

Barley smiled a thin smile. "Remember him? Who'd have thought ...? Lordy, Tom, you sure never know, do you? Anyway, the widow's got all those coins he left her, and I understand she earns more than enough to keep herself in fine style by lending them out to people who are starting and running businesses. Hell of a lot more convenient for all parties than hauling hundred-pound sacks of corn or potatoes around to make payments with. Anyway, what do you think of handling the attackers' gold coins that way?"

Tom considered the angles.

"I'd suggest going about it a little differently. The basic idea's good. It's smart to head off charity cases before they begin, if possible, and I think giving each widow something will go a long way toward that goal, and demonstrate some morale-boosting community support in the process. But a full ounce of gold is not a sum we could likely duplicate for other widows in the future: it's too huge an amount. More men will be killed at some point, and then what, after we've given the present batch of widows an ounce of gold each? Bad feelings, I'm afraid.

"So what I think I'd do is deposit all fourteen ounces with Miz Strewk. Out of the interest received, the police department can then pay *some* amount in silver each month to the widows. Decide on an amount you're confident you can match in the future, when sooner or later more widows' pensions will be required.

"Oh, and another thing: fourteen ounces of gold is one *hell* of a huge sum of money. Demand a hell of a fine return on it from Miz Strewk. If she's not willing to pass on to the police department damn near *all* the interest she earns off that capital, threaten to use it to set up a competing bank. She's old but she's sharp as a tack: won't take her long to see reason. In her own 'white collar' way she's not all that different from the Scouse Brothers."

"Good thinking, Tom; I appreciate your counsel. Let's do it that way. I'll ask Judge Parker to oversee the investment agreement with Miz Strewk and the pension arrangements for the widows. Well, I'm headed for Woodside Baptist. You coming?"

"Of course, Chief—that's why I was waiting around after the trial."

There was a moment's silence.

"You did what you had to, you know. You're a stronger man than I am, Chief. You don't take refuge in dithering. I'm glad you could do it. We all owe you a great deal—for things you may not even realize."

"Ah well...Kind of you to say so. That grave better not be deeper than about four feet: I *told* Patterson not to have the men waste a whole lot of energy. We got a shitload of grave-digging still ahead of us."

The grave was, indeed, not much more than four feet deep. It amounted to a trench about six feet wide, into which the attackers' bodies had been laid crosswise, side-by-side, touching each other at the shoulders. The trench looked to be about twelve feet long. The freshly executed prisoner's body was being added to the previous six.

The row of bodies, still dressed in the bloody clothes they'd been wearing, their status not warranting precious cloth for shrouds, reminded Tom of war-atrocity photos he'd seen all his life.

Corpses in pits, he thought, heartsick: the archetypal news photo of the 20th century. *We sure haven't wasted much time getting off to a brisk start in the 21st.*

Sophie joined Tom and the Chief at the graveside.

"I sent Tim back to the shop with the Gravely the minute they'd finished digging," she said, a bit accusingly. "He has no business seeing things like this."

"No, I suppose not," replied Tom, hugging her. "But I'm not entirely sure. When nobody knew at first if there were other attackers in other parts of town, I posted him with a carbine to guard the shop, the steam Gravely, and you. I tried to impress on him the importance of not shooting unless you absolutely, *absolutely* have to shoot. This sight makes it pretty clear why. Gunshots are not something actors get up from, so they can report to Makeup for freshening and then be on their Marks again for the next Take of a scene. Gunshots do not shoot the pistols out of bad guys' hands, leaving them gnashing their teeth in rage at the good guy but otherwise unharmed and ready to be arrested. Gunshots don't kill only the bad guys, either.

"If The Collapse has achieved nothing else of value, I hope it has at least ended, for a very long time, the moronic, cartoon-portrayal of guns and what they do. Cowboys-and-Indians, Cops-and-Robbers, Valiant Soldiers versus Enemy Fanatics—God, how I wish every stupid viewer of that crap could be forced to stand *here* for an hour, staring down into this pit-full of carcasses."

Parson Miller joined the small group: Tom and Sophie, Chief Barley, a couple of the deputies who'd transported the last body, four woodcutters, reassigned from firewood cutting to a three-hour shift with the digging teams, and a handful of townspeople who, for whatever reason, had decided to attend. Parson Miller's service consisted simply of a brief reading of Scripture, a plea to God to accept the souls of these unknown men, and a plea to the living to allow God's Judgment, which the living can never understand, to take the place of their own.

The gravediggers resumed their work even before the small group had dispersed, filling in the trench with the loose dirt.

290

As Tom and Sophie said goodbye to Chief Barley, Sophie hugged him tightly.

"*Thank you,*" she told him forcefully.

"Yess'm," he replied softly, and headed back to his office to see if there had been any word about Dick Peters and the thirteen men still out with him, and to finalize arrangements for Bill Parton, his Citizens Patrol deputy whose burial would be one of the next day's ten.

As he neared the station, a deputy came running out to meet him.

"Gotta radio call, Chief—from Dick! They're at the Amish place!"

Barley hurried inside, where he struggled to make out enough of the faint signal to learn what had happened.

"Yeah, Chief, This is Dick. Hear me ok? All right. Well, we never caught the two guys. Snow came down almost as soon as we were on their trail, so tracking wasn't easy. They'd slip out of the woods every so often and cross a field or pasture—bare dirt where the wind had blown the snow off—so they wouldn't leave much sign. Then back into the woods again at some other place, where we couldn't see them. Delayed us a while each time they did that before we'd finally pick them up again. It was pretty clear they were drawing away from us, increasing their lead. They were definitely heading south, though. Copy?"

"Copy."

"Only thing south of Mountainview for miles and miles is the Amish, and I figured we wanted to make sure these guys didn't go there. So we gave up tracking them and formed into a long column and headed straight for the Amish, fast as we could, not trying to be quiet about it. I figured we'd at least drive them away from the Amish and set up a screen along the edge of that settlement to encourage them to move on past instead of trying another attack. Copy?"

"Copy."

"We've got thirteen guys now—all but me—strung out in a long, shallow arc around the east edge of the Amish place, staying out of sight but moving around a bit now and then and calling to each once in a while to make sure the killers know we're there. My guess is these two guys are not crazy: they're going to keep on heading south instead of trying a suicide-charge against the line we've established. Come nightfall, we'll pull in a bit closer together but still maintain as much of a line as we can. Copy?"

"Copy."

"I couldn't get radio contact from the ground. So I went into the Amish settlement to see if I could get up in the top of their tallest building. Some kinda barn or something. They got all bent outta shape over my rifle. Told me to take it out of their home. So I went out and left it with one of our guys and came back. They're kind of worked up over it, but not too much to allow me to get up in the rafters of their highest barn. That's where I'm talking from now. They've supplied food and water to take to the guys, and we have our sleeping bags, so I figure we'll stay put here for a couple days, to give the killers an incentive to keep moving on. How's that sound to you?"

"Sounds good, Dick. We'll keep a continuous radio watch here. Can you try to call in each day around dusk and dawn?"

"Will do."

"Ok. Good job. Glad you could work things out with the Amish about the guns. Be as diplomatic as you can with them. We're going to need those people in all sorts of ways for years to come, remember."

"Yeah. Ok. That's all I got. Talk with you again tomorrow around dawn. Over."

"Dawn tomorrow. Over."

Three days later, Dick Peters and his tired, cold, disgruntled men trudged their footsore way eleven miles back to Mountainview from the Amish community. They'd found not the faintest trace of the remaining two attackers. Their own frustration about their mission's inconclusiveness was matched, they found, by a sense of expectant dread that hung like an invisible pall over Mountainview's entire population. The people of Mountainview seemed to be waiting, breath drawn, for some other shoe to drop. Were there… *others…*slipping quietly through the surrounding forests…*out there…?*

"You too?" asked Tom one evening, two weeks later, when Sophie had laid aside her book, gotten up from the couch they were sharing in the library, put on some water for tea, idly leafed through several other books, chosen one, read two paragraphs, put it aside too, and decided she didn't want tea after all when the whistling kettle sounded.

"Yeah. Me too."

They were in most ways very privileged, living vastly above the standards of anyone else in town. They had two small fluorescent lights that made it possible for them to read after sundown, yet which drew so little current they could be powered by the car batteries Tom kept charged in the shop below. Using the same batteries they could also play tapes and CDs. Tom needed to run the steam Gravely for the generator in his shop each day to power his shop equipment, so there was no added cost for the secondary benefits they received in their home, such as having the only truly well-heated house in town, and being able to use the electric well pump to provide running water, and keeping the battery-bank charged for their reading-lights and music.

And yet, in mid-March, living better than any other people in Mountainview, with the worst of the winter's cold behind them and the days beginning to lengthen, they still could not stop their restless fidgeting and pacing.

Tom sighed, putting his arm around his wife on the couch and pulling her to him.

"'Nother day, 'nother delay…" she muttered, wriggling herself gently into place against him, careful of his still-tender healing rib.

"The university *will* get started, Tom: I just have to take it easy and roll with the postponements and keep the Big Picture in mind. I know that. It's just irritating. At least the restaurant operation's doing well. We're clearly going to make a financial go of it. If business continues improving, Maybelle plans to cut back her hours with the woodcutting crew she's been cooking for and put the time into expanded restaurant hours. The money should work out about the same either way for her, but she enjoys being her own boss at the restaurant. If she and Owen don't end up moving to the Amish community, I think we might eventually do a deal where she buys out my half of the restaurant business, and I rent space there to do university classes outside the mealtime hours. *If* the university ever actually gets going, that is."

She gnawed gently on Tom's free arm, chewing out her frustration on this improvised doggie-toy.

"You seem to be muttering vile language and pacing around in circles a bit more than usual, whenever I come through the shop."

"Yes; I am," Tom admitted. "It's a slow go, trying to put together a steam engine out of assorted gasoline engine bits and pieces. I'll get it done—I *have* to have it working, to power the shop's generator by spring, when the steam Gravely's going to be needed fulltime for farm work. It's just…I can't *concentrate*. I live every day sort of…*listening* …waiting…for some other catastrophe…all day long, half-expecting at any moment I'll hear another outburst of gunfire."

He drew a long breath. "We need to send out that patrol to Grayson we've been intending for so long."

In the two weeks since Dick Peters and his men returned from the Amish community, there'd been no further sign of the two men they'd been tracking. It was assumed—or at least hoped—they had continued on south, leaving the area permanently. But the maddening inconclusiveness of the matter, the lack of any resolution, greatly undermined whatever closure might have been achieved when the townspeople had suspended all regular business for a day and turned out in unison for the ten funerals.

In truth, the suddenness and ferocity of the attack and its death-toll, striking totally without warning, had left Mountainview with a bad case of the dreads-and-jitters. It was hard to live each day just waiting, passively, feeling like a target—never knowing if some unseen person in the woods at that very moment might be carefully lining up the cross-hairs of his scope on the back of one's neck. It was becoming necessary—psychologically, if for no other reason—that the people of Mountainview reached out to probe their surroundings, explore them, and reassure themselves that the countryside all around was not crawling with unseen killers.

Grayson, and its continuing baffling silence, just twenty-five miles away up Rt. 12, was, Tom thought, as good a direction as any for an initial armed probe.

When he took his thoughts to Chief Barley, Tom was relieved to find the Chief had already begun planning the expedition, however reluctantly.

"Come on, Tom: if there were any people in Grayson we'd have heard something by now. I think all of them, or nearly all, must be dead. Granted, there's always some risk of our scouting party being ambushed by anyone who may still be alive, but that's not what worries me. I'm far more concerned about *why* they may all be dead: disease. We sure as hell do not want to bring back here any epidemic that may have killed off all of Grayson. Tell you the truth, I'd just as soon *never* go there."

He worked energetically with his pocketknife, deepening the initials he was carving into a corner of his wooden desk—initials Tom could see were already very deeply carved.

"Oh well…" he sighed, "there's popular sentiment building. Might as well try to steer this grand adventure in as safe a direction as possible, since I can't block the idea."

He shoved a pencil and paper toward Tom.

"Add your requests to the shopping list. I'm having anyone who expresses an interest jot down whatever items he thinks it most important for us to get when we go to Grayson. We'll go over all the entries before setting out, condense and prioritize them, and have a clear plan in mind about what things we'll try to find, and where and how we'll find them.

"Anyway," (viciously digging the initials even deeper) "it's already having a good impact on morale. Half the goddamn people in town running around with smiles on their faces, writing their Letters to Santa…"

Tom himself smiled, despite the Chief's plain irritation, but after a moment the smile was replaced by a more serious look of concern.

"You know, Chief—it sounds crazy to say this—but bear with me a moment while I do some pondering out loud. First, I share your concerns about disease. I think that's probably the greatest risk Grayson poses for us. But it may also be very important to us *when* any epidemic struck.

"Grayson's population was about 4000? Maybe 4500? That means there must be a lot of vehicles there—let's say 8000 or so. If Grayson's population was killed off fairly suddenly, early in The Collapse, many of the vehicles may still have some gas or diesel remaining in them. And perhaps there might be some left in the storage tanks at gas stations.

"We could, I suppose, devote not just one but *several* trips to siphoning or pumping out all the gas or diesel we could find in Grayson and hauling it back here to squeeze the last drop of use from our own vehicles, generators, farm machinery, and so forth. There must be tank trucks of various sorts in Grayson, so if there's fuel there we could use them to haul it back here. Suppose, just theoretically, we could scavenge enough gas and diesel from Grayson to allow us to scrape by here in Mountainview for one more year, using the strictest economy. I really can't imagine we could get *more* than that amount of fuel from whatever remains of a town of 4500 or so."

"Well, no," Barley agreed, his puzzlement plain on his face. "I suppose, offhand, a year's worth of fuel would be about the most we could reasonably hope to scavenge. So?"

"I think there would be big consequences for us—both positive and negative. And I'm not sure which would be bigger in the long run. On the one hand, finding fuel in Grayson would be a huge break for us, giving us additional time to produce the steam engines we're going to need. On the other hand, finding fuel in Grayson would work to delay the closure we also badly need: the acceptance that our world now is permanently different from what it was before The Collapse, the wholehearted commitment we must have to build ourselves a new society, not just hang on day by day in hopes someone or something will 'save' us.

"To be honest, Chief, in the long run I'm not sure whether I *want* to find any gas and diesel left in Grayson."

"Well; I guess we'll find whatever we find. If they're all or nearly all dead, I suppose you're right: any fuel remaining will depend on how soon they died. Draw up plans for what the expedition should do in whatever fuel-vs-no-fuel scenarios you consider likely. And we'll just go there, and wing it, and hope we don't bring back some sort of plague to Mountainview."

The plan decided on by the third week of March was to take Johnson's big, thirty foot long hay wagon, pulled by Invincible, plus one of the horse carts the Scouse brothers had made from the back of a pickup truck, pulled by the mule. Twenty well-armed men would go on foot—with food, water, camping equipment and animal fodder hauled in the carts. And one man ("Not me, for damn sure!" exclaimed Tom) would ride Trigger, to scout ahead of the party.

Hockley Beener asked his new assistant, Starshine, to scavenge the entire town for suitable handheld radios, and from her results he selected five for the expedition. The plan was for the group to maintain radio contact with Chief Barley in the police station. When the expedition had reached the limit of a radio set's range, one man would halt there with his radio to serve as a relay. The expedition would continue until it reached the limit of its contact with that relay-man, at which point a second relay-man would remain behind while the expedition continued. Using however many relay links it took, the expedition intended to maintain contact with Mountainview, should urgent reinforcements have to be summoned, or urgent warnings sent.

The lists of most-desired items to be sought were, after great discussion, finally condensed into a total somewhat approaching realism, and priorities agreed on. Dick Peters, appointed by Barley to head the expedition, selected his twenty volunteer infantrymen from more than twice that many applicants, making certain each was armed with the most suitable weapon available. Including the AR-15's and 30-.06's taken from the recent attackers, plus the best weapons the town of Mountainview already had, the twenty infantrymen were indeed far more heavily armed than a comparable-size urban police force, and almost as lethally equipped with small arms as a military unit.

Owen Paks, though refusing to carry a weapon, absolutely insisted on going as Invincible's handler, and his demand was accommodated. As Barley privately told Dick Peters and some of the others "Tell Owen 'no' and you won't have to walk all the way to Grayson for a war: you'll have one with Owen right here and now."

Peters, with a wink to Tom, declared "RHIP: Rank Has Its Pratfalls" and decided to ride the valiant Trigger himself. The mule would be led, in turn, by whichever infantryman could be inveigled into the chore—not a plum assignment because of the mule's occasional tendency to bite.

At the start of the last week in March, in a bitter-cold gusty wind under a clear sky, the column assembled an hour after dawn in front of the police station. Last-minute checks of radios and supplies were completed, Mountainview's three clergymen offered brief prayers, and the column set off down Main Street to Rt. 12, then north toward Grayson.

Tom, at fifty-nine much too old to be of any use as a foot-soldier, and with his broken rib not yet fully healed, silently waved goodbye to the expedition with a doubly intense feeling. As the column moved away, he was hit hard by having to bid farewell not just to the expedition but to his own former days as a more vigorous younger man—something he had put off accepting till well past time reality demanded its acknowledgment.

"Let's hope it works out," Chief Barley said to him quietly as the column rounded a corner and was lost to view.

In a sober way—laying to final rest any fantasies about "outside help" while providing the supplies vital for Mountainview's own self-help—it did.

Chapter 35
Grayson I

The infantrymen, walking easily on the flat, smooth road with no significant weight in their packs, had no trouble making twenty-two miles in eight hours. At that point, in the late afternoon, about three miles from Grayson in a shallow draw next to a trickling creek, Peters brought the column to a halt.

They posted pickets around the perimeter of their camp and staked out Invincible and the mule with food and water. They hung a large kettle of salted pork and pinto beans over one campfire on an iron tripod, and set water pots on another fire to boil for tea and the later washing-up. They tied tarps along one side of the big wagon, from the top of the wagon sides right down to the ground, securely roped to the bottom of the wheels, to form a windbreak, then they spread their sleeping bags out in that shelter. Peters, meanwhile, used the day's remaining light to cautiously ride on toward Grayson a bit, then in various other directions, carefully scouting all around the camp while their food was cooking.

"I've seen no human signs in any direction," he later told the party as they ate supper. "We'll be up by dawn, and moving within an hour to cover the remaining three miles, so I expect to reach Grayson before nine o'clock tomorrow morning. That'll give us all day long to make a very cautious approach and entry, once we reach town. We'll leave the wagons, with a three-man guard holding one of the radios, outside town—the wagons turned around and heading back toward Mountainview in case they need to pull out in a hurry. I expect to enter the town in two groups on foot. Beyond that, we'll just have to see what things look like once we get there."

Dick Peters reported their situation and plans back to Mountainview by radio. They had had to station only a single relay midway between their camp and the town to maintain contact. Responding to Peters' report, Chief Barley emphasized again the vital necessity of every sanitary precaution the party could possibly take. After signing off, Peters then repeated his and the Chief's concerns to the party around the campfire.

"Look, men: forget the John Wayne stuff, OK? You're sufficiently well armed and numerous nobody's likely to take us on in a fire-fight. If anybody did, I'm confident we'd come out on top. What I want you to think—instead of John Wayne—is Louis Pasteur.

"Our biggest risk in Grayson tomorrow is likely to be disease. So I'm going to go over this once again: Do *not* eat or drink anything you find there. The outside of that sealed can or soda-pop bottle, or your own hands, could be contaminated. Do *not* try to hide some nifty little item you find and sneak it back to Mountainview as a souvenir: you might be bringing back germs on it that could kill us all. Do *not*, if you can possibly avoid it, go into confined indoor spaces where rats and the fleas from those rats will be especially concentrated. Ordinary rats, no bigger than this (Peters cupped one hand) can carry ordinary fleas, no bigger than this (he indicated on the tip of one finger) which can carry, for example, the Black Plague bacillus—not even big enough to *see*."

He turned both palms up, registering futility. He looked closely at each man, making certain he was getting through.

"And *that disease*—on more than one occasion—killed about a third of all the people in Europe." He paused. "You get my drift? Even John Wayne on a busy day didn't kill that may people. So I'm telling you again: the greatest risk tomorrow—for ourselves *and* for all our families in Mountainview, when we return—is disease. Louis Pasteur and his sanitation will be a lot more helpful to keep in mind than any John Wayne-style gunslinging.

"Now let's get to sleep. As each picket comes in to wake his replacement, try to get up and take position as quietly as you can, to let the others stay asleep. See you at dawn."

The next day dawned frosty and clear, drawing the men close around their two campfires. The men stamped and shivered, easing out the aches and soreness from their night on cold, hard ground. In short order, they wolfed down massive amounts of pancakes with butter and molasses, fried strips of pork, and three gallons of boiling-hot tea.

Peters himself carefully supervised the spraying of each man's wrists, ankles, boot-tops, and pants-cuffs with the last of Mountainview's precious insect repellant. He checked that each man had his pint bottle of Clorox bleach-and-detergent sterilizing solution, and that his canteen was filled with drinking water they'd brought from Mountainview.

They struck camp, harnessed Invincible and the mule, checked their weapons one last time for their own peace of mind's sake, and began the short march to Grayson.

A quarter of a mile before the town limits, they reached the bridge that carried Rt. 12 across Possum Creek. The bridge was still in fine shape, as was the narrow little two-lane blacktop county road. But near the Grayson end of the bridge, about thirty feet from the bridge itself, the party could see a crazy jumble of vehicles. Cars, pickups, various old farm trucks, and a new-looking school bus formed a chaotic traffic jam that blocked the pavement.

They halted on the south side of the creek, gazing, perplexed, down the length of the little bridge—hardly forty feet long—studying the chaos near its north end.

"Turn the wagons around here," Peters told his men. "Owen, you'll stay on the hay wagon with Invincible, of course; and Jack, you stay with the mule. Bring them both water and some feed, but keep them in harness. Jed, stake out Trigger with some water over there in the ditch, but leave him saddled and bridled, then take cover behind that bridge abutment.

"All three of you: make sure you keep checking upstream and downstream, as well as across the creek toward Grayson. See those feral dogs on the Grayson side? Don't allow 'em to cross the bridge and get to your animals on this side. Keep a close ear to your radio. If we pass the word, or if you think there's trouble and we can't get through to you, head back toward Mountainview as fast as you can. Don't pull up till you get to Bob Fox, the radio relay guy about halfway back to town. He'll be our assembly point if there's trouble and we have to retreat and re-group. Everybody got that?

"OK: Jim, take your men across the bridge and then get on the left shoulder of the road heading toward town. I'll have my men on the road's right shoulder, about ten yards behind you. Don't bunch up. Take things slow and easy. Check carefully all around you all the time. Don't rush—we've got all the time in the world. Got it? OK, let's go."

In the clear, cold, morning silence the two files of men slowly crossed the little bridge and took their positions, along the shoulders of the road, for their entry into Grayson, a quarter-mile ahead. Dick Peters was second in line in his file of men, on the road's right shoulder.

"Looks like a panic," the point man said to Peters just behind him, gesturing at the jumble of vehicles. "I think they were all going Hell-for-leather toward that narrow little two-lane bridge, and they ran together before they even reached the bridge itself. See here?" he pointed along the shoulder, "you could easily just pull off the blacktop two or three feet, drive along the shoulder around these vehicles, then pull back onto the road and cross the bridge. Must have been what those Amish did with their wagon, assuming this mess happened before they came through here."

He thought a moment, puzzled. "But why didn't anybody else do that? We've seen no vehicles, or even any signs of people, all the way between here and Mountainview."

Peters cautiously studied several of the vehicles. A few had one or more doors open, and no sign of occupants inside, though there were human skulls and assorted other bones strewn about the road in the area of this grisly traffic jam. A few vehicles had one window slightly open. Peters grunted softly as he peered in to find clean, white, large-bones from human remains—skulls, pelvises, tibias, femurs—still inside these vehicles, obviously too large for animals to extract through the window and drag away.

But, truly baffling, most of the vehicles had neither doors nor windows open. Peters grunted again as he peered inside several of these to find not merely scattered, well-cleaned bones but fairly complete corpses, often including men, women, and children: entire families he assumed. No scavengers larger than insects had been able to gain entry to the closed vehicles, and their grim work was still not complete.

"Panic, yeah ...," Peters said, taking a deep breath. "This traffic jam looks like the way bodies pile up near theater exits when there's a fire. In the stampede a single person falls, trips the one behind him, who trips two others, and in no time you have a pile of bodies blocking access to the exit—which may be a perfectly usable open door to safety. Like the bridge here. Evidently those two cars there in front collided, each racing to get to the bridge first, and they blocked all the rest. Could have been nighttime, so nobody saw you could just drive around the blockage using the shoulder here."

He stood looking in puzzlement at the death-scene around him, still not able to comprehend the missing element.

"But regardless of their panic—whatever that was about—once the road was blocked why didn't everyone just get out of his vehicle and run? Hell, *swim* the creek, if they were too panic-crazed to simply walk across the bridge like we just did. Look here: family upon family just sat in their cars—in summer heat I assume—with all the windows up...until they *died?* And nobody from town came here afterward, to remove the bodies for burial, instead of leaving them to the animals? What the hell?"

After a bit more thought, he began going from one vehicle to another, checking something in each driver's area.

"Look here, at the position of all the ignition keys: I think every one of these vehicles was left running! I'll bet they all just ran, sitting here, till they ran out of gas."

The scavenging animals had included plenty of rats, judging from the amount of droppings covering the scene. But most of the spooked and jittery men, anxiously wanting to leave this traffic-jam-of-the-dead, had more pressing concerns on their minds than rats or ignition keys or whatever Peters was yammering on about. They waited, shifting uneasily, eyeing two packs of feral dogs that were slinking about on opposite sides of the area, just far enough away to feel safe from the men and from each other.

"Don't waste ammo on them as long as they stay away," Peters told the men. "But keep an eye on them and take down the leader if they start acting like they're going to try rushing us. These are domestic dogs gone wild: they don't have an instinctive fear of Man like wolves would, so they may be more aggressive. Also, considering what they've been eating ..."

At last, Peters gave the word and the two files of men walked cautiously on, keeping to the shoulders of the road, finding bones but no signs of living humans as they covered the quarter mile to town. Peters, who had been lost deep in thought during their slow, careful progress, halted the two groups at the edge of town.

The men, so near to entering their objective, were beside themselves with frustration. They stood anxiously fidgeting, never taking their eyes off the feral dogs that had silently followed them from the bridge. The men were wound up tight, ready for exploring, or attacking, or fleeing, or scavenging, or discovering survivors they could rescue—or bargain with—or...*anything* but yet another damn halt while that damn Peters slowly scratched his damn ass and pondered the damn meaning of life.

"Thyson Chicken ..." Peters said thoughtfully to his band of furious, jumpy men. "Anybody work for the Thyson Plant here?"

"*Fuckin' crazy* ..." one man muttered in disgust, carefully speaking just softly enough to allow Peters to pretend not to hear it.

"Anybody?"

Silence.

"Well ...," Luther Meadows said tentatively, raising his hand, as he'd been taught in school. "I di'nt exactly *work* for Thyson ..."

Snickers from several of the men. Luther didn't exactly *work* much for anybody—though he'd been employed plenty of different places.

"I was, uh, night watchman—I mean Uniformed Plant Security Officer," he hastily corrected himself. "With Burns Protective Services. We handled security for the Thyson Plant."

With an inward sigh, Peters thought to himself 'Great. Oh well…best I can do,' and directed a hearty, man-to-man nod toward hapless Luther.

"Would you happen to know if they used any dangerous materials there at Thyson? Say…in their chicken processing operations maybe? I'm thinking maybe some kind of poisonous chemicals…?"

"Oh yessir. No doubt about that. Their chilling-and-freezing plant for that chicken processing they done was huge—and it run using ammonia, which is deadly, that's for sure. I know that for a fact. Ever' hour on the hour, I had to step outside the guard-shack and look up at a orange windsock, just like they got on these helicopter landin' pads. And I had to write down in my logbook whichever way the wind was a-blowin' based on that windsock—and whether it was strong, medium, or light. Or if it was dead calm I had to write that down too.

"An' my Captain—Cap'n Johnson—he said if ever the 'mergency sireens was to go off at the plant, about a leak of that ammonia, or if we had a fire or somethin', I was to head the plant workers upwind when they evacuated. And if I had to call the 'mergency number he give me—which he wrote in red ink on the front cover of the logbook—I had to be sure to look at the latest entry in the log and tell the Fire-n-Rescue, or Police, or whoever answered, what the wind direction was, so they'd know which way to get there from."

"Thank you, Luther. I think that's going to be very helpful."

Peters thought a moment, then said "OK. I think before going into town we'll just slip right along the edge of town to the Thyson Plant first. It's almost directly across town from here, up at the north end. Shouldn't take long to get there—couldn't be more than a couple of miles. Jim, you keep your squad on the left edge of the road; we'll be on the right side a little ways behind you. Let's still take our time and look all around us. Be careful not to bunch up and give anybody too good a target. But I do believe, men, the odds of meeting any hostiles have just gone way down.

"Except, maybe, those little puppies," he added with a grin, gesturing to the feral pack that had shadowed them, gliding silently just a few yards away. "they're just a lovable bunch a lapdogs—looking for a quick meal. Try not to stumble and fall down, lest they think you're it."

In less than an hour, they were at the entrance to the Thyson Plant. From the guard-shack at the plant gate, they removed the death-notice and obituary for the town of Grayson. It was the guard's logbook. On the page for Thursday,

303

August Twenty-seventh, in the block for the hour from 02:00-03:00, was a scribbled entry:

GAS ALARM 02:17 CALLED NUMBER NO ANSWER HOLLERED NOBODY AROUND STILL CALLING 02:22 OH SHIT I'M

The 02:00 wind observation entered at the top of that hourly block was FROM NORTH. GENTLE.

Peters carefully folded the page and placed it in his shirt pocket.

"It had to have been something of that sort," he told the stricken group of men standing around him, tightly gripping their rifles with nothing to shoot at.

"Lethal gas, drifting slowly right across town from one end to the other, just after two a.m. I see no bones around here: looks like the plant was deserted, probably went broke in the economic collapse—then most likely not properly maintained. Looks like there was nobody left here but one security guard—and him with no one at the other end of the phone when the poor bastard tried to call.

"A few people must have been awake at that hour. Maybe some of them phoned their friends and relatives—or ran out in the streets and screamed to sound an alarm. But an alarm for what? How many would have been thinking clearly enough, at two a.m., to recall what that particular automatic siren signal from the Thyson Plant meant, and then note the wind direction, and then think to move immediately *crosswind*, not downwind—without waiting to help Granny, without stopping to get dressed, without even putting on shoes…"

He shook his head.

"So a terrified small handful of people tried to head south out of town, creating that traffic jam just short of the bridge, where the gas cloud caught up with them, closed car windows or no. There must have been a few handfuls of others, especially on the east or west edges of town, who ran frantically from their homes in the dark, heading by sheer luck in what proved to be the right direction—out of the gas plume. Some probably just kept running in panic till they collapsed or were too lost to find their way back. Others probably stayed closer, wandering around the neighboring woods and fields till dawn.

"If they'd gathered up enough courage to return to town then, they'd have seen such awfulness they probably wished they were among the dead: an entire town populated by nothing but thousands of gassed corpses—filling the houses, spilling out onto the front lawns and the sidewalks, littering the streets …

"There was a toxic gas leak from a chemical plant in Bhopal, India—back in the Eighties, if I recall—that killed over 10,000 people. But that didn't happen with an entire *nation* collapsing around the affected community: there were aid programs and re-building efforts and other resources that could be directed to Bhopal. At least they could tend to their dead. I expect any survivors who returned to this horror here eventually just…quit. People will do that, you know. When the horror and the hopelessness become too overwhelming …"

He checked again for anything more he should recover from the guard shack. Seeing nothing, he turned back to his sickened, silent men.

"Well. Good news: looks like it was not a disease epidemic that killed them. That makes things a bit safer for us and for the people we'll return home to. Bad news: there are still bound to be diseases here in great number. We've got an entire town that was full of unburied corpses—over four thousand of them—and which offered unlimited hiding and breeding places for rats, with good protection from their natural predators: crawl spaces under the houses, the basements and attics of large buildings, sewer tunnels, and so on.

"Under ideal conditions, which this town provided, a rat population can grow so fast you can't imagine it. The handful of rats that survived the gassing—perhaps a few high above ground in the Courthouse attic—plus all the rats from the surrounding countryside that would have swarmed into town during the next days and weeks, drawn by unlimited food and cover, must have set off a population explosion beyond description.

"Any dogs or cats that were roaming outside town, or that ran away in time and thereby escaped the gas, have gone feral, of course. The good news is they'll most likely stay here in town now, with limitless rats as their food source. They'll have easier pickings here than they'd find roaming the countryside. Having them stay here is certainly better for us, too, even twenty-five miles away.

"Incidentally, regarding certain kinds of animal populations becoming concentrated: when it warms up in spring and the snakes start moving around, guess where they're going to make a bee-line for as well."

Peters smiled a thin, grim smile.

"I don't think anyone could have created a more effective roadblock to prevent travelers moving along Rt. 12 toward Mountainview. Grayson, here, is a cork in the bottle. In a couple of months, by late spring, nobody with a lick of sense would go into Grayson. In essence, this place is becoming a biological minefield: a town of 4000 or more unburied corpses, now crawling with rats and the diseases they carry; plus feral dog and cat populations, which, along with skunks and coons, will soon become reservoirs of rabies, since there's no more pet vaccination; plus, by late spring, half the timber rattlers and copperheads for a dozen miles around, drawn into town by enough rats to make this place Snake Heaven.

"Any travelers with enough smarts to still be alive today would realize entering a 'dead-town' like Grayson is crazy. On foot, of course, they could detour around Grayson and swim or raft across Possum Creek at some other point if they were determined to head our way. But I don't think any wheeled traffic is going to find the approach through Grayson to that Rt. 12 bridge very attractive.

"Men on foot, carrying everything they own on their backs cross-country, amount to nothing more threatening than refugees or bandits: only groups with wheeled transport, like ours, can constitute a genuine military force. I think Grayson will block vehicle traffic along Rt. 12 effectively enough to improve our safety for many years—in a perfectly 'natural' way, with no artificial, manmade barriers to give away the presence of any other communities still alive down Rt. 12 past Grayson."

He looked around him at the dead town.

"Speaking of vehicle traffic…I suspect we're not going to find fuel here for any motor vehicles. See the gas station on the corner? Burned out—either deliberately by vandals or accidentally by scavengers trying to get whatever was left in the storage tanks. And see the house there, down that street—and then again three houses on past it? Those large bones in the front yards are from some cow or horse-sized animal. I'll bet they were horses. I'll bet people in Grayson had pretty well run out of motor fuel by the time the gas leak killed them, and those were horses they were using for transport."

Before the expedition left Mountainview, Tom had provided several of the men with small, case-hardened metal punches, only two or three inches long and easily carried in a shirt pocket, but hard and sharp enough to puncture a car's gas tank. As the expedition entered the town, men quickly checked vehicles they came upon, kneeling beside them, reaching under with their mental punch, giving it a smart tap with a rock to puncture the gas tank—and finding every tank was empty.

When his men had gotten consistent results for two blocks, Peters said "I expect we'd better go with our plans for the 'no-fuel-remaining' alternative. Keep checking for fuel every now and then, but let's head for the two motorcycle shops we'd planned on. I think The Collapse and resulting halt to gasoline and diesel deliveries meant there was very little fuel left in Grayson by the time the ammonia leak hit them. And I expect any survivors who trickled back into town afterward must have pretty well scavenged whatever fuel still remained, either using it to drive out of town heading north, or else just staying here and using it up before they died.

"Who knows—maybe some enterprising fellow who survived the gassing came back into town, loaded up a tanker truck with whatever he could pump out of service station tanks, and then headed north with it for barter. If so, and if anybody managed to get any use out of it, good for them. But I don't think we're likely to find any fuel left here."

He sighed, and muttered to himself something several of the men found puzzling. "Probably just as well…"

They headed down the deserted street toward the center of town.

Chapter 36
Grayson II

The increasingly clear absence of fuel sobered the men, who had nearly all secretly harbored dreams of finding abundant gasoline and diesel that would allow life in Mountainview to return to what they had known before The Collapse. But the plans Tom had previously drawn up for the 'no-fuel' contingency gave the men instructions to implement right away, preventing any aimlessness or downheartedness. Using the town maps and the phone book Yellow Pages for Grayson they'd brought from Mountainview, the men eagerly set about acquiring other items they'd dreamed of since The Collapse.

One group headed first to Grayson Honda and Pete's Power Sports, two motorcycle dealers only a couple of blocks from each other. The men were overjoyed to find exactly the Crown Jewels Tom had implored them to bring back: Honda 650 motorcycles.

Those 650cc bikes, Tom had explained, used the largest single-cylinder, air cooled engines commonly available in the U.S. They would be ideal for conversion: simple enough to avoid the complexities of multiple cylinders and water cooling, yet large enough to produce significant power when converted to steam. Motorcycles, he had explained, were the only widely available source for such engines. Only Honda, Suzuki, Kawasaki, and BMW made single-cylinder bikes with engines that large; of those four, only the Honda and Suzuki were air cooled; and of those two only Honda had dealers in virtually every city and town on the planet.

"Good old reliable Honda," Jim Payson exclaimed triumphantly, "I knew they wouldn't let us down!"

Grayson Honda and Pete's Power Sports each had a brand new XR650L on the showroom floor. To compound the good fortune, in Pete's repair bay were two off-road versions of the same bike—XR650R's—which used the identical engine. One bike, with some of its gauges removed and dangling at the ends of their wires, had apparently been in the shop for electrical work of some sort irrelevant to converting the engine to steam. The other bike, fully intact, must have had some repairs completed, or was perhaps in merely for routine servicing.

While some of the men rolled their four prizes out onto the street, others, as instructed, looked about them for a nearby structure with an eight-foot ceiling. An add-on garage for a nearby house, with the garage door standing open, filled the bill. Using a heavy hammer and a tire iron from the bike shops, the men bashed the sheetrock off a portion of the garage wall, exposing the studs, then bashed loose four of the two-by-four wall studs, which were a bit less than eight feet long. The men used wire and pliers from the bike shops to secure one of the two-by-four's across the handlebars of each bike, tying it tightly in several places.

With a man at each end, the eight-foot two-by-four provided plenty of leverage to hold a bike upright and steer as the pair of men pushed the bike along the street. Each pair of bike-pushers removed the empty backpacks they'd been wearing, wired their backpacks' shoulder straps together at the top, to make a set of "saddlebags," and hung them across the bike's seat. They filled these "saddlebags" with items from the bike shops: hammers and hacksaws, files and drill bits, open-end wrenches and socket wrenches and screwdrivers, welding rods and lapping compound, sheets of gasket material and cans of WD-40 and Loc-Tite and ether starting spray. To their delight, the men found two unopened five-gallon jugs of 10W-30 motor oil. Wiring the handles of the jugs together, they placed them across one of the bikes as saddlebags.

"With good, smooth pavement to push these on, and no hills, I expect each of these four bikes will carry 700 pounds or more," Jim pointed out. "Sure beats trying to haul stuff out on our backs—or bringing our draft animals into town where those dogs might be tempted. Tom knew what he was doing when he dreamed up this idea."

The motorcycle teams proudly rolled their treasures down the middle of the street, keeping a wary eye out for dog packs, as they hurried to join three other teams that had been sent to the town's pharmacies. In all three cases, entering pharmacies had proved to be a time-consuming business: locked doors had had to be smashed open, and the crowded aisles very carefully investigated to avoid the risk of inadvertently trapping rats, skunks, or any other creatures that might attack if left no line of retreat. The three pharmacies' riches, though, proved well worth the scavengers' toil and trouble.

By the time the motorcycle crews reached them, the pharmacy crews already had their backpacks stuffed with loot, yet had hardly begun their work. After a bit of searching, the men found rolls of heavy, plastic leaf-bags that had not been chewed by rats. Into these, they dumped shelf-loads of aspirin and similar painkillers, vitamin pills of every sort, non-prescription medicines, insect repellents and insecticides, boxes of syringes and hypodermic needles, racks of assorted common-prescription eyeglasses and non-prescription sunglasses, tweezers and scissors, razors and blades, and anything else that looked useful.

They were disappointed to find the boxes of paper dust-and-pollen masks had been fouled by rats, so the men continued to use their bandannas over their mouths and noses in hopes of reducing the amount of germ-laden dust they inhaled.

Moving behind the counter into the prescription area, the men went shelf-by-shelf, checking the prioritized lists Doc had given them, finding a fair number of his "most-desired" items. Much of the prescription stock was well past its expiration dates, or had been ruined by not being refrigerated or by being frozen, but they took any items on the list that seemed even possibly usable, along with a *Physicians' Desk Reference* and a *Merck Manual.*

They were disappointed, but not surprised, to find the prescription painkillers locked in safes that were far too heavy to move and too strong for amateurs to break open. Also disappointing but not surprising was the absence in these retail pharmacies of scalpels and other medical instruments. Still, with their backpacks and leaf-bags full of treasure, securely tied together and slung over the motorcycles to be rolled away, they knew they had acquired an enormous lifesaving haul.

One of the pharmacies, located in a corner of a Safeway, tempted the men with the potential of raiding the grocery store for items such as shoe and boot laces, reams of white bond paper, quart plastic jugs of charcoal lighter fluid, and—most desperately craved—edibles such as coffee and spices. But the accessible food in the grocery store had produced such an indescribable rat population over the past seven months the men had to forgo entering the area. The sheer volume of dried rat droppings, inches deep in some places, made the likelihood of stirring up disease-laden dust particles too great—and the men assumed the flea concentration in the area must be as horrific as the rat population obviously was.

Still, the men's delight at their success was sufficient, for the moment at least, to hold at bay the horror of the necropolis they were so hurriedly looting. They rolled their heavily laden motorcycles down the middle of Grayson's streets on their way to their next major objectives, steering around the occasional pelvises and skulls and other large bones no animals had bothered to drag off into hiding before devouring the flesh and cracking the bones for the marrow.

En route to the two hardware stores that were next on their list, the men passed the Grayson County Bank. Sadder but wiser, regarding the nation's pre-Collapse economic realities, they weren't even tempted to look inside.

"Suppose every teller's drawer, and the bank vault itself, were all standing wide open: what would there be in that so-called 'bank,' that *storehouse of wealth*, that ever did have any value—even then, much less now?" remarked Dick Peters with a bemused smile.

"They've got maybe a hundred thousand 'dollars' or thereabouts, in stacks of worthless paper banknotes that are not even usable for writing paper because of all the official-looking high-cockalorum printed on them to gull the innocent. Even before The Collapse, those banknotes were backed by nothing, redeemable for nothing (except other banknotes just like them) and worth nothing.

"This bank, like any other, also no doubt has a ton or two of 'coins' that are just as worthless: zinc, base-metal slugs. Hell, not even the hundreds of pounds of so-called 'pennies' they've got there are worth anything for their copper: there isn't any, except for a thin copper wash over the near-worthless zinc the coins are actually made of. When a so-called 'penny' no longer even contained a pennyworth of copper, that pretty well told you what their so-called 'dollar' was worth!"

"Well," Jordan Grant pointed out, "There'd be some awfully nice things in the safe deposit boxes. Too bad they're far too secure for us to break open. Can you imagine the number of *real* coins folks put away in there over the years, and the precious metals and gemstones in their jewelry ..."

"Ain't it the truth," Peters replied wistfully. "Tells you something about the world people were living in by the time of The Collapse, doesn't it? Even among the dumbest, everybody understood you wouldn't put the nation's official currency—wads of hundred dollar bills—in your safe deposit box. They'd be worth far less in a few years when you took them back out. The things people paid a bank to store securely for them were things they knew actually had value: gold or silver coins and bars, jewelry, gemstones.

"Everybody understood that the nation's official currency—the visible sign of a nation's honor, bearing its 'full faith and credit,' the sacred bond between a government and its people—was in fact a fraud. Only a jerk would 'save money' by actually saving the 'money' his government (under penalty of law) demanded that he use. What people did was exactly what anyone with a lick of sense does when he receives a counterfeit twenty: pass it on to somebody else, so he's not out twenty bucks. The citizens *knew* they were getting counterfeit bills from their rulers!

"But instead of raising what was once quaintly termed a 'hew and cry' they chose to pass the phonies along to some other sucker. 'Long range' financial planning amounted to finding ways to get rid of the government paper that was every day becoming worth less—before it became, in fact, completely worthless. What a rock-solid basis for the largest economy on earth!"

Rolling their valuables past the Grayson County Bank's "million-dollar" hoard of rubbish, the men made a brief stop at a Staples office supply store. They found enough ballpoint pens and assorted pencils to fill one of their big leaf bags, and they found enough little 8"X10" kitchen-wall-sized blackboards and boxes of chalk to fill another. The rats had left unspoiled enough reams of white bond paper for the men to devote one of their bikes entirely to carrying 750 pounds of that item. But two other finds gave them the greatest satisfaction.

"Fountain pens! Hot Damn!"

Bob Feller smashed open the glass display case to scoop up several dozen of the dusty, long-forgotten treasures, and checked carefully through the store in hopes (not realized) of finding more.

"Chalkboards are great for school and some other uses, but obviously not for keeping long-term records," he explained. "For recording things on paper, ballpoints and pencils will last only so long, and we can't make replacements for either. Fountain pens, though, will last for generations—and ink for them is something we *can* easily make. They'll be a heck of a lot better than quills!"

As they loaded about 200 pounds of the store's other most prized item, computer floppy discs, onto one of the bikes, Bob held one up alongside a fountain pen and remarked "Who'd a thunk it? Fountain pens and computer floppies: the two most precious items these days for preserving knowledge. Talk about an odd couple, where old-fashioned meets new-fangled ..."

The four motorcycles were by now each carrying about seven or eight hundred pounds. In addition, each of the nine men not pushing a bike had about eighty pounds in his backpack. Dick Peters decided to bring this material back to the wagons, remain camped overnight, and return to Grayson briefly the following day. By walky-talky, he relayed the decision, and a summary of their results so far, back through the wagon-camp party at the bridge, through the radio link they'd posted midway from Mountainview, and on to Chief Barley.

The scavenging party arrived back near the wagons at the far end of the bridge by late afternoon. They halted on the road about thirty feet before reaching the wagons, and began unloading their goods, removing them from the makeshift saddlebags and spreading them out on the blacktop. They thoroughly sprayed their treasures and their clothing and themselves with insecticide, then used a pump-up garden sprayer with Clorox/detergent mix to lightly mist their goods.

"It's about the best we can do—for fleas or other insects and for any disease organisms as well," Dick Peters judged. "At least we haven't been tromping around all day in a plague zone, still crawling with whatever virus or bacteria were involved.

"When I had him on the radio and explained the absence of any epidemic," Peters reported with a grin, "the Chief said he was looking forward to his first decent night's sleep since this whole expedition was dreamed up."

In the late afternoon, cooks heated rabbit, potato and onion stew in a huge cauldron hung over the campfire on a chain from an iron tripod. They baked cornbread in a cast iron dutch oven nestled in the coals of the other campfire, and sprinkled tea leaves in two kettles of water put on to boil for the precious, steaming mugs of tea the men held close in the growing chill.

By nightfall, the men had stowed the day's loot—hopefully bug and germ free—in the huge hay wagon and the mule cart. Most of those who had been to town then stretched out in their sleeping bags, tired and pleased in equal measure.

The three men who had remained with the wagons, supplemented by another three men, continued their picket duty—concentrating especially on the little bridge, where the glowing eyes of the feral dogs moved constantly, eerily, back and forth, weaving around and around through the darkness, just at the bridge's Grayson end. By this time, the scent of the mule and two horses was well in the dogs' nostrils, and there was no question they were keenly interested.

Helping to keep them on the Grayson side of the creek, and off the bridge entirely, was a large bonfire the men built near the Grayson end of the bridge. As the logs blazed on the concrete roadway, the men periodically pushed coals and embers off to the sides of the bonfire, eventually forming a line clear across the narrow little bridge. It could easily have been jumped by the dogs, and eventually no doubt would have been, once their fear of the unfamiliar expedition party diminished. But for this night the newness of the situation and the existing fire proved sufficient to keep the dogs wary enough to stay off the bridge. At least as comforting, it also provided enough light, with its flames reflecting off the white concrete roadway and bridge walls, to shoot anything that tried to pass.

The next day, shortly after dawn, well fed and sprayed once again with insecticide, the scavenging party cleared a space in the line of embers across the bridge and rolled their motorcycles back toward Grayson. Competing to provide gruesome details, they called goodbyes to the three men remaining with the wagons, urging them to resist any attack by the feral dogs, and helpfully describing for them the likely consequences of any failure to repel such an attack. A victim's belly and entrails would be the dogs' first area of concentration, most of the men emphasized.

The scavengers' primary objectives for the day, Peters rehearsed for them as they walked, were the Grayson Medical Clinic—not much more than a glorified doc-in-a-box, but the best the town could offer by way of medical facilities—plus two hardware stores, a farm-supply store, and any other promising source of paper.

Paper? some of the men grumbled in disgust—with a whole town full of really great stuff to take?

"Not quite as sexy as guns and ammo, or knives and axes, is it?" Dick Peters said to them in good humor, realizing it was part of his job to explain.

"But think of it this way: any of you guys know how to make paper? Trust me, it's a hell of an involved process. We won't be able to attempt it for years, perhaps not for a decade. What do we write on in the meantime? We're not going to slip back into the condition of illiterate savages, we're civilized people. And we're not on some weekend campout. We're keeping *civilization* alive: for however many decades, generations, *centuries* it takes to re-build. Paper was one of Man's greatest inventions, absolutely vital for recording the information he needed to help him rise out of barbarism. You can easily forget how important paper is, until you have none. It's a lot like air: try doing without, if it seems too commonplace to have any value."

The men understood, quietly appreciating not only Peters' explanation but his consideration in providing it, and they rolled their four mechanical beasts of burden along the road to Grayson in good spirits.

The Grayson Medical Clinic, their first stop, provided a fine assortment of basic instruments and supplies. The men collected scalpels and curved suturing needles, forceps and retractors, syringes and hypodermic needles, stethoscopes and thermometers, blood pressure cuffs and two basic lab microscopes. They found some usable prescription medicines, three gallons of surgical disinfectant, and—in cardboard cartons stored safely in a metal locker—three gross of the sterile latex gloves Doc had especially begged for.

"How about dental stuff: aren't we going to look for that too?" asked one of the men as they rolled their laden bikes away from the medical clinic.

"Actually, no," Peters said. "It seems odd, all right, not raiding a dentist's office, but Doc pointed out some things to me before we left Mountainview.

"In the first place, ever looked at a modern dentist's drill—the whole thing, not just the part he sticks in your mouth? That apparatus is *big*—and heavy and cumbersome—and would need to be removed from its floor-and-chair mounting for transportation, then re-installed in comparable fashion for use back in Mountainview. We could do all that, if we decided to. But for a drill to be of any use, once you've drilled a tooth, you need amalgam, or filling-material, to finish the job.

"Amalgam was expensive, and dentists before The Collapse saw no point in buying large quantities of it merely to sit in a stockpile: their suppliers could easily provide more by overnight delivery whenever the office supplies ran low. So, as Doc pointed out, all the dentists in Grayson put together aren't going to have enough amalgam in stock to last us any considerable time. And without it, a drill would have little value.

"Also, Doc pointed out, modern dentistry depended so heavily on the use of X-ray equipment—which we'll not have again for generations—that lugging back a modern, high-tech drill would not be practical. The scalpels, forceps, and related medical stuff we've just gotten, plus the equipment Doc already had and the opium we're producing, will make old-fashioned tooth-pulling bearable and efficient—and tooth-pulling will be about the state of the art for dentistry in Mountainview for decades to come."

When the expedition reached two hardware stores, the next stops on their planned route, they found plenty of items the men had been dreaming of. They filled bag after bag with hand tools of all sorts; fish hooks, firearms and ammunition; axes and hatchets and knives; whetstones and grindstones and files; nails and screws and nuts and bolts; cigarette lighters, matches, candles and lighter fluid; rat poison and bug spray and mousetraps.

Many of the hardware items were hellishly heavy. When two of the bikes had about seven or eight hundred pounds apiece loaded on them, Peters decided to dispatch those two, with half the men, back to the wagons. Four men pushed the two loaded bikes, with five others carrying about 80 pounds apiece in their backpacks, rifles in hand, keeping a wary eye on the ever-present feral dogs that maintained their distance but never left the men.

The remaining eight men pressed on a few blocks further into town, toward a farm store that was on the planned list of targets. On their way, they passed the offices of the *Grayson Clarion,* the county's weekly paper. To their disappointment, they found huge supplies of paper, much of it unspoiled, but all in a form they couldn't use: enormous rolls of newsprint, which must have weighed nearly a ton apiece.

Making their way past the back of the printing plant, nervous at being in the close confines of an alleyway instead of the wide streets where they felt safer, the men noticed a standard delivery panel truck backed up to the loading dock of a store. "JoAnn's Patterns and Fabrics" said the name on the loading dock door.

Dick Peters regarded the closed delivery van for a moment, considering.

"That delivery truck looks rat-proof. Let's take a peek."

Using a heavy ball-peen hammer they'd taken from the hardware store, the men bashed open the lock on the truck's rear cargo door where it butted up against the store's loading dock. Gingerly, not certain what might come scurrying out, they pushed the door up with a stick, ready to jump back.

Nothing came out. The men cautiously peered in. Several shrugged, much more interested in getting out of this creepy, close-quarters alleyway than in gazing at some damn truck full of cloth.

"Gentlemen," Peters announced with a grin, "you have just made yourselves heroes to the female half of Mountainview. There is very damn little cloth to be found in this town which hasn't been ruined by rats and other animals, or by the elements. This is the first sizeable batch I've seen. Hooray for watertight, rat-proof truck bodies. Get out your plastic leaf bags and load 'em up! Meanwhile, you two slip carefully into the store itself and see how many sewing needles, knitting and darning needles, crochet hooks, safety pins and straight pins, scissors, thimbles, ribbons, measuring tapes, buttons, and suchlike notions you can find."

Skeptically, a couple of men climbed up into the truck full of cloth.

"Oooohh—won't *this* make me a pretty pair of drawers," cried Jordan Grant, prancing about with a bolt of pale pink flannel, printed with daisies, he'd hauled off one of the racks in the truck.

"You'll be glad enough to have it some cold winter," Peters replied with a grin, removing a bolt of heavy denim from another rack and showing it to him as he passed it outside for loading on the bike. "This denim's strong, and durable as hell, but it's going to feel pretty stiff and raw the first dozen times somebody wears it. And if you think *denim* might chafe your girlish skin without any drawers, just wait and see what our first attempts at linsey-woolsey feel like.

"Linsey-woolsey: flax and wool ..." Peters smiled an evil, knowing smile. "Think in terms of crushed plant stems interwoven with crude, pencil-thick globs of wool to make a sort of homespun 'cloth.' Ever worn clothes made out of a burlap sack—only rougher? You men are gonna have the experience of learning firsthand why one of the manufactured items pioneers craved most—even more than muskets, powder and lead in some cases—was soft, machine-made cloth."

The bolts of fabric and sewing supplies, together with the medical items they'd already salvaged, fully loaded one of the group's remaining two bikes. The men proceeded to the farm store they'd been heading for, only to encounter a particularly hard disappointment. It took but a single look through the double doors, once they'd bashed them open, to see of rack after rack of priceless, heavy work clothes, all chewed and destroyed by nesting rats and other animals; shelf after shelf of sturdy leather work boots, gloves, and belts, all chewed and destroyed by animals; bin after bin of seeds, bulbs, and assorted plant materials, all destroyed by animals.

The droppings were so deep on the floor, and the possibility of finding anything usable so slim, the men just turned away in heartsick silence.

"Grayson Farm Supply: the *one* store you'd count on to have everything a Robinson Crusoe would need," muttered one of the men bitterly.

They trudged back through town, heading generally toward the Rt. 12 bridge at the south end, keeping an eye out for any promising-looking stores. When they came across a Kinko's Copy Center, Peters was glad once again he'd patiently explained to the men the value of something as un-sexy as ordinary paper.

There were enough unspoiled reams of bond the rats hadn't yet gotten to, in the middles of pallet-loads, for the scavengers to fully burden their remaining motorcycle. Understanding the paper's value, the men were able to shake off some of their low spirits from the Farm Store letdown and head back toward the wagon camp feeling their time and effort had been well spent.

On their way, they passed the last of the major objectives the expedition had planned to visit: the Grayson County Library. It was heartbreaking to think of the priceless materials inside: many, many tons of books, magazines, films, recordings, and similar items. The expedition had nothing remotely near the transportation capacity to haul so many tons of material—nor was there any place in Mountainview to store it safely if they could have moved it there.

Considering these realities, the expedition's planners had decided to content themselves with safeguarding the library's contents as best they could for the time being, in hopes much of it might survive until Mountainview acquired some way to transport it and some place to house it.

Accordingly, Peters instructed his men to search carefully for some way to enter the library building without causing damage. In time, they found a back door, formerly a staff entrance, with an old and sloppy latch they could trip with a "slim-jim" used to open locked cars, then re-lock behind them when departing.

Having gained entry, the men carefully examined the library building, verifying there were no signs of any water damage from roof leaks, no windows left open to allow access to water or animals, and no other signs of immediate threat to the library's collection. The books, packed tightly together on shelves, were not accessible enough to make convenient nesting material for rats or mice. To extend some protection from those pests however, the men scattered throughout the building more than a hundred pounds of mouse and rat poison they had scavenged earlier from the two hardware stores.

"Rats are intelligent enough to become trap-shy and bait-shy when some of them are killed," explained Peters to the men. "Possibly, if enough of them are poisoned in this building, they might become inclined to go elsewhere— especially with an entire town to serve as 'elsewhere.' Mice probably won't be driven out as successfully, but they're a lot less destructive than rats, and in any case this batch of poison is about all we can do at present. If the roof keeps out moisture for the next several years, there's a pretty fair chance most of the library's collection will remain usable. And maybe, in years to come, we'll have the resources needed to haul tons of this material back to Mountainview, and someplace built to store it once we get it there."

He spoke wistfully, torn by the pain of leaving such priceless material behind. "Till then, I guess this is about the best we can do."

When the exploration party reached the wagons, just past One in the afternoon, they found the first group had already unloaded their bikes, sprayed their cargo and themselves for bugs and germs, and loaded their treasure in the wagons. The remaining men hastened to do the same. As they did so, Dick Peters took two men with shotguns for a guard, selected a tire iron and an "Oklahoma credit card"—a piece of plastic tubing—from their loot, and went back across the bridge to the ghoulish traffic jam at the Grayson end.

He pried a crumpled fender away from where it pressed against the front tire of the car nearest the bridge, reached into the car and shifted it from Park to Neutral, and gestured to one of the two men to help him push.

"Let's just roll it onto the end of the bridge and get it toward the middle of the road a bit, so as to obstruct both lanes. That'll be enough to account for the bridge being blocked, and all the rest of these vehicles sitting back here—especially since this car will have caught on fire for some reason."

After he'd rolled the car into place, Peters checked several of the pickups in the traffic jam, peering through the windows at the dashboards, till he found one he wanted.

"Perfect: a pickup with an auxiliary fuel tank," he explained. "When the driver was killed the engine would have kept on running till it drained the main tank—but there'd have been no one to manually switch over to the auxiliary. Let's hope there's some fuel left in that one."

He stuck one end of the plastic tubing into the auxiliary tank and blew into the other—producing no bubbling but merely a gentle hiss of air.

"Damn. Well, let's try another one."

He looked through all the other vehicles in the traffic jam but found no others with dual fuel tanks. Nor, after several tries with his tubing, did he find any single-tank vehicle with any fuel—either gas or diesel—remaining in its tank. In the bed of one of the pickups, however, he did find a chainsaw and a mostly full, two-gallon can of gas/oil fuel mix for it. And in a battered farm truck nearby, he found a 100-foot spool of three-quarter-inch polypropylene rope.

"Yes! Plenty of gas and oil to light off this rope. Poly rope burns hot as hell—and burns clean, leaving no plastic goo behind. I shoulda been a fire-bug," he gloated, as he draped masses of the rope over each tire of the vehicle they'd pushed onto the bridge. He removed the valve-stem from each tire, allowing the air to escape.

"Don't want a tire exploding and maybe putting out this accidental fire we're about to have," he explained.

He checked to ensure there were no signs left of their former wagon camp on the other side of the creek, scattering the remains of all the fires except for a small pile of still-glowing coals left from the bonfire the men had built near the Grayson end of the bridge. He took the brush and dead tree limbs left over from the firewood supply the wagon-guards had accumulated, and stuffed the wood into the car, dumping it onto the car's front and back seats. He left all four doors open.

"A handful of wood-ash in a burned out car won't be noticed by anybody," he explained, "if there's even any left after a few weeks' wind and rain."

He carefully poured some of the gas/oil chainsaw fuel onto the brush in the car's front and back seats, then used the remainder to soak the rope wadded around each tire.

Peters and the two men returned to the wagon-camp end of the bridge and took one final look around. It was Two-thirty on a clear, calm, cool March afternoon.

"I think we're ready," he said, gazing across the bridge at Grayson.

Silently, he uttered a moment's prayer for the people of the town. At least it had been very quick for nearly all of them, he consoled himself.

The expedition's two wagons moved out. The "pusher-teams" rolled the four motorcycles behind them. The infantry walked along both sides of the road, one of the men leading Trigger. As the expedition moved off, Peters scooped up the last glowing coals from the bridge bonfire and tossed them at the fuel-soaked car a few feet away. In moments, the gasoline, brush, and plastic rope blazed up, making a fire that would obviously be hot enough to ignite the car tires as well.

Peters turned away and caught up with the rest of the expedition heading home to Mountainview.

"Once those car tires light off, they'll smoke and smolder for days," he explained to the men. No feral dog's going to be interested in squeezing past them to cross that bridge for a long, long time. By then, there will be no scent of men or horses on our side, or any other reason for dogs to be attracted. They'll pretty much stay on their side, I think.

"When the weather warms up, in a couple of months, and Grayson's alive with rattlesnakes and copperheads, in addition to all its other charms—rats, and rabid skunks and coons and feral dogs and cats, and so forth—that town will be as effective a barrier to travel as anything possibly could be. Only a crazy man would try to force his way through a deathtrap like Grayson once that biological minefield's fully activated. And for what purpose? There's not the slightest indication that any living people at our end of the bridge tried to block the road: it's been blocked in a perfectly 'natural' and 'understandable' way by a burned-out car."

Peters went on, spelling it out for the men. He needed to get it off his own chest, needed to make sure his men understood, needed to be certain they too gained the closure which he considered the single most important treasure they were taking back with them from Grayson.

"We owe those people a great debt. I can't imagine any of us returning any time very soon—at least not for several years, till the biological hazard is reduced. The people of Grayson have given us everything they had to give: They've given us the crucial supplies we'll need, while we learn to make our own way in the world. They've given us the awareness that we're going to have to *do* exactly that, not just sit on our asses waiting to be 'rescued.' And they've given us as much safety from attack as they could possibly provide, while we're learning how to stay alive in this new world. God bless the poor bastards who died there in Grayson, in the old one. Their gruesome end has done as much as anything could have to keep Mountainview safe and unmolested. We owe them a great deal. We in Mountainview are duty-bound—in memory of those thousands of Grayson dead—to *succeed*: to keep our tiny flicker of civilization alive, to grow it, and in time to rebuild from it a better world than the one that ended so horribly for those people, choking to death in terror, in the blackness of that awful night."

Chapter 37
Renaissance: With Steam and Electricity's Help, a Light Begins to Dawn

As Dick Peters had hoped, the expedition's impact on Mountainview's morale proved every bit as important as the physical items the men brought back. For the first time since The Collapse, people in Mountainview were freed from a debilitating, unrealistic fear—that the countryside around them might be alive with potential attackers—and an equally debilitating, unrealistic hope—of "rescue" by some outside savior.

Empowered by their new realism, as spring touched the fields and pastures with the first faint traces of green, the people of Mountainview began to accept the time-horizon for what they now understood would be their generation's lifelong task: laying foundations for a new civilization to replace an old one that was irrevocably dead. Mountainview's ham radio operators still maintained a reasonably thorough listening watch on the frequencies most likely to be used for any short to medium-range transmissions—those of about twenty to 400 miles—but heard nothing at all.

By mid-April, Tom completed work on the 3.5 HP steam engine he'd been constructing from assorted gasoline engine parts. He connected his ungainly monstrosity by a flat leather drive-belt to a Gravely generator in his shop, fired the boiler till he had steam up, and savored a mixture of relief and long-awaited satisfaction when the engine *chuff, chuff, chuff'd* steadily on the concrete shop floor, driving the generator to provide electric current for his shop equipment.

"We'll now be able to rent out the 4 HP steam Gravely full-time for plowing, tilling, woodcutting, hauling things in the cart, pumping irrigation water, and all of Mountainview's countless other machine-power needs," he told Sophie that evening. "This new 3.5 HP engine I'll keep full time in the shop, generating power to run the shop tools."

His eyes sparkled with excitement as they sat together on the couch in the library after supper, sipping a glass of hard cider, enjoying a rare break from the long working hours they were both putting in. "And—finally—I'll be able to sell some power to other people!"

Seeing she didn't get it, he explained.

"Unlike, say, a gasoline engine—which you can start when you need it and stop when you don't—a steam engine requires a considerable period of firing in the firebox before the boiler builds up steam to working pressure. Once you've done that, it's far more efficient to keep the engine running than to stop it, let it cool, and fire it up again later.

"This new engine, for use only with the shop's generator, will provide electric power constantly while it's running, even though I'll only need that power for the shop tools intermittently—or not at all when I'm eating lunch, sleeping at night, or away from the shop taking a day off or working on something else. The engine, though, can be kept running, say, twenty-two hours a day, or thereabouts, to power the generator—requiring only that someone occasionally put more wood in the firebox and remove the ash, monitor the oil and boiler-water levels, and periodically pump more water into the boiler. All the electric power generated when I'm not using it I can sell."

"How? For what?" Sophie asked in puzzlement.

"Well, for a start probably just by running an extension cord to any next-door neighbors who want to use their electric well pump to pump their own water, as we've been doing. Till now, they've had two choices: buy water delivered by Bill Etter with his mule cart, or fetch it from the creek themselves. Now they'll have another option: buy power from us to pump their own water.

"In addition, there are all those car, tractor, truck and assorted other batteries that have been cluttering up the showroom floor these many months. I've got over a hundred of them I bought or bartered for at the start of The Collapse. I've kept them fully charged, so they've still got plenty of life in them. I expect some people will want to buy some of them to power a cassette tape or CD player, or a light to sew or read by sometimes in the evenings, now that I can sell them power to keep the batteries charged."

"How would you transmit the current? Surely you can't just string extension cords all over town from your generator."

He grinned.

"Tell you the truth, I *was* initially considering something nearly that crude.

KISS, after all. But Hockley's working out a method that will mostly use the town's existing electric wires. Every house in town is on the old electric grid, of course, and the wires are all still in place: it's a matter of using switches to route the current from the generator here in the shop to specific houses that purchase electricity.

"Eventually he may even set up meters, so I can sell to multiple customers simultaneously and bill each one for the amount of current actually consumed. At first, though, we'll just charge a flat rate per half-hour block of time. Harry Homeowner can buy the generator's entire output sent to his house for a pre-arranged period: say, every Tuesday from three to three-thirty a.m. He can use it to run his well pump to store the coming week's water, operate power tools, recharge his batteries, or whatever. As a sales incentive, the time slots will be first-come-first-served: the earliest people to sign up will get the most convenient hours.

"Hockley will be one of our first customers. The work he's been doing— storing on computer files basically every cultural artifact Starshine brings him: books, pictures, music, films—requires more current than his existing solar cells can produce to keep his computers' battery banks charged. That's why the past few weeks I've been physically hauling cartloads of charged batteries over to him and bringing his here for recharging. Believe me, we'll both be happy to just send him the electrons down a wire—a lot less work than lugging those damned batteries back and forth!"

Tom kissed his way along the nape of Sophie's neck to one ear, which he gently nibbled.

"If I knew anyone with a restaurant, I bet I could sell her power too. Just think of being able to offer 'Premium Dining' from, say, five-thirty to seven-thirty each Sunday, when for a mere extra twenty-five percent your patrons can enjoy electric lighting and recorded music, or a DVD movie played on that huge TV set you got for the university's use…or even the luxury of *electric fans* during the coming summer's heat …"

"Why Mr. Jeffson," she murmured, wiggling slightly as his hands roamed, "you make such a compelling case. Do all your prospective customers receive such a *personalized* sales presentation?"

"In the finest traditions of the electric utilities industry, Honey, we don't merely serve our customers—we do everything we can to *service* them."

"Now wait just a minute with the *servicing* part. Really, Tom …" she giggled but wiggled free of his grasp. "Really; be serious a moment. How are you going to find time to tend a steam engine running in the shop twenty-two hours a day, plus all your other work?"

"Tim's coming to work at the shop full time. With spring here, and the steam Gravely increasingly being hired out for agricultural work he can't do with one leg—plowing, for example—I think his engine-operator skills will be perfect in the shop, tending the new engine here full time. If you're OK with it, I'd like to clean out the backyard shed and refurbish it a bit so he can live there. He's amazingly mobile, with his crutch. Still, being able to live where he works, and working at a fixed location, like the shop, will make things more practical for him. And from my perspective, I couldn't ask for a better deal than a live-in, full-time engine operator."

"One who operates the engine twenty-two hours a day? Seven days a week?" she exclaimed. "That certainly *is* full time, isn't it! Just out of curiosity, what do you intend to pay for such working hours? And what are you going to charge people for the electricity you plan to sell?"

"Respectively," said Tom, "A. as little as I can; and B. as little as possible until I can change that to as much as possible. What's the point of owning a public utility if you don't use it to sweat your hired help with starvation wages while bankrupting your customers with extortionate charges?"

But then, seeing she was on the edge of going ballistic, he reluctantly abandoned the enjoyment of making her crazy and reviewed for her some concepts that to him seemed as obvious as gravity—but which for her were apparently brand new ideas.

"Look: if Tim can get better pay from anyone else, he should grab it. But he won't. I happen to think his work's excellent, so I'll just outbid any other offer he might get, and thereby keep him as my employee. But I won't bid more than I have to for him because I'm going to pass the cost of his wages on to my electric customers, and I want to keep their bills initially low enough to encourage plenty of people to sign up, thereby maximizing our own income.

"This system of competing financial interests—the employee, the employer, and the customer, each making the best deal he can for himself—is called 'free enterprise.' It works. Unlike certain other plans that have been tried.

"As to the issue of eventually charging as much as the market will bear for my electricity: if potential customers don't want to pay my price they just don't buy any. They haven't got electricity now, so it's no comedown for them. In practice, once I have power for sale they'll simply have an additional choice. Before, they could hike to the creek and carry their own water, or pay Bill Etter to haul it to them by mule cart. Now they'll have the third option of paying me for power to run their own well pump. Neither Bill nor I will be able to overcharge, will we—now that people can choose whichever service they prefer."

"OK," admitted Sophie, "It sounds fine in theory."

She thought further.

"But in practice it looks to me like it would be more easy and efficient, and therefore cheaper, to run current through a wire so someone can use their existing well pump, rather than having all the labor and expense Bill Etter does: feeding, grooming, and caring for a mule, loading a water tank at the creek, hauling it all over town, hand-pumping the water into people's storage tanks, and on and on. What if your electric service undercuts his costs to where he can't stay in business?"

Tom laughed.

"What a dilemma you face! You can't decide which to be more alarmed about: will the wicked capitalist gouge people into paying too *much* for electric power to pump their water—or will the fiend allow them to pay too *little,* thereby putting Bill and his mule cart out of business! Well, let me guide your concern: worry about the latter. I fully intend to drive Bill's water cart out of business as soon as I possibly can."

"*See!*" she burst out, "Dog-eat-dog! Pure cutthroat capitalism! I'm sure it will give you great pleasure to destroy a valuable, socially productive business like Bill's—which happens to provide his livelihood, you know: it's how he makes a *living.*"

"It won't be much longer, once I get the electric service in operation," Tom announced smugly.

But because she was so genuinely upset about Bill Etter's pending business failure, Tom hugged her close. Gently, he explained junior highschool-level economics to his genius-IQ wife—who had received her postgraduate degree from one of California's most prestigious universities, and had therefore never been exposed to concepts even slightly educated people had understood for the past 500 years.

"You are right: hauling water throughout Mountainview by mule cart is a frightfully inefficient and labor-intensive and therefore costly business, compared with sending electric current through a wire for people to run their own well pumps. The people who've actually been *paying* that high cost (unlike certain limousine liberals living above the Gravely shop, who've always had electric power) want very much to pay less for their water. Maybe they hope to buy a warmer coat, or have meat four times a week, instead of only three, on the money they could save with lower water bills.

"If I can underprice Bill Etter enough to run him out of business that's simply another way of saying I can save many Mountainview families significant amounts of money, which they can use to improve their living standards. And in doing that, I'll be making enough money to improve our own lot in life as well."

"Swell consolation for Bill Etter, facing the loss of his livelihood!" Sophie retorted.

"But see—Bill's not going to lose his livelihood. He'll change from hauling water in his mule cart to hauling hay or grain or firewood."

Tom paused a moment, organizing his point.

"Ever watch those guys who've been delivering firewood all winter, pushing those two-wheel garden carts all over town? Think that would be fun, delivering two or three hundred pounds of wood at a trip? Say, about three-quarters of a mile roundtrip for the average delivery? With about one and a half *tons* to be delivered throughout Mountainview *daily*? All winter long? That's sheer, brute coolie-work, Sophie, in which men are used as draft animals!

"If my electricity can replace Bill Etter's mule for providing water to people, and Bill then seeks new work hauling firewood in his cart—ton at a time, with Bill riding on the cart, not walking—that will, in turn, free up those coolie-gangs who've been slaving all winter as draft animals.

"Some of them may learn to make or repair shoes, and others may get work tending a farmer's expanding herd of cattle, swine, or sheep, and others may become carpenters, or candle-makers, or sharpeners of saws and axes and knives. Believe me, *any* of those choices—and a hundred others like them—are better for the individual *and* for his community than for him to spend his life pushing carts of firewood all over town like a draft animal—or a Medieval peasant.

"Human life after the Renaissance became better than it had been through the preceding Dark Ages. Anyone could see at a glance that living conditions were improved. But the real change—the revolution—that made possible those improvements in living standards was invisible: a huge leap forward in people's basic economic understanding.

"You're alarmed that I might exploit Tim by underpaying him for his work. And then alarmed that I might *over*pay him, resulting in excessively high bills for my electric customers as I pass the cost of his pay on to them. And then, on further thought, alarmed yet again that on the third hand I might *undercharge* those customers, driving Bill Etter out of work.

"Your anxiety centers around trying to determine the 'correct' price for each of those transactions. It's a dilemma all socialists endlessly grapple with—and have yet to solve. The Soviet Union's gigantic bureaucracy, GOSPLAN, struggled for seventy years to determine the 'correct' price for every item in the nation—every raw material, every service, every durable good, every consumer good, every last worker's precise pay rate …

"They failed completely, of course. But what's really amazing is that anyone could have been so stupid as to try. No group of humans, however brilliant, with any amount of computer assistance, could ever process the infinite amounts of constantly changing data necessary to determine 'correct' prices and wages.

"Long before Socialism's 20th Century debacle, the Medieval Catholic Church had attempted the same hopeless task—relying, I assume, on faith and prayer in lieu of computer assistance. The Medieval Church was convinced it could achieve fairness, economic justice for all, by determining the 'Just Value' of every good and service. By setting the 'correct' prices and wages, and carefully monitoring all Christendom's adherence to them, the Church would prevent economic unfairness, ensuring that all people paid exactly what they 'ought to' for every item, and received exactly what they 'ought to' for their money or labor.

"The resulting economic inefficiency and stagnation was a major reason the Dark Ages were so dark. It was only after the revolution of Renaissance ideas broke the Church's Medieval stranglehold, and the earliest stirrings of capitalism became possible, that the improvements the Renaissance produced in people's living standards could be achieved."

He gave her some time to consider her knee-jerk loathing for free market economics, and reflect on the insoluble problems man had always created every time he'd attempted to set up some sort of "Just Value" alternative.

"Can you, by careful, conscious thought, regulate the processes of your own body?" he asked her. "Just one single body? By consciously monitoring when and how forcefully to contract each chamber of your heart, what rate of secretion to maintain for every gland, what carbon-dioxide and nitrogen and oxygen percentages to maintain in the blood, what rate of cell division to maintain in every part of every organ, where to direct what levels of antibodies in response to every infectious threat. And on and on, nearly *ad infinitum*— just for one individual body?! Simply asking the question makes clear the absurdity of such an attempt.

"I don't claim the body always regulates itself perfectly, of course. People die of cancer and heart attacks and diabetes and a thousand other things. But I do claim the body 'works itself' better than you could ever consciously 'work it.' In like manner, I don't claim free market economics will always produce a perfect outcome: completely fair and efficient and optimal in every way. But I do claim—and I think even a passing acquaintance with history will confirm—that free markets work better than any of mankind's attempts over the centuries to set up any type of 'Just Value' alternative.

"When an educated person, as devoutly future-oriented and 'Progressive' as you are, holds basic economic beliefs straight out of the darkest chapters of Dark Ages Catholic theocracy, I suggest your 'Progressive' education— from kindergarten through graduate school—has missed a few chapters in Man's long story. Centuries ago, the Catholics themselves, thank Heavens, moved far beyond such economic primitivism. I don't think anyone still believes in 'Just Value' economics any more—except our most 'Progressive' elements, lost in the little echo-chamber of academia, insulated from the real world, where teachers and students can safely parrot their moral certainties back and forth to each other."

Tom's love for Sophie had led him to risk such frankness. And Sophie's tremendous intelligence and intellectual honesty enabled her to pay off on the risky bet Tom had made.

"You may have a point, Tom. I want to think about it more. I think it is true that I was born and raised and educated in what—I've begun to realize—was a very closed culture." She smiled ruefully. "A culture in which one 'correct' worldview did exercise the hegemony we otherwise deplored so much."

Intelligent as always, she saw the ramifications of the point she'd just made.

"Maybe I've become so close to Maybelle and Owen," she mused, "because I can *understand* them. Their own background and upbringing—in the world of Brother Stainfuss and the Foursquare Baptists—was also a pretty closed environment, full of intensely righteous moral certainty but with little room for fresh new ideas. And yet Maybelle and Owen are willing to consider a major change, like moving to the Amish community. While still holding to the fundamentals of their faith, they're courageous enough to re-think how they can best put into practice their deepest convictions."

Sophie and Tom fell silent for a time.

"Even you, of all people," she said with a smile, "may have undergone some changes; even you, a person who placed his deepest faith in the cool and rational avoidance of any unverifiable belief whatever. A person who had built a mighty fortress, *Ein Feste Burg,* on the unassailable mountaintop of his aloofness, his eternally uncommitted, agnostic skepticism. Who'd avoided the slightest weakness by avoiding even the slightest faith in or commitment to— anything. Whether to any belief system, religious or secular; or to his own species, humans in general; or to any specific community, be it the former United States, or the town of Mountainview, or the Amish settlement; or even just committing to a single individual: a wife, for example.

"When someone that devoted to massive non-commitment helps his townspeople survive, as you're doing with your steam engines; and helps his community build bridges to another community, as you've done with the Amish; and even—heavens!—loses himself so far as to actually *get married ...*"

She grinned. "What surprise have you in store for us next, I wonder: marching down the aisle next Sunday during Altar Call at Foursquare Baptist? Running for Chief Barley's job as the candidate of Mountainview's Green Party? Now that you're on the slippery slope of *commitment ...*"

"Well," Tom slowly considered, "since committing to marriage has turned out to be such a fabulous change for the better—so much more so than I could ever have dreamed—I've been thinking about marrying two or three more women ..."

He hugged her tightly, knowing well what a wicked jab she could unleash to his ribs if allowed freedom of movement. She made a mental note on her own private scorecard, for matters to be dealt with in the fullness of time, then returned to the subject at hand.

"But while we're pondering these philosophical issues, which will take some time, how about the practical ones, Tom? Even with Tim in the shop full time, how are you ever going to be able to do all the work you're considering?"

Tom was engulfed by such a wave of pride in his wife, and the affection it intensified, that he required a moment to collect himself.

"Well, first, Tim won't be working twenty-two hours a day. When I'm in the shop I can easily tend the engine myself. Also, those two Amish boys of Caleb Yoder's, the twins Jacob and Joshua, are hot to learn about steam engines. They're just finishing up that cider press they've been building, and it looks like they've done a really nice job with it. They've asked me if I'll take them on so they can remain here, enjoying the exciting big city life in Mountainview instead of returning to the Amish community. They've gotten Caleb's approval, and Owen and Maybelle are happy to keep them on as paying boarders, so it looks like I have two new steam engine assistants.

"I'll train them to operate the steam Gravely, and they'll do nearly all the actual operation of the machine. In another week or two, spring will be far enough along for the Gravely to be in use pretty much from dawn to dusk, seven days a week, so it will take two operators to run it. Say thirteen hours of operation daily, times seven days a week, makes ninety-one hours weekly total, or about forty-six hours for each of the twins as Gravely operator. An additional nine hours each, working in the shop, will bring each of them up to a basic fifty-five hour work-week.

"Because the twins' work schedules will be staggered—one of them arriving in the shop before I arrive each morning and one leaving the shop after I leave each evening—and because I'll tend the shop generator myself while I'm there, that will leave mainly the middle of the night for Tim to tend the machine. But he'll have plenty of other work to keep him occupied.

"I can't tell you what incredible good fortune we've had, with the expedition to Grayson bringing back those four Honda 650 motorcycles: four simple, large, single-cylinder, air-cooled engines with gearboxes to match—and all of them identical. I couldn't ask for anything better to convert to steam. As I work on the first one, learning how to do the conversion, Tim and the twins during their shop hours can copy much of my work on the remaining three. I'll still have to do some machining operations they can't yet handle, of course; but nevertheless, we're about to re-achieve a *huge* leap in Man's work productivity: from handcrafting items, one at a time, to producing identical batches with interchangeable parts.

"I've reached an agreement with the Mountainview expedition for sharing the benefits of the four machines. I'll own the machines, convert them to steam, train operators for them, and rent them out. The police department, on behalf of the expedition that obtained the machines, will get half the net revenue from them—that is, the rental fee minus expenses for boiler fuel, operators' pay, and maintenance. I'll get the other half of their net revenue for converting the engines to steam, maintaining them, and managing their rentals and their operation. The engine operators will get a paycheck for work that's far less brutally exhausting than what they'd be doing otherwise. The parties that rent the machines—to cut firewood or fenceposts or building lumber, to pump irrigation water, to blow air for winnowing grain, or whatever—will perform those tasks quicker and easier, and therefore cheaper, than they could without mechanical power. So their prices to Mountainview consumers—for the wood they've cut, the crops they've irrigated, the grain they've produced—will be lower than would have been possible without machines. So all the people of Mountainview—especially us, with our half of the machines' rental income—will live better.

"The police department, which initially paid its employees with gasoline from the Department's tank plus rations from an old Civil Defense stockpile, has been able to make payroll—barely—after both those items ran out by using its portion of Bill Etter's water delivery profits and by using the interest Miz Strewk pays on the gold coins taken from the people who attacked us back in February. Chief Barley's delighted that the Department's portion of the income from the four motorcycle engines, once they're converted to steam, will allow him to give his people a badly needed pay raise.

"And as for us, if I can continue in this capitalist fashion, doing quite well by doing the community some good, I hope to become rich enough in the years ahead to mostly retire from work and devote myself to pursuing other interests—such as supporting a certain university, for example."

He refilled their glasses of hard cider and snuggled closer to her on the couch.

"All in all, things in the Steam Engine Department, Mrs. Jeffson, are looking very bright indeed. How's tricks these days in higher education?"

Chapter 38
On the One Hand,
Tis a Mixed Blessing to Be Simple...

"Absolutely standard, I'm afraid, Professor Jeffson," Sophie replied, with a sad little wave of her glass. "The faculty and administration are spending their time canoodling on the sofa, getting drunk; not one single deadline for the university's much-delayed opening is being met on schedule; and the eternal hatred between 'Town and Gown' looks set to erupt any minute into full-blown warfare."

"So? Sounds normal enough."

"Before the '*Gown*' part even *exists?*" she wailed.

"Hmm. OK, that's different. But what's the holdup with the Grand Opening? The Department of Humanities, I am pleased to announce, will offer the renowned Professor Jeffson's course on the *Antigone*—a dramatic work in which some old dead white European male points out that once we appoint Rulers to rule over us we are all—Rulers and subjects, good people and bad people alike—doomed.

"Professor Parker, of the Law Faculty, has told me he will ignore his assigned topic and conduct instead a seminar on why the fact that we humans are doomed matters not a whit, because any society's death is merely the precondition for a successor society's birth, and there are many fascinating books to be savored which explain this process and demonstrate how intriguing it all is conceptually, especially for an old, old man who's really only been interested, all his life, in beautifully written books setting forth Grand Theories whose conceptual loveliness is exceeded only by their practical uselessness.

"Professor Barley, I am given to understand, of the Department of Political Science, has cobbled together some load of cock-and-bull for his course on 'Democracy: Athen's Gift to Mountainview'. As if Democracy—selecting our leaders by means of pandering-competitions called elections, which got us into the present mess—offers any hope of escaping our inevitable doom.

"Plus, if all the forgoing were not enough, for long-term perspective I look forward to auditing the course on natural selection, in which the esteemed Doc Billings, Chairman of the Department of Natural Sciences, will survey the state of contemporary speculation about the evolution of life forms, from their possibly virus-like beginnings in the primordial ooze to today's *Homo sapiens*. Without, of course, addressing whether that change represents progress or regress—scientists having sense enough to sidestep any such value judgments.

"Rounding out the university's first-semester offerings, by the way—just to tip you off, in case you don't know—I have reason to believe Professor Hockley Beener, *wunderkind* of the circuit board, may stray slightly from his acknowledged field of expertise to undertake an impassioned exegesis of the love poems of Robert Herrick. I loaned him the book.

"Starshine got so far behind with the laundry she ran out of wearable blue jeans and work shirts one day and had to grit her teeth and put on an actual skirt and blouse. So now poor Hockley's doomed as well. Head-over-heels; no hope.

"But aside from the shame of a promising young computer scientist snared by a woman and sliding into the degradation of Eng. Lit.—well, that plus the Doom thing—how could the university present any real problem?"

"Evolution."

She said it in such a tone of hopelessness Tom's heart instantly went out to her.

"Brother Stainfus," she added, by way of explanation.

"Ah."

At first he tried to cajole her out of her gloom.

"Well, hell, Sophie: you and the Righteous Brother are on the same, sternly disapproving side here, aren't you? Natural *selection?* Survival of the *fittest?* Social *Darwinism?* Ug! Double-plus-ungood I should think—were I some kind of 19th Century primitive, such as a Socialist or a Christian Fundamentalist."

"Oh, *Tom*!" her very real distress tore at his heart, "what am I going to do? Doc's course topic has gotten out. How could we change it now, in response to outrage from the Foursquare Baptist Church? I *would,* personally. I swear to God this is *not* an issue of 'face' or pride or ego. If it were just that I'd recant and retreat and beg Brother Stainfus on my knees for forgiveness. I'd change the course to a discussion of why fossils—which do not indicate the existence of extinct species, and are not more than 4,000 years old, and don't exist anyway—are fully explained in the Book of Revelations or something. I'd do *anything* to avoid starting the university off by tearing the community apart!

"But, Tom, if a university operates only at the pleasure of some religious group's veto-power, is it really a university—or a Sunday School? What about its responsibility to uphold its teachers' right to free-inquiry? And its students' right to learn? And *everyone's* right to q*uestion?*"

She had begun to weep silently, not willing to admit she was doing so, but betrayed by the twin streaks of moisture Tom saw on her face. She twisted one corner of the lap-robe they shared until Tom feared she might tear a piece off the blanket.

"California crazy-woman," she sobbed softly, "c-c-come here to corrupt good people and tear apart a peaceful community with the Godless, heathen troublemaking of Outsiders."

Tom pulled her to him, gently stroking her hair, holding her tight.

"Well, you know, Sophie, during the decades in which tenured leftist radicals from the Sixties exercised nearly complete control over most of America's leading universities—very often an extremely heavy-handed control, dictating the sorts of professors who could be hired, the sorts of things they could teach, the sorts of opinions that were and were not acceptable from students, and what effects such opinions had on the students' grades—an awful lot of Politically Incorrect people felt the same anguish Brother Stainfuss is now causing you."

He sighed, wishing there were an easy answer.

"Does it all boil down, in the end, simply to power?" he mused. "The strongest faction just rams its own values through, and that settles that? There used to be large, well-funded, and very powerful academic industries devoted to making precisely that argument—so long as *they* were the most powerful faction, of course.

"Post-Modernism, Deconstructionism, Multi-Culturalism: these academic gangs and their fellow-travelers all shared a tendency to deny any absolute values—such as the rights of teachers, students, and ordinary people you just mentioned. Instead, these gangs, controlling much of academia for decades, very explicitly accepted the existence only of relative values, which were socially created or socially granted by—naturally—the strongest faction in any society. The academic gangs emphatically denied that any society had ever done otherwise—that in fact the very idea of even *attempting* to do otherwise was foolish, a mere exercise in self-delusion, or 'false consciousness.'

"Even students with no interest in philosophy or political science or any such area of public-policy concern—kids who just wanted to become dentists, or CPA's or whatever—still had to get their BA or BS before they could receive professional training. And to make it through the 'gate-keeping' of those first four years many of them soon realized they had better learn to keep their heads down, and keep their opinions to themselves, and keep a ready line of politically approved, shuckin'-an'-jivein' patter to trot out for their professors and student-aid counselors and Correct-Thinking fellow students whenever necessary.

"Was there much room, or respect, at Berkeley for the cautious conservatism of traditionalists: people who give great weight to the social values deeply embedded in our society because those values have proved useful for thousands of years in guiding the lives of untold billions of people? Square and stodgy old notions like honoring your marriage vows, living unostentatiously within your means, earning a day's wage by a day's work, paying your bills, defending your country: the sorts of eye-rollingly un-cool values Grant Wood naively thought he was satirizing, rather than honoring, in *American Gothic;* values of such hilarious squareness they'd set the Parisian or Greenwich Village café intellectuals to rolling on the floor. But which may last a bit longer (and do Mankind a bit more good) than all the most fashionably stylized posturings of the Trotskyites, Dadaists, deconstructionists, post-modernists, and similarly pretentious cafe intellectuals there ever were or ever will be.

"Brother Stainfuss and his Believers are very often stupid. I'll grant that. Generally goodhearted, honest, hardworking, decent-living, generous, salt-of-the-earth souls, no question. But dumb? Oh Lord! Downright dumb as pig-dribble. Though you're too polite to come right out and say so, I'm not.

"But, Sophie: how much of a screwed-up mess have Brother Stainfuss and his benighted backwoods yokels ever caused the larger society—compared to what we were treated to in just four or five decades from The Best And The Brightest?

"Remember these glorious triumphs: The War on Vietnam? The War on Poverty? The War on Drugs? The War on Terrorism? The Racial Bussing fiasco for schoolchildren? The 'Race-Norming' scandal of colleges secretly altering college admission test scores? The 'temporary' (soon changed to permanent) use of 'quotas' (soon changed to 'goals') to fight racial discrimination in employment by discriminating against whites? A truly shameless exercise in rent-seeking that was soon expanded to favor women,

and 'the gay/lesbian/bisexual/transsexual-and-transgendered-community'—
and God knows how many other groups pushing and shoving before The
Collapse, eager to join in the fight against favoritism by getting on the list for
favored treatment!

"Good Lord, Sophie, some of the government's pet pressure-groups—like
the invention called 'Latino'—weren't even *groups*! 'Latinos' are not of one
race or skin-color: they range from purest Caucasian whites to Negroid blacks,
with every shade of brown in between; they're not a linguistic group: they
speak a variety of tongues from assorted forms of Spanish to Portuguese to
Haitian and other Creoles; they're not of a particular economic class or
geographical origin: the palest Spanish royalty, who's never been out of Madrid
except on his chartered jet to ski at Gstaad, is as much 'Latino' as the darkest,
starving Brazilian rag-picker.

"Those two 'group members'—from different continents, from different
races and economic classes, with different appearances—can't even
converse, because they speak different languages.

"And yet—in areas from education to hiring to SBA loan-approval to kid-
glove treatment by the press—the former was just as entitled to special favors
(in the cause of fighting favoritism) as was the latter. And *both*—on the first
day they set foot on U.S. soil—were entitled to official favoritism over the son
of a poor-white Appalachian coal miner or share-cropper, whose people had
lived here, helping to build the nation, and dying in its wars, for 200 years!

"The scam called 'affirmative action'—cooked up by the academy's
Deepthinkers, and providing tax-funded jobs for armies of government
Enforcers— went far beyond the normal, routinely corrupt cynicism of
government *realpolitik*. Even judged by its own supporters' vague, feel-good
emotional desire to help the downtrodden it was very often, in practice, flatly
counter-productive!

"However much Brother Stainfuss and his band of simpletons may damage
their own lives by clinging to various goofy or downright stupid beliefs, *none*
of those people has caused anything remotely close to the social damage done
just in my lifetime by The Best and the Brightest. So I'm not the ideal candidate,
Sophie, to express great anguish and outrage about what has befallen your
university, now that—with the help of Brother Stainfuss—the worm here in
tiny little Mountainview has finally turned."

But his irritated sigh itself turned into a helpless shrug, which slowly
morphed into a grin.

"Still. *God*, what a moron! And you wonder—given a range from the

Foursquare Baptists at one end of the spectrum to The Best and the Brightest at the other—why I have so little use for human beings?"

He chuckled. "Think we'll only have to go as far back as the 1920's and re-fight the Scopes Monkey Trial? After all, Copernicus and Galileo and that bunch, a long time before the 1920's, came up with at least equally shocking and impious notions—for which the Godly ancestors of Brother Stainfuss no doubt wanted them burned at the stake.

"But assuming Brother Stainfuss and his *current* followers now grudgingly accept that all celestial bodies do not revolve around the earth, as Copernicus concluded 600 years ago, your whole Evolution Problem may simply require allowing time to run its course. Give Darwin about 500 more years to slowly seep in, and perhaps he won't fill the Righteous Brother with any more outrage than Copernicus now does."

Tom admitted, with a grin, "This suggestion does, of course, depend on the assumption that the Foursquare Baptists have by now succumbed to the Copernicans' heretical ideas—or at least heard of them. If they haven't yet— or if you're in too much of a hurry to give things another 500 years in Darwin's case—perhaps some other strategy would be called for."

"*Ha. Ha. And Ha.*"

She tried to make it sound bitter, but it came out so small and sad and forlorn Tom regretted his petty lack of magnanimity. Uncharacteristically, he struggled to rise above his true nature and make some gesture toward a positive contribution, perhaps even something helpful, or at least well-intentioned. He considered for a time.

"Have you invited the three preachers—Stainfuss, Parson Miller, and Call-Me-Bob—to teach?"

"Teach? Or preach?" she replied bitterly. "The idea is to start a *school*, Tom. With the Methodist and two Baptist churches running multiple services and Sunday School classes all day Sunday, plus more of the same on Wednesday evenings, plus church-group activities almost every weekday, plus the Vacation Bible School now being planned, *surely* people here get enough religion."

"Not the point," Tom replied. "Being left out of a big new thing in town— the university—*that's* the point. I think Stainfuss has a legitimate beef. Sign him up to teach a course—and the other two as well, naturally—and I'll bet the heretical horrors of Darwinism will quietly slip right back into the moldering grave they were just dragged out of.

"Look, Sophie, try it this way: just repeat to yourself all those lofty-sounding,

Politically Correct notions you so devoutly believe in—then (here's the novel idea) actually try implementing them.

"*Diversity?* Allow some into your university, starting with the creationists' nitwit alternative to evolution, for example.

"*Multi-Culturalism?* Try some: allow people from cultures very unlike the prevailing secular-humanist orthodoxy of the elites to participate in your university.

"*Social Justice?* Perhaps there are more approaches to that goal than just those of the orthodox, tax-and-spend socialists. Call-Me-Bob, for example, passionately wants faith-based social uplift programs of every sort; Stainfuss advises us to pray for justice in the next world while living righteous lives in this one, and submitting to a Devine Plan we cannot understand; Parson Miller believes we should generally be nice, lend a hand to our neighbor on occasion, and not get carried away too far in any particular direction.

"*Liberal Open Mindedness?* Well, OK—you get the idea, right? Your orthodox, Politically Correct leftist slogans, Sophie, are, in many cases, perfectly fine ideas. For heaven sakes, try *implementing* them! Even in—of all unlikely places—a supposed haven for intellectual freedom such as a university!"

And so it came to pass that three more courses were added to the university's forthcoming offerings.

Call-me-Bob led an inquiry into the possibility that followers of the Black (i.e. covert) Madonna were actually an occult (i.e. hidden) splinter-group within the early Church, devoted to avoiding the misogyny of St. Paul's thought, secretly attempting to preserve early Christian concepts that Pauline orthodoxy had nearly stamped out, until the Qumran and Nag Hammadi discoveries of the 20th century indicated those concepts were central to some of the earliest Christian teachings.

Parson Miller offered a standard survey of church history that, typically, included far more widely accepted facts than Call-me-Bob's course—and far fewer huge new exciting ideas.

Brother Stainfuss—the ball having been neatly placed in his court—was caught in a painful dilemma. He at first considered teaching a much-ballyhooed "creationist" alternative to Darwin, assured of a full and enthusiastic class by simply instructing his church members to attend. But then it occurred to him to wonder what *other* classes his followers might then be tempted to attend, and what perils those classes (indeed, this whole, frightening, secular-education-thing in general) might lead them into. These were not comforting thoughts.

Uncertain as to which alternative to take with his flock—whether to make participation in the new university mandatory or prohibited—Brother Stainfuss settled for an uneasy compromise. He offered a survey course on Old Testament genealogy, trusting in an endless string of "begats" to deter most potential students and put any remaining ones to sleep, thereby hopefully allowing the whole issue of the university to return to what he prayed would be merciful obscurity.

In the first week of April, Sophie's enterprise held its Grand Opening. It was officially dedicated as "Mountainview University"—Sophie having quietly backed down from earlier threats, including "The New School for Progressive Social Policy Research."

For thirty cents silver, people were invited to attend a day-long Gala. They were offered a Greek (or, strictly speaking, in some respects "Greek-like") banquet featuring lamb or goat with rice, hummus, tabouli, dolmas, pita bread, baklava, and tea.

Tom, who contributed the last fifty pounds of rice left from his Y2K staples, did so with mixed emotions. He loved rice, and he knew he would almost certainly never see any again, not considering it likely that trade with places as far away as the Carolinas would resume in his lifetime—even assuming there were any survivors in such areas still growing rice.

"This university had better turn out to be really *good*," he mused only half in jest, hefting the two six-gallon plastic buckets into the Gravely cart to take them to the restaurant.

"Amazingly," Sophie told him, "we can produce nearly every ingredient for most common Greek dishes except rice, olives, and lemons—with a few bits of artful dodging, admittedly. I suspect, for example, the Greeks were inclined to wrap their dolmas in grape leaves just because they didn't have fresh spring collards like we do. Anyway, next year we'll have our own grape leaves aplenty."

In the crowded restaurant, there was a continuously running program of travelogues and PBS documentaries on Greece, which Starshine had ferreted out of peoples' long-forgotten collections of video tapes for Hockley to enter into the computer and display on the restaurant's huge TV screen. Interspersed between the video tapes were still photos, drawings, and paintings of Greece, ancient and modern, that Hockley had scanned from books Starshine had brought him. There was a surprising variety of Greek music from various records, tapes, and CD's she'd located.

There was a demonstration of what, to be kind, might best be called "Greek-like" dancing presented by the Methodist Young Marrieds Group, and a performance of Greek folk songs by the Mountainview Baptist Youth Association.

Olanda Priddy displayed on a table the embroidered tablecloth, Greek doll, and two scarves a former beau in the U.S. Navy had sent her from Athens, and Bub Ford displayed one of the prized pieces in his gun collection, an 1890 bolt action Mauser that, although technically made under contract for Turkey, might well have been captured in Greece.

Chief Barley, lending his official weight to the gala, made a brief speech formally opening Mountainview University.

"We are today," he noted, "in some ways back where so much of our culture began: ancient Greece. The past nine months have been tougher than any of us could have imagined. No wonder we sometimes fear to think about our future. But a knowledge of ancient Greece can help provide some reassuring perspective. The people of that time and place were far poorer than we are; they lived a far harder and more desperately dangerous life than we do; their dry, thin, stony land offered far less promise than our own lush fields and forests.

"And yet, at this University we're opening today, you can see pictures of buildings the Greeks built 2500 years ago which still astonish us; and you can read and discuss plays they wrote 2500 years ago, which still engage and enthrall us; and you can debate ideas about government they implemented 2500 years ago which are still with us today. The more we know of our past the more grounds for hope we have for our future—and the university we're opening today can give us that vital knowledge of the past.

"In addition, our University offers courses concerning material from long before ancient Greece—the time of the Old Testament, for example—and also much closer to our own era: right up to the very latest theories about the origins of human life.

"So I urge you all to look over the course outlines you'll see at the tables over there, and sign up for any you have an interest in, as your time permits. As you'll see, classes will be conducted during various daytime and evening hours, working around the needs of the restaurant. Each class will run for the next three months, thru the first week of July. And, for this first semester, each class will cost just one dollar silver.

"For the old-fashioned among us, we have a surprisingly large assortment of books to rent, at one dime per book per week. And for all of us—old and new fashioned alike—we have just about every book, movie, and picture owned in Mountainview now available in several locations on computers, which the University will provide you the use of for a penny an hour. And that, my friends, is a bargain. The money all goes back into the University's operating costs, and we hope to expand the course offerings every semester.

"And, yes, Mountainview University will eventually—soon, we hope— offer formal BA and BS degrees. We are not ignorant savages. We will not become ignorant savages. We will build a new and better world out of the sufferings of The Collapse—and we will do so, in no small part, through the learning transmitted here at Mountainview University.

"I now declare this school to be officially open for business, and I thank you all for your attention, and I will not grade as tough in my course as Judge Parker's likely to in his, so I urge you to sign up for mine while there's still room. Thank you all."

Barley stepped down to laughter and applause. And as Tom hugged Sophie, discretely offering her his handkerchief, he could sense beneath her unexpected emotional release just how important her university was to her. It was, he realized with a mixture of pride and dread—and a brief, stabbing pain of loneliness—the most important thing in her life.

Chapter 39
Out of Bondage

In their new world—no longer immersed in a constant bath of radio, television, movies, advertising, and celebrity trivia—the ordinary people of Mountainview discovered to their surprise they had the time and desire to focus on more significant matters. The university was a hit right from the start, enrolling over two dozen serious and motivated students aged seventeen to seventy.

"You know, Tom, the more serious people from our past, who actually read books, were not inherently superior people to the dumbed-down, apathetic, aliterate serfs populating the government's plantations by the time of The Collapse," Judge Parker said one day in mid-April. "They just had the good fortune to live before a small handful of slick operators discovered the immense profit to be made by hooking the populace on electronic heroin, and then supplying them with it, 24/7, through their television sets."

Tom, surprised and intrigued yet again by the "extremist radicalism" of his old friend, silently raised an eyebrow. The Judge continued.

"Centuries from now, people will look back on our own society before The Collapse—and the obscene profits a tiny handful of people extracted from it—with much the same revulsion we now feel toward those 19th century British who at gunpoint opened China to the opium trade, providing an inexhaustible market for Britain's cheap, Indian-grown opium, and relieving China's population of its valuable silver, shipped by the ton back to a small handful of English businessmen.

"Who, by the way, felt no shame whatsoever at their behavior. After all, no Chinaman was forced to buy opium. Nor was there any personal ill will on the part of the sellers. '*It was just business*'—As Rupert Murdock or Ted Turner, or Sumner Redstone would have told you in our own day, very indignantly, if you had accused them of enslaving people or peddling narcotics.

"You mail out millions of unsolicited credit cards to the childlike masses, to hook them on a lifestyle where they pay 18% interest to buy the plastic crap you then shill to them nonstop on television. And the same electronic spew hawking your wares also serves as an electronic lobotomiser, dumbing the marks down to where they're so focused on having a good emotional wallow with Oprah (between commercials) they're not even conscious of their addiction or its cost.

"In economic terms, you've combined wage-slavery with the drug trade—but so cleanly, through the modern marvels of electronics, there's not a trace of muck on your own hands, nor the least blemish on your public image or your private conscience."

Judge Parker smiled thinly, looking out his library window at his neighbor's one-and-a-half acre backyard, which a man was tilling with the steam Gravely, *chuff-chuff-chuffing* up one row and down the next, about half finished turning the lawn into cropland. The old Judge gestured toward the scene.

"I see Bill Kelson's putting in a corn crop. He's expanded his hog operation to where he'll need every bit of corn he can raise or buy. And from what I've tasted of his pork, he'll have eager customers lining up for every pound he'll sell.

"Bill used to have the 'Glam-R-Nailz' franchise in Grayson, you know. Had three storefronts in the seedier parts of town, where girls who'd dropped out of high school could spend half their weekly minimum-wage paycheck—or their welfare check—having three-inch-long green plastic fingernails with embedded rhinestones glued on: for only $9.95 down and the balance carried on their Mastercards at 18-21%. Bill had a real goldmine going, from what I hear. He didn't think he was doing anything squalid. But look at him now."

The Judge gestured again at the soon-to-be-productive corn field.

"You know, Tom, a lot of what we left behind in The Collapse was well worth leaving behind."

Tom chuckled. "So the old University of Virginia graduate's going all Jeffersonian on me, eh? Let's hear it for the moral superiority of the yeoman-farmer and his honest agrarian toil, far from the vice and corruption of big cities like Grayson."

But Tom's smile faded, changing to a more serious look of genuine curiosity. "Really, though, how *is* this new life we're living—apart from being so morally pure and all? How's Mabel doing with her plant-growing, now that her hobby of selling fru-fru to yuppies has become something very different, done in deadly earnest? And how's Arlene-the-Moonshiner doing in her log cabin out at the distillery and salt-works?"

"Super and terrific, in brief," the Judge replied. "I'll admit I've been surprised myself at just how well things are going. Mabel's got six fulltime gardening employees hard at work setting out the annuals; and next week she'll start Al Jenkins and his crew to constructing a huge greenhouse along the entire south side of the house here.

"Al's promised to have it finished before fall, of course." The Judge grinned. "And if it takes Mabel and Arlene both, using the whip in shifts, I'll bet that's a deadline he'll actually meet."

"As for Arlene ..." The old man shook his head in delighted wonder. "She's *happy,* Tom! For a while, after The Collapse, we were deeply worried about whether Arlene was going to make it. I think things could have gone either way. But now she and Billie are really churning out the booze and salt—well above the early projections, it seems. I suspect they're in the process of getting modestly rich off their share: they've asked me to keep a discrete eye open for any small parcels of investment cropland that might come up for sale.

"They're also negotiating with Bill Etter to use his mule cart to haul salt to the Amish, which those folks need in quantity for their animals, among other uses. On his return trip, he'll bring back the sugar syrup they crush out of their sugar beets and grain sorghum, which we use for sweetener and the still uses to make alcohol. Chief Barley's overjoyed to leave all the headaches of the transportation arrangements and barter negotiations in Arlene's hands—and she's absolutely in her managerial-and-dealmaking element. *Arlene's going to make it, Tom!* You and your Sophie may well have saved my daughter's life. I thank you for that—more than I can say."

He halted suddenly, unable to speak further.

"Well," Tom demurred, turning his attention to the scene outside the window, where the steam Gravely steadily worked, as the old Judge collected himself, "Mabel and Arlene are doing things vital for the lives of all of us in Mountainview, and for the Amish as well. Without the plants and the salt Mabel and Arlene produce, I'm pretty sure we'd all die off.

"Speaking of the Amish community, though, I guess you heard Klara Yoder completed her month's intensive medical training with Doc and has returned to the Amish. I hear she had a lot of quiet, behind-the-scenes negotiating to do there, but eventually they agreed to maintain a radio link with Mountainview. Supposedly, it's just so Klara and Doc can join forces in the event of a serious medical case at either location—but I suspect in time it'll gradually develop into a broader communication link."

Tom grinned. "A *radio*, after all, is not a *telephone*—as I understand Klara explained to her Elders, over and over again."

The two longtime friends re-filled their glasses, sharing some of the last of the Judge's genuine whisky from the old days, as the shadows began to lengthen outside the library window.

"So you accuse me of Jeffersonian quaintness in my declining years, eh?" the old Judge mused. "Well, he always was willing to place his bets on freedom, despite its undeniable inefficiencies, wasn't he? To the everlasting fury of the Hamiltonians, those worshippers of efficient, centralized corporate/state Power: the Power to 'make the trains run on time,' the Power to behaviorally engineer an improved 'New Soviet Man'—the Power to make the 20th century orders of magnitude more horrific than any other in human history, in terms of government-produced mass slaughter, suffering, and devastation.

"Very well, I confess: I do think what the good life really boils down to is freedom. But achieving and maintaining it's more complicated than might at first be obvious: there's a bit more to it than just slay the tyrant, throw off the yoke, and declare 'Mission Accomplished.'

"For the good life, we must have freedom from want, obviously: enough food, clothing, shelter and the like to avoid the bite of poverty. Also, freedom from degrading, animal-like physical drudgery: the freedom that machines like your steam engines offer us. I hear, by the way, you've got a regular assembly line going now at your shop, with the Yoder twins and Tim helping you convert those four motorcycle engines to steam. Thanks to you, we haven't lost our precarious grip on the mechanical age, and regressed to the draft-animal status your machines give us freedom from.

"Freedom, in its larger sense, also involves freedom from the crippling effects of ignorance. The two Yoder boys in your shop, who were already skilled with livestock, are now becoming steam engine mechanics as well; Klara has received substantial medical training; the Amish community now has a radio so either group can summon help in emergencies; and Mountainview has a promising university, backed up by the fine collection of material Hockley and Starshine have stored on computer. All well and good: I find the achievements downright impressive.

"But other people have also had all these freedoms: from economic want, from crushing physical toil, and from pervasive ignorance. Yet if the result is no more serious—fosters no more human dignity—than *'Heather-and-Jason-shop-The-Galleria'* then why bother?

"I think in some ways the most precious freedom we've stumbled into here in Mountainview is our freedom from…as best I can put it…from *shallowness* or *triviality*.

"We're not bathed every waking moment in a flood of electronic babble urging us to be desperately concerned about whether Liz or Rosie or Opera has lost or gained five pounds; or whether the latest celebrity criminal will get away with it or not; or whether we ought to have the green-and-orange—or maybe the black-and-purple—three-inch plastic fingernails pasted on; or whether we can hustle enough of a bonus this year to trade our new BMW in on a Lexus; or whether we'd be more youthful and popular if we put zero down on a balloon note for a bigger McMansion in a newer development; or ..."

He sat silent, for a moment, recalling the grossness and silliness—the truly breathtaking vulgarity—of their former world.

"I don't think, by the time The Collapse came, we even realized how deeply we had been taken hostage by the incessant, omnipresent flood of electronic *drivel*: relentlessly consumerist, least-common-denominator oriented, and compulsively *shallow*. Reclaiming the freedom to live lives not immersed in commercially manufactured trivia may, in the end, be the most far-reaching of the freedoms we've acquired.

"Of course most people today still generally choose to immerse themselves in trivia. Little people, by definition, will almost always confine their attention to small thoughts about small matters: Millie's angst about that dress stuck-up-Maggie wore to church last Sunday; Buck's irritation at Bo's stubborn refusal to admit the Moose really are better than the Kiwanis; little Sally's dread that if Meg tells Bob what Janie said about Bill she'll just *die*.

"But there's all the difference in the world between the natural process of little people concentrating on the little trivia they find or invent for themselves, versus the artificial process of being *force-fed* trivia deliberately manufactured by commercial interests for commercial gain. It's the difference between geese healthily pecking about on their own for corn, versus their being restrained in cages, with funnels forced down their necks, into which corn is poured until the goose's liver is destroyed—in order to fetch the farmer top dollar for pate foie gras.

"So, yes, I *like* our rough-hewn new world, Tom. I think people are freer—at all levels up and down the social and economic scale—than they were in the old one. And if that marks me as hopelessly Jeffersonian—well, I guess there are worse fates."

"No doubt," acknowledged Tom with a smile. "Of course I share your preference for the Jeffersonian ideals. But I wouldn't dismiss too quickly the importance of *using* the Hamiltonians' contributions as a means toward achieving the ends we both desire."

"I think, Judge, the vital thing is to combine both tributaries into a single river: finding effective ways to select the desirable aspects of progress and efficiency—from Hamiltonian or whatever sources—then putting them to use in the service of Jeffersonian ideals.

"We're using computers, for example: those cold and soulless agents of manipulation playing a key role in your example of credit card debt-slavery. But with Hockley's genius, and Starshine's abilities, we're using *our* computers for good: to permanently store and easily access the information that will free us from the provincial ignorance which was always the dark side of Jefferson's rustic yeomanry.

"Likewise, we can accept and turn to positive use all sorts of 'capitalist' innovations—from steam engines to interest-charging banks—and seize the benefits they can offer us today, instead of rejecting them as forever tainted by their part in the Dark, Satanic Mills of a blighted era long ago. We must manage to finally *get over,* somehow, the lingering emotional residue of kneejerk anti-capitalism—the dead hand of Karl Marx, still reaching out from the Industrial Revolution's cruelties of more than two centuries ago—and free ourselves to look more pragmatically for *what works* in our new world.

"For one thing, we must get beyond kneejerk, anti-capitalist government-worship in order to achieve some means of sustainable funding for social services and medical care for us all. Groups like the Amish, out on the far edge of the feared and demonized 'Religious Right,' achieved that milestone of progress centuries ago—in stark contrast to the repeated failures of our own Lefties, whose deepest passion in governing was usually: first, to deliver paybacks to their hated enemies, the capitalist rich; second, to deliver payoffs to their constituents and booty to their friends—welfare benefits and 'jobs for the boys'—by increasing government's size and power; and, usually a distant third, incidentally address whatever social need was at issue.

"Our Lefties, worshipping at their Hamiltonian altar of State Power (serving a jealous God indeed, and not about to place any other God before Him) never did achieve the lasting cradle-to-grave social safety net the profoundly anti-government Amish have been accustomed to for three hundred years. The leftists, though, certainly damaged or destroyed plenty of societies with the fraudulent tactics they resorted to for funding their government programs.

"The leftists of our time—typically ranging from agnostic to rabidly atheist—demonstrated a truly touching belief in miracles, especially that of the Loaves and Fishes. Omnipotent Government *would* miraculously somehow provide care for all—no matter the resources available. And if the necessary wealth wasn't there, why merely pretend it soon would be, via Ponzi financing. Or just print up additional bales of paper banknotes, and claim those bales of worthless paper represented the actual wealth necessary to fund all the well-meaning social programs one's heart (or re-election needs) might favor.

"We in the larger society democratically chose to be dishonest, and we've reaped our reward. But the Amish have proved to me that dishonesty is *not* compulsory; the disasters it brings in train are *not* inevitable.

"Now that we're freed from an endless torrent of media drivel, more able to focus our attention on matters of substance, perhaps we can increasingly take the route Klara Yoder typifies: making carefully thought-out use of progress—whether in medicines, medical tools and techniques, or radiotelephones—to serve the interests of a humane, human-scale society.

"Freed from a constant force-feeding of trivia by the media, we may now have the opportunity to build a more serious culture based on lasting values, as the Amish have done, while still retaining the ability to profit from progress if and when specific aspects of that progress really do profit us. Regaining a Jeffersonian culture will take some careful steering between the dangers of the Amish way—their blanket rejection of nearly all innovation to preserve their humane society—and the dangers of our own, secular way, upon which our society foundered: a mindless preoccupation with *anything* sufficiently new, noisy, and vulgar—no matter how socially destructive—so long as a tiny handful of billionaire media hustlers could further enrich themselves by pimping it."

Tom's anger, his bitterness left over from their pre-Collapse world, had scarcely cooled in the year since that world had ended. The passion in his voice surprised his friend, the old Judge.

"Television!" Tom spat out. "In support of my contempt for the social depths we had reached—and those who had helped us reach them—I offer as evidence the values actively promoted, 24/7, by America's television-culture: from the shallow, infotainment-quality 'news' programs and the sitcoms and 'reality shows' of the four broadcast networks to the more narrowly targeted but at least equally mindless, vulgar, and socially destructive programming on the 'narrow-cast' networks like MTV and Black Entertainment Television.

"The 'Vast Wasteland' charge was, of course, leveled against television from its beginning, and it was true from the beginning. But back then it was not so terribly important, because most of what television presented was only moronic—as opposed to malignant. Big difference. If you didn't want to waste your time you just didn't watch TV: problem solved. Simple.

"But television's impact changed over the years, as its content descended from the moronic to the malignant. I think television (and other media, but TV was egregious) played a crucial role in the downward trend of the nation's academic standards, until it became commonplace to see two quite distinct student bodies in American universities: Asian kids mastering math, physics, or chemistry and American kids taking sociology, education, or marketing— or, if even those fields were beyond them, working on their self-esteem by pursuing the so-called 'Studies' offered in feminist, gay, Black, Hispanic, and similar support-groups.

"I think television also played a critical role in the economic slide that— funny coincidence—exactly paralleled the one in education. Mens' hourly take-home pay in this country, adjusted for inflation, reached its highest point in 1973. Then, ever since America's first generation of television-raised children became its first generation of television-raised workers, the nation's real economic growth stagnated. Before the end, the U.S. had become almost entirely a casino economy, based on the twin fantasies of intrinsically worthless paper money and the childlike hopes of the pitiful that they could 'strike it rich' in some quick and easy Big Deal.

"I give you the breathtaking idiocy of the dot-com bubble, where five trillion dollars returned to the thin air it had been created from, POOF, while TV-raised Joe and Josephine Sixpack sought investment counsel from—of course—television. The multitude of 'bubble-vision' investment shows catering to the TV generation's mentality featured—to give just one example among many—the financial genius of a wildly optimistic, Get-Rich-Quick hostess in a low-cut blouse and short skirts named the Money Honey."

The old Judge grinned. "Yeah, I saw that one once. Good enough looker, in a Las Vegas sort of way, but she talked too fast for me. I was so busy trying to keep track of which of the three walnut shells the pea was under I couldn't keep up, minute-to-minute, with which company's IPO was going to double my money the quickest."

He signed, thinking of his own financial ruin after accumulating the soundest, most conservative, most completely secure investments. "Not that investing, in the long run, worked any better than gambling ..."

"Exactly!" Tom replied. "Exactly. In the end, when the ignorance of the vulgarians had spread widely enough—no longer just a personal trait of individuals but now a systemic trait pervading the whole economy—it no longer did any good to be an ant instead of a grasshopper, for the world of both collapsed equally.

"And that may have been television's most destructive impact: the harm it did responsible, capable people by assisting our society's decline into apathetic, vulgarian ignorance. Until eventually even a meaningful degree of self-government—the nation's founding idea, its reason for existence—became no longer possible. Television proved very good at making money, lots of it, by furnishing mindless diversion to people who had less and less interest in running their own lives, and showed less and less capacity for doing so with each passing year—who willingly handed over all that hard and boring stuff to Government, asking only in return for a bit of mindless titillation in the present and the politician's promise of endless prosperity in the future: the sort of happy, hazy dream sucked from the opium pipe that television had become for the masses.

"The dreamily dependant, especially when they're kept trustingly childlike and entertainment-saturated, don't make ideal material for thoughtful, informed, and capable self-government. Consider, for example, the steadily shortening length of campaign 'sound bites' directed over the years to a television-oriented, intellectually impaired electorate. Or read any of the Federalist Papers, or Lincoln-Douglass debates, and contrast the sophistication of their ideas with the mental level political speeches and 'debates' had reached in the last few years before The Collapse—then tell me television's impact on our attempt at self-government was anything but disastrous.

"Are we to think all this decay in such widely different areas, educational, economic, civic—leading finally to the complete destruction of a terminally vulgarized, dumbed-down nation in The Collapse—merely *happened*, by chance, to coincide exactly with the rise of the television-culture? That the wealth of a tiny handful of media owners—short-term geniuses but long-term-fools—increased astronomically; the mental, financial, and social functioning of the television-addicted masses declined catastrophically; the electronic-heroin's impact on the society and its pervasiveness throughout the society expanded exponentially—and it was sheer chance that all these things happened simultaneously? With no causation whatever? Please!

"I think that a medium which at first merely provided no benefit—a Wasteland—was changed by the shortsighted, Get-Rich-Quick artists (getting rich quickly from it indeed) into a force that did active harm. No longer merely a Wasteland, it became a toxic dump, leaching ignorance, apathetic dependency, and vulgarity into the society's cultural groundwater; and thereby poisoning people far from the source. So by the time of The Collapse, merely avoiding television yourself would no longer prevent your being harmed by it. Because by retailing public degeneracy for private profit, television had fatally weakened the society all around you.

"Don't get me wrong: I'm against outlawing literal drugs, however harmful, and I'm equally against outlawing the metaphorical opium distributed electronically by television—for the same reason in both cases: prohibition and censorship, in addition to their many other failings, simply don't work. The approach has been tried forever, and merely makes its advocates into figures of contempt.

"In the case of censorship, for example, whether of television or anything else: censorship of *what*—by *whom*? The moralistic Religious Right always loved anything with sufficient amounts of John Wayne or Rambo-style patriotic gore, showing heroic US troops slaughtering the men, women, and children of the Evildoers—from Redskins to Ragheads: rackin' em and stackin' em in high-piled, mangled, bloody heaps. But show the most sublimely beautiful work by Botticelli or Rembrandt, with a female breast exposed, and hysterical screaming immediately erupted to shield our youth from such an obscenely awful sight.

"A well-organized chorus of Blacks proudly affirmed the 'authenticity' of their Gangsta Rap, celebrating drug dealers gunning down their rivals and pimps beating their ho's—but shrieked with impressive gusto for the banning of *Huckleberry Finn* because in the nation's most profound anti-slavery masterpiece Twain's heroic character is Nigger Jim.

"The Lefties at ACLU would fight like demons for such tax-subsidized 'art' as a crucifix in a jar of urine—and fight just as hard to censor, forbid, and prohibit anything they found *really* appalling from the world of religion—such as a moment of silence at a high school graduation.

"Censorship—the very idea—has been proved so ludicrous, so often, by the idiocies of so many disparate groups it's not worth an intelligent person's consideration.

"But I think some sort of 'screening' process which (unlike censorship) actually works is becoming possible for us here today. Partly, it's becoming possible because our economic realities today no longer offer a financial incentive to rich men to slop pig swill to the masses for personal profit. And partly it's becoming possible because today's economic realities put us directly in touch—every single day—with the real, the physical, the concrete. And that leaves us with less time for, and less susceptibility to, manipulation by abstractions: by skillfully produced Technicolor bullshit.

"Suppose, for example, you or your husband or your father actually killed a man; personally; up close; with an ax; frantically struggling for survival. Let's just see how much use you then have for Rambo-style, don't-spare-the-ketchup, shoot-em-up trash.

"Or, for example, suppose you've spent weeks in brutal stoop-labor under a sweltering sun planting potatoes, which you eventually dig out of the near-frozen ground in a bitter autumn wind, fervently hoping there will be enough to keep you from starving. Let's see whether you're more likely to devote your precious few leisure moments to 'art' celebrating pimps-and-ho's or to genuine, lasting works of music and literature.

"Or suppose you face the prospect of freezing—you, personally—if you can't cut firewood fast enough to keep pace with the winter's consumption. Then see which you'll find a more meaningful part of your life: the silly, sniggering blasphemy of a four-year-old's potty-mentality, or earnest prayers of supplication to a deity.

"So our circumstances, perhaps, may save us. Our culture will improve—despite all our stupidity and vulgarity and other flaws—because today's realities will force it to."

"I think you may be right," Judge Parker mused. "And perhaps we'll be 'saved by our circumstances' in another respect as well. By necessity, for a long time to come, we'll be living in small groups. That means our governments will remain limited in power, small in size, local in extent. Governments will, in other words, be our servant, not our master. And they will perform—or be altered or replaced."

"Well," Tom replied. "That's clearly the case for the present. We're obviously going to live in small communities for the foreseeable future. But do you mean to say the only choice we'll *ever* have is between living in small societies with workable government or growing again into large ones with corrupt, abusive, and inefficient government?"

"I think so," the old student of Man and Man's law replied. He gestured toward the books shelved floor-to-ceiling in his paneled library. "At least that's what all these, consistently, tell me. History, it seems, is basically the story of how nations, in every place and time, expand until they collapse.

"Human beings, Tom, are somehow not *meant* to live in huge groups. I am convinced of it. We can do so, of course: vast empires from Mesopotamia to the Soviet Union to the former United States prove it. For that matter, we could live under water, I suppose, if we were determined to do so—willing to put up with the enormous costs, inefficiencies, and other drawbacks. But *why*? Humans are meant to live on land. And they thrive best (the bulk of them, long-term, I mean, not a tiny handful of privileged, parasitic Rulers and their courtiers, living, short-term, off all the rest) when they remain in small enough communities to make small government possible.

"Look at what—at least for the past 500 years or so, far longer than any competitor in the modern age—has been one of the most stable, safe, prosperous, enlightened, and altogether desirable societies on earth: Switzerland. (I speak of it in the present tense because if any nation on earth survived The Collapse it would be Switzerland, and I'll bet it has.)

"That happy country was always tiny—compared to suffering-wracked dinosaurs like the vast British, Soviet, and American empires—but still not small enough for the shrewd Swiss. So they divided their tiny nation into twenty-three states, or cantons. Three of those being still too big, they subdivided them into half-cantons! And they kept most of the governing power of their loose confederacy firmly in the hands of these local cantons.

"They do have a President, of course, like any self-respecting nation. He (or she, the last I heard) is appointed from a group of seven central-government officials, taking turns on a round-robin basis to serve a one-year term. Most Swiss wouldn't normally know or care which technocrat happened to be their nation's President in any given year, any more than they'd normally have reason to know or care who was currently Superintendent of Public Waterworks and Drains. So much for *imperial glory*, in one of the most humane, successful, and *secure* nations Man has ever devised!

"Perhaps the 'secure' part surprises you? In a dog-eat-dog world, the small-scale, low-key Swiss approach must be militarily risky? Well—unlike the U.S. in the War of 1812, and Russia countless times—since Switzerland became a nation some 500 years ago, it's never once been invaded.

"As the saying goes: 'Switzerland doesn't *have* an army—Switzerland *is* an army.' Every able-bodied male over sixteen is required to keep in his home an assault rifle (a real one, a fully automatic 'machine gun,' not the sort of semi-automatic that used to get people like Barbara Feinstein all worked up) with sufficient ammunition for regular practice plus emergency use. That's just a basic civic requirement for ordinary citizens: the militarily more serious civilians are issued anti-tank rifles, mortars, heavy machine guns, and similar ordnance …

"In the 1930s and '40s, Adolf Hitler, just across a common border, lusted mightily for Switzerland: for control of its strategic location, its precision industries, and it immense hoard of gold. But although he was willing to take on the British Empire and the Soviet Empire simultaneously—and for a time had both those empires on the run—he decided not to mess with Switzerland. That should give people a clue!

"In brief: small is workable, Tom. It can be done. Man can choose to live in the small societies he seems best suited for. He can insist on remaining a citizen—an active shareholder in a polity small enough for him to keep a very close eye on the 'hired help'—his government. Or he can choose image over substance: imperial glory over mere day-to-day efficiency. He can choose to be downgraded from a citizen to a mere subject—a powerless speck in a vast, impressive-looking empire—but *what* a splendidly impressive-looking empire! Comes down to wisdom, really—the ability to learn from experience: our supposed difference from the instinctually programmed lower creatures.

"Without acquiring wisdom, Man will no doubt go right on building huge nations, and upon their collapse immediately set about constructing the next huge mega-state on the rubble of the former one: termites rebuilding a kicked-over mound, their new one identical to the previous one. History—my own coldly rational God—is completely indifferent. History will show us conclusively that pounding your thumb with a hammer hurts; but History couldn't care less whether people choose to learn from that and change, or go on repeating the same behavior, over and over, world without end. So I can't tell you want we *will* do in future, only what we *could* if we chose to.

"I agree with you, Tom, that in terms of their size and culture and government—and in many other respects as well—each of our two present groups provides half the answer. We need to find ways of combining these halves—retaining the Amish success at keeping humane social values in a human-scale society while adding secular Mountainview's success at remaining open to progress and innovation.

"I think our two groups also need each other in a much more basic way: genetically. I'm not an expert, but I suspect over time neither community will have enough genetic diversity to avoid harmful inbreeding—certainly not the Amish, with only three dozen or so people, and probably not Mountainview either, with only around 400. But because the two groups' bloodlines are completely different, intermarriage between them will probably facilitate both groups' survival."

"Bringing together the two halves …," Tom said, nodding, "that's the big project—the 'make-or-break' project—that will mean long-term success or failure for us all. And here's a practical aspect of our 'joining the two halves' project: how are we and the Amish going to divvy up the land between our communities?

"Obviously," Tom pointed out, "the eleven miles or so lying along Rt. 12 between Mountainview and the Amish community is ideal land for both groups: it has that nice blacktop road running through it, providing infinitely easier access to either community than is the case in locations away from the road, where you have to drag yourself and everything else cross-country, through fields, forests and pastures.

"Chief Barley, along with the Amish Elders, has investigated the land's ownership, and to everyone's surprise almost none of it's owned by anyone currently living in either community. Jed Hospers has fifty-some acres just outside the Mountainview town limits on the east side of Rt. 12, but otherwise, best anyone can tell, the land between our two communities seems to have been owned by various commercial entities—banks, mortgage companies, and a timber company—plus a few absentee private owners, mostly from Grayson, who are now dead and almost certainly have no living heirs. So how do we and the Amish lay claim to the land?

"Mountainview's population is roughly eleven times that of the Amish," Tom continued, "so should we get eleven times the land they do? Hell, we're stronger: why not just take it all? Surely we can reject that option, can't we? We're not Huns or Visigoths in the 5th century—or Americans eying northern Mexico in 1846. I assume we're capable of something reflecting a bit more sophisticated, long-term enlightened self-interest than a simple 'law-of-the-jungle, might-makes-right' approach."

The Judge grunted his agreement, but didn't comment further.

"What I'm suggesting to Barley—and I'd like you to help sell this to him, if you agree—is to divide the 'ownerless' land along Rt. 12 evenly between Mountainview and the Amish. They're not presently as numerous as we are, but their population growth rate is higher, and in just a few generations they'll have plenty of need for the land and plenty of people to settle it.

"But—here's a vital point, I think—I don't want to see the land divided in half so the Amish get the half nearest them and we in Mountainview get the half nearest us. Instead, to encourage increasingly strong ties between the two communities, let's divide the land so the Amish get all of it on the west side of Rt. 12, from their community to ours, and Mountainview gets all of it on the east side of Rt. 12, from our community to theirs.

"As you'll recall if you drove that stretch of Rt. 12 in the past few years, the land to the west is generally cleared and was used mostly as pasture for scrub cattle, to the extent any of its owners did anything with it. The land to the east of the highway is more grown up in timber, of varying quality. We in Mountainview, with our steam engines, are better equipped to harvest and process the timber. And the Amish, who have more livestock than we do, would get better use from the cleared pasture-land.

"Both our communities, I think, would benefit if we built three wooden towers: one in each community where that community joins Rt. 12, and one midway between the communities. The map shows Rt. 12 traces a fairly straight line between our communities, and the terrain it crosses is very gently rolling: no major curves or hills between Mountainview and the Amish. With towers that provided an eye-level height fifteen feet above ground, according to my figuring, you could see from each tower to the next. Place one man in each of the three towers, with binoculars and a scoped rifle, and most of the terrain between our communities would be under visual surveillance—with much of it under effective rifle fire as well.

"Communications would be possible via Morse code light signals, using a mirror in daytime or a lantern at night, thus providing redundancy in the event of radio failure. And the security would not only be from human threats but also from things like animal predators, fire, and breaks in the pasture fence-lines. I assume our local coyote population is increasing rapidly, and before long it will certainly be joined by wolves, moving down the Appalachian ridges and valleys from Canada. The Amish, I think, will become willing to use firearms to defend their herds and flocks against animal predators, so long as the towers are built on Mountainview property—the east side of Rt. 12—thus not requiring that firearms be brought onto Amish land.

"I'd suggest using timbers we'd cut from our side of Rt. 12, plus Amish labor, to build eight-foot-by-eight-foot towers two stories high, fully enclosed on the ground floor, with window-openings secured by locking shutters. A ladder against an inside wall would provide access to the upper floor. The upper floor would have a roof to keep it dry, and windows in the walls all the way around, removable in summer for ventilation. A tiny stove on the ground level would serve for cooking and wintertime heating. An eight-by-eight, two-story tower would yield 128 square feet of floor space, or enough for the sleeping bags of about ten men.

"The towers, especially the one in the middle, would therefore make convenient bunkhouses for work crews, providing all-weather accommodations and avoiding the alternative of either traveling daily to and from one of the communities to a worksite or else camping out in all weather.

"If we can achieve the necessary agreements, both communities would benefit tremendously from the expanded pastures for animal production and the expanded opportunities for woodcutting, all of them with convenient frontage on a paved highway, and all of them served by a chain of communications/security/bunkhouse facilities.

"I don't know whether the Amish would decide to auction off their portion of the land or hold it as a 'commons' property. Here in Mountainview, I have no doubt our portion of the land would be divided into tracts and auctioned off by the police department—or possibly leased in some cases if a sufficiently attractive purchase bid was not obtained. Either way, the income to the police department should be enough to cover all its operating costs for many years. Will you support the idea, and offer your legal assistance to Barley in drawing up the necessary paperwork?"

The judge carefully considered the issue for any objections or unresolved questions, but could find only one.

"You say the Amish would get the west side of Rt. 12 and Mountainview the east side. But for what distance? Surely not west to the Pacific Ocean for the Amish and east to the Atlantic for us?"

Tom grinned. "Hey, your guy Jefferson thought on that kind of scale: the Louisiana Purchase—then Lewis and Clark? But I'm game for any distance the parties can agree on as reasonable. How about initially two miles in each direction from Rt. 12, with the understanding that the issue will be re-visited at some specified time—say in five years—and revised or extended then as circumstances warrant? Two miles east and west from Rt. 12 would pretty much cover our valley floor, which is roughly four miles wide for most of its length."

"Sounds sensible," the judge agreed. "I'd be happy to endorse the plan to Chief Barley, and offer my services to him and to the Amish for any negotiating or paperwork required to implement it. The paperwork shouldn't take but a day or two, and building the three towers—assuming you wait till the spring plowing-and-planting rush is over, could surely be done within a month or two.

"Since we're looking into the future here," the judge continued, "there's another issue I'd like to see agreement on: the eventual 'colonization' of Grayson. I realize it's not sensible, because of the risk, to attempt that in the next few years, even if we had the manpower and other resources to spare. But eventually—perhaps in as little as five years—I think the issue will arise. There are just too many valuable resources in Grayson for it to be kept out of play indefinitely.

"For example, exploring house-to-house 'prospecting' for gold or silver coins, gemstones, and other precious objects will at some point become hugely profitable, perhaps setting off our own little 'gold rush' on a relative scale comparable to the California Gold Rush. Less romantically, things like window glass, tools, lumber, and other construction materials obtained from Grayson's houses will become the basis for men's fortunes in the years ahead. The Grayson County Library collection is priceless. I'd like to see some agreement reached about how such treasures are to be dealt with."

"Good point," agreed Tom. "How about an Amish/Mountinview agreement that both communities will prohibit their members from going to Grayson for the next five years, with the same penalties imposed for removing any item from Grayson as would be imposed for stealing the item from their own community? After five years—or earlier with mutual consent—the issue of Grayson will be re-visited and a more detailed agreement drawn up concerning the use of its resources.

"One issue I'd like to see nailed down is a 'first-priority' commitment to have a team of workers occupy the Library, as soon as we have a telephone connection between Grayson and Mountainview, to scan items from the library into a computer, sending the data back here to Mountainview for easy access and safekeeping on discs. That would be infinitely easier than physically moving the materials back here and constructing a physical building to house them."

The judge made some notes and said he would speak to Chief Barley the next day to urge the Amish/Mountainview land agreement and a Grayson-colonization agreement be moved forward without delay.

When the two men parted in the chilly mid-April dusk, each was looking happily ahead with great faith toward things yet unseen, instead of morosely back at things seen all too often. But to some extent, the men's touchingly rationalist, naively Jeffersonian faith in Freedom's power to produce endless improvement gave them a less-than-perfect view of the future—as if through a glass, seen darkly.

For Jefferson, however wise, lived long before Freud. And neither of Jefferson's two disciples in Mountainview accorded sufficient weight to the fact that human pain and desperation can sometimes make us forge our own fetters.

Chapter 40
Utopia Postponed

If it *was* merely coincidence it was certainly a grisly one. It occurred at dusk, in the last week of April. Bill Robinson, the Citizens Patrol lookout manning his post near Dean Jacobs' presently unoccupied woodpile on the east edge of town, saw the man emerge from the treeline and start across the intervening pasture toward Mountainview. The man's clothing (apparently composed of layer upon layer of rotting rags) and his appearance (obviously the wild hair and beard had not been trimmed in the past year) were immediately striking.

The man left the treeline at almost exactly the same point from which the nine attackers had launched their murderous dawn assault just two months earlier.

Urgently scanning the fields and treeline for signs of any other men, Robinson bellowed as loudly as he could "HALT! STAY WHERE YOU ARE!"

The man continued to advance. Visibility in the twilight was rather poor, and getting worse.

Robinson fired a warning shot in the air and shouted again "HALT! WHO ARE YOU?"

The man started, briefly, at the crack of the gunshot, and began to remove something from his backpack. That was all it took for Bill Robinson to reach his decision and sound the emergency signal on his air horn: three longs—pause—and three more longs.

Everyone in Mountainview knew the meaning of that one: all lookouts to assume the highest alert status, all residents who could do so report to their nearest lookout post for volunteer service, and all off-duty Citizens Patrol deputies report to the police station on the double.

Robinson, still frantically searching the shadows of the darkening treeline and the adjoining fields—but unable to locate signs of any other men there—screamed again "HALT!" and fired another shot in the air.

By this time, the man had located what he'd been fumbling for in his pack: a roughly square black object of some sort, about the size of a thick, hardcover book, which he waved threateningly in Bill Robinson's general direction.

Two Citizens Patrolmen flopped down beside Robinson in his lookout post, out of breath from their run but quickly checking and cocking their weapons. Several townspeople were sprinting toward the scene, ready to serve as messengers or however else they might be needed.

"I *still* can't see anybody else in the trees!" Robinson, in anguish, briefed the newcomers. "Could be some kind of trap—or it might just be some lone nut. Why won't he halt? What the hell's that black thing he's threatening us with—some kind of bomb?"

One of the just-arrived deputies pointed out "Well, if he's got anything military-grade there—like Semtex or C4—that much of it would shatter half the damn windows in Mountainview. Also, Bill, if he gets very much closer, there won't be a whole lot left of us or these nearest two houses either."

"I'm not going to shoot him just yet," Robinson replied in agony, peering desperately through the shadows to pick up anything, *anything*, that might be hiding in the darkening treeline, sweating as he gripped his Remington .30-.30.

"*All of you*," he turned and shouted urgently to the growing group of Citizens Patrol deputies and townspeople, "O*n the ground*! *Flat*! *Take cover!*"

"Get back!" shouted the people just arriving in the lookout post, passing the word to the rapidly growing throng converging on the scene. "Get back! Take cover!"

The man was now less than a hundred feet away, still coming toward them, holding the black object aloft and defiantly shaking it at them. They could now hear he was shouting at them too.

One of the deputies, flat on the ground beside Bill Robinson, pleaded quietly with him, his voice hoarse with strain. "You're senior here, Bill. What you say goes. But Jesus Christ, he's getting awfully close. There's a lot of our own people clustered here now. If that *is* a bomb ..."

At that moment, for the first time, they could make out the words the man was shouting.

"*...And I looked and beheld a pale horse: and his name that sat on him was Death...*"

"Revelations!" Bill Robinson said, with sudden comprehension, nearly sobbing with relief. "It's some religious nut. That's a Bible he's waving. *Hold your fire men*! *Safe your weapons!*"

He got to his feet. A moment later, the wild-looking creature came to a halt before him. Robinson stood in the dimming twilight, quivering, panting, every muscle trembling from the massive overload of adrenaline blasting through his system.

Using every last trace of self control, determined not to allow sobbing to betray his indescribable relief at how close he had just come to killing the man, Robinson spoke to him, deadly slow and quiet.

"Don't you *UNDERSTAND* the goddamn meaning of the word *HALT?*"

"Let not your tongue defile the Name of the Holy!" screeched the nut, waving his Bible in Bill's face with renewed vigor. "Take not the Name of the Most High Almighty in vain! Fear Him who …"

Almost in slow motion, with a bizarre, surrealistic gracefulness, Bill drew back his right fist and slammed it with all his adrenaline-charged strength into the man's solar plexus.

The nut, his ravings chopped off in mid-word, thumped onto the ground like a 160-pound sack of grain dropped from a second story hay loft. He lay there in dead silence, the center of a shocked and frozen scene which by now included over a dozen Citizens Patrol deputies and townspeople.

After what seemed an eternity, the nut was able to get some air into his lungs and begin puking. He puked and puked and puked, occasionally emitting something between a strangled whimper and a moan, then resumed his puking again.

Robinson sent messengers to the police station and all the lookout posts, to report what had happened and direct all parties to stand down from the alert. Looking around, he sought out the deputy who had just pleaded with him to kill the man.

"Take command of the lookout post here till I get back," he ordered, wanting to give the man immediate responsibility and authority. In part, he meant to display his confidence in the man for public consumption, but mostly he wanted to offer the man all the private reassurance and support his vote-of-confidence could provide, to help the man work his way through the horrifying second-thoughts and might-have-been's that would begin pressing in on him about now.

"It could have been called either way," Bill murmured to the man, too low for anyone to overhear. "I was just lucky. We all were."

Gathering a wad of the nut's filthy rags in one meaty hand, Robinson jerked him to his feet and headed toward the police station with him, the man's arms and legs flopping loosely, puppet-like, as Robinson half carried, half marched him down the street.

By mid-morning of the next day, Chief Barley had had enough. He'd tried sympathetically to elicit information from the man the previous evening, fed him supper and given him the town's jail cell as accommodations for the night, then at breakfast the next morning tried again to get something meaningful out of him—all without success.

"*Borderline case my ass*," the Chief muttered in frustration to Doc and Judge Parker, who he'd asked to come take a look at the man and render opinions. They sat in Barley's office, down the hall a few feet from the jail cell, where the nut lustily banged on the bars to emphasize each point of the extremely loud and lengthy sermon he was delivering: a detailed catalog of the most horrific tortures and torments awaiting the unwary, as outlined in various blood-soaked passages the nut bellowed at top volume from his Bible.

"He's not entirely irrational," Barley pointed out to Doc and the Judge. "I don't think we ought to be under any obligation to 'institutionalize' him at our own expense. Listen to him. He speaks in complete sentences. Aside from the fact that it's crazy, that sermon he's bellowing undeniably strings together actual Bible verses in a logical pattern. Hell, he's a better public speaker than I am! He's not *our* problem: I say kick him in the ass and send him on his way. And don't forget: he's *survived* all this time, Judge. Don't tell me an insane person—so mentally incompetent he's morally entitled to our care—could have managed that."

"I wouldn't tell you any such thing, Chief. Sanity or insanity is a medical issue; I deal with legal matters: two different fields entirely. A legal man has no more business ruling on questions of sanity than a plumber has ruling on questions of trigonometry. You need the advice of someone in the medical field." The Judge pointed at Doc.

"Oh come off it, Judge," Barley protested. "Legal people issued rulings about mental competence all the time before The Collapse."

"They shouldn't have, though," the Judge replied. "And since it's now *after* The Collapse this one's not doing so any longer. It's a medical issue; you need a medical opinion." He pointed once again at Doc.

"From a *veterinarian*?!" exclaimed Doc. "Three grown men are going to sit here suggesting a psychiatric competency ruling be issued by a *veterinarian*? And you think *he's* the crazy one?! Give me a friggin' break!"

It was the second time the issue had been "hot potatoed" round the circle, and all three men were keenly aware they were once more back where they'd begun.

"Bastard's getting on my nerves," muttered Barley, leaning back in his chair to kick the office door closed, reducing the noise level a bit.

"I'd ream Bill Robinson's ass for not shooting him when he could have—except, in all fairness, he couldn't have known the bastard would be like *this*."

The Chief sighed a long, bitterly regretful sigh. "Our best chance since The Collapse to learn something about whatever places he's traveled through…and we can't get him off Jesus long enough to say a single useful word."

With repeated vigorous gouging, he deepened the impressively deep initials he was carving into his wooden desk with his pocket knife.

"I wonder where he has been, and how he survived," Doc mused. "It really is amazing, isn't it?"

The Chief grunted. "I guess there are lots of vacant farmhouses where he could have sheltered through the winter. Some of them would have had seed grain and other edible stuff stored, with some firewood cut and more easy wood to be had by breaking up the furniture and outbuildings. We found a dozen or so wire snares in his backpack, so I guess in good weather he got enough rabbits, squirrels, birds, turtles, snakes, and whatever to keep him going. I don't think he was too choosey: there's some raw, half-eaten bits in his pack that look like they have black and white skunk fur on them.

"Frankly, I don't give a damn. Whatever he did before he can do again. He's not one of our own, and I can't see adopting him. I want an 'expert opinion'—and I don't care what kind of goddamn expert it comes from—stating he's mentally competent and not in need of being confined at our expense."

Doc and the judge sat silent. Barley fumed. A glance out the window showed the small crowd of hangers-on lounging about the sidewalk and listening to the jailhouse sermon was slowly but steadily growing.

A knock on the door, and a grunt from Barley to come in, produced Tom, with a puzzled look on his face.

"Do you consider yourself a qualified expert in some field?" Barley snapped at him, in lieu of hello.

"I do, sir. As Chairman of Mountainview University's Department of Humanities, I regard all matters humane as being within my area of expertise. Also steam engines, to some extent. Why?"

Barley explained—Doc and the Judge still remaining stubbornly mute.

"Well, Chief, I kind of think both Doc and the Judge have a valid point. I'll tell you whose opinion I'd get on this: Klara Yoder's."

The men sat silent, taken aback by this option coming out of the blue.

Tom continued, speaking mostly to Chief Barley. "You need an expert opinion to support whatever you decide to do with him. From the sound of him, that guy needs a bit of healing. Klara's an expert healer and she'll give you an opinion. Two birds, one stone. Call her on the radio and ask her to come by tomorrow."

And so, around noon the following day, four worried men of mature age and considerable bulk found themselves losing a long, intensely whispered battle in Chief Barley's office against one slight, serenely untroubled woman, of considerably fewer years and scarcely any bulk at all.

"There's just no *reason* for you to actually go in there *with* him!" Tom hissed urgently, repeating the same argument Barley, Doc, and the Judge had just made. "You're going to *talk* to him, right? Well, talk through the bars. No harm in that. Just common sense. Who knows what he'll do?"

"Now he sings," Klara pointed out, somewhat unnecessarily given the volume at which *The Old Rugged Cross* was thundering from the cell. "He sounds not so worried. I wish you could be not worried too. Sometimes for what the psychiatry books call 'anxiety' is good to have a little valerian tea. I make you some soon and you see."

She delivered this with such a perfectly straight face Tom wanted to kick her.

But then, content with her little thrust, she relented and smiled winningly at her four gallant knights. "Do not have 'anxiety' about me. I wish only good for him, so he will do me no harm."

If I hear that from those damned Amish *one more time*…Tom gritted his teeth.

But at last, having gently, implacably argued the four burly men into a defeated pulp, she led the way down the hall to the cell, where Barley unlocked the door. She stood outside it, smiling at the wild-looking man sitting on the cot inside, who had left off singing upon the group's arrival.

"Hello. I am Klara Yoder. Can I come in please?"

The man looked up at her in surprise, stood, made vague gestures of dusting off his layers of rags and tidying the beard that went halfway down his chest, and muttered softly "Yes ma'am."

Klara stepped into the cell. Closing the door behind her, she turned and pointedly gazed through the bars at the four men crowding close outside. They shuffled slightly and looked down. She held her gaze firmly on them. There was a bit more shuffling. One or two cleared his throat. The silence lengthened.

Finally, like half-trained bears being sent to their kennel, the men one after another slowly turned from the cell door and grudgingly lumbered down the hallway back to Barley's office.

Whereupon, turning to her patient with a smile, the slight woman said "What is *your* name?"

"I am The Testifier! I bring the Word of fire to warn a corrupt and evil world. I am come as a witness to unspeakable horrors that walk abroad in these Final Days!"

"Yes, but do you have another name? From long ago, before these terrible days began?

The wild man was silent for a good while, looking down, thinking things over. Then he said softly "Jack Carter."

Klara nodded and smiled encouragingly.

"So ..." she said gently, the word and her own inflection completely open-ended, her voice opening any door in the world the man might wish to walk through, her manner relaxed and friendly—but most of all just *interested* in the human being she was with.

There was another silence. After it had gone on awhile, the man turned the cell's one chair to face the cot, gestured to the chair, and moved to seat himself on the cot.

When she sat, he did so as well. Anxiously, he then softly asked her—his concern clearly genuine—"They threaten you? When you were in their office all that time? I'll do whatever I can to help: the Hosts of the Lord Almighty will forsake not the afflicted who call upon Him."

Klara considered her reply. *Nature has given us women such great power as healers*, she thought to herself—pleased by her power and a bit saddened, too. *With even the slightest willingness, we can harness and turn to positive use the deepest biological drive males possess: their instinct to protect us. Any man still breathing contains a huge force inside him, just waiting for someone to direct it toward the good.*

"No, no," she said gently to the man; "they do nothing bad. They asked me to come here to meet you. They are fearful about you. They are frightened, and their fear makes it hard for them to think how best to help you. So they ask me."

"They fear *the truth*!"

She smiled gently. "Don't we all?"

But here she had found his limits—beyond which he was not willing to go with her at present. Instead of replying to her he resumed his singing, blasting out "Rock of Ages" with sufficient volume to prevent himself having to consider her challenge.

Four heads poked out of Barley's office doorway. After waiting long enough to make sure her patient did not wish to interact with her any further, she rose and motioned the men to come.

"He is troubled, but I think he knows he is troubled," she told the men, back in Barley's office. "Perhaps he comes to us because some part of him knows he needs our help to stay alive. If he and I eat together, I think in one or two days maybe I learn more things to tell you. Anyway, while I am here, I have many more questions for Doc about medical things."

And so a storeroom was made available in the police station, a cot set up in it, and Klara moved in. She spent most of her time with Doc in his veterinary office, assisting him with the small trickle of patients who came there with various complaints, and studying further in the many areas her intensive medical internship had opened up.

Each morning, noon, and evening, she brought into the jail a large breakfast, lunch, or dinner for two prepared by Chief Barley's wife, Betty, next door. Dining with her patient, she gently steered their conversation toward his history: where he'd come from, how he'd survived, what he could tell her about what he'd seen in the outside world. It was a slow process, interrupted many times by long spells of Biblical ranting, singing, and sermonizing, but by the evening of the second day she was able to provide an opinion to the men in Chief Barley's office.

"I think he will not do harm to other people. He wants to help people, but does not know how—like us," she added parenthetically, with a slight grin. "But I think he cannot live just now without our help. If he receives such help—food and clothes and a place to stay and some simple work to do—I think in time he can tell us about what he has seen. He cannot tell about towns or places on a map because he did not have any map: he was just walking wherever God sent him. And he has much confusion between what he saw and what he dreamed.

"But I think with care and rest, and a simple, plain life—same thing each day, so as to be boring—sometime in the future he will know better which things he has seen and which he has dreamed. Maybe he will have important information to tell you then, maybe not. But without our care he will not be able to live. So he must have care."

"Not in *this* damn jail," muttered Barley, sick to death of the preaching and singing, but resigned to the decision—in truth, secretly much relieved that he'd not been the one forced to make it.

To everyone's surprise but Klara's, there proved no need to confine the patient: having the audience he clearly craved, he was not the least bit inclined to lose it by running away. He was taken out to Jensen's place at the edge of town, given a hot bath, shave, and haircut, and two suits of work clothes, and installed with a cot, rag-rug, and old chest-of-drawers in a former storage shed in the back yard.

Jensen, a widower getting on in years, and a bit deaf, agreed to oversee the man—partly for the weekly one dollar silver the police department was willing to pay for his keep, and partly because Jensen himself was just plain lonely. It had gotten hard to have no one but himself around the place. After their two children had grown up and moved to Atlanta, he and Mae had cared for her dotty old father throughout the man's final years. Then there were summer visits from the grandkids to look forward to. At the time of The Collapse, Mae had been visiting the kids in Atlanta. He'd heard nothing since from any of them.

Bereft of wife, children, and any other relations, Jensen had kept the old gelding, Trigger, which he'd gotten for his grandchildren to ride, until its presence became more of a painful daily reminder than he could stand, whereupon he'd sold the idle beast to the police department. But lately, he'd almost begun to wish he had the useless creature back, merely to feed and take care of, so lengthy and still and quiet had his endless days become.

Jensen found, to his pleasure, that he enjoyed the patient's presence—especially his endless, shouted, bloodcurdling sermons—rather as some people used to enjoy keeping a mostly ignored television on, simply to fill their quiet solitude with background noise.

Given an occasional suggestion by Jensen, the patient was perfectly willing to bathe and shave once in a while, and generally take care of himself. Very early in his stay—following a discussion when Jensen discovered his guest was setting snares for barn rats—the patient was strictly forbidden to assist with the cooking in any way whatsoever. But he was just as happy to do the dishwashing and occasional laundry instead, so matters worked well for all concerned.

Before returning to her own community, Klara had told Jensen it was important for the patient to have some simple work to do. So Jensen took down a big, old fashioned crosscut saw from where it had been hanging idle in the barn, oiled it, and led his charge to the woodpile out back of the house.

It seemed a match made in heaven: the preacher appeared to enjoy sawing as he bellowed his dire warnings culled from a vivid but theologically narrow range of blood-soaked Biblical texts. Various townspeople began dropping by for a few minutes now and then to marvel at the sermons, which made little sense but offered a bright spot of noisy drama in an otherwise quiet, post-electronic world. Old Jensen's formerly long days, now that he had the constant drone of preaching in the background and the comings and goings of entertainment-starved townspeople to divert him, became happier. And the rows of cut-and-stacked firewood at the woodpile began growing to impressive dimensions.

The town's three previously installed preachers faced an especially delicate predicament in defining their relationship to someone who either conceivably was, or most definitely wasn't, a member of their own fraternity.

Call-Me-Bob had decided immediately upon hearing the man—judging mostly by his concentration on the Book of Revelations—that modern psychotherapeutic techniques were called for. In the progressive and enlightened seminary Call-Me-Bob had attended, even the slightest interest in the Book of Revelations was thought to constitute at least five or six of the "seven early warning signs" of mental illness.

"Unfortunately, Call-Me-Bob's courses in pastoral psychology had been more theoretical than practical; and coming from what now seemed an infinitely long-ago, pre-Collapse world, they didn't have quite the relevance to current conditions one might desire. So Call-Me-Bob, feeling both guilty and impotent, didn't move to interact in any way with the patient, but maintained a careful distance, confining his involvement mostly to occasional discrete monitoring of the patient's living and working conditions to ensure there was no capitalist exploitation of him in those matters.

Parson Miller was a respectably educated and respectably behaved man in a vocation that (he privately rued) contained more than its fair share of…colorful…individuals, whose formal education he (privately) did not hold in high esteem. The wild Holy man, or Holy wild-man, or whatever the ranting preacher was, touched a sore spot in Parson Miller, who admitted (to himself, in the *strictest possible* privacy) that he would really just as soon have made his career as an Episcopal (not Baptist) clergyman, charged with the spiritual care of prosperous, well-educated professional people and business-owners (not "salt-of-the-earth" villagers) preferably in a bustling, medium-sized city with an element of "cultured society" (instead of a place like…uh…)

Honest enough to (privately) admit the truth, and decent enough to feel (privately) ashamed of it, Parson Miller (privately) resented the Bible-nut who'd stumbled in from the backwoods. Clearly, the man's ravings demonstrated no formal theological training, so he was not a fellow man of the cloth. And just as clearly, the practice of intensive psychotherapy (seemingly indicated here) was a medical, not pastoral, matter. So Parson Miller decisively distanced himself from any involvement with the ranting nut—and yet was a decent enough man to feel both guilty and impotent at having done so.

Brother Stainfuss hardly knew *what* to make of the new arrival. Beyond any question, there was a tremendous theological Message in the man's description of these days as the End Times, and of present-day people as being, for the most part, Hell-bound sinners who had turned from the One True Salvation onto a path heading toward Indescribable Torment. And the *vivid detail* with which the man described the countless tortures of Hell awaiting the Unsaved! It was so lurid Brother Stainfuss himself was taken a bit aback, gulping as he experienced simultaneous envy at the power of the preaching and squeamishness at the extent of the horrors revealed.

This new Shepherd, should he decide to do so, might steal much of my flock, thought Brother Stainfuss with alarm. Then he immediately felt guilty for having had such a thought. And then immediately pointed out to himself that it was *not* just a matter of stealing one's flock, but—infinitely more serious—perhaps leading it astray, away from the One True Salvation.

"There were, for example, disturbing references to Mary repeatedly sprinkled through this man's high-volume sermons. Mary...Hmmm. Well, it was not proof positive the man had fallen for some sort of Papist Anti-Christ doctrines—praying to statues, and burning incense, and bedecking their Papist "temples" with gold and silver and jewels, and similar abominations. But the matter would bear careful watching.

Under a variety of pretexts, therefore, Brother Stainfuss began to find reasons for casually dropping by the vicinity of the newcomer's sermons. Considering their volume, it wasn't necessary to get very close. After all, he told himself sternly, he obviously had a moral duty to investigate this man and his sermons—not *spy* on him, exactly, but... Nevertheless, he couldn't help feeling guilty, as if he actually *were* spying.

For surely, reckoned Brother Stainfuss—whose mental processes did not much incline toward nuanced shades of gray—this new preacher must be *either* a True Prophet, come to save them all—*or* a False Seducer, sent to lure the unwary into eternal suffering. Yet, struggle as he might, Brother Satinfuss could not entirely decide which. The harder he wrestled with the problem, the less able to resolve it he seemed to be.

Feeling intensely guilty about what might be considered "spying" based on unworthy motives and suspicions—and intensely impotent at his inability to decide which of only two possibilities (sanctified or diabolical) the preacher represented—Brother Stainfuss skulked miserably about on the fringes of Jensen's woodpile, listening to the sounds of sawing and preaching. He wished his over-scrupulousness in religious matters had not cast him into such a torment of guilt and impotence. If only, he yearned, he could be like those other two—Call-Me-Bob and Parson Miller—easy in his conscience, and calmly at peace in his faith.

For many in Mountainview, though, the ranting new preacher's next impact on the town was to be, at least indirectly, a more keenly felt loss than their clergymen's peace of mind.

Chapter 41
New Dreams for Old

When Owen came by the Gravely shop one Sunday afternoon in mid-May, a couple of weeks after the new preacher's dramatic arrival, he had Maybelle with him. This was rather unusual because, though the two couples enjoyed each other's company, they were so buried by their workloads they seldom had much time to socialize except on their various jobs. Owen and Maybelle wore expressions of trepidation mixed with joyous relief, clearly the result of some major decision they had reached.

When Tom ushered them up the stairs, calling ahead to Sophie, she burst out of the upstairs door and ran halfway down the steps to meet them, as if she had guessed some wonderful news, opening her arms wide to hug Maybelle and Owen in a fiercely joyous hug, urging them to come on up and tell her everything.

Maybelle, obviously on Sophie's wavelength, bubbled over with pleasure and began to babble; Owen blushed like a fourteen-year-old at the attractive, well-endowed Sophie's exuberant embrace, and pawed silently at the stair carpet; Tom, who had been caught up in a particularly frustrating problem involving linking the camshaft to the push-rod of a water injection pump for the Honda 650 motors he was converting to steam, watched the scene with half his mind. Whatever all the emoting was about, it didn't seem likely to solve *his* problem. Why were people such damned nuisances, constantly interrupting in the middle of important things?

Sophie immediately sensed the ceremonial nature of the visit: she insisted the group sit in the library, instead of around the kitchen table. Pushing a plate of molasses cookies into Maybelle's hands to take to the men, she threw some tea leaves into the pot, added kindling to the fire under the kettle, and busily arranged cups and saucers.

In moments, the cookies were distributed, the tea was ready and poured, and there was an expectant hush as Maybelle, with gravest solemnity, focused a Nancy Reagan-like Enraptured Gaze upon her husband for his announcement of their big news.

"Uh," he told the carpet, "well. Looks like we're gonna have a baby. And, um, also...decided to move to the Amish. Nothin' really wrong with here," he attempted to explain, "but me an' Maybelle...um...we think maybe the Amish would be a better place to raise a kid. Sort of—I don't know—sort of safer, maybe. Or somethin'. With a kid, it's pretty important" he advised them all, in conclusion.

Sophie, knowing full well how long and how deeply Owen and Maybelle had yearned for a baby, hid her face against Maybelle's neck as she hugged her fiercely again, trying not to let anyone see how much she was crying.

With the two women thus engaged—and with Owen, having completed his manly duty at making the announcement, now lapsed into a much-relieved silence—Tom gathered the conversational ball had been passed to him. Oh well; you couldn't think sensibly about the push-rod anyway, just trying to visualize it in the abstract: you had to physically hold it and turn it and actually *see* the various possibilities.

"Hey, that's great!" he told Owen. "When's the baby due?"

"Eight months. About. Maybelle's got it figured out in weeks. 'Bout eight months."

"Well, hey, that's great!" repeated Tom lamely, casting an eye over at the two hugging, weeping women for a little help with this conversational business. Receiving none, he searched for some other lifeline.

"And you're moving to the Amish community? Gee, Owen, I'm glad you've decided. I know you've been considering it for a long time. I think you'll like it: they have some really great people there. You know Sophie and I think the world of them. I've always been tempted myself...Some of the ideals they practice...the way they live...In a way, I envy you and Maybelle: you two have more guts than I do. What made up your minds?"

Owen took a deep breath, wanting badly to explain in some fashion that would not embarrass his wife and him before these two older, more worldly people he and Maybelle so admired.

"Well," he began, struggling to explain rationally a decision that had been reached by intuitive, not rational, means. "That new preacher. Over to Jensen's, you know? He shouts. And seems like he mostly preaches the End Times, and Hell's Torments, and how most people ain't gonna be saved, and all that. And, you know, me an' Maybelle have went over to Jensen's a few times to hear him. And, well...we was just kind of surprised, you know, at how close he is to Brother Stainfuss. With the shoutin' about the Hellfire Torments,

I mean. And after a while I says to Maybelle 'If bein' real loud makes preachin' into True Gospel, then bein' real loud woulda made that rock music the kids used to listen to into quality music.' And of course that don't make no sense at all: I heard some of that stuff.

"And then, uh, couple days ago, Maybelle tol' me we're gonna have a baby. And we just looked at each other a long while, and we finally said 'let's go join the Amish, and have it there, and be part of them.' Because, well, I just don't think we hold with the Foursquare Baptists any longer, so far as what they believe—especially for a little baby, where you gotta give it every advantage you can in life."

He struggled onward, relying on sheer effort to communicate his points.

"Killin' and stuff. Killin' people. And torments. Don't want that sort of thing around our baby. So, anyway, we decided. And yesterday I rode Invincible over to the Amish and back, and ask Amon Yoost if we could join them, and they all met together right then and there and said they'd love to have us. And we all prayed on it. And so we figured we'd tell you."

"Thank you for doing so, Owen. It's an honor you've done us. I can't explain it, entirely, but I think Sophie and I will look back on this day, and your decision, as a major event in our own lives—an event that gives us both so much hope and happiness, and so much pride in you and Maybelle, and what you're doing."

Tom sat silent a moment, then continued.

"Well, hell, you two aren't *kids,* for crying out loud. But, you know, neither Sophie nor I ever had actual kids of our own. And—tell ya the truth—we're as proud of you two as if you were our kids. If you ever need some Godparents for the baby ..."

"That's wonderful!" exclaimed Maybelle, hearing Tom's offer and unable to restrain herself. "Would you?" She looked at Sophie.

"With all the pride and pleasure in the world," Sophie said quietly, drying her eyes. "You couldn't give us a more wonderful gift."

And so, after another round of tea and some more cookies, the group moved on to a buffet supper Sophie and Maybelle improvised from leftovers. Tom dashed down to the backyard shed where Tim was living and asked him to take over in the shop. And the conversation over supper expanded into practical considerations involving Owen and Maybelle's forthcoming move.

Chief among these was ownership of the Frankenstein's Monster the now-thriving restaurant had evolved into. Engrossed in her university, Sophie had hoped to sell her half of the restaurant to Maybelle. Now Maybelle wanted to sell her half to Sophie.

"Sounds like you both would be happy to sell it, or at least rent it, to some third party," Tom pointed out. "Why don't you ask around in the Amish community, Maybelle, to see if anybody might want to move here and take it on? And Sophie can look around here in Mountainview to see if anyone capable might be interested. Meantime, if necessary, you could close the restaurant for a couple weeks of 'summer vacation' while Owen and Maybelle are moving and you're finding the right person. Any rent from the restaurant and from your house here in town should provide a nice income while you're getting settled with the Amish. Do you know yet what you'll be doing there, Owen?"

"Horses," Owen replied proudly. "They seen what I done with Invincible, and figured I could handle horses. I'll help with everything: breeding, foaling, training—doing all the feeding and grooming and regular care—right on up to working 'em for plowing and timber-skidding, and so forth, just like Invincible. I'll miss him, I gotta confess: Invincible is one fine horse. But I'll get to see him now and then because I'll be bringing the Amish mares here to be serviced. So we won't really have to say goodbye completely."

"Ah hell," Tom burst out, surprised by the strength of his own emotion, "you and Maybelle won't have to say goodbye in any way: you two will be back and forth between the Amish and Mountainview all the time. There's going to be pretty continuous cooperation between the two communities as the land between us along Rt. 12 is developed. I'll bet the Amish will come here regularly: to attend the university, to work for wages in Mountainview, to receive medical care beyond what Klara Yoder can provide in their own community, and—especially the young folks—just in search of broader horizons.

"You'll see: you and Maybelle will be part of two communities now instead of only one. And you'll just be the first of a growing list of people in that situation if I have my way. I want our two communities to come together. Each has things the other needs. And you two are the perfect couple to start the trend."

But it was no less emotionally wrenching, two weeks later at the end of May, for Mountainview to see Owen and Maybelle depart. They were greatly loved and respected throughout the village. For people who had suffered the loss of friends, family, and their entire world in The Collapse any additional loss was acutely painful.

Almost as if she had heard Tom's wish for closer ties between the two communities, Klara Yoder arrived in the big hay wagon that came to get Owen and Maybelle.

Ever since her month's medical internship with Doc, and her later stay of three days when the raving preacher, Jack Carter, made his dramatic entry into Mountainview, Klara had adopted the practice of visiting the town for a few days every couple of weeks to further her medical training and to check on her patient. The townspeople were becoming accustomed to the young woman's visits, and, with the typical well-meaning nosiness of villagers everywhere, had begun to take it upon themselves to find her a husband. After all, at the age of twenty-seven...!

So despite their heavy hearts at seeing Owen and Maybelle leave Mountainview, the big hay cart piled high with furniture and other possessions, the townspeople's sadness was at least somewhat tempered by the prospect of having Klara in their midst for three or four days, to be invited to at least a month's worth of meals, and subjected to the most cunningly planned chance encounters with an assortment of carefully vetted young men who met the standards of the town's self-appointed cupids.

Klara, her tact and courtesy never slipping an inch, steadfastly failed to notice the town's romantic efforts on her behalf, and went her calmly professional way, accompanying Doc when he saw patients, studying in his office between times, and dropping by to chat with her own patient, Jack Carter.

The instant Klara was occupied elsewhere, poor Doc was besieged by a swarm of townspeople dropping in—purely by chance—to casually review the many advantages of marriage—especially if, for example, a young man were thirty years old, just four years out of veterinary school, and had the opportunity to acquire a wife and a nurse simultaneously. "Two for the price of one!" as every casual visitor, pleased by his own originality, did not fail to jokingly remark.

It finally got bad enough Doc took to suddenly assuming an air of grave medical concern the moment he detected the first hint of what he privately called "The Seven Early Warning Signs of marriage-talk."

"Stick out your tongue!" he would interrupt his casual drop-in, peering at him in sudden alarm. "Have you been feeling feverish?"

Idly fingering a horse syringe of horrifying size, which he kept in his office for the moral effect it produced when displayed before a wide-eyed patient, Doc would ponder thoughtfully a long, long moment, then finally advise his time-wasting caller "Well, keep an eye on your tongue there, in case any redness develops. And if you start to feel feverish I want you back in here without delay, understand?"

"You know, Klara," Doc mentioned one evening after their last patient, when they were finally alone together, "if you don't give in soon and marry me you're going to have half the town under your psychiatric care. They just plain can't stand it. It's driving them nuts."

She sighed. "Also are problems with my own people. But, you know, is not so simple. Which place would we live?"

"Which do you want? Name it and it's agreed."

"Well, but is also the religion …"

"So I'll convert."

"Perhaps…I don't know…maybe is better for the woman to convert …"

"Fine. Let's both do it: I'll switch to Mennonite, you become an agnostic."

"Now you are making fun," she said softly, anxiety mixed in with the confused turmoil of her feelings, the desire she felt for Doc countered by her trepidation over problems she could all too clearly imagine in her community's response to him, and to her marrying him.

She gently patted him on the shoulder. "Let's wait. Maybe we think of some way…maybe something happens …"

"I'll wait for you, Klara. You know that. I figure I've still got fifty years or so left in me, and I'm not going anywhere. I'll wait for as long as it takes you to reach the right answer—which, to give you a hint, is yes."

They stood, unable to find further words.

To ease the moment, he smiled and changed the subject. "How's your preacher doing?"

"Better, I think. Fewer people now listen to him because his preaching is becoming less exciting. Is a good sign, I think. Perhaps soon he becomes completely boring and just talks in a normal voice about minor things, so people pay him no attention. Then we declare him cured—just like everyone else— and he can become a real preacher." She deadpanned it with only the tiniest hint of her mischievous grin that made Doc's heart stop and turned him weak with desire every time he saw it.

"But really," she added, "I need to look up eclipse of the moon some small time past, to get its date. Have you an almanac?"

Doc's silent, raised eyebrow and fishy look stated eloquently enough what he thought of this method of treating lunacy. But he looked through his shelves until he found the previous year's *Information Please*, then thumbed its astronomical section.

"April Twentieth," he showed her. "Nearly complete lunar eclipse, as viewed from the mid-Atlantic seaboard, beginning two-seventeen a.m. local time."

After a moment's silence, he ventured "Ah...Klara? So ...?"

"So I think perhaps many people were killed one time, few months after The Collapse, but in some place rather far from us," she replied gravely, lost in thought. "And also, are other kinds of people still living. Bad people; not so far away. I tell you more when I talk with him further. Let us hope in the meantime his preaching becomes so boring he loses his audience at last, and is ready for a new career."

Chapter 42
Celebrating—or Commemorating?

By June 4, it was no longer possible to pretend there would not soon be a Fourth of July—no matter how delicately people tiptoed around the subject.

The spring plowing and planting had never been done in such frantic fashion before—or at the cost of such physical toil—but finished they finally were, and everyone briefly caught his breath. Jacob and Joshua, the Yoder twins working for Tom operating the steam Gravely, were brown as Indians and even more muscled than they had been, from their long hours keeping the machine in nearly continuous operation, dawn till dusk, seven days a week. In their scant spare time, they filled in at the shop, helping Tom and the young Tim finish converting the four Honda 650 engines to steam.

One of those engines was to be used to pump irrigation water from various points along Sandy Run, at the edge of Mountainview, into the adjacent fields of corn, wheat, and oats. Another two of the stationary engines were intended to power large circular saws, cutting tree trunks into firewood, fenceposts, and building lumber. The remaining engine Tom hoped to use for powering a generator throughout the rest of the summer, producing enough current to run (alternately) the freezer and chill-cases at Jared's Coneco Handimart, so fresh meat and dairy products could be stocked. In fall, once temperatures dropped, the engine would be relocated to power a large fan for winnowing grains by blowing the chaff away from the kernels, then to power mechanical corn huskers, and then to power grinding mills, producing wheat flour and corn meal, and then for grinding silage to make animal fodder.

The Shop's own steam engine, devoted to producing electric power nearly around the clock—for running the shop tools and for sale to townspeople—had been moved outside until the next fall's cool weather made its heat welcome indoors once again. Tom's electricity sales, fully subscribed for every available half-hour time block he had available, were bringing in a handsome income. Any townspeople able to afford the twenty cents silver Tom charged for a half-hour's electricity were at last able to pump their water electrically, and use electric tools and fans, and recharge batteries to operate lights and music players and computers.

Mountainview's crops of all sorts were thriving under the hot summer sun, and its production of animals, from rabbits and chickens to hogs and cattle, was increasing by the month. Moonshine and salt from the still and the evaporator went regularly to the Amish community, and return loads of sugar juice, crushed from the Amish sugar beets and grain sorgo, enlivened the diets of Mountainview residents and fed the still for new batches of moonshine. Cut and split firewood—for cooking, steam engine fuel, and the winter's heating needs—accumulated in huge quantities, row upon row, in the town's various woodlots, and more trees were continuously being felled, bucked, and hauled to town for additional fuel-wood, fence posts, and lumber.

It was a lush, bountiful time. Every day, each person's hard, hot, dusty work produced concrete, tangible results: supplies of food, fuel, clothing, tools, equipment, and other necessities to add to the growing inventories that spelled survival for the people of Mountainview. It was harder work than most townspeople had previously done—especially those whose jobs had involved moving papers in slow circles while seated behind an office desk—but it was more deeply satisfying as well. On balance—despite all the sunburn, sweat, blisters, skinned knuckles and aching muscles at day's end—almost all the former office workers were astonished to discover that hardly any of them yearned for the previous life of airconditioned irrelevance, insulated by paperwork from the real world, in which more serious people than they did the countless things more serious than paperwork which are necessary to meet life's physical needs.

It was deeply *satisfying,* people discovered, to actually produce something *real*—something your family could eat, or wear, or use as a tool, or heat the home with next winter—instead of something that merely altered the commas and rephrased a few minor points in the third draft of the latest corporate memo about the enhanced drive toward achieving ever-greater maximization of staff work efficiency in these challenging (yet opportunity-filled) times, with their unprecedented need to trim ruthlessly any resources not directed toward vital aspects of implementing the organization's latest quarterly Mission Objectives.

Part of the reason people found such satisfaction in producing tangible products was that they had specific, concrete needs for those products to meet. Consequently, the products they made or bought could actually satisfy those needs: Goal achieved. If you need shoes, and you make or buy a sturdy, comfortable, affordable pair of shoes, then you have met your need: mission accomplished; job completed; contentment attained.

This was a far different world than most people had lived in before The Collapse. For in that consumerist culture the shoes themselves were merely a pretext. What people were *really* after was not a goal so concrete and specific (and achievable) as mere shoes, but instead an amorphous, intangible (oftentimes not even articulable) need for footwear proclaiming the wearer's membership in some Platinum Executive-Elite Prestige Club.

But in a world where everybody had had the same credit cards, to buy the same $250 sneakers, how could such expenditures make *any* particular owner a *real* member of the Platinum Executive-Elite Prestige Club? No tangible product, ever, could possibly satisfy the impossible yearning for status—which is attained by what you are, not what you own.

For shoe salesmen, a population composed entirely of chronically insecure Imelda Marcos clones, chronically titillated by advertising, was a dream come true. But for the ordinary person it meant spending $250 on shoes which, a day later, still left him feeling unsatisfied—'missing out,' somehow on the sizzle that had been promised but not delivered—scanning the next week's shoe store ads for a *better* pair of shoes, ones that would this time actually *deliver* on the ad-man's whispered promises.

In their new, post-Collapse world, it became clear even to ordinary, unreflective people that, overall, they were happier in a world where they could satisfy a need for shoes with a pair of shoes, and thereby chalk up a success—instead of spending unlimited money on unlimited piles of shoes that still left the same unappeasable hunger and a sense of emptiness and discontent and failure to achieve what they sought.

Still, despite their satisfaction with the work they were now doing, and with their lives in general, people couldn't avoid the fact that June Fourth meant only one more month until the Fourth of July. And everyone in Mountainview knew the significance of the latter date all too well: the day the terrorists had set off four little nukes, insignificant little puffs, really, that had blown down a huge nation's entire economic house of cards in The Collapse. It was not a date any person wanted to remember, nor one any person could forget.

"Yes, I suppose we'd better get out in front of events and plan *something*," Tom said, agreeing with Chief Barley as they sat in Barley's office, sharing some fried chicken for lunch. "How about if we invite the Amish over again, like we did at Christmas, for some sort of party. That went over well. Maybe it'll help take people's minds off the grimness, and let us celebrate the positive side of things. After all, we *are* still here. Who'd have bet on that, a year ago?"

With misgivings, but seeing no alternative, Tom and the Chief agreed to promote a Fourth of July visit by the Amish, for a day of feasting, music, celebrations, and dogged mutual support in a heroic effort to "accent-u-ate the positive" and get past the awful anniversary.

The plan almost ran aground before it got underway. The Amish, misunderstanding the invitation as being to a standard Fourth of July celebration, politely but firmly declined. They did not consider it seemly to celebrate the birth of the U.S. or any other earthly State, they explained, and they did not observe the former nation's birth any more than they served in its armies or participated in its welfare programs or made use of its courts.

After hasty consultation in Mountainview, Chief Barley contacted Klara Yoder by "medical" radio and explained that this year's festivity was actually meant to celebrate the first year's success in surviving The Collapse of the former nation. It would actually be the present-day Amish community and Mountainview the festivities would honor, not the corpse of a former nation that had died in The Collapse. With this explanation, the invitation was accepted and the planning for a new kind of Fourth of July began in earnest.

When the big day finally arrived, two wagon loads of the Amish pulled into town just after nine on the clear, hot July morning, with the humidity already building and puffy white cumulus clouds suggesting possible late afternoon thunderstorms. In their wagons, the Amish had brought their contributions to the expected feast, omitting none of the "seven sweets and seven sours" required for any respectable Amish banquet.

In addition, they brought things for games: hoops for rolling, sacks for sack races, horse shoes and stakes for horseshoe-pitching, rope for a tug-of-war, a plywood "donkey" and its tail for "pin the tail on the donkey," a ball for dodgeball and kickball. The Amish boys had marbles and the girls brought their favorite dolls, and the adults brought stories and recipes and reminiscences of bygone times, and their memories of the Christmas Celebration and the friends they'd made then.

The Mountainview and Amish boys immediately clustered together, vigorously punching each other in the shoulders to demonstrate their total lack of interest in girls. The Mountainview and Amish girls immediately clustered together, competing in their expressions of pained loathing and disdain for the juvenile conduct of the boys, who, in any case, they most emphatically had not even noticed. And the adults from both groups sought out friends they'd made

382

previously, to catch up on all the vital news and gossip they'd missed since the past Christmas.

With numerous games going on simultaneously, on the playgrounds of Mountainview School and throughout the town's wide, mostly unpaved streets, there was no lack of excitement. The children of all ages played till exhausted, then collapsed on the ground in the nearest patch of shade till they were ready to wash down some more food with a glass of cold sassafras tea or birch beer and resume playing again. For the Amish, this was normal and predictable children's behavior—though admittedly this festival was of greater size and excitement than most were accustomed to.

For more than a few bewildered Mountainview parents, their children's behavior was at first disconcerting. Little Heather and Jason galloped off to play made-up games with other children, for example, instead of needing to be constantly entertained, supervised, and directed minute-by-minute in activities totally planned by adults. To the dark misgivings of some of the more Progressive Mountainview parents, the children wore no helmets. And did *all* those games use only equipment certified as one hundred percent totally child-safe after extensive testing in university laboratories? It was unfamiliar ground, and a bit worrisome.

The kids regarded it as normal to play till exhausted, collapse till recovered, then play some more—all without boredom, fussing, whining, and demanding "what *else* is there?"

Parents who had spent a large portion of an entire month's take-home pay to herd their pack of hot, bored, and quarrelsome children through the high-priced plastic wonders of Disney World were dumbfounded. Here were kids having the time of their lives in a spontaneous tug-of-war contest—and all it required was for the adults to hand them three dollars worth of rope and get out of their way! Who knew? It was delightful, of course…but…well…for some of the more Socially Advanced among the Baby Boomer parents it took a bit of getting used to.

On the street outside the restaurant, teams of men from both communities presided over huge iron grills, glowing with sufficient heat to put to shame most medium-sized steel mills, and bearing sufficient quantities of roasting animal flesh, slathered in various highly secret sauces, to feed…perhaps one might say "to feed an emerging small, new nation."

Inside the restaurant, within the cooling breeze of electric fans, women of both communities glanced out the window toward the billowing smoke and their menfolk from time to time, rolled their eyes at each other, and served up mountains of salads, vegetables, breads, desserts, and savories of every sort.

A bizarre assortment of music blared from the restaurant's speakers—ranging from weepy ballads by inexcusably over-the-top Irish tenors, to brass band polka tunes, to the *William Tell Overture*, to Appalachian hammered-dulcimer folk tunes, to the theme from *2001: A Space Odyssey*.

By early afternoon, all present had—according to their priorities—played their way to exhaustion, chatted their way to a complete understanding of what was *really* going on behind the scenes in both communities, and/or gorged themselves to stupefaction.

Doc had had a chance to ask Klara her opinion concerning slides he'd prepared of some especially interesting intestinal parasites, which required that he and she take their food and drink, leave the public hubbub, and retreat to the quieter confines of his medical office for extended consideration of the matter. Owen had had a chance to tell Tom how much he and Maybelle were enjoying life among the Amish. Maybelle, very much the center of attention in the restaurant, had taken full advantage of countless opportunities to present in minute detail every aspect of her pregnancy to every woman from both communities. Many of the parents from both communities had occasion to remark to each other how much the other's children had shot up just since Christmas, and to commiserate with each other on the speed with which shoes and clothing were outgrown.

At a brief ceremony in the early afternoon, Chief Barley thanked Amon Yoost and Caleb Yoder for their community's crucial role in helping Mountainview get past a milestone that some in Mountainview had confided to him they feared might be too painful to endure.

"The former United States of America, begun on July 4th, 1776, is now just another closed chapter in Man's long history—as dead and gone as Babylon or Carthage," Barley told the assembled people. "Whatever we may have thought of that nation, we all lost loved ones and we lost our accustomed world in its passing. And we mourn our common loss.

"This new society we're building together—whatever it's eventually named—should, I suggest, take for its founding the date that triggered the Collapse of the old one: a day, exactly one year ago now, on which four relatively minor terrorist bombs exploded, killing probably less than two hundred thousand people in a nation of three hundred million—but thereby collapsing a society which, we discovered too late, was economically and morally hollow: rotten at its core.

"I am not as well versed in the Scriptures as most of you are, but I will confess I have endured many nighttime hours of heartache because I could not get out of my mind a certain Biblical expression that has kept running through my head, over and over. I refer to the acid, scathing, contemptuous moral indictment expressed by the phrase 'whited sepulcher.'

"Let us, I urge you, commemorate on this day every year two equally important things: first, a quiet, non-belligerent, non-jingoistic pride in our own achievement, because we have stayed alive to begin the long rebuilding process. And second, equally important, let this date commemorate our determination to learn from the failures which collapsed the nation previously celebrated on this day.

"If we can do that, perhaps we can build on bedrock with heavy timbers, to form a new society that will endure. Then, perhaps," (the amply padded Chief concluded with a smile, gazing fondly over at the last of the steaks and sausages faintly smoking on the grill and the remaining slabs of apple pie and carrot cake on the tables in the restaurant) "then perhaps we can ensure that our descendants, and theirs, will have more substantial nourishment than cotton candy and Wonder Bread, however brightly colored, skillfully packaged and heavily advertised those might be; let us have—and *value*—the *substantial* foods that come from the earth, not some whipped-air concoctions from a task-force composed of a corporation's chemistry lab, advertising department, and cost accountants. *Genuine* food, I repeat—bought with genuine money—not paper scrip whipped up by a government printing racket in response to focus-group meetings and poll results.

"Perhaps we can ground our values deeply enough in the real, the substantial, the *genuine* to avoid that fatal addiction to mere *image* and surface *appearance* that marked those slick operators whose shallowness too often set the tone for the now-dead world where they thrived. Perhaps we can at last truly value the steak, not the sizzle; the substance, not the show; the item itself, not its style or the extent of its hype.

"But speaking of food—as I sometimes tend to do when Miz Barley gets crazy notions about dieting—I think there's still a bit left. So thank you all for coming, and let's not let anything go to waste: building a whole new world's not a job you take on without just a tiny bit more steak and a second piece of pie."

As one wiseacre after another in the crowd shouted "*Second* piece of pie?" the Chief waved happily, grinning, and stepped down from the apple crate he'd been on, urging his friends Amon and Caleb to join him as he moved toward the remaining food.

By the late afternoon, parents were collecting their children and the Amish were harnessing their two draft horses and packing up their belongings for the return trip. The visitors set off by about six, assured of sufficient light remaining on this long summer day to reach home. They were pursued by such clearly heartfelt calls of farewell, and such profuse thanks for their visit, that the Amish were somewhat taken aback.

It was only when the last waves and shouts from the Mountainview residents had receded into the distance that the visitors fully grasped how badly the people of Mountainview had needed them to get through this day. Reflecting, and discussing the matter quietly, the Amish came to appreciate that for themselves, living apart from any worldly government, July Fourth had never amounted to anything more than the day after July Third. But for these kindly English, with their sad, inexplicable commitment to the Powers and Principalities of this world, July Fourth had obviously been a very deeply meaningful date, signifying to them this year the loss of something they had held very dear.

It pleased the Amish that their visit had made possible the distractions of the festival—the food and fellowship and games and hubbub—that eased the painful passage of the anniversary date. They were stricken at recalling how nearly they had declined the invitation because they had not at first understood the commemoration's intent, nor the depth of their neighbors' unspoken plea.

"We must learn to do better," Caleb mused quietly to Amon in the wagon. "We do not understand well enough the English ways. But they are good people, of that I have no doubt. And the more contact I have with them the more I agree with something their Tom and their Chief Barley have said to me more than once: our communities need each other if we are to survive. Our two communities, they have said, form the two sides of an arch. We must think beyond the strange words they sometimes use, and look to the meaning in their hearts.

"The speech this afternoon of the Chief, for example. Granted: it was not said in the way we would have said it. But Amon, look to the sense of what he was saying: the importance of the real over the image, the lasting over the transient, the substance over the vapor. Is not that what we too believe, though perhaps in different words? I think we must work to become closer. However different many of our outward appearances may be, we are as one in the beliefs that matter most.

"And, do not forget," he told Amon quietly, "we are fellow survivors of a shipwreck, clinging to the same raft. We are all in the sea together, fearing and fighting the same waves. I do not think the Ordnung, which commands us to be separate from the worldly, instructs us also to separate ourselves from our fellow victims of a shipwreck. I want us to live and work more closely with these English—for all our sakes."

The Elders quietly reached agreement that this would become their policy. During the three hour trip back to their community they considered the best ways for gradually raising the issue among their fellow believers, and how to explain most clearly the reasons for their commitment to closer cooperation.

But—as generally ought to be the case in a healthy, well-ordered society— the members of the Amish community were actually somewhat ahead of their leaders. In the coming days, any close doctrinal parsing of the detailed reasons for increased cooperation with the English was buried under an avalanche of excitement set off by Abraham Hite the day after their return. He announced a plan that even a few months ago would have been mind-boggling: he and his wife Rebecca and their seven children—Mennonites of unquestionably devout faith and exemplary behavior—had decided to move to Mountainview!

Their beliefs were not the least bit in question, Abraham explained: they all intended to continue in the faith of their birth, as devoutly as ever. They merely intended to be practicing Mennonites who lived henceforth in Mountainview.

His present acreage, Abraham explained, was, as everyone knew, not ideally productive land. As his family had grown, they found themselves harder and harder pressed to win sufficient gains from the land to get by financially. During the past winter, when he had spent a couple of months in Mountainview building a cider press, he had seen any number of opportunities for well-paying enterprise—one of the most promising being the restaurant Sophie and Maybelle had started. During the July 4th visit, he and Rebecca had examined the restaurant and discussed it with Sophie and Maybelle, who were looking for someone to operate the business while renting or buying it. After much discussion of terms, and considerable thought and prayer, he and Rebecca had decided to move to Mountainview and enter the restaurant trade.

They would, at least initially, occupy Owen and Maybelle's Mountainview house. With renovations Abraham could do himself, the house would accommodate his entire family. Owen and Maybelle, who had been living in a room rented from Mrs. Stoltzfus while looking for a house in the Amish community, agreed to occupy the Hite place on an "even-steven" basis, with no cash payments due either party. In future, this house-exchange might be made permanent by legal transfer of deed if the parties so desired.

While Rebecca worked full-time at the restaurant, assisted by the older children, Abraham would divide his time between the restaurant and wage-paying jobs, which were plentiful in Mountainview. They had reached agreement with Maybelle and Sophie to purchase the restaurant in equal monthly payments of eight dollars silver, spread over the next ten years—and this purchase would include the land and building the restaurant occupied, which Maybelle and Sophie had purchased outright from Mr. and Mrs. Gump once the restaurant's success became apparent.

Abraham and Rebecca Hite would continue the existing agreement under which the restaurant rented its facilities to Mountainview University during the restaurant's off-hours. That would bring in, initially, two dollars silver for each month of the coming September-June academic year, with payments for subsequent academic years to be re-negotiated as the University expanded.

It was entirely possible in future, Abraham concluded, that people from the Amish community taking courses at the University—especially unmarried young women—as well as others who simply wished to do wage-work in Mountainview for a spell, might wish to room and board at the Hite residence in Mountainview. There they could be assured of a home environment meeting the highest standards of Mennonite propriety in every respect. Any interested persons should discuss the matter with himself or Rebecca, who would be delighted to quote them highly attractive prices, and reserve any room(s) required.

And so, a development which only months earlier would have aroused shock and dismay received widespread approval from the Hite family's Mennonite neighbors. Several of them began entertaining notions, that would previously have been excessively daring, of spending a few months away from their home, living among the English, and studying or working to accumulate money from wage-paying jobs in town.

Those Yoder boys, Jacob and Joshua, for example, were learning about steam engines and other metal-shop work, and they appeared to love every minute of it. One could only imagine the silver coins they must be carefully putting aside, week by week, to buy land, animals, and equipment when they decided to marry. Any girl fortunate enough to catch the eye of so enterprising a young man would enter married life enjoying the independence of her own family farm, instead of working such land as the young man's father chose to set aside for their use, but not owning it for many years till it was received through inheritance.

Perhaps—to raise an even bolder possibility—a person might not even return to full-time farming at all! Though big city life held no attraction for anyone in the Amish community, several people there could imagine the advantages of living on the edge of a Mountainview-sized town, with several acres extending out from the house for a bit of truck-gardening or small-animal husbandry, while enjoying the security of weekly wages from a town job and the excitement of such a bustling community. Amazing new vistas were opening up.

Chapter 43
Signs and the Interpretation of Signs

Brother Stainfuss, to his dismay, was lately having to edge ever closer to hear Jack Carter's preaching as its volume steadily diminished. Furthermore, there seemed increasingly little purpose in doing so: Carter was clearly losing his gift of tongues. There was less fire and color in his testimony with every passing day. The Spirit, clearly, had moved on from Jack Carter—leaving a disillusioned Brother Stainfuss to wonder what he'd once found so compelling in the man's testimony. For all the Living Word of Fire to be found in Carter's more recent subdued musings, Brother Stainfuss glumly concluded, the man might as well have been Episcopalian.

But he continued dutifully monitoring Carter's preaching, in part because that woman, Klara, had sought him out a couple of weeks ago and asked him to. Brother Stainfuss, whose entire life had been bound up in his Call to preach, had never found occasion to wed. But he secretly admitted to himself that if such an opportunity had ever occurred, he could not imagine any woman he'd find more compelling than Klara. Her people, however peculiar, were certainly not the least bit inclined toward heathen or Papist ways, of that he was quite confident. And as for the woman herself, the quiet way she had of looking at you when you talked—really *looking* and *listening*—made Brother Stainfuss feel acutely conscious that he was a man and she was a woman; a woman, furthermore, who was genuinely interested in what he had to say. He was, strictly within his most secret heart of hearts, thoroughly smitten by Klara. Not, of course, that he would ever declare himself or pursue the matter.

But Klara had sought him out—him, personally!—and quietly asked him about Carter's preaching, and had asked him to tell her if he felt there were changes, and had asked if he heard women's names mentioned. And then— which sealed his opinion that Klara was a woman who possessed powers and gifts herself—she had asked him to tell her if Carter referred to an occasion, some couple of months past, in which God had sent a sign by causing the moon to be covered and its light to be obscured.

Now obviously, if God were to send a sign, this was exactly the sort of sign He would send. "But sign of what?" Brother Stainfuss asked himself for the umpteenth time, straining his eyes up into the black night sky in search of a clue, as he strolled, in his recently adopted custom, past Jensen's place. To him though, it seemed, was not to be given the interpretation of Signs.

It was scarcely ten p.m., but Mountainview these days rose with the dawn, and so its people were fast asleep in the early darkness. Brother Stainfus, in a carefully offhand explanation distributed here and there, had allowed as how lately he'd been troubled with wakefulness, and had found a brief stroll in the cool night air useful to settle him and invite slumber.

What, he racked his brain, as he walked his evening mission, could the hiding of the moon's light, some two and a half months ago, be a Sign of?

He'd quietly passed his objective, the sleeping Jensen place, turned, and just headed back toward the Parsonage (as he called the tiny, four-room shack he'd inherited from his parents) when he heard the sound from the shed in Jensen's back yard, where Carter slept.

"*MARY!*"

Brother Stainfuss heard it again, clearly now, a cry from Carter in his sleep. "*Oh! My Mary!*"

Quickly touching his pocket Testament, as a charm against Papistry, should the cry indicate idolatry of that sort, Brother Stainfuss froze in the darkness and listened.

"*Sorry! Oh, sorry! Oh, sorry!*" the mumbled sleep-talking continued, with an intense anguish, an indescribable remorse, that wrung the heart of Brother Stainfuss. And then there was only silence.

After a time, Brother Stainfuss walked slowly along the dark, deserted street back to his little Parsonage to spend a sleepless night himself.

When he arose, still awake in the early dawn, he knew what he must do, however difficult: he must notify Klara. She would understand the meaning of what he'd heard, and make things clear. But to notify her he must deal with Doc, for in Doc's office was the medical radio-telephone used to contact Klara at the Amish community.

On his early morning trip to the medical office, Brother Stainfuss had to summon all his resources to fight back his deep visceral loathing—and, yes, he admitted it, his fear—of this atheist, Darwinist medical man: Doc, who undoubtedly thought himself so preciously educated, so scientifically adept with his books and instruments and learned terminology that he no longer needed to heed God's Eternal Word; Doc, who no doubt looked down with a well-bred, painfully polite tolerance on the world's less favored men, those striving to live righteous lives in fearful obedience to the Lord God Almighty; Doc, who (Brother Stainfuss could imagine this with humiliating clarity) probably chuckled privately with others of his upper-class, educated sort about the lack of culture and refinement of humbler men such as…well…Doc: who had the radio in his office, which Brother Stainfuss must now beg use of to get through to Klara with his news.

"Good morning. I need to send a message to Klara. She would want to know. On the radio?"

A sleepy Doc—his first eye-opening mug of tea not even brewed yet, much less savored—blinked blearily at the little preacher, trying to make sense of his words.

"Klara? Message? Uh…sure. Um. Let' see: there's the transceiver there. On the wall. Want me to make contact and then give it to you?"

So Doc had called—raising a surprised Mrs. Yoder at work in her kitchen, who sent little Elisha running out to the barn to fetch Klara away from a colicky calf—and then handed the transceiver to Brother Stainfuss, whose embarrassment and anxiety were only intensified when he realized he would have to confess he did not know how to operate the device.

But before that humiliation, a now more awakened Doc quickly sensed the problem and explained, making the matter into nothing.

"You hold down this button when you're talking. Then let it up to hear Klara when she answers."

Doc explained it quietly, Brother Stainfuss noted, so Klara on the other end would not have heard that he needed the instruction.

"Klara?" In his panic of initial mike-fright, like all radio novices, Brother Stainfuss had forgotten to hold down the Transmit button. Doc gestured with a gently pointing finger.

"Klara?" croaked Brother Stainfuss again, this time successfully getting through. Doc gestured to let up on the button.

"Yes, is Klara here. Who is this please?"

"Klara, it's Brother Stainfuss. Ah…um…he cried out in his sleep last night. He cried out 'Mary' and he said 'sorry, sorry.' He was badly troubled, Miz Klara. I could hear from his voice he was very sorely afflicted. And I thought I should tell you."

No reply came through, and after a moment Doc gently touched him, gesturing for him to let up the button he'd been holding down with a white-fingered death grip.

"Hello? Are you there? I repeat: thank you for the message, Brother Stainfuss. I will plan to come right away to talk with him. I should arrive by noon. Do you hear me?"

"Yes," Brother Stainfuss was able to transmit successfully. "Yes, Miz Klara. I hear you. Thank you. Thank you."

And with dazed relief he handed the instrument to Doc, who spoke a few brief words with Klara and formally signed off.

Doc, very far from being a fool, sensed how much it had cost the little preacher to come to his turf and beg the use of an instrument that, to him, was new and complicated and fearsome.

"Would you have some tea with me, Brother?" he asked gently. "I have something I've been wanting to show you."

Nodding mutely, sinking into a chair beside Doc's medical desk, Brother Stainfuss sat in a sort of light-headed, sleep-deprived daze while Doc brewed the two mugs of tea. Placing the filled mugs on the desk, and taking a deep, grateful pull from his own, Doc glanced at the battery-level indicator on the car battery beside the desk, then turned on the computer.

He clicked and clacked on various buttons, doing some sort of computer-mystery operation Brother Stainfuss had never learned about. The screen slowly came to life in a deep, dark, blue-black color. As Brother Stainfuss privately phrased it, retreating in his anxiety from the fearful unknowns of computers to the bedrock certainties of Scripture, the screen before him was "without form, and void."

Then another key clacked and there was light. And the light was in the form of tiny pinpricks—not scattered at random, but arranged in a beautiful pattern. There must have been millions of them, swirled across the screen's blue-black void in countless beautiful spirals, near and far, large and small.

The two men looked at it, struck silent by its beauty.

"It was taken by the Lick Observatory, Mt. Hamilton, California, looking toward the Andromeda-31 galaxy."

The men sat silent again, held by the wonder.

"Our Sun, our Earth, our entire Solar System," Doc said, "if they were in this photo, would be too tiny to see with the naked eye. The light from those furthermost stars—those over there—there took millions of years to reach us."

He paused to gather up his own courage to make the offer.

"I was looking at several of these pictures the other day and thought of you.

393

Printed out, in large size, they might make powerful posters for a church or Sunday school, or to illustrate a sermon. If you'd like, I can show you how to bring them up on the computer and print the ones you want. It's not hard—you'd get the knack in a couple hours or less—and you could then do a lot of other things, too. Some of the Biblical concordances, commentaries, translations, maps, and other things that were put on computer are simply astonishing. We still have quite a few that people saved on their own computers before the internet went down. While we're waiting for Klara, why don't I show you how to work this thing?"

"Yes," Brother Stainfuss nodded in a sort of daze, his eyes and mind still overwhelmed by the immensity of this one tiny portion of God's splendor.

Doc settled him in front of the screen, his hands on the computer's keyboard and mousepad, and began.

When Klara arrived, just before noon, she met briefly with Brother Stainfuss in Doc's office and then went to visit Jack Carter, who was working silently in Jensen's woodlot. She had brought some assorted makings for a picnic lunch, hastily acquired from Doc and Brother Stainfuss, and sat privately with her patient under a shade tree as the two of them talked and shared a long, long meal.

After lunch, Jack decided to take his first time off from work since he'd been at Jensen's. He went for a long, quiet walk beside Sandy Run, heading east out of town. At some point, well distant from the community, when he had found the right place overlooking a bend in the babbling little stream, he moved some heavy rocks into a sort of outline of a grave. And then he sat on a fallen log beside it and wept.

Klara, after they'd finished the picnic and their long talk, had returned to Doc's office to give him her report.

She was tired, Doc saw—so deeply tired he was frightened for her. He wanted to forbid her to do anything like this ever again. He would beg her not to. He would do whatever it took. Perhaps he could *bribe* her somehow... She sat beside his desk, drinking deeply from a mug of tea, and his fear for her exhaustion was actually physical in him. He would hold her here, by force, until she agreed ...

"Good news we have now, I think," she began. "Jack will have good times and bad times, he and I agree—probably for the rest of his life. But is no more need to pay Jensen for keeping him. He is now 'cured' we have decided—anyway, cured enough to be much like the rest of us. He will stay where he is for another month or so, working at the firewood, until he finds another job he likes and a place he wants to live. Is no big hurry for that, he says: he likes cutting wood at Jensen's, and having his own shed there to live in.

"We think he has now about as good an understanding as he will ever get to separate what he has only dreamed from what he has actually experienced. In his dream last night he lost his wife, Mary, once again—and he now remembers some of what actually happened. It was very good that Brother Stainfuss called me, I think, so Jack and I could talk about his dream while it was still so recent. I will tell you now what Jack and I believe he experienced— as best we can understand it.

"Jack was salesman from Houston, Texas, selling X-ray machines for hospitals and for industrial use. He was very good salesman, and won a prize from his company: two weeks deluxe vacation for him and his wife to visit Washington, D.C. They had a lovely hotel in Arlington, Virginia, just between Reagan National Airport and the Pentagon, so close he says they can easily walk to either of those places if there is any place to walk. But there isn't, he says: impossible to walk because there is only huge roads for cars. This part I don't understand, but he told me it's normal…Maybe cars—I guess—are too valuable to waste space letting people walk in such high-level, important places as Washington?

"Anyway, during their vacation's second week, he says, he and Mary get on a tour bus to go on a Fourth of July day-trip to Civil War battlefields in the Shenandoah Valley, small distance west of Washington. The bus has just left their hotel, going west on Highway 7 maybe only ten or fifteen minutes, when the atom bomb explodes behind them, right where they were. Jack says there is horrible flash, and flying debris everywhere, but the bus windows are not broken and no one inside the bus is hurt. He can watch the mushroom cloud climbing behind them. There are some damaged buildings and a few small fires breaking out around them, on each side—but behind them looks very, very bad.

"The bus continues quickly out of town, sometimes driving over lawns or sidewalks when the street is blocked. He says they keep going west on Highway 7, not knowing what else to do, very afraid to go back because Jack has seen the mushroom cloud and he knows from selling X-ray machines that near that cloud will be death.

"They go past a town called Leesburg, Virginia. He remembers the town's name because just behind them, at that place, many other cars make a huge crash which blocks the road to any more traffic. So once again, their bus leaves behind a terrible thing, like escaping the atom bomb earlier. After Leesburg they go about fifteen miles more, he thinks, up a small but steep mountain, until the bus is stopped by a man on the road pointing a gun, and forced to pull onto a small side-road. Then thieves come from the woods on each side and make all the passengers get out.

"The thieves, he said, took anything they liked from the passengers, and also they took the diesel fuel from the bus, which they pumped into a home-heating oil truck they had. After the passengers were searched and robbed, they were free to go away. Some turned back toward where they'd come from; some went to either side of the highway, looking for a farmhouse or some place to stay; Jack and Mary continued west on Highway 7, walking till it was dark.

"He says they walked and walked: the days and nights of this time blurred into one another and he doesn't know how long it was. Sometimes a farmer would give them work for a week or two, with room and board, and then give them some food to take when they decided to move on; sometimes they found orchards or gardens they could steal from; sometimes they were hungry.

"From what they heard farmers and other people say, there were no more airplanes flying to return them home to Houston. Mary had some distant cousin, she thought, who lived somewhere in this area, and the best they had for a plan was to try to find her.

"The days and nights blurred together, but he thinks they spent the rest of July and part of August walking around from farm to farm in the same general area this way. I think they were in a kind of shock from the mushroom cloud they had seen behind them on the bus—rising from where they had been just minutes before. Jack had seen color photographs, from his training courses, showing what radiation does to people ...

"At some time—maybe it was late August, we don't know—they were walking across a small, wooded mountain where few people lived. They were planning to head west toward a town called Berryville. Suddenly there was a large explosion a few miles ahead of them on the mountain. It was a deep, rolling 'BOOM,' with a trail of black smoke rising above the trees. But this was not a mushroom cloud, so they were not so afraid for radiation, and they continued walking as they had been.

"After several hours, they reached a place where they saw a smoking, blackened hole in the side of the mountain. It must have been a military place of some kind, they thought, where explosives had gone off by accident. There had been coils of barbed wire around this place, but much of that had been blown away by the explosion. Trees had been stripped of their bark and limbs by the blast. Going a little bit ahead, Jack saw pieces of humans which the fire had spit out of the hole in the mountain, and he told Mary not to come further.

There was obviously no one still alive inside the mountain.

"He remembers the boots especially: several boots—perhaps half a dozen—which had been blown off people and were lying about on the ground. Some had only the feet still in them, but others had six or eight inches of splintered leg-bone still sticking up out of the boot. They were all heavy military boots, he said, like parachute soldiers wear.

"He says he saw some arms and legs, too, but he remembers looking especially at two torsos which were missing most of their arms and legs. The torsos had on Army uniforms of some kind. On the left shoulder of one he saw a patch which said 'Special Forces' and on the right shoulder was a patch saying 'Presidential Detail.' He looked at another torso, and that one had no left shoulder, but on the right shoulder was again 'Presidential Detail.'

"All this took, he believes, perhaps one or two minutes in total.

"He was in shock, vomiting sometimes from these things he saw, and he turned from the scene to go away, waving to Mary where he'd left her, and pointing her to a distant location where he'd join her, so she wouldn't come closer.

"She waved back to him in agreement, and started in the direction he'd indicated. And at her first step, when her foot came down, she exploded. There was a loud 'THUMP' and Jack saw in a pinkish mist one of her legs fly in one direction and part of the other leg fly in a different direction, and there was very little left, and his mind shattered into pieces and he turned and fled, running until he fell from exhaustion. As soon as he could get up he ran some more until he dropped again. And he did this over and over—for how long he does not know.

"He didn't remember until his dream last night which things at that place of evil actually happened and which were fever-dreams from his sickness.

"He remembers almost nothing from that point on. He tried to explain me it was like what he called a 'bad acid trip,' where the unending horror never stopped, month after month.

"He must have found food, water, and shelter—since he remained alive—but he has no memory of doing so. After some time (one, two, three months?) he remembers he was in an abandoned farmhouse and he saw there a Bible and he read in the Book of Revelations. And he said that, too, was like some 'bad acid trip,' so he decided maybe the Bible was the only thing that understood him, and knew what he was going through. So he took it with him, and often he would read it, grateful that he was not the only one.

"He remembers nothing else that actually happened in this time: the other memories he carries from these days, we are pretty sure, come from the sickness inside his head, not from things actually happening outside him. There was screaming, and flames, and demons, and death and killing.

"He had no map and no plan, and he has no idea where he traveled or how he arrived here or how much time had passed. He must have found shelter during the worst of the winter. He does not remember. The only thing he can tell us is that one night God sent him a Sign: the moon was covered over, and went dark.

"Very soon after this Sign—perhaps the next day, he thinks—he came upon a settlement of people. He lay in the woods and watched them. We have talked carefully about this, and we think that what I inform you now is actual, not a dream. He says the settlement, about as big as Mountainview, contained some people who carried whips and clubs, and many other people who worked almost without stopping from dawn to dusk. If the workers stopped, the people with whips and clubs beat them. Some got up and returned to work; others never got up again.

"He decided God's Sign had been sent to warn him away from that place. Because April Twentieth was the date of the eclipse, and he arrived here on April Twenty-eighth, I think that settlement is maybe not so far away.

"The next things he remembers are meeting me in the jail here, and then eating and talking with me, and then going to Jensen's and cutting wood, and all the while trying his best to tell people—to warn them of the terrible things he had seen—just like in the Bible. Slowly, we have come to understand that there are only these few things I have told you which he can truly remember. All the rest is gone in sickness.

"We talked about Mary, and he understands now that when he waved her in a certain direction, and she started that way and blew up, his mind shattered because he had not kept her from harm. He had failed her, and in his terror he failed to find some pieces of her to bury, and he could not accept anything so horrible. So he mostly left this world and went to some other place. But not entirely. And now he has come back to us—at least on his good days. And perhaps there will be more of those ahead, we hope. And so we thank God."

Doc had moved to her during the telling, and held her tightly, and after she had finished they were silent together for a long time.

Chapter 44
In a World Turned Upside Down:
Real Leadership for Real Americans

Tom placed the water injection pump's flange in his bench vise, carefully tightened the jaws to securely hold it, and began to file down a slight projection, drawing the hand file across it gently in careful, rhythmic strokes. After he'd completed this step, automatically checking the resulting smoothness with a thumb while his conscious mind strayed elsewhere, he sank tiredly down into the rocker beside his shop bench. It was hot in West Virginia in early September, though the electric fan on the floor beside him, powered by the steam-driven generator just outside the shop, helped somewhat. His tiredness was increased by his lack of sleep the previous night.

Chief Barley had come to supper, for a worrisomely half-official, half-personal visit. Officially, he'd come to discuss with Tom and Sophie what Klara had learned from her patient about a slaveholding settlement apparently not far away, and to solicit Tom and Sophie's thoughts about the implications that discovery might hold for morale and security in Mountainview.

But as the evening wore on, the Chief's deeper motives for his visit became plainer. He was getting tired, he confessed to them. Every single day since The Collapse it had been vital to accomplish more than was reasonably possible, always using fewer resources than the minimum required for the task, living constantly under the ever-hanging possibility of catastrophe for the community from any of a dozen different directions if they failed to achieve the impossible.

"I'm not up to it any longer," he told them, quietly pleading. "Look, I'm a small-town cop: capable of running a three-man police force, handing out the occasional speeding ticket, and keeping the kids' Halloween mischief to a reasonable level. That's all. I don't have the brains, education, or ability in the areas necessary to 'run' Mountainview—and I never have had. I've been faking it ever since The Collapse, and we've all just been lucky. I'm too tired,

Tom, to keep on doing it any longer."

The evening had continued into the late hours. Chief Barley really had no one except Tom and Sophie he could speak to in this way. Both those people understood the Chief's position—with a clarity that deeply anguished them—but they understood Mountainview's position with an equally painful clarity: the job was essential to Mountainview's survival, and the town had no one else as well equipped for it as Barley.

"You want me to tell you it's ok for you to step down," Tom said gently, putting a hand on his friend's shoulder. "But all I can truthfully tell you is that the job's essential and we have no one else as capable. And if staying on means you burn out at some point and collapse—well, I still can't change the facts, or lie to you about them: the job's essential and we have no one else as capable."

Sophie, digging her nails into her chair's upholstery, said softly "I'm sure in one more year... We'll be more secure by then—economically and in all kinds of ways—and we'll have had the time to prepare some replacements, season them in the job, see how they work out..."

But Barley was at the end of his rope—he wouldn't have brought up the matter with Tom and Sophie if he hadn't been—and the inconclusive session went on deep into the night.

For the moment, Tom thought wearily in his shop, sitting in his rocker beside the work bench, Barley would hold. The long evening's discussion had eked out that temporary, unstated victory. But he knew it was only one small success in what would be a long, long struggle—with the odds against the Chief steadily growing, month by month, until his resignation or collapse, whichever occurred first.

Feeling an ache inside him that was actually physical, Tom admitted to himself he knew pretty well which that would be. Barley was an overwhelmed, overweight man in late middle age, eating unwisely, exercising little, and living every day under the unbearable grinding of intense stress. You didn't have to be a cardiologist, Tom thought...And we're not ideally equipped here in Mountainview for the very latest in open-heart surgery ...

Tom prayed it wouldn't happen too soon.

"Every month ...," he pleaded silently to a Deity whose existence he alternately denied and despised, "every single month will make a difference, perhaps a crucial one. Mountainview *is* becoming stronger each month, in all kinds of ways, just as Sophie said. Just let him last long enough. And then give us more luck than we have any right to hope for in choosing his successor. Please."

Tom turned off the fan and threw the master breaker, shutting down the shop's electrical system. Then he switched the generator over to the standby-load they used whenever current was not needed elsewhere: charging the many batteries stored in the Gravely Dealership's former showroom and at Hockley Beener's house.

Then he left the shop and walked the short distance to Sophie's former restaurant, now her beloved university. He found her in her tiny "office"—a shed in the side-yard squeezed in between the restaurant and the outhouse. As he'd suspected, Sophie was sitting vacantly, too distracted by the previous night's discussion to get anything accomplished. He kissed her and took the other chair. They didn't need to speak for a time, each of them knowing the other's mind.

Finally, Tom spoke.

"Well—whatever else, my love, we've made it through the first full year since The Collapse. Despite the horrors and hardships of that time, we have established a beachhead: we are still alive and we are still civilized. From this starting point, our descendants can begin the long, slow slog of human progress back toward the 21st Century we so suddenly dropped out of.

"But this time, perhaps we can achieve a society valuing substance over style. Where people find contentment by having a sufficiency of goods with actual, tangible value—rather than addictively, compulsively, endlessly chasing every piece of insubstantial froth peddled by marketers hustling 'image' and 'prestige' and 'pizzazz.'

Where people buy their substantial goods using real money having actual value, rather than ginned-up little slips of 'make-believe' paper, or—worse yet—mere debt-based promises to pay the bill sometime 'later,' in a 'later' they've never thought much about except to hope it never comes.

Where people would rather actually *own* a simple, modest cottage than tenuously, temporarily, feel '*Important*,' camping in a fabulous, balloon-note-McMortgaged McMansion—of which they actually own not a single two-by-four, or windowpane, or roofing shingle.

Where coping with our serious problems has produced a new, more serious, kind of citizen: one impressed more by actualities than by promises, by roots in good soil more than by castles in air.

Where these more serious citizens are determined to *remain* citizens, and not be reduced to mere subjects. And who therefore take care to ensure that their government, kept strictly limited and local—'bound down with chains of iron' as Mister Jefferson put it—remains their servant instead of becoming their master."

Speaking wistfully now, instead of venting the anger Sophie had so often heard from him in the past, he said "A society, in other words, like our former nation was meant to be—before that founding dream died and was laid away to rot inside the majestic, splendidly imperial Whited Sepulcher the country became."

He took from his pocket a one-ounce Silver Eagle, turning the large, heavy coin slowly in his fingers, gazing at its portrait of Lady Liberty striding toward a dawn, bearing symbols of Beauty and Abundance in her arms.

"With an indescribable amount of hard work and determination—and a great deal of luck—our descendants in some distant generation might once again enjoy the privilege, ease, and luxury our own generation so foolishly threw away.

"Let us hope those people, in that distant future, will have gained wisdom enough to hold onto such a precious inheritance."